D1236124

THE GATEWAY
CHRONICLES

BOOK 3

To Fallon & Sydney, Enjoy the journey!

THE WHITE THREAD

KB.

BY

K. B. HOYLE

TWCS
PUBLISHING HOUSE

First published by The Writer's Coffee Shop, 2012

The Writer's Coffee Shop
(Australia)   PO Box 447 Cherrybrook NSW 2126
(USA)   PO Box 2116 Waxahachie TX 75168

Paperback ISBN- 978-1-61213-328-7
E-book ISBN- 978-1-61213-108-5

A CIP catalogue record for this book is available from the US Congress Library.

C. S. Lewis quotation
Mere Christianity. New York: HarperOne, 1952

Cover image by: © Carlos Caetano/© Sergiy Serdyuk/ © Akihito Yokoyama
Cover design by: Megan Dooley

www.thewriterscoffeeshop.com/khoyle

ABOUT THE AUTHOR

The Gateway Chronicles 3: The White Thread is K. B. Hoyle's third published novel. Ms. Hoyle lives outside of Birmingham, Alabama, with her husband and three children. She is a teacher at a local classical school. Follow her on twitter @kbhoyle_author.

ALSO BY K. B. HOYLE

Book One of *The Gateway Chronicles: The Six*
Book Two of *The Gateway Chronicles: The Oracle*

DEDICATION

To Julie and Brad

Special Thanks

As usual, this book could not have been possible without the help and support of many, many people. A special thanks to Hayley German Fisher, Kathie Spitz, Caryn Stevens, and everyone on the TWCS team; Beth Mitchell and Yvonne Lovelady; to Katie Foust; to Mariah Lawrence, Hannah Pryor, and Bethany Carter; to Schledia Benefield; to Melissa and Wally Bell; to John Granger (*How Harry Cast His Spell*, SaltRiver, 2008) for e-mailing me all those ring composition charts; to Donna Huber (@Girl_Who_Reads) for your excellent reviews and marketing help; to Beth Mitchell, the Blackwell family, Abby Holcombe, and Elise Helton for helping me out with free childcare so I could write; to the ladies of my writers group for your excellent critiques; and to all my students for your enthusiasm and support.

"The proper motto is not 'Be good, sweet maid, and let who can be clever,' but 'Be good, sweet maid, and don't forget that this involves being as clever as you can.'"

C. S. Lewis

CHAPTER 1

THE DISAPPEARANCE

Disappearance of Teenaged Boy in Rural Upper Michigan Confounds Law Enforcement; Investigation Continues . . .

Darcy Pennington sat up straight in bed, her eyes going wide as she took in the photograph accompanying the Internet article. It was an old picture, but it was undeniably him. A quick read down the page confirmed it.

Colin Mackaby, son of Lawrence and Rebekah Mackaby of Manhattan, New York, was vacationing in the Upper Peninsula with his family when his disappearance was reported on February 13th. The boy has had previous run-ins with the law and was initially thought to have run away from the camp at which his family was staying, but an area-wide search has turned up no leads. No residents in the nearby town of Logger's Head recognized the boy. Police task forces have scoured the woods for miles around the camp with body-sniffing dogs, but no traces have been found. Police now fear a possible kidnapping and request that locals report any suspicious vehicles or persons. A hotline has been set up at the phone number listed below, and the Mackaby family is offering a reward of $50,000 for any information leading to the recovery of their son . . .

Darcy scanned the rest of the article, but it was nothing more than a description of Colin and what he had been wearing on the day he had disappeared. She leaned her head back against her headboard, her heart thumping within her chest. "Oh, Colin . . . what have you gotten yourself into?" she murmured.

"Hey! Furniture Girl!"

Darcy closed her eyes slowly, praying Brandon Cooper would lose her in the crowd. She shouldered her way past a hand-holding couple and ducked around the corner into the school's math wing. Just a few more steps and she'd be at her locker. She could see Sam's bright head bobbing as she stood along the wall, her blue eyes scanning for Darcy among the mass of students.

"Hey, Sam," Darcy said, pulling up beside her and shooting a glance over her shoulder. She exhaled, relieved she couldn't see Brandon Cooper anywhere. Then again, it was difficult to pick out any familiar face in the milling crowd. "How'd you do on the math final?" Darcy spun the dial on her locker combination and peeked surreptitiously over her shoulder again.

"Pretty good, I think. Mrs. Cranston said the grades would be up by Friday. Who're you looking for?" Sam frowned, looking down the hallway.

"Guess." Darcy swung open her locker and bent over to paw through the detritus of almost a year's worth of textbooks, worksheets, notebooks, and old tests.

Sam sighed. "Oh. So he's bothering you again, huh? If only you could tell him—"

"Tell him what, exactly?" Darcy pulled a couple strands of hair out of the corner of her mouth and peered up at her friend. "That I travel to a magical land every summer where I have magical powers and might be engaged—ish—to a prince?"

Sam's eyes filled with mirth. "Well, if you put it like that—"

"It sounds crazy, I know." Darcy extracted her biology notebook with a great deal of difficulty, sending random papers and chewed pencils skittering down the hallway between people's feet.

"Well, you have to admit," Sam said, retrieving a few papers for Darcy and shoving them into her hands, "it would probably get him to leave you alone."

"*And* get him to start another rumor about me. As if it hasn't been hard enough being 'Furniture Girl' all year. Even Mr. Richards calls me that sometimes!"

"Mr. Richards is one of the football coaches, isn't he? Maybe Brandon talks about you at practice."

Darcy groaned. "Oh, Sam, stop, please!"

"These yours?" A deep male voice asked in Darcy's ear and she jumped, but it was only Lewis, blinking owlishly at her and holding out a handful of papers. "I found them on the floor over there and thought I recognized your handwriting."

"Thanks, Lewis." Darcy shot him a half-smile and snatched the papers, shoving them into her locker before slamming it shut. She straightened and shouldered her bag. "Come on, guys, two periods of biology review and we're done for the day."

Sam gave a strangled groan as she pushed away from the lockers and attached herself to Darcy's side. They maneuvered their way back into the main flow and let themselves be swept along. Lewis loped easily in their wake; he had finally hit puberty, but he seemed all but oblivious to it. Although he had grown several inches and his voice had lowered several octaves, he still held the demeanor of the small, quiet boy who was used to being teased. It didn't help that he refused to shop for new clothes, so most of his shirts rode too high on his waist, and his pants, which had been long on him at the beginning of the school year, were now dangling two inches above the tops of his sneakers. Sam pestered him about it, but Darcy just shook her head in bemusement and kept her comments to herself.

They ducked into room 323 and made their way to their customary lab table by the windows in the back of the room. Lewis hated sitting in the back of any class, but Darcy and Sam despised biology so much that he had made this exception for the one class they all managed to have scheduled together.

"Sit!" Mr. Finch barked over the sound of the bell ringing. "I have one hour and thirty minutes to make sure you succeed on your exam tomorrow. Don't waste my time and I won't waste yours. Use the first thirty minutes to compare notes with your lab partners . . ."

As Mr. Finch continued to speak, Darcy was distracted by the cheerleaders at the next table, texting under the lab desk and giggling with their heads together. Darcy sniffed in disgust. She may not be perfect, but a school rule breaker she was not.

The closest cheerleader, a white-blonde-haired girl named Sydney, looked up and speared Darcy with an icy glare. "What's your problem, Furniture Girl?"

Darcy looked away and absorbed herself in pretending to study her biology notes while Sam and Lewis prattled on about the structure of DNA . . . or RNA . . . or something. Darcy rested her head on her hand and sighed as she listened to the cheerleaders' derisive laughter. *Finish the week. Just finish the week.*

"Sam, did you get the e-mail I sent you last night?" Darcy whispered out of the corner of her mouth, glancing at Mr. Finch to make sure he was still busy on the far side of the classroom.

Sam stopped talking mid-sentence about RNA and gasped, turning huge eyes on Darcy. "Oh my gosh, *yes!* I can't believe that!"

"If it hadn't been so late, I would've called you, but I technically wasn't even supposed to be on the Internet at the time." Darcy looked around Sam to Lewis. "I copied you on the e-mail, Lewis, did you get it?"

"No," he said, paging through his notes. "I was studying for *biology.*"

"Well, read it when you get home . . . it's about Colin. I finally found him."

Darcy had been looking for information on Colin Mackaby, ever since returning from Alitheia the previous summer, but she was alone in her curiosity about Colin and what role he played in their other-worldly adventures. Sam and Lewis had long ago written Colin off as a nut job and an overall bad guy. Darcy, though, couldn't forget the haunting vision of Colin crying over his broken ribs on the dock at Cedar Cove, nor how his left palm had not borne the scar she'd thought they'd shared. She knew he had to have some answers for her, but he had been like a ghost all year. She hadn't been able to find him on any social networking sites, hadn't found an e-mail address, and hadn't even found anything about his parents until the article she'd uncovered the night before.

She wondered why it had taken so long for the article to turn up, seeing as Colin disappeared in February and it was now June, but it had looked like a scanned page from a small local newspaper. Perhaps they hadn't posted it to their website until recently. She'd looked for further information, but all she'd found was a quick update stating Colin Mackaby was still missing.

"Well?" Lewis stared at her, surrendering studying biology to talk about Colin. "What did you find?"

Darcy shook her head, glancing meaningfully to Mr. Finch who was inching closer to their workspace. "Later," she said.

"Doesn't it kind of remind you of what happened to Eleanor Stevenson?" Sam asked, swinging her bag at her side as the three of them walked down Milwaukee Avenue, heading to Darcy's family's store. Every other day Darcy was expected to go straight to the store after school to complete various menial tasks—without pay, of course. Sam and Lewis usually accompanied her, even though it lengthened their usual route home, and Darcy always appreciated the company.

"That's what I thought at first, but now I'm not so sure."

"Why not? She disappeared at Cedar Cove, and now Colin has, as well."

"But they found her body, Sam," Darcy said. "Colin's just . . . gone."

"Maybe he wandered off and froze to death somewhere," Lewis said, sounding grumpy. "It would serve him right."

"Lewis!" Darcy reprimanded him. "That's horrible! If you had seen . . ." She trailed off and shook her head. "His dad is awful! I'm more concerned about Colin having been *murdered* by his dad than having wandered off. But I guess I don't really think that happened, either."

"So what *do* you think happened?" Lewis asked.

"Honestly . . . I think he's in Alitheia."

"But I thought you said—" Sam started.

"But he can't have gone through the gateway!" Lewis interrupted.

"I know, I know!" Darcy responded to both of them. "I don't think he's died, like Eleanor has died in our world, but I *do* think Tselloch found a way to draw him through."

Lewis shook his head. "I don't know, Darcy. Rubidius said it was highly unlikely for people to get through without a gateway."

"Well, do you have any better ideas?" Darcy asked.

Lewis sniffed and pushed his glasses up on his nose.

They drew up alongside Darcy's dad's store, and Darcy glared up at the sign with gritted teeth. It looked just as awful today as it had the day Darcy had tearfully begged her father not to put it up. For their family Christmas picture earlier that year, Darcy's dad had insisted they pose on a couch in the store. They all had dressed up in their matching Christmas sweaters, and a professional photographer had arranged them artfully on the couch as they smiled cheesy pasted on smiles. Darcy had thought that had been the end of it.

Later, she'd heard her dad ordering a four-by-six print and thought that was rather small. And then the print arrived—not four by six inches, but four by six *feet*—not for hanging in the house, but for hanging outside the store. "Pennington Furniture Surplus" it read, the hideous picture beside it with the new caption "A *Family* Store."

The sign had gone up the week before Christmas break and, thanks to Brandon Cooper and his network of friends, by the time school resumed after Christmas, everybody was calling Darcy "Furniture Girl" and approaching her in the hallway to say "nice sweater," or "are you for sale along with the couch?" She'd been mortified, but as much as she'd pleaded with her dad to take the sign down, he'd merely insisted that the teasing would pass.

Darcy stared up at it, pursing her lips, and then yanked open the door, a small bell chiming above her head.

"We'll meet you inside," Sam said, staring down at her phone. "My mom wants to know what time I'll be home, and she's got Lewis's mom on the house phone wondering the same thing." Sam poked Lewis in the ribs. "Your mom says to turn your phone on."

"Sure, whatever." Darcy waved a dismissive hand and let the door close behind her. Cold air and the smell of leather and upholstery blasted her in the face. Her dad looked up from the back corner where he was wooing a potential customer. He waved her forward and returned to his sales pitch Darcy sighed and meandered to the back of the store, weaving her way between the scattered floor displays, and came to a halt with her arms crossed several feet from her dad.

" . . . think I'm going to keep looking," the elderly lady was saying.

"Well, if you change your mind, here's my card. You can call me any time of the day or night, and remember we offer the warranty package with the free stain protection treatment thrown in to boot!" Her dad held out his card and shook the lady's hand.

The bell over the door chimed again, and Darcy turned to see Sam and Lewis entering the store. The old lady narrowed her eyes and looked from Darcy to the other two, as though the mere presence of teenagers boded mischief for her day.

Darcy's dad turned to her, his eyes weary. Darcy knew business had been tough lately, but she was surprised at how old he suddenly looked and some of her irritation melted away.

"Dad—"

"Put your bag in my office, Darcy, and grab a broom." He rubbed his hands over his face and looked around at the floor displays as if deciding where to have Darcy begin sweeping.

Darcy ignored her dad's directive. "Everything okay, Dad?"

"Hmmm? Oh, everything's fine. Just tired. But I just finished some interviews and hired on a boy to help in the back over the summer. I think he's about your age. Brandon Cooper, you know him?"

Darcy's jaw dropped as her arms slipped down to her sides. "*Dad!* He's the one who started all those rumors about me this year! You hired *him?*"

Allan Pennington frowned. "Are you sure, Darcy? He doesn't seem the type."

"Of *course I'm sure.*" Darcy stomped her foot and threw her bag onto the nearest chair in frustration.

"Well, if that's true, then working together will give you a chance to mend your differences." He walked away from her, his attention already on the next task at hand.

There were a whole lot of things Darcy wanted to say to her father's retreating back, but her concern for him warred with her frustration. She contented herself with merely throwing a silent fit as another customer entered the store. Chad, her dad's regular salesman, moved forward from the counter to greet the customer and Sam threw Darcy a sympathetic grimace from the front of the store. Lewis had settled into an armchair with his notebook on his knee.

"Broom, Darcy," her dad called over to her as he held his office door open. "I need the store swept and dusted before closing. If Sam and Lewis want to stay, I have plenty of jobs for them to do around here as well." He disappeared into his office.

Darcy huffed and shouldered her bag in resignation. She detoured to the front of the store on her way to the office. "You'd better get out of here," she muttered to Sam and Lewis, "or my dad's going to put you to work."

"Darcy." Sam's gentle hand on her arm stopped her as she turned away. "Only one month until Cedar Cove, and then . . . well, you know." The corner of her mouth lifted.

"If I survive until then," Darcy said.

CHAPTER 2

THE OTHER ORACLE

Later, Darcy lost herself in a magical land of opportunities, a land where she could shed the teasing and the heartache of the school year and become an entirely different person, a place where reality was turned on its end. Darcy became not the teased girl living with the outcasts on the margins of society, but a girl desired by a boy who wasn't a prince but a star athlete and the object of more than one girl's attentions.

Ah, the Internet! Darcy thought, snuggling down into the pillows against her headboard. She had made it to the end of the week, through all her second semester finals, and had earned her computer privileges for the weekend.

A soft *bloop!* announced she had a new message. *"How was your week?"* it read.

Darcy chewed her lip and thought about how to answer. *"Well, I survived,"* she typed back. *"Finals went okay, but my dad hired that guy I told you about to work at the store over the summer. Ugh."*

She waited a few seconds before, *bloop!*

"Who? That Brandon kid?"

"Yeah."

"If he gives you any trouble, I'll come and beat him up for you."

Darcy flushed with pleasure and smiled. Perry was always saying that sort of stuff to her now. He had never come out and *said* that he liked her, per se, but his attentions over the year had increased to the point that Darcy felt safe in her assumption that he did, in fact, like her. They had been through a lot together their previous year in Alitheia. Who could blame them for ending up liking each other?

She often had this conversation with herself because she knew the one person who *would* be hurt if she found out how often Darcy and Perry spoke these days. That was why it was one of only three secrets she kept from Sam.

The house phone rang downstairs.

Bloop!

"You there?"

"Yeah, sorry," she typed. *"How was your week?"*

That was all Perry needed to ramble on about all the sports clinics and training sessions he was involved in at the moment. His school in Iowa had let out a week earlier, and he was free to pursue his extracurriculars to his heart's content. He had also, this year, kept up with his Alitheian forms every morning, so he would be in much better shape than he'd been in last year to resume his role as warrior when they returned to the other world. Darcy hoped Dean had been as wise.

Darcy's door opened, and her mom poked her head in. "Darcy, Sam called. She and Lewis are coming over and I invited them to stay for dinner. She said you weren't responding to her texts."

"Oh, okay. Thanks, Mom, I'll be down in a few minutes."

Darcy fished in her pocket for her phone as her mom closed the door. "Dead," she muttered, flipping it open and closed again. She tended to forget about such trivial things as putting her phone on the charger when she had a chat date with Perry on her mind.

Sam hadn't said anything earlier that day about coming over, and Darcy wondered what had come up. She felt a stab of regret about cutting off her chat with Perry, but he had been going on about soccer for at least ten minutes now, and she knew he would continue for a while yet unless derailed.

"Hey, I'm really sorry, but I have to go," she typed, interrupting him midstream.

"Okay, that's cool. Same time tomorrow?"

"Sure!"

Darcy's fingers itched to type something more personal, but she hesitated. Did she really want to be the first one to say it?

"Hey, Darcy?" he typed back after a moment.

Darcy's heart skipped a beat. *"Yes?"*

The pause while he typed his message seemed interminable before finally, *bloop!*

"I'm really looking forward to seeing you in a month."

Darcy let out the breath she'd been holding. That was as personal as they ever got with each other. *"Me too,"* she typed.

"See ya."

"Bye."

Darcy closed her laptop and stretched the kinks out of her back. At least everything about her Internet life was good, even if her school year had stunk.

She reached the bottom of the stairs just as the doorbell sounded. Veering right, she swept open the front door. It recently had become gratifying to see her friends looking the age they had looked at the end of their last year in Alitheia, just before they'd gone home and reverted to their original ages. They lived each year twice, but they didn't age exactly the same in both worlds. While Sam had lost some weight in Alitheia last year, she had lost even more this year in their world, and although most people would still classify her as overweight, Darcy viewed her as the incredible shrinking girl.

She popped open the storm door and stood aside for them.

"Hey, come on in."

Sam bounded inside with wide eyes and a flushed face, and Lewis followed behind her, clutching a stack of ancient-looking books to his chest.

"What's up?" Darcy asked as she closed the door.

"Not here!" Sam said. "Let's go upstairs."

"Actually," Darcy's mom said, rounding the corner from the kitchen, "I'd like you three to sit out on the back patio and keep an eye on the coals while I make up the salad. Roger's out there and I don't trust him around the hot grill."

"Ugh." Darcy wrinkled her nose.

"Really, Darcy! You can discuss whatever secretive things you have to discuss out there. He won't bother you. Now go on!" Mrs. Pennington shooed them toward the back door with her salad tongs.

They stepped out onto the red brick patio, and Darcy searched for her brother. He had hit the magical age of twelve, and with it had come all the delightful accoutrements. He had grown taller and more stringy-looking with great big hands and feet. He had also taken to wearing his curly red hair long and only deigned to look at people by peering sidelong through a curtain of curls. His attitude had changed from energetic playfulness to disdainful, sullen silence. Darcy didn't think she would ever admit this out loud, but she longed for the days when he had tagged along in her wake, pestering her into playing with him.

She spotted Roger in the back corner of the yard under the spreading maple tree, texting with a friend on his new smart phone—a bribe from her parents to get him to be kind to them again. It hadn't worked. He ignored the arrival of Darcy and her friends, so she figured they were safe to talk at the patio table without being overheard.

They pulled three chairs out to sit down at the table. Lewis deposited his armful of books on top of it, and the smoke from the grill made the air shimmer like a gateway behind him.

"What is all this?" Darcy asked without preamble, picking up a book and examining it.

"Some ancient literature, books on Greek mythology, and whatnot," Lewis said, turning one of the books over in his hand.

Darcy knit her brows together. "And you brought this over here . . . why?"

Lewis looked to Sam and then back to Darcy. "Well, we thought maybe we could research the Oracle at Delphi and find some clues to help us rescue Yahto Veli when we get back."

Darcy snorted. "I'm *way* ahead of you."

"What?"

She set the book down on the table and leaned forward. "I already researched the Oracle at Delphi ages ago—like—right away when we got back. I didn't find anything useful, *and* I used the Internet. You *do* know about the Internet, don't you, Lewis?" She gestured toward the pile of books.

Lewis scowled at her. "So shoot me if I like to use real books printed on real paper! If you're not interested, though, I'll just go." He started to gather his books, but Darcy sighed and put a hand on his arm.

"You can't leave. My mom has already doubled all the portions of the dishes she's making tonight. And . . . I'm sorry, it's just that . . . I really don't think there is anything that we can learn about the Oracle in Alitheia from an oracle that existed in ancient Greece. What's to say there are any similarities at all between them?"

"But that's just it," Lewis said, excited. "There *are* similarities, from what you've told us, at least." He sat forward and held up his fingers to count off. "One: they are both collectors of stuff. Two: they both apparently know the future of all things. Three: they both speak in riddles. And four: they both have powerful magic defenses."

Darcy chewed on that for a moment. "I don't remember the Oracle at Delphi having strong magic defenses."

"Sure it did!" He grabbed an ancient tome from the tabletop that read "*The Histories* by *Herodotus*" on the spine. Darcy shivered, her left hand clenching into a fist to hide the oval-shaped scar left by the Oracle's curse. She was still a little leery of old history texts.

Lewis paged through, utterly focused. He stopped after a few minutes and scanned the page. "I doubt you would find this story on the Internet," he said. "I don't think it's very well known."

"What's it about?" Sam asked, leaning forward to read over his shoulder.

He tilted the book away from her, grumbling about her reading over his shoulder. "It takes place right after the Persians got through the pass at Thermopylae." He looked at Darcy while Sam squinted and cocked her head. History was Darcy's best subject, and she tended to remember it well. She nodded for Lewis to continue.

"Xerxes split his army into two divisions, one to head to Athens to destroy it, and the other to go up to Delphi and take all the treasure and stuff. Long story short, when his soldiers got near the Oracle's shrine, all the sacred weapons were lying outside the temple and a supernatural war cry came from within. Then this massive storm broke out and the earth shook and a part of the mountain broke off and crushed a ton of his soldiers. The rest of them fled and the Oracle was safe, along with all her treasure."

"That's in *here?*" Sam snatched the book from Lewis and peered at it. "But it looks so boring on the outside!"

Darcy ignored Sam's comment. "But, Lewis, nothing like that happened when I went to see the Oracle."

"Yeah, but my point is that last time, you went as a petitioner. This time you will be going as an aggressor, and who knows how the Oracle will respond!"

"But these comparisons between the Oracles are all *hypothetical*," Darcy said in frustration. "Even our going to the Oracle is hypothetical." All discussions of rescuing Yahto Veli always came back to the same thing: would they be *allowed* to attempt to rescue him, or would they be constrained by their duties to the prophecy? Lewis's and Sam's faces fell; they understood what she was thinking.

"Besides," Darcy said, "the Greeks believed that the Oracle at Delphi had the power of the god Apollo behind her. The Oracle in Alitheia is not a prophetess—or a *god*, even—it's just . . . an *entity* . . . a *thing*." Darcy gestured helplessly. She found it difficult to communicate with Sam and Lewis, who had not been there, what it had been like to stand before the Oracle. Only two other people knew what she was talking about. One of them was now a captive in the Oracle's lair, and the other was the alchemist Rubidius, who seemed strangely resistant to rescuing Yahto Veli.

Of course, Colin Mackaby might also know something about the Oracle in Alitheia, but now that he had disappeared off the face of the earth, there was no way for her to ask him.

"It might be a god. You don't really know," Lewis said quietly.

Darcy stared at him, her brain replaying the Oracle's demand for payment, Yahto deciding to stay so that she could escape, the black hand coming out of the darkness to snatch him away . . .

Supernatural *stuff* in Alitheia was run of the mill, and all sorts of creatures and beings could be classified as "gods," she supposed, but she had never thought of the Oracle like that. The only entity she ever had thought of as a god in Alitheia was Pateros, and only because he seemed to be more or less in control of everything that happened there. At least, that was how the Alitheians talked about him. Wasn't he more powerful than the Oracle?

Lewis took her silence as encouragement to continue. "The Oracle manipulated *time*, Darcy! Seven months passed in one hour. You can't deny that is pretty powerful."

"More—or less—powerful than a year passing in only a couple seconds?" Darcy shook her head. "Don't forget that's what Pateros does for us every year in Alitheia. I'd like to know who'd win in a showdown between the two."

"Time is not a constant," Sam said.

"*What?*" Darcy asked in exasperation.

Sam shrugged. "I don't know. It's physics, or something. I heard my dad talking about it with a friend."

Lewis looked at Sam with a quizzical expression, one eyebrow raised, and Darcy closed her eyes and shook her head. "Anyway," she said, "I just don't know—"

"Darcy! How are those coals coming?" her mom called through the kitchen window.

Darcy pursed her lips and stood up to peer into the grill. "They're white!" she called back. She sat back down and tried to remember what she had been about to say, but a shadow fell over her shoulder.

"What do you want, Roger?" Darcy asked through gritted teeth.

"Nothin'. What *is* all this?" He looked up from his phone long enough to tap his finger on one of the books.

"They're books, you know . . . reading? You *have* read a book before, haven't you?"

"Isn't school out for the summer?" Roger grunted. He put his ear buds in and slunk away.

Darcy rolled her eyes. A car door slammed out front, announcing the arrival of her dad. "We'd better put all this away if we don't want to have to answer any more questions." She had answered her fair share of awkward questions that year, such as, where had she gotten that big scar on her palm? Her mom was still convinced that Darcy had inflicted it on herself. And in a way, Darcy guessed, that wasn't too far from the truth.

"Come and get the steaks, Darcy!" her mom called again from the window. "And if Sam and Lewis want something to drink, they're going to have to come and choose something out of the cooler in the garage. They're not going to get out there by magic, you know!"

Darcy raised her eyebrows and smiled at her friends.

CHAPTER 3

THE PIN PRICK

Steaks, salad, laughter, chatting with her friends and her parents, Roger's face lit up by the light of his phone . . . it was a good, diversionary, late spring dinner. They ate on the patio and pulled out a game of *Drop Site* to play as soon as the dinner dishes were cleared. Darcy loved playing cards— it was one of the few activities she could enjoy with her family; even Roger played most days.

The fireflies began to light up the growing shadows in the yard before Sam and Lewis stood to leave.

"Well, just a few more weeks, kids," Darcy's dad said as they picked up the cards. "How do you all feel about heading back to camp this year?"

"Great!" Sam answered. "I can't wait!"

"And you're sure your folks don't mind having Darcy in your van for the drive up?"

"They don't mind at all! With Michael away for the summer, it's just me and Abby. We've got plenty of space." Sam beamed.

Michael Palm, Samantha's older brother, was in Ann Arbor beginning a summer term at his university, and Sam's parents had invited Darcy to ride with them to Cedar Cove. Darcy was only too happy to take them up on the offer since the Palms were always on time to camp, not to mention she wouldn't have to spend the eight-hour drive alone with Roger in the back of the Penningtons' van.

"Well," her dad said, "tell your mom and dad we can take some luggage off their hands if they'd like some extra breathing room."

made her so sick, so her mom chalked it up to a freak stomach bug. Darcy said nothing to discourage the idea.

She lay in bed on her side, staring at her laptop's screensaver as it scrolled through images of her favorite artwork. She felt much calmer than she had the night before, but no less nervous. Her nightmare was becoming a reality; she was becoming one of the tsellodrin—the men and women in Alitheia who gave themselves over to mindless slavery at the hand of Tselloch. Darcy's transformation was so slow, she hoped it meant she was fighting it with everything inside her and that perhaps Rubidius could find a cure . . . if she could muster the courage to tell him.

It was after lunchtime now, and Darcy's stomach growled. She couldn't tell her mom that she didn't *really* have the stomach flu, so she'd had to accept, without complaint, nothing more than chicken broth and two saltine crackers for her meal.

In a few hours she would have another chat date with Perry, but the thought brought her no joy now. She couldn't tell *him* what was going on with her. She doubted he would find her acquiescence to Tselloch their first year very impressive at all.

Darcy passed a hand over her eyes and rolled onto her back. She needed to talk to someone, badly—someone who would listen and not judge. With a deep sigh, she reached for her cell phone.

Sam answered on the third ring. "Darcy? I thought that you were sick! Your mom called my mom. Is everything okay?"

Darcy listened to Sam's chatter with her eyes closed. Her body jittered, like it did when she was trying not to cry. "No—ah—Sam, I need to talk to you."

Darcy poured out the whole story, starting with her time in the dungeon, when Tselloch had visited her as the black panther and when Darcy, in desperation, had reached out for him just before her rescuers arrived. She told Sam about her fears of becoming a tsellodrin and her nightmares and the coldness in her fingers, and she ended with what had happened in her bathroom the night before.

Darcy finished her tale, and a very pregnant pause greeted her on the other end.

"I'm coming over," Sam said, and she hung up the phone.

CHAPTER 4

EAST MOORING

The passage of a month had dulled the shock of the pinprick. Darcy felt relieved that Sam now knew about it but at times wished she would just drop it. Darcy felt as though she had a terminal illness with no idea how long she had to live, and Sam constantly reminded her of it by being sometimes anxious for her and other times confident that everything would turn out okay. There was one refrain, however, that Sam repeated no matter what mood she was in.

"Darcy, you *have* to tell Rubidius! *Promise me* you'll tell Rubidius as soon as we get there!"

"Sam—I—"

"So secretive back there!" Kathy Palm's voice broke into their whispered conversation. "Sam's barely said two words about Cedar Cove the entire drive."

Darcy sat back, thankful for the reprieve, but Sam just looked annoyed. "Mom," she said, "we're having a private conversation!"

"Okay, okay. I just thought you girls would like to know we're almost there."

"Really?" Sam sat up straight in her seat to peer out the window like a small child. In fact, she so resembled her little sister Abby, who was sitting in the row in front of them, that Darcy almost laughed out loud.

Out the window, the blue lake glided past them, and Mariner's Point was visible across the bay. Darcy felt a flood of warmth course through her. The drive had gone much faster with Sam as a companion rather than her brother. She watched the brown buildings disappear into the trees, imagining the brownstone castle that stood there in Alitheia, its watchtower piercing the sky. She wondered what security they would find this year when they returned, and whether Tselloch would still be held at bay, the environs of the castles still protected. Darcy had been so consumed all year with thoughts of Yahto and Colin that she had barely stopped to think about what else went on in Alitheia while they were away.

The van slowed and swung to the right, the tires crunching over gravel as they made their entrance to Glorietta Bay, the east side of camp. She became aware that she was about to see Perry and she hadn't looked in a mirror since the rest stop in Menominee. She yanked her ponytail holder out of her hair and let her long waves fall about her shoulders. With a shake of her head, she attempted to run her fingers through the tangles.

"Here," Sam said, and handed her a travel-size brush with a mirror on the back. "I'm all finished with it." Sam's cheeks were bright pink with excitement.

"Thanks!" Darcy brushed out her hair and reformed her ponytail. As the van came to a halt, she turned the brush over and checked her complexion. Several days at the pool with Sam and Lewis had given her a heavier-than-usual dusting of freckles, but she noted with pleasure that her eyes looked bright and she didn't look too tired or pale. *Not bad!* she thought, but her hand shook as she handed the brush back to Sam.

Outside the car, they stretched and blinked in the bright sunlight. Being at Cedar Cove was like being wrapped in a blanket of pure nature. Human voices sounded almost intrusive to the quiet serenity of the cedar-strewn forest, even in the parking lot. The soft buzzing of insects and the calls of the gulls sounded right and normal to her ears. Darcy gazed around, eyeing the moss-covered boulders and wild strawberry plants that peeked through the ferns. A baby toad no larger than a teaspoon hopped onto a rock next to the car, and she poked Sam to draw her attention to it.

"Cute!" Sam said, but her attention was almost immediately diverted. Walking toward them from across the parking lot were two familiar forms. Sam grinned from ear to ear and grabbed at Darcy's hand.

Dean strolled at Perry's side with his hands in his pockets. He still had a couple inches on Perry, but Perry was catching up. He looked great to Darcy . . . except for his hair. This year he had cut his normally gorgeous blond hair into what Darcy recognized as a ridiculous parody of the latest boy pop singer's style. It looked like Perry had combed all his hair forward and then stuck his head backward out the car window at highway speeds to cement it that way. Perry's smile faltered as he got closer; Darcy's distaste must have shown on her face.

"Hey girls!" Perry stepped around a boulder near the front of the van and Dean walked around the other side. Perry's eyes flickered from Darcy to Sam and back to Darcy. He gave Sam a quick hug and then approached Darcy. She forgot all about his hair in that moment as he hugged her, and she breathed in and closed her eyes. He smelled of sunshine and cotton, and he lingered a brief moment longer than he had with Sam.

She beamed at him as he pulled away. "Hi!" she and Sam said breathlessly at the same time.

Dean grunted and waved. "Helloooo! I'm here, too, you know."

"Oh! Sorry, Dean." Sam stepped forward to hug him, but he hung back.

"I didn't mean that I wanted a *hug*—that's Perry's thing—but a little acknowledgment would be nice."

"Hi, Dean," Darcy said dryly. She glanced back at Perry; he was watching her with a slight smile.

"Boys! Just what I need. Help with the bags, will you?" Sam's dad intruded and dumped two loaded suitcases at Dean's and Perry's feet.

"Sure thing!" Perry said and leapt to the task. He didn't seem to mind the excuse to flex his muscles.

While Perry and Dean wrestled with the bags, Sam took Darcy by the arm and drew her toward the lodge. "Wow!" she whispered. "Perry looks *amazing*. I love his haircut."

"Really?" Darcy asked, wrinkling her nose. "I think it looks a little . . . I don't know . . ."

"You don't like it? I think he can pull it off!"

They entered the lodge together and stood in the cool reception area. It was still pretty quiet since it was earlier than when Darcy's family usually arrived, and Darcy enjoyed savoring the arrival at camp without having to rush off to dinner. A few giggling children ran past them and slammed into the crash bar on the door, heading out to the boardwalk.

"I wonder if Amelia's here yet," Sam said. "I'm going to go ask." She trotted over to the reception desk, and Darcy moved back to the front door to look out at the parking lot.

Dean and Perry were almost to the door, each carrying two suitcases. They seemed to be trying to outdo each other, and they took the last twenty feet at a sprint. She swung the door wide for them at the last second and tried to get out of the way, but Dean lunged forward with his suitcases and slammed her into the doorjamb.

She ducked aside, feeling stupid for getting in the way and rubbing her shoulder where she'd hit the door.

"Hey, watch it!" Perry said sharply to Dean. He dropped his suitcases by the umbrella stand and put his hands on Darcy's shoulders. "You okay? Sorry about that."

Darcy stared up into his sky blue eyes. "I'm fine," she said in a very small voice.

"Okay!" Sam marched back to them, faltering as she saw Perry's hands on Darcy's shoulders. Perry dropped his hands and put them on his hips.

"What's up?" He turned his full attention on Sam.

She blinked once and then continued, "Amelia's family has been here since about lunch, so she's probably out at their cabin—"

"Yeah, we've already said hello," Perry said.

"Well, Darcy and I should go and see her, so do you guys want to come with?" She looked hopeful.

"Nah, we said we'd help your dad with a few more things. We'll see you girls at dinner." He and Dean turned to the door. "Hey," Perry said, turning back to them, "when's Lewis getting here?"

"I don't know, probably in an hour or so. They were still packing their car when we pulled out."

"Cool. See you later."

Sam watched his back through the pane of glass in the door while Darcy stood next to her doing the same. "Oh, Darcy," Sam murmured. "Every year I think I'll be over him, but I never am. And he never treats me as anything more than a friend!"

Darcy cleared her throat. "Come on," she said, heading to the opposite door. "Don't pine. Let's go see Amelia!"

Darcy shook her head at Amelia Bennet, who was sitting across the table from her in the dining hall. She and Sam had told Amelia earlier about the article detailing Colin's disappearance from Cedar Cove that year, and they'd wondered if his parents would still show up this week. Sam had checked discreetly with the front desk and found that they were still registered to come, but a scan of the dining hall confirmed they were not there yet. Darcy would understand if they didn't make it; she didn't think *she* would want to return somewhere a family member had gone missing from, either.

As they finished dessert, Darcy felt another stab of annoyance that she hadn't been able to maneuver to sit next to Amelia so they could confer in whispers. Rather, she was seated across from Amelia, who sat between her parents, of whom she was a perfect combination. Both of them were tall and willowy like Amelia, and she had her dad's hazel eyes and her mom's straw-colored hair. Mr. and Mrs. Bennet were very prim and proper, and from time to time Mrs. Bennet looked askance at Roger, who hadn't put down his phone once during the entire meal.

Darcy tapped her foot, waiting for everybody to finish up so she and Amelia could meet with the others. She knew nobody else was as bothered as she was about Colin's absence. In fact, the rest of them all seemed rather relieved.

"At least *this* year we won't have to worry about him sneaking around after us," Sam had said just before dinner.

"But that's a moot point if he's already *in* Alitheia," Darcy had pointed out.

Darcy still felt rather cheated by his absence. She'd wanted to corner him and *make* him tell her how he'd been able to transport himself to Alitheia, even just as an apparition. She'd wanted him to explain why he'd had an Oracle scar on his hand in Alitheia and not in their world. And most of all she'd wanted to know, once and for all, whether or not he was in league with Tselloch. Only he could answer these questions, and she'd waited all year for the opportunity to ask them. Coupled with her frustration was a fear for his safety. If he *was* in Alitheia, then he had to be with Tselloch, and what did Tselloch want with him anyway?

After what felt like an eternity, the adults at the table finally pushed back their chairs and began gathering up the dishes. Darcy jumped in to help them, and her mother raised her eyebrows skeptically; the sooner they got everything cleared up, the sooner Darcy and Amelia could escape. Sam joined them and they made even faster work of it.

"Make sure you're in the room by ten o'clock!" Darcy's dad called after her as she and the other two girls scampered off through the crowded dining hall.

"The boys are out here," Sam said, dodging the rack of dirty dessert trays and leading them outside.

"Well, where to?" Perry asked as soon as they joined them.

"I want to check out their cabin," Darcy said before anybody else could make a suggestion.

"Whose cabin?" Lewis said, frowning at her.

"The Mackabys' . . . you know, East Mooring."

The others looked at her, a little exasperated. "Darcy, nobody knows what happened to Colin. What possible good could it do to go out there?" Sam asked. "Let's go find a private spot and talk about things that are *a little more important*."

"Come on, please?" Darcy clasped her hands together. "Let's just go out to East Mooring and look around—it'll only take a few minutes! Then I'll drop it, I promise."

"I'm game," Perry said, shrugging a shoulder. Darcy smiled at him.

The others quickly, if reluctantly, capitulated once Perry did, and they began to make their way to the door.

"So, what exactly is she hoping to find?" Amelia asked Sam.

Darcy didn't hear a response from Sam, and she didn't really care. She led them through the campsite, ignoring the greetings of people who were busy setting up their tents and campers. She could hear Perry, Dean, and Lewis discussing Colin's disappearance in low tones.

"It's weird, isn't it?" one of them whispered.

"Serves him right if he *did* get his butt frozen to death," another replied disdainfully.

East Mooring was set quite a distance from the rest of camp, sheltered by a good fifty yards of forest from those families who pitched tents and campers instead of staying in the lodge or the cabins. It had its own private beach and dock and was one of the nicest places to stay at Cedar Cove. The cabin itself was dark and abandoned, as it was still registered to the Mackaby family, but none of them were there.

Darcy climbed the steps to the door and the rest of them hung back. She tried the handle, but it was locked. Cupping her hands on either side of her face, she peered through the screened window, but all she could see were shadowy forms of a neat sitting room and kitchenette. She descended from the door and began a circuit of the cabin, brushing cobwebs aside in the tall grass that grew from the foundations of the cabin. A rustle behind her announced that at least one of her friends was following her.

It didn't take long, and she arrived back at the front to find Amelia, Dean, and Lewis waiting and looking bored. Perry and Sam emerged from the woods behind her a moment later.

Darcy put her hands on her hips and looked left to right. Deciding the beach was the next best place to check, she headed in that direction. This time everybody followed her.

"What exactly are we looking for, Darcy?" Amelia called, a hint of annoyance in her voice. "If you *tell* us, we can help you."

"Anything . . . clues . . . I don't know, exactly," Darcy responded. "Just let me look, okay?"

"It's fine, Darcy," Sam said. "We're behind you."

Darcy nodded and walked slowly along the small, private beach. She felt nothing tangible—nothing that compared to the tingles she'd felt her first night at Cedar Cove two years before—but she *did* feel an inexplicable draw to East Mooring. She walked out to the end of the dock and peered around before turning back. Off to one side she could see a game trail heading off into the woods behind the cabin, and she set off to follow it.

"Where are we going now?" Dean asked.

"There's a game trail over here that I want to check out," Darcy answered. "You don't have to come if you don't want to. I'll be right back."

"Darcy, you shouldn't go into the woods alone. We're coming with you," Sam said, huffing as she hurried across the sand behind her.

The trail was so narrow it only allowed for a single-file line. Darcy led with Sam behind her, and Perry, Dean, Lewis, and Amelia brought up the rear. Her heart began to beat faster. She trotted along but, after only a few minutes, she lost it. The trail came to an abrupt end in a pile of rocks.

Darcy stopped and frowned, her hopes falling. The forest was thick here, and no sign of the trail showed behind the rocks. She'd felt certain they would find *something* here. Now that her investigation had come up dry, though, she felt more than a little foolish. She turned around and shrugged. "Nothing, I guess. Sorry."

"Can we go back now?" Amelia called up to her.

"Yeah, go ahead!" Darcy gestured that they should turn back around. As she dropped her hand to her side, she noticed a dark wisp of fog curling around her sandaled feet. "Wait," she said as the wisp vanished on the breeze.

Amelia and Lewis were already around a bend and out of sight, but the other three stopped and looked curiously at Darcy, following her eyeline to her feet.

"What is it?" Sam whispered.

"I thought I saw—"

Sam's teeth began to chatter and she wrapped her arms around her chest. "Whoa, did it just get really cold?"

"There it is again," Darcy said, pointing toward the forest floor. A very thin, inky ground mist curled and undulated in their direction, but after another moment it vanished.

Darcy looked up and turned wide eyes on Dean and Perry. Perry's mouth was hanging open and Dean had gone white.

"It can't be here," Perry whispered. "It's a *spell*—"

"What *is* it?" Sam asked in a high-pitched voice. "Guys?" She tried to back down the trail, but Perry was frozen behind her.

The fog appeared again, just at Darcy's feet, and she felt its iciness caress her toes. An irrational fear brought back horrible memories of darkness, and panic gripped her soul. She jumped backward and it disappeared again. "Let's get out of here."

Dean turned and sped down the trail, Perry, Sam, and Darcy hot on his heels. They burst out onto the beach and threw themselves down onto the sand, gasping for air.

"What the . . . What on *earth* took you guys so long? And what's wrong with Sam?" Amelia's expression changed from annoyance to alarm as she wrapped her arms around Sam, who had dissolved into tears.

"Darcy?" Lewis said. He'd been cleaning his glasses on his T-shirt and had put them back on hurriedly when they'd reappeared. "What did you find?"

Darcy sat up and dug her hands into her hair. "It's difficult to explain . . ." She dropped her hands to her knees and looked to Perry for help. He was lying on his back staring up at the sky, oblivious to her petition.

Dean answered for her instead. "It was like a part of this spell we ran into on our way to the Oracle, outside of Fobos. But it's—"

"Impossible," Perry finally spoke. "Totally impossible! How can it be here? How can any magic work *here?*"

"Do you mean the fear spell?" Lewis asked. "The one that almost killed you guys?"

"Yeah, but this was a lot smaller. Outside of Fobos it was huge, and it was everywhere!" Dean gestured in a wild arc.

Sam's sobs had subsided into hiccups and she stood unsteadily. "Well, whatever it is, can we get farther away from it?" she asked in a shaky voice.

"I'm sorry, Sam." Darcy jumped up and brushed off her legs. "I shouldn't have insisted that we come out here. It was stupid."

"It doesn't matter, Darcy," Sam said, brushing off her apology.

"What does this mean for us?" Lewis asked as they picked their way back toward the campsite.

"It means we *really* need some answers," Darcy said. "I say we try to get through the gateway in the morning."

CHAPTER 5

EARTH, WIND, FIRE, AND WATER

"Oh, for Pete's sake!" Darcy grumbled, using one of her dad's favorite expressions. She was standing in front of the gateway, passing her arm back and forth between the two trees that marked the spot, and nothing was happening. She knew she shouldn't feel so surprised; the moment they had arrived they'd been able to tell that the gateway wasn't open. The two trees looked like ordinary mundane trees, no telltale shimmer betraying a magical portal, nor any magical critters pointing the way or leading them through, though they'd scoured the area for a good half hour looking for one.

Footsteps crunched through the underbrush, and Darcy looked over her shoulder to see Perry ducking under a low-hanging birch limb to get to her side. "Anything yet?" he asked quietly.

Darcy shook her head and put her hands on her hips. "Nope."

"I suppose that serves us right for trying to get through earlier than usual. I guess it's on a timer, or something." He scratched his chin.

"How are the others?" Darcy peered back through the woods toward Gnome's Haven. "Are they getting really tired of waiting?" It had been close to two hours already and, though they all had agreed to wait it out, Darcy knew the lunch bell would be ringing at any moment.

"They're fine. Sam and Dean climbed the rock and Amelia's been boring us all to death talking about Simon." He snorted. "As if I really care that he graduated with high honors."

Darcy chuckled. Amelia's relationship with Simon had lasted longer than any of them had thought it would, but now he would be heading off to college in another state, and Darcy doubted they would stay together much longer. "Give her a break," she said. "They've been together for a year, so they must *really* like each other."

"Hmm," Perry responded, reaching up to tuck an errant strand of Darcy's hair behind her ear.

Darcy froze and they stared at each other, the silence broken only by the distant sound of a clanging bell. Darcy cleared her throat and looked down. "That's the lunch bell," she said unnecessarily. Perry had been attending Cedar Cove with his family since he was a baby. He knew what the lunch bell sounded like.

"We should head back," Perry said. "If we don't show up for lunch, our parents will freak out. We can come back over on the ferry as soon as lunch is over."

Darcy hated to admit that he was right. She frowned back at the two trees, desperately wanting answers. Waiting even a few more hours to return to Alitheia felt as though it might as well be another week.

Before she knew what she was doing, she had fallen to her knees amidst the ferns before the two trees. "What are you doing?" Perry asked, but his voice seemed far away. She held her hands out before her, her palms facing up in a gesture of supplication. She didn't know what compelled her, but she slid her eyes closed and thought of Pateros—not as the great bear that had saved her life more than once, or as the golden eagle that led them home each year, but as the gentle stag that had watched her from the woods. *Please*, she thought, mouthing the word without speaking it aloud.

Perry gasped beside her, and she knew her request had been granted even before opening her eyes.

"I'll go get the others, you stay here," Perry said, and he crashed away through the underbrush.

Darcy opened her eyes and looked up at the shimmer that had formed between the trees. She stood and held out her cold hand toward it, brushing the surface and feeling little shockwaves pulse through her.

"What did you *do?*" Sam huffed up beside her and staring in awe at the gateway. "Perry said that you prayed or something?"

"I didn't do anything," Darcy said. "I just asked."

"Well it worked," Dean said, looking appreciatively at her. "I was beginning to think we'd have to—"

The gateway flickered, and they drew in a collective breath. "Come on, guys, all together!" Perry said, and they pushed en masse through the gateway.

Going through the gateway together made the passage less than comfortable. Darcy felt as though her face got suctioned and for a moment she couldn't breathe. When they broke apart, Darcy opened and closed her mouth several times, trying to make her ears pop. She noticed her friends making similar faces.

The forest in Alitheia was silent. No gnomes or fairies were visible, and the shimmer between the trees had disappeared. The landscape was still vividly colorful, but it felt abandoned, like an empty auditorium.

"I guess they weren't expecting us so soon," Lewis said.

"Obviously," Perry muttered. He stretched and flipped his hair out of his eyes. "What should we do? Wait here?"

"I'm hungry," Dean said. "We should have thought about lunch."

"Why did Pateros let us through if they aren't going to come and get us for a couple hours yet?" Sam wondered aloud.

"Because Darcy *asked* him to," Amelia said. She shook her head. "We should have just waited."

Darcy felt a stab of anger. Here they were, back in *Alitheia*, and they all were grumbling! "I'm not going to mope around here," she said. "I'm heading to Gnome's Haven. Maybe we can get a message to them that we've arrived. Or, if worse comes to worst, we'll just hike to Kenidros. It's not like we don't know the way."

"Darcy's right," Sam leapt to her support. "We shouldn't just wait here. Let's go."

"All *right*," Amelia huffed. Although annoyed, Darcy didn't blame Amelia for being cranky. Amelia hated leaving her family—not to mention Simon—for so long every year, and she covered up her pain with a brittle exterior. Darcy knew Amelia would probably cry herself to sleep for a few nights, but she always snapped out of it.

Retracing their steps in Alitheia always felt strange. Alitheia was a parallel world to theirs, in the vicinity of the active gateway at least, and in some ways it felt as though they hadn't really gone anywhere. Sure the colors were brighter, but until they first sighted something otherworldly, or a structure that existed only in Alitheia, Darcy couldn't quite register that they were in another realm.

The fairies were silent at the moment, though, and when they reached the house-sized boulder that was Gnome's Haven, the various cubbies and nooks were empty and dark.

"This isn't right," Darcy murmured.

"Where are the gnomes?" Sam asked anxiously. She moved closer and examined a few of the cubbies.

"Maybe this is what it's like here all the time, when nothing's going on, I mean," Lewis said.

"Maybe . . ." But Darcy didn't know if she believed that. Gnomes were too playful to spend most of their time tucked away in their tunnels.

"There's one!" Dean shouted, pointing to a rosy-cheeked, fat female gnome who had poked a head out of her tunnel and squinted at them.

"Hello!" Sam leaned over to her. "Can you tell us where—"

"Ppppthhhhh!" The gnome stuck out her tongue at Sam and blew a raspberry. Then she popped back into her hole.

Sam blinked and wiped gnome spittle off her face. "Well, that was rude."

"At least we know they're still here," Perry reasoned. "What do you think, Darcy?"

Darcy looked at the hole into which the gnome had disappeared. "I don't know," she admitted. "Maybe they're scared of something." She searched for a familiar cranny. "I'd like to see if Brachos will come out."

She found his crevice with relative ease. He was, after all, the first gnome she had ever seen, and the position of his home was emblazoned in her memory. In their world, his home was just a shallow dip, but in Alitheia it opened up to a tunnel that burrowed deep within the rock. Darcy lowered her face close, but not too close, mindful of the face-full of spit Sam had just received. "Brachos," she called softly, and then a little louder, "Brachos!"

She heard some scritching and scratching, and a few pebbles rolled out of his hole before his bearded face popped out. Gnomes didn't speak human speech—although they did imitate human words from time to time—and he wasn't a high animal, so Darcy couldn't use her mind speaking abilities, but she knew that he, like all Alitheian magical creatures and high animals, could understand human speech. "Hello! We—we're back!"

Brachos made a noise in his throat that sounded like a handful of pebbles grinding together.

"Right, ah . . . I guess that was obvious. There's nobody here to meet us, though. Do you think—that is—is it possible for you to deliver a message for us?"

Brachos lowered his eyebrows and waved his short little arms at her as he launched into a stream of aggravated chittering. He punctuated his rant by growling and slapping his hands on the rock, and finally he shook his head and popped back out of sight.

"What was *that* all about?" Perry asked in the silence that followed his disappearance.

"Ummm . . ." Darcy looked at Sam, who was covering her mouth with her hand and trying not to laugh. "Sam!"

"What? It was funny, you have to admit! Still," she lowered her hand and sobered, "he seemed pretty upset about something. I don't think he's able to help us."

Darcy and the others nodded. "So what next? Should we hike to Kenidros?"

"What if we miss them?" Amelia asked. "They're probably bringing the *Cal Meridian* again, and what if they set off early and we miss each other in passing? If I were Captain Boreas, I'd be pretty ticked off if I got my ship all ready for nothing."

Darcy had to admit that was logical, but it meant they'd have to hang out where they were for another two or three hours, and that would make everybody even crankier.

"And then they'd worry about us," Lewis said.

Darcy sighed. "Yeah, you're right. Let's at least go down to the shoals, though. If they come in on the ship, it would be best if they could see us right away."

"And then we can pass the time by skipping rocks, or something," Sam said. She often tried to best Perry at rock-skipping, but Darcy was still the only girl who had ever done that, and that had only been under the strange power that had come upon her on her first night ever at Cedar Cove.

They picked their way over to the bridge that led from the rock shelf down to the shoreline, and Darcy couldn't shake the feeling that something was amiss.

"What happened here?" Perry asked, bending down to examine the planks near the bottom of the bridge where it terminated suddenly.

The last ten or twelve feet of the causeway, which usually extended down into the water, had been blasted away. The distance to the shoals wasn't too great to jump, though, and Perry and Dean hopped down to help Darcy, Sam, and Amelia. Sam blushed when Perry took her hand, but he was already looking at Darcy. Lewis slid down after the girls, shooting daggers at Dean with his eyes when Dean mockingly extended a hand to help.

They gathered around on the rocks, staring at the twisted and charred chunks of wood that now made up the end of the pier. Pieces of the causeway were scattered over the shoals, and some were caught up in tide pools among the rocks. Darcy picked up a splinter and turned it over in her fingers. Feeling a sudden tingling sensation between her shoulder blades, she raised her head and looked around. Nobody was around but them. The sea extended beyond the point like a stretch of blue satin, and a few gulls winged in the still air above them. The only thing that looked strange was the faint curl of smoke rising above the trees no more than a quarter-mile down the shoreline.

"I see it, too," Lewis said in her ear. "I think there's someone down there."

"Where?" Perry asked, squinting in the direction they were looking.

"There, where the shore bends inland. You see the smoke?" Darcy pointed.

"Oh," he said, turning to Darcy and Lewis with a gleam in his eye. "We should go check it out."

"Are you crazy?" Darcy asked and shook her head. "Listen, I'm the queen of bad decisions, and even *I* can see it would be really stupid to go down there. It could be tsellodrin, for all we know, and we don't have any weapons or anything!"

"Ah, come on, it's not tsellodrin. When have you ever seen a tsellodrin light a fire? Plus, the isthmus is protected, remember? By 'old enchantments,' or whatever."

"*Somewhat* protected," Darcy corrected him. "It's not failsafe."

"I bet they're cooking something," Dean chimed in wistfully.

"And what makes you think they'd give us some of it if they are?" Darcy asked.

"Darcy's right," Amelia stepped in. "It's a bad idea. We should just wait here."

"We could go and check it out and get back long before the ship arrives," Perry argued. "Aren't you at least a little curious?"

"Curious, yes, but what if it's those people, or *creatures*, that did this?" Darcy gestured to the wreckage around them.

"We don't need to go looking for trouble," Amelia said, nodding in support. "It always seems to find us anyway."

Perry scowled at Darcy as though she'd betrayed him. Darcy had to admit that a year ago she would have capitulated to *anything* Perry had wanted to do so badly, but she liked to think she had learned *something* over the last few years.

Perry made his next move.

"What do you think, Sam?" He turned his most winning smile on her. "Don't you want to go and check it out?"

Ooh . . . that's low, Darcy thought, feeling a sting of anger that Perry would use Sam's feelings for him to get what he wanted.

"Sam, you don't have to agree with him," Darcy said.

Sam opened her mouth, her wide baby-blue eyes, blond curls, and clear complexion making her look young and vulnerable. "Oh, don't ask me! I hate being put on the spot." She buried her face in her hands.

"Come on, Sam, we need to take a vote. All in favor of going?" Perry, Dean, and—to Darcy's great surprise—Lewis all raised their hands.

"Lewis!" Darcy glared at him.

He took off his glasses and cleaned them so as not to look her in the eyes. "I'm really hungry," he muttered, "and kinda curious. It doesn't mean we have to *talk* to them; let's just go take a look."

"All in favor of *not* going?"

Darcy and Amelia raised their hands. Sam remained unmoving.

"Come on, Sam, you have to vote," Perry urged.

"Well . . . if I vote to stay, will the three of you stay, too?"

Perry looked at Dean and Lewis. "I don't know, maybe we'll go. The three of us can handle ourselves."

Darcy sucked air in through her teeth and crossed her arms. She'd known that he could be stubborn, but this was ridiculous! Right at this moment, she hated Perry's stupid pop-star haircut and the absurd shoes he was wearing that were shaped like actual feet, complete with a spot for each toe.

Sam turned pleading eyes upon Darcy. "We really shouldn't split up!" she whispered. "If they're determined to go, we should go with them and get it over with. I bet we can get back in plenty of time."

Amelia tisked and rolled her eyes. "You're just giving him what he wants, Sam."

"Still . . ."

Darcy huffed and dropped her arms. As much as she hated to concede, staying together was wiser than splitting up, even if it meant being forced into something every fiber of her being screamed out against. "Okay, fine!" She wanted to smack the look of gleeful triumph right off Perry's face. "But if we do this, we're going to be smart about it!" She jabbed a finger at Dean. "He's going to have to go in alone to check it out with his talent before any of us get too close!"

"Of course!" Perry said, spreading his arms. "Give me some credit." He flipped his hair and turned down the shoreline.

Darcy exchanged an exasperated look with Amelia before hurrying to catch up with Perry, hoping at least to keep the boys from blundering things up too badly.

She jumped from rock to rock, occasionally losing her balance on a wobbly one and almost falling into the water. It did nothing to improve her mood.

Three or four miles down the coast, off the isthmus onto the mainland, they would eventually come to the ruins of Paradeisos, but the smoke column was much nearer than that. Already they were close enough to smell the burning logs and roasting meat. A man's gruff voice drifted across the water, and Perry and Darcy motioned for the others to stop. Crouching low, Perry led them away from the sea and toward the tree line. They crept into the shadowy woods and fetched up against a car-sized mossy boulder. Darcy saw movement out of the corner of her eye and jumped, but it was just a fairy disappearing into a fern stalk.

"Okay," Perry whispered, "Dean and Sam will go forward and check it —"

Sam squeaked at her name. "Why me?" She stared at Perry like he was about to throw her in front of a freight train.

"Because you can tell, just by looking at them, whether or not they're trustworthy," Perry said matter-of-factly.

"It's not that simple!" Sam said. "If they don't know we're here, they have no intentions toward us at all, good *or* bad. I might not be able to sense anything!"

"Still, I think you should go," Perry insisted. Then he smiled at her again. "Come on, Sam, it's no big deal. Dean can cloak you with his magic. You *can* do two people at once, right, Dean?"

Dean shrugged. "Yeah, I mean, we just got back so I'm a little out of practice, but that's pretty basic for me now."

"Great." Perry didn't give Sam a chance to argue. "So, like I was saying, Dean and Sam will go ahead and check them out. If they seem pretty harmless, then we can go and ask for something to eat."

"Stupid," Amelia muttered.

"We don't have to tell them who we *are*," Perry said.

"Look at how we're dressed!" Darcy said. "How are they *not* going to know?"

"Oh, yeah . . . well . . . Come on! We came this far. What do you want to do, turn back?"

"Yes!" Darcy and Amelia said at the same time, and Sam nodded vigorously.

"I'm sorry, Perry," Sam said. "I shouldn't have agreed to this."

"We're going back," Darcy said. "And if you boys have any brains at all, you'll come with us . . ." She faltered and looked around. "Wait a second, where's Dean?"

The others looked around, too, startled, but Dean was gone.

"Yes!" Perry said happily. "Probably got tired of listening to you all bickering and went to check it out."

Darcy closed her eyes and shook her head. "This is bad; this is *really* bad. He shouldn't have gone alone."

"What do you want to do, Darcy?" Sam was back in her camp.

Darcy sighed. "I think we should go and keep an eye out for him."

"But if he's using his magic, you won't be able to see him," Amelia said.

"I don't want to keep an eye *on* him; I want to keep an eye out *for* him. He hasn't practiced his talent in a year. If something goes wrong, I want to be able to warn him . . . or help him."

"Should we all go?" Lewis asked. He suddenly looked very nervous.

"No, I'll just go with Sam. If you'll come," she added, and Sam nodded.

"I'll come, too," Perry said, standing and brushing dead leaves off his legs.

"Fine, whatever. Will you guys be okay for a few minutes?" Darcy addressed Amelia and Lewis, avoiding looking at Perry.

"We'll be fine," Amelia said. "Just hurry."

Darcy, Sam, and Perry nodded and began to pick their way through the woods, staying close to the shoreline to keep their bearings. Before long, they came to a break in the trees through which they could see an inlet. They ducked behind trees as they spotted a group of about ten men clustered together in a makeshift camp at the far end of the cove.

Darcy breathed very slowly. Snatches of conversation floated across the water, but she couldn't make out anything distinct. "I can't tell if Dean is around there." Perry peeked around a tree as discreetly as he could.

Darcy nodded and looked over to her right. "Sam?" she whispered. Sam shook her head and shrugged, and Darcy understood that to mean Sam couldn't tell anything yet.

"Okay, let's move a little bit closer, *quietly!*" Darcy snapped as Perry stepped on a dead stick, snapping it loudly.

Like stealth army soldiers they flitted from tree to tree. It might have been fun, Darcy thought, to hum her own theme music and throw in a roll here or there, but the current situation didn't call for that, and Darcy was in no mood for it besides. They moved slowly around the inlet, inching closer and closer to the camp, finally stopping where they could hear the men and the crackling of the fire. They lay on their stomachs in three-foot-high beach grass, hidden behind a small cluster of sun-bleached rocks.

Darcy poked Sam and raised her eyebrows. Sam turned wide eyes on her and mouthed something, and Darcy shook her head and brought her ear closer to Sam's mouth.

"I feel very uneasy, like, *magical* uneasy," Sam said in the lowest of whispers.

Darcy turned to Perry and poked him in the ribs, more forcefully than she had Sam. It was more of a jab, really. She inched toward him and opened her mouth to deliver Sam's message.

"Hey! What's going on with our food?" one of the men in the camp shouted.

Darcy and Perry popped up and poked their heads over the rocks, trying to see and stay hidden at the same time. *Dean!* Darcy thought. *You idiot!* A hunk of roasted meat hung suspended in the air and then vanished, the great majority of the men in the camp roaring indignantly and rushing toward the phenomenon.

Darcy heard the thumping of tennis shoes over rocks and looked panic-stricken at Perry and Sam. Dean was running right at them, about to lead the men pursuing him directly to their hiding spot.

A breeze above them ruffled their hair as Dean cleared the rocks in a flying leap and fell, still cloaked, into their midst. The smell of roast meat came with him, and hot fat dripped onto Darcy's forearm, burning her.

"Ouch! Drop the meat, you idiot! Let's go!" She and Sam were already scrambling to their feet.

Dean popped into sight then, holding a sharp stick on which the meat was speared. He looked dumbfounded. "What are you guys doing here?"

"We came to make sure that you wouldn't get into trouble, which *obviously* you did! Now let's *get out of here!*"

The shouts of the men grew louder; they had been spotted. Dean dropped the stick and together the four of them scrambled for the cover of the trees.

"Why—did—you—have—to—steal—their—meat?" Darcy asked breathlessly, dodging trees and boulders.

"I could tell they were—bad guys," Dean answered, much less winded, as he bounded over a boulder. "I—didn't want to come back—empty handed!"

Sam cried out behind them. Darcy skidded to a stop and swung around to see Sam lying on her side, her foot stuck at an odd angle between two rocks. "Dean, Perry!" Darcy shouted, and the boys turned about and hurried back.

"It's my ankle," Sam wailed. "What are we going to *do?*" They had disappeared into the trees, but Sam's cry had drawn the pursuers in their direction. They were almost upon them.

Darcy extricated Sam's foot while Perry and Dean looked around for something to fight with. "Diplomacy first!" Darcy huffed at them as Sam whimpered and clung to her shoulder.

"What does that word even *mean?*" Perry picked up a large branch and brandished it like a sword.

"It means try talking to them!" Darcy said as the first of the men reached them and drew up short. He was rather short and very ugly, wearing a shirt that must at one time have been white but was now a gray-spotted yellow.

The other men piled in and looked to him for instructions. With a quick motion of his hand, the men had them surrounded. Darcy could see now what Dean had meant when he said they were "bad guys." They smelled of alcohol and smoke and they leered at them, eyeing Darcy and Sam in a way that made Darcy shiver and lower her eyes. She heard a thump as Perry dropped his branch.

"Smart," the leader said. He moved closer and Darcy heard the clear metal *shing* of a blade being drawn from a scabbard. Unable to bear not seeing the action, she looked up anxiously.

"I can't believe it," the man said, eyeing them incredulously.

"Look at how they're dressed!" another said. He was unusually tall and had a huge mole on his forehead.

"What a spot of luck for us," said the first man. "It's the blessed *Six*, come right into our hands to *save us*, isn't that right?" His eyes had lost their incredulity and now were cold like marbles. "Course, there are only four of you here. Where are your friends, darling?" He leered in Darcy's face. She set her jaw and looked away. "They're close by, I'd bet," the man shouted to his companions. "Find them and bring them to the camp!"

Four men peeled away into the woods while the others stayed to bind Darcy and her friends. They were not gagged, though, so whoever these men were, they were not afraid of being overheard. The men dragged them back to the makeshift camp and seated them back to back near the fire. A few minutes later, the four men returned with a struggling Amelia and an unconscious Lewis between them.

Once seated, Lewis woke slowly, his glasses gone and a large red lump above his left eye. "He tried to defend me," Amelia whispered to her friends. "Who *are* these guys?"

Darcy didn't have a good answer for her, so she turned instead to the men.

"Tselloch is doomed to lose someday, you know," she said.

"Tselloch!" the leader growled. "I don't serve that shadow spawn."

"Then you're on our side!" Darcy said.

"*Your* side?" He sneered at her. "And what have *you* done for us, eh? We serve ourselves! We don't need some prophecy or magical bear to help us survive." He spit on the ground. "We reject any who seek to enslave us to their way of thinking."

Darcy looked away. She could hear them now discussing sums of money, and had no trouble figuring out what that meant.

"Whoever they are," she said to her friends, "they're going to hold us for ransom."

"Makes sense," Sam said, her head down, breathing shallowly with her eyes closed. Her ankle was almost twice its normal size.

"So what do we do?" Perry asked. He'd been rather quiet for the last fifteen minutes.

"We try to escape," Darcy said. "They're not going to kill us now that they know who we are. We're worth way too much money."

"Escape," Amelia said. "And how are we going to do that?"

"Just give me a sec, okay?" Darcy closed her eyes and concentrated hard on the fibers in the ropes binding her wrists. She'd been at it since they'd first been tied up, and she could finally sense the knot coming loose. With a quick wiggle and a final shake, the ropes fell from her hands, but she kept them behind her back.

"Excellent!" Perry whispered. "Quick, do us, too!"

"Give me a minute, I'm tired." Darcy closed her eyes. She was out of practice but not nearly as weak as she had been the year before. "I'm going to try to trap them. I don't have the energy to set you all free and do that, too. Your legs are free, though, so be ready to run. And don't forget to help Sam!"

Darcy searched around for something she could use and settled on the trees. Down close to the water as they were, the roots of the ancient cedar trees all around them were exposed. The men were conversing right on top of a thick bundle of roots, if she could just . . .

She squinted and concentrated on penetrating the roots with her magic. She had to use her hands to direct the magic—she was too weak not to—so she raised them carefully, praying the men wouldn't notice. The roots began to rise from their beds and twine themselves around the men's feet. They made very faint creaking sounds, but they were too busy arguing about sums of money to notice.

Beads of sweat popped out on Darcy's forehead, and she paused for a moment as black dots clouded her vision. Pulling the roots from their resting places felt like pulling a tightly strung bow, but she willed them to move once again. If she could trap their feet, she and her friends might have a chance to get away.

One of the men stepped forward and tripped over a root wrapped halfway around his ankle. "What the——" He looked left to right and spotted Darcy. "She's using her magic!" He pointed wildly at Darcy, his other hand going for his sword.

The meeting of men broke apart in confusion as those who were partially trapped extricated themselves with much grumbling and cursing, and the leader shook a root off his boot and lumbered toward Darcy with a sneer.

Darcy slouched back, exhausted, and watched him approach. As he got closer, she could see that the whites of his eyes were yellow with malnutrition and several of his teeth were rotted.

"Witch!" he spat in her face. His breath was rancid. "You dare use *magic* against me?" He raised a hand holding a curved sword, his clamped fist shaking. She met his eyes and saw his unwavering intent to kill.

He swung down his arm, but his sword spun out of his hand and landed somewhere in the woods far away. Darcy and Amelia gasped as Sam cried aloud. The man snarled and whirled around as a loud foghorn sounded in the bay. All of them looked up to see the golden ship that had just weighed anchor, its deep blue sails billowing and snapping in the wind.

"Yes!" Perry cried out as the man called out orders to his men. In a moment the six were each taken into the grasp of one of the ruffians, blades held at each of their throats.

"If you want them," the bladeless leader called out, standing before them and gesturing to the six, "you'll have to pay for them!"

Darcy almost laughed at the man's foolishness as a familiar figure on deck made a flicking movement with his hand. *Rubidius.* A rock soared through the air and smashed into the leader's head. He crumpled to the ground instantly.

A couple of the men dropped their weapons and ran for the woods, while a few others tightened their grips on their captives. Rubidius, the master magician, looked furious standing on the deck of the ship. His wild hair blew around him, his sleeves were rolled up, and Darcy could almost imagine that his eyes were flashing with fire.

With another flick of Rubidius's hand, the tree roots rose and—as Darcy had tried to make them— trapped the men escaping into the woods. Once they were immobilized, Rubidius raised a sheet of water from the bay and advanced it toward the men still holding the captives. The wind blew the salty water into their faces, and Darcy turned her head away, coughing and sputtering. The arms of the man holding onto her began to shake, and she wriggled madly, breaking free. She sloshed over to Sam and Amelia, their captors already having abandoned them, and they huddled together.

The now sodden men tried frantically to escape, but Rubidius was not finished. He rose what remained of the fire into a curtain of flames, cutting off their escape to the woods. Darcy felt the heat of the flames as she watched, and the steam rising from the clothes of the men nearest the fire gave her an idea. Summoning her last reserves of magical strength, she grabbed a gust of wind and pushed it toward the fire, hot ash blowing up into the eyes of the remaining men. They cried out in pain and grabbed at their faces.

A golden circlet of light flashed into being in the air around them. Darcy squinted and jumped back, the bright light momentarily blinding her. With a crack and a soft *boom* the light contracted inward and touched her chest. She looked around, her eyes wild and confused, and saw Rubidius, the light touching his chest as well. It pulsed against her heart, and she felt her strength return and her magic intensify. She gasped aloud as the light shot outward in an expanding circle that vanished almost instantly, leaving the air tingling with golden ripples in its wake.

The remaining men fell to their knees and raised their hands above their heads in surrender. Rubidius let the water and the fire subside, and sailors from the ship began to pile into coracles and row ashore.

Darcy looked to Rubidius, her eyes full of relief and wonder. She wanted to ask him what had just happened to them, what that golden ring had been, but from the shore she could see that his face was drawn. He crossed his arms and glared at the six of them.

He looked positively livid.

CHAPTER 6
A DIFFERENT WELCOME

Darcy watched as the men were ushered below deck to the two small holding cells aboard the *Cal Meridian*. Rubidius stood at her side with his arms crossed and, although he hadn't yet said a word to them, he continuously huffed and muttered to himself.

"Foolishness!" he grunted. "Childish behavior."

Darcy winced with each harsh utterance. She should have been firmer with Perry and Dean; she never should have allowed this to happen. In fact, she never should have tried to get through the gateway ahead of schedule. Why would Pateros allow them through early if the Alitheians weren't yet ready for them?

Once the prisoners were secured and the coracles on board, Boreas, the golden-haired captain of the *Cal Meridian,* called out orders to his crew, and they pulled in the anchor to make way. Crew members took to the oars to row them out of the cove, and Darcy steadied herself with both hands on the gold-painted banister as the schooner lurched into motion. Finally, Rubidius looked down his nose at her, and Darcy cringed under his gaze.

"How did you know where to find us?" she asked in a small voice.

He sniffed. "Brachos brought a message to the low castle that you had arrived early, and from there they sent a message to Ormiskos. We left as quickly as we were able and, when we arrived, we followed the smoke. We had *assumed* that you would stay *put*." He arched an eyebrow angrily.

Darcy assumed that by "low castle" Rubidius meant Kenidros, the second of two castles built in Alitheia's history, and the nearest to the gateway's location.

"We're sorry," Darcy said as penitently as she could.

"Darcy and Amelia wanted us to stay at Gnome's Haven; it wasn't their fault," Sam added. She was leaning on a pair of makeshift crutches, her ankle bound between two sturdy planks of wood. Only a grimace here and there betrayed the pain she was in; she was holding up admirably.

"Humph!" Rubidius said. He studied Darcy, his eyes more shrewd than angry. "Perhaps we should have been ready for you. We assumed you would come at the same time as the two times before."

"We should have," Darcy said. "I asked for it to—that is—I asked *Pateros* to open the gateway early, and he did, but just for a minute or two."

Rubidius made a sound of surprise, knitting his brows together and looking befuddled.

"Why do you think—"

"I do not know," Rubidius answered without allowing her to finish. "Perhaps . . ." he trailed off and squinted toward the shore. The ship was already coming abreast of the shoreline where the destroyed causeway sat. "Perhaps that is why."

He pointed, and Darcy's hands on the railing grew white at the knuckles. She almost screamed, trying to scramble backward, but Rubidius blocked her way.

"Calm yourself, Darcy," he said, placing his hands on her shoulders. "It is only an apparition."

Her friends leaned over the railing, gazing at the figure at the burned end of the pier. They had never seen him before. Darcy, however, recognized him immediately.

His preternaturally tall form was swathed in robes of deepest black that matched his skin, as dark as ink. His hair was long and smooth, hanging about his shoulders, and his facial features were aquiline and appeared chiseled from stone. Darcy stared at him in terror, her heart pounding within her chest, when she noticed in his face the outline of cedar limbs. She could see through him. Rubidius was right; he was only an apparition.

"Who *is* that?" Sam asked.

"It is Tselloch," Rubidius answered matter-of-factly.

"*What?*" Sam shrieked as the others backed away from the side of the ship. As they watched, Tselloch's form flickered and vanished.

"It wasn't really him," Rubidius said. "He's able to project himself—an image of himself, that is. He's become quite adept at it, and he is getting bolder." He looked up at the wheel deck where Boreas was watching them. The captain's face looked grim.

"So, it wasn't—it wasn't—it—"

"No, Sam, it wasn't him in person."

"Isn't it about the time that we usually arrive?" Lewis asked quietly.

Rubidius looked over at him. "Yes."

"So . . . he knows where the gateway is," Darcy said, "*and* what time we arrive."

"As we thought he might," Rubidius reminded her.

Darcy's mind filled with the image of a man falling from the sky, the words "follow me" etched in blood across his chest. She closed her eyes to erase the memory.

"Could he have done anything to us? In that form, I mean?" she whispered.

"We do not know the extent of his power, but I do not believe he could have physically hurt you. Talked with you, frightened and discouraged you, deceived you, even. But hurt you . . ." Rubidius shook his head. "It is unlikely. Unless he can enchant in that form—"

"And now he knows for certain where the gateway is located," a familiar voice cut in. Torrin descended the left staircase from the upper deck and brought with him a scent of earthiness and sweat. "Perhaps he only suspected last time, but now his suspicions are confirmed."

Rubidius seemed unfazed. Darcy suspected he believed Tselloch to have known the gateway's location long before now.

"Why don't you place a guard on the gateway?" she asked him, ignoring Torrin as the shaggy-haired scout clasped hands with the boys and bowed to Sam, Amelia, and herself.

"Obviously because we do not want to draw undue attention to it. There are others—" Rubidius stopped himself and took a deep breath.

The ship was heading out into deeper water and the sails had taken over for the oarsmen. The breeze picked up and ruffled Rubidius's beard, and Darcy shivered as the cooler air raised goose bumps on her arms.

"The ancient enchantments, coupled with the newer protection provided by myself and other magicians, have served very well to keep the peninsula secure as of late," he said at last, calmer.

"Secure?" Perry asked, his voice rising. "Then what was all *that* about?" He gestured back toward the inlet where they'd been captured.

"And why was the pier blown up?" Darcy asked.

"Those are . . . separate, but related, issues that have nothing to do with Tselloch. At least, not directly," Rubidius said. "The enchantments do not protect against those who do not serve the Shadow."

He was quiet for a moment as he gathered his thoughts, and Darcy thought he looked weary. She wondered how much energy it took him to perform magic like he'd just done.

"Increasingly, as of late, some people have become . . . disillusioned with the state of affairs in the land," Rubidius began again.

"What does *that* mean?" Sam asked.

Rubidius glanced at Sam. "It means they lived miserable lives under Tselloch's rule, and they do not see how life is any better now under the regency of Lord Tullin. Tselloch and his servants still roam the land, and the promised Six," he inclined his head at them, "are not—in their eyes—fulfilling the words of the prophecy."

"How are we *supposed* to fulfill the darn prophecy if we're never allowed to go out, find Tselloch, and fight him?" Perry asked. "It's not our fault we're not allowed to do anything!"

"Calm yourself, Master Perry," Torrin said, leaning his side against the railing and watching the conversation with interest.

Darcy looked fearfully from Rubidius to Perry, expecting the volatile alchemist to explode in anger, but he seemed too weary to make that sort of response. Instead he merely said, "They apportion equal blame to you as to those of us who have sought to protect, guide, and teach you. Although, really, they blame most of this land's ills on magic itself. They have thus rejected and scorned their magical abilities, and they persecute those who do practice their talents. To use magic against them is considered a crime punishable by death . . . according to their rules, at least. Most of them now live as petty thieves and ruffians, but their numbers swell every day that Tselloch remains free."

"We *have* to do something about him," Perry said. "Rubidius, we can't sit around being trained forever!"

Darcy's heart sank as she listened, understanding now why Rubidius was so reluctant to allow them to launch a rescue mission for Yahto Veli; it would detract from their purpose in Alitheia. The people of Alitheia needed them—they needed a morale boost. Darcy swallowed hard and studied her fingernails.

"But what about the destroyed pier? Did those men do that?" Amelia asked.

"No, Tellius did that," Rubidius replied, chuckling.

"What?" Amelia and Sam said at the same time. Darcy merely looked up, interested despite herself.

"Yesterday," Rubidius said, "we sailed around here to search for the men who captured you today. They've been causing trouble in this area for some months, and Tellius wanted to confront them directly. We couldn't find them, but we located their camp on the shore at Gnome's Haven; their fire was still smoldering. They've scared most of the fairies and gnomes into hiding, as I'm sure you've noticed. They had also left an *unsavory* message carved into the pier . . . a welcome for you six, you could call it. Tellius wanted to burn it off using his fire talent, and I thought it would be good practice for him. The fire they'd left still had some burning embers, so Tellius had what he needed to work with. Well, he was rather angry about the message and he let his talent get away from him a bit—"

"A bit?" Dean laughed. "You mean he blew up the end of the pier?"

"It was a good learning experience," Rubidius insisted, looking ruffled. "He singed a few hairs, and I guarantee he will not let his temper get the best of his talent again!"

Darcy snorted and shook her head. Fire, like air, was a very volatile element to control. Earth and water were more stable and easier to master. "So, he's gotten pretty strong, then?" she asked Rubidius.

"Stronger," Rubidius allowed. "Indeed . . . stronger. He must learn quickly, of course, if he wants to be able to maintain his claim to the throne."

"What does his magic have to do with his right to inherit the throne?" Lewis asked.

"It shouldn't have any bearing on it," Torrin said. He seemed no longer capable of staying out of the conversation. "But in this present climate, the people want to look ahead to a strong leader. If Tellius were to neglect his magical instruction, word would get out, and those still loyal to the Ecclektos line would lose faith in him. There is already a movement among the nobility to leave Tullin on the throne beyond Tellius's seventeenth birthday."

Darcy gasped, feeling indignant for the young prince. She looked from Torrin to Rubidius. "But Tullin wouldn't agree to that, would he?"

Rubidius hesitated. "No. He loves Tellius like the son he never had, but if the voice of the nobility gets loud enough, he might not have a choice."

They had rounded what was Whitetail Point in their world and skimmed across the waves, fast approaching Kenidros. The single watchtower was already visible above the tree line where it pierced the sky.

"Why are you telling us all of this?" Darcy asked after a moment of silence.

"You asked, didn't you?" Rubidius sounded peeved, more like himself.

"Is it because you want us to understand why we can't rescue Yahto Veli this year?" she ventured.

A muscle tightened in Torrin's jaw, and Rubidius looked at her sidelong, the wind making his bushy eyebrows dance. He said nothing but held her gaze steadily.

"Oh, Rubidius, is that really what you're trying to tell us?" Sam asked.

"I think you should go below deck and change your clothes," he said, breaking his gaze with Darcy. "You'll find your things in separate berths."

"Pants?" Darcy asked Rubidius with raised eyebrows after coming back out on deck. They had sorted through the clothes in the berths to discover six sets of linen pants and plain white shirts. The only thing that had distinguished one outfit from another was the magical object lying atop each pile of clothes. Darcy had put the heavy Ecclektos family ring on her left index finger; it was finally too tight for her thumb.

Rubidius looked down and inspected her attire. "Good, you have your ring," was all he said.

Stupid, worthless, pointless ring that does nothing special or magical whatsoever, Darcy thought impatiently. She waited in silence for Rubidius to get around to explaining the pants.

"Yes, yes . . . we thought it would be best for you to arrive less conspicuously this year," he said finally.

"Why? Because of the people?" Darcy squinted ahead to where the seawalls enclosed Ormiskos Bay. Men in the towers were already shouting orders to open the gate.

"Yes," Rubidius said, turning shrewd eyes on her. "As much as you might want to believe that I seek only to discourage your quest to rescue Yahto Veli, I seek also to open your eyes to the way the Alitheians might view you, especially due to what happened during your last visit."

Darcy felt a hard knot gather in her stomach. "You mean, because I wasted almost an entire year going to see the Oracle?"

"Word of your journey did escape the palace, I'm afraid." Rubidius looked serious. "Darcy, I place a heavier burden of knowledge upon your shoulders because I expect you to be able to bear up under it. There are those who will despise you now. Are you prepared to face opposition from the people?"

Darcy laughed humorlessly. "You should see how people pick on me at school." She sobered. "Won't they know it's us when they see the *Cal Meridian*, even with these clothes on?"

Rubidius's eyes twinkled. "We have taken the *Cal Meridian* out every day for two weeks. Only the very astute will figure out what day it is that you are to arrive. Some believe you have arrived already."

"Oh . . . well, great, I guess." Darcy felt strange entering the bay as though they were delinquent teenagers out after curfew.

With a great churning of the water, the sea gate closed behind them, sealing them in to the cove. The castle of Ormiskos lay directly ahead, gray-stoned and five-towered. Fishing vessels sailed about and people swarmed on the docks and in the streets of Ormiskos Prime, but very few of them looked their direction with more than vague interest, and Darcy felt both relieved and a little hollow inside.

"What, no parade this year?" Perry came up behind them, and Darcy rolled her eyes.

Darcy felt unsettled as they entered the castle and were greeted cheerfully by supporters, most of whom Darcy didn't know or even recognize. Voitto Vesa was absent from the gathering, as were Eleanor, Tellius, and Cadmus.

Neither Borna Fero nor Wal Wyn were around either, but Tokala, the handsome soldier who'd accompanied her on her Oracle journey, came and greeted Darcy with a hug that lifted her off the floor. Tormod, the yellow-haired half-Alitheian grunted at her from across the chamber into which they'd been ushered. No one else even looked familiar.

They were then taken to their rooms high in the west wing and left alone to "refresh themselves" before they ate an early supper. It all felt . . . weird. Darcy had so looked forward to seeing her Alitheian friends and—although she wouldn't admit it—had counted on a much warmer welcome. She felt almost as though she wanted to cry, but she held herself together.

Sam had been hurried off to the infirmary to see Nurse Dembe about her ankle, but Amelia was changing into a dress in her chamber. Darcy took the opportunity to change as well. Her wardrobe, as expected, was stocked with colorful medieval garb, but Darcy chose a dark gray gown with long sleeves. *It suits my mood*, she thought bitterly as she slipped it on.

A knock sounded on her main door and Darcy thought it odd that Amelia hadn't just used the side doors that connected their chambers. "Coming!" She unlocked the door that led to the hallway and opened it. "Oh . . . Hi!"

Perry stood on the other side of the door, dressed in a blue doublet that brought out the color of his eyes, his linen pants tucked into high black boots. His sword was strapped around his waist; he was rarely without it in Alitheia. "Can I come in?"

Darcy glowered at him, though she wasn't really angry anymore. "Sure," she said, stepping aside, leaving the door open after he entered.

"Look, I just wanted to say—acknowledge, really—what a complete idiot I was earlier today. You were right. We shouldn't have gone to check out that campsite."

Darcy nodded and let a smile play on her lips. "Yeah, well . . . I guess it kept us from having to confront Tselloch's apparition, or whatever that was, so . . ." she trailed off and shrugged.

"Friends?" Perry held out his hand.

"Friends." Darcy took his hand.

He grasped it tightly and stepped forward.

"Oy! Perry, where did you go, man?" Dean shouted down the hall just as Amelia appeared at the still-open door.

"Didn't you hear me knock, Darcy?" Amelia asked, bustling in wearing a pretty lavender gown.

Darcy guiltily yanked her hand out of Perry's, feeling her ears turn bright red and hot. Amelia scrutinized her, and Darcy might have imagined it, but she thought she saw understanding cross her face.

Dean appeared a moment later wearing a doublet like Perry's and looking much more grown up than usual. "Should have known you'd be down here," he muttered, filling the doorframe. Amelia shot Dean a piercing look and then her eyes narrowed on Darcy. She definitely suspected something.

"Lewis went to see about Sam's ankle, and he also said something about getting a new pair of glasses. Course, I don't know what they'll have for him here—" Dean continued.

"They make glasses in Alitheia," Darcy said, hoping to draw Amelia's attention to anything other than Perry and her. "Badru had some last year, remember?" She'd been amazed that the master magician who had accompanied her to the Oracle had wound up in the end with his glasses still intact and on his face.

"Oh yeah." Dean shrugged. "Well, what do you guys want to do until dinner?"

"I'd like to go to the infirmary, too," Darcy said. "I bet Sam could use some more company."

"Let's all go," Perry said.

The walk from the west wing to the infirmary was rather winding and lengthy. They passed through much of the castle to get there, going down and then up several flights of stairs. Amelia led the way, as she knew the castle well, having lived there while the rest of them had travelled to see the Oracle. She told them about various rooms as they passed. A tea room over here, and over there a dance room where she and Sam had taken lessons . . . She had something to say about almost every door, but there was one she passed with barely a glance. It opened to a short flight of stairs leading down into darkness.

"What's down there?" Dean asked, pausing to peer down the stairs.

Amelia frowned. "I have no idea. That door was always locked last year."

They continued on and finally reached the sick ward to find Sam lying in a bed by a window with her foot elevated on some pillows. Lewis lay in a bed next to her with a compress bound to his forehead. "She insisted," he muttered, jerking his thumb toward Nurse Dembe who was busy with another patient.

"Indeed I did," Nurse Dembe said, straightening and looking their direction. She stiffened unexpectedly and bowed. "Your majesty."

"Nurse Dembe," Darcy said, embarrassed. "Don't . . . I'm not—"

She was interrupted by a flood of people surging into the room, one of them hurrying determinedly toward them. *Tellius.*

"Is she okay? Lady Sam . . . is she hurt very badly?" he asked. "I only just found out you'd arrived, and when I heard one of you was injured, I had to come here first. I'm sorry I wasn't able to greet you right away, but I was busy in the war room."

Darcy and the others stared at the young prince in dumbstruck silence. Much of the awkwardness of his adolescence had melted almost completely away in the year since they'd last seen him. His complexion was still pocked with red bumps, and he hadn't lost all the gangliness of youth, but his attitude and composure seemed much more mature. Darcy wondered if he'd taken etiquette lessons in their absence. He was fourteen now, Darcy reminded herself, and in the fall he would turn fifteen and they would be the same age for the first time, if only until March when Darcy turned sixteen.

Tellius had not yet looked at her. He was bent over Sam, asking Nurse Dembe her about her leg. "It's only a sprain," Darcy heard Sam say.

Darcy shot a look at Perry and found him staring at Tellius as though he had a sour taste in his mouth. He looked from the prince to her, and Darcy almost smiled. He was weighing his competition. She wanted to laugh aloud and say don't be ridiculous, but the more she studied Tellius, the more she understood Perry's unease.

Tellius straightened at last and looked down at Darcy, and she had to admit he qualified as good-looking now. His dark hair was long and hung almost to his shoulders where it curled around the high collar of his doublet and, although he was tanned, his freckles were still visible. "Hello," she said, abruptly shy.

He smiled and took her hand. Drawing it to his lips, he kissed it very lightly and said, "Welcome back," before dropping it to her side. He turned to Amelia and did the same, then clasped the forearms of each of the boys in greeting.

Darcy puzzled over his manner. It was—particularly with her—so easy now! Her eyes widened as her brain worked. Tellius believed the oracle Darcy had received the year before meant they no longer had to get married. *He's free*, she thought, bemused that he felt he could just be himself now, with all the pressure off.

A member of Tellius's entourage stepped forward and cleared his throat. "Your meal, my lords and ladies, is waiting."

"Oh! Can I come down?" Sam tried to sit up in bed, but the nurse pushed her back.

"I'm sorry, my lady, but no. You may go," Nurse Dembe addressed Lewis, "but I will keep Lady Sam here for the night. We will have a healer coming through in the morning," she addressed Sam, "and I would like you to be here in case he arrives very early. I will have a tray brought up for you."

Sam's face fell and Lewis said, "I'll stay and keep you company. I have to wait for some new glasses, anyway—I'd probably just bump into a lot of stuff if I went."

"Thanks, Lewis." Sam shot him a grateful look but still seemed disappointed.

Darcy and Amelia exchanged a glance. "We can stay, too," Darcy said.

The nobleman who had announced the dinner sniffed unctuously. "The meal is to be a banquet celebrating your arrival. How are you to be greeted if you are not present?"

"Oh, right."

"It's okay, just go on," Sam urged them. "Lewis can stay with me, but the rest of you should go."

Tellius offered Darcy his arm, and she took it, feeling rather foolish until another young man from his entourage offered an arm to Amelia. They waved goodbye to Sam and Lewis and exited the infirmary. Tellius held back a little until he and Darcy were walking at the rear of the pack.

"I have something for you," he murmured when he seemed satisfied nobody would overhear them.

"What?" Darcy whispered back, trying to ignore the looks Perry was shooting them over his shoulder. She was resting her right hand as lightly as she could in the crook of Tellius's arm, mindful as always of the coldness. It wouldn't do to have Tellius asking questions about what was wrong with her hand, but he seemed thoroughly distracted anyway.

"A sword."

"A . . . what? A sword?" Darcy wondered why he thought this should be a secret.

"When the servants were cleaning your chambers for your arrival, they found it under your bed and removed it to the armory. I thought it might be important, so I got it back for you."

Terra's sword. It was the sword the tsellodrin had used to take the life of her friend, the oread Terra, at the end of their adventures the year before. Darcy had kept it and vowed to learn to use it to avenge her friend.

"It *is* important. Thank you for retrieving it," she said, touched by Tellius's thoughtfulness.

He shrugged, but seemed pleased with himself nonetheless.

"Why did they take it away?" Darcy asked him.

"It's considered an improper weapon for a woman. Swordplay is generally left to men and narks."

"Oh . . . so I can have it back, but I can't learn how to use it, is that it?"

"Do you *want* to learn how to use it?" Tellius asked, even quieter than before.

"Yes!"

"Then I'll teach you." He smiled sidelong at her. "Meet me tomorrow in the weapons room of the west wing before sunrise, and I'll give you your sword and your first lesson."

"Won't Rubidius and Eleanor be angry?"

"Eleanor is away. I'll handle Rubidius."

CHAPTER 7
LESSONS WITH TELLIUS

Eleanor Stevenson was with Cadmus at Kenidros, assisting with the younger Ecclektos's training. Rubidius had taken over almost sole responsibility of Tellius's education, so Eleanor had been spending more time with his brother. Tellius had assured Darcy that Eleanor was eager to see them, but that she wouldn't arrive for a few days, at least.

Darcy had taken that information to bed with her after the banquet and, in anticipation of her early-morning lesson with Tellius, had set her old-fashioned windup alarm clock for four-thirty. The clock had come out of Sam's pouch the year before, when the Oracle's call had necessitated that Darcy take a bitter potion several times throughout the night. She was happy to have it now, because she wasn't a natural early riser and knew she would never make the lessons without it.

When the alarm went off the next morning, Darcy turned it off and lay in bed blinking blearily up at the shadowy ceiling. Feeling discombobulated, she tried to remember where she was and what she was supposed to be getting up for. It was comfortable under her down comforter, and the dark room about her was quite cold. The servants had lit a fire in the grate before bed the night before, and it had now burned down to embers. In a few hours the summer sun would warm the bricks of the castle, the heat eventually penetrating to the inner rooms, but that was a long way off.

She groaned and rolled over, burying her face in her pillow. *Oh yeah, sword lessons.* The concept was much less appealing now that morning had arrived. But Tellius would be waiting for her. She pushed herself up, her long hair falling in curtains on either side of her face, and dangled her feet over the edge of the bed. She hugged her nightgown to her body and shivered, wishing she could stay on the carpet, but it didn't extend all the way to the wardrobe at the far end of the room.

Tiptoeing across the cold flagstones as though walking on hot coals, Darcy reached the wardrobe and searched for something appropriate to wear. Only dresses hung inside, but she still had the linen pants and shirt from the day before. She slipped them on as quickly as she could, braided her hair, took a quick look in the mirror above her washbasin, and slipped through her door and into the hall of the west wing

It was very dark except for the weak light of low-burning gas lamps mounted high on the walls at ten-foot intervals. Shadowy figures of guards stood at either end of the long hallway, but she knew they wouldn't bother her as long as she stayed in the west wing.

Still, she felt the urge to tiptoe, even though the plush carpet runner would hide any sound of footsteps, as she passed a couple of doorways and came to the weapons practice room. She had never had a reason for spending time in here before, but she knew the walls of the long, high-ceilinged room were covered with racks of various types of weaponry. The door was closed, but Darcy could see a sliver of light escaping through the crack at the bottom.

She knocked lightly and, when Tellius didn't come to the door, turned the catch and pushed it open.

The lights were ablaze, and Tellius was seated on a bench at a long wooden table on the far side of the room, fast asleep with his head resting on his hand. He looked disheveled, wearing the same clothes he'd had on the night before. Darcy stood in the doorway in indecision over whether to stay or go, but then she noticed he had a sword out on the table before him —her sword.

She closed the door and walked over to him. Sitting down gingerly on the bench beside him, she looked at the weapon. As she'd noticed the year before when she had taken it from Terra's fallen body, the sword wasn't at all beautiful or ornate. In form, it was too thin to be a broad sword, but not thin enough to be a rapier. It was also rather short, but not as short as a Roman gladius. It was plain and iron-gray, its hilt and pommel wrapped in black leather.

Darcy decided to risk drawing it toward her, but Tellius started the moment she moved it. He dropped his head from his hand and jerked awake, his hand falling immediately upon the sword and gripping it. Darcy jumped back. "I'm sorry! I didn't mean to wake you; I was just trying to see my sword."

"Wha—oh! Of course, here," he handed it to her hilt first and then rubbed his face with his hands. "I didn't mean to be asleep when you arrived. I apologize."

Darcy smiled as she heard him talk. His phraseology was so different from that of fourteen-year-old boys in her world, but of course one would expect a prince, especially one raised among adults as Tellius had been, to use proper diction. "It's fine," she said. "Don't worry about it." She raised the sword in one hand, feeling how the weight was distributed and thinking it was a light enough weapon for her to handle.

Tellius stood and stretched. "Are you ready?"

"What?" Darcy swung around to face him, sweeping the sword in a wide arc as she did so.

"Careful!" he said, taking a step back to avoid the blade. "Actually, why don't you give that back to me for the time being? You won't be starting with an actual blade, anyway." He held out his hand and Darcy turned it hilt out and placed the sword in his grip, her ears blazing.

"I'm sorry, I didn't mean to make you nervous," she laughed uneasily.

"You didn't; it's all right. I know you are not used to handling a long blade." He went to a large chest against the wall and began to root around in it, pulling out several scabbards to try the blade in before he settled on one. Sliding the sword into its place, he put it back on the table. "There, now you can safely take it back to your room for storage until we're ready to use it." His smirked as though he were trying to keep a straight face.

He must think I'm an idiot. "Okay, so if we're not starting with real swords, what are we going to use today?"

"These." Tellius went to the wall and pulled down two wooden practice swords. They looked like children's toys.

"Let me guess," Darcy said. "Those are used for training, like, ten-year-olds, or something?"

Tellius laughed. "Actually, I started training with one of these when I was five." He must have noticed Darcy's sour expression, however, because he added, "Listen, we have to start somewhere, and the beginning is as good a place as any."

Darcy sighed. "Fine." Her head was still muddy because of the early hour and, as she stood, she stretched and stifled a huge yawn.

Tellius handed her both of the practice swords and began to unbutton his doublet. Darcy's attention was drawn back to his attire and the deep circles beneath his eyes. "Were you up all night?" she asked as he slipped out of his doublet and rolled up his shirtsleeves.

He shrugged and reached out a hand for one of the swords. "Most of it," he admitted.

"Why?" Darcy asked.

He looked reluctant to answer, and Darcy wondered if she were prying into things that were none of her business. He twirled the sword absentmindedly as his eyes cast about the room. "There are . . . many issues to deal with in Ormiskos right now. I don't *have* to take part in all the meetings, but Cousin Tullin encourages me to, and I agree with him. If I make it to be king someday . . ." he trailed off.

"*If?*" Darcy asked. "Of course you're going to be king!"

His eyes bespoke sadness at her words, and she wondered again at how much he had grown up over the past year. "We really should start, if you'd still like to do this," he said at last. "I should send you away before Baran arrives to prepare for morning forms."

"Of course, yeah, let's start."

Tellius began by showing her the proper ready stance and how to hold her sword. "Two hands," he kept reminding her. "You only fight with one hand if you are carrying a shield, but that takes a lot more strength and control than you have right now. We'll get to that in the future." He took her through several forms that the men practiced every morning. In addition to strength and agility training, the forms were a way for them to remember the positions and movements of swordplay. "After doing this enough times, the motions become automatic," Tellius said.

The light in the room began to change, and Tellius looked to the window that looked down upon an inner courtyard. "You should probably go back to your room now," Tellius said, holding out a hand for her wooden sword. "Baran will be here soon, and I should change, as well." He nodded toward the door where a staircase led to a landing above it. This chamber, like the library, was connected to the royal suites one floor above.

Sweaty and exhausted, Darcy handed the practice sword to him, noting that although he still looked tired, he had barely broken a sweat. "Thanks," she said. "I really appreciate you doing this for me." She walked to the table and retrieved her sword and scabbard.

"Where did you get it?" Tellius asked, his voice coming from across the room where he was putting the practice swords back in their holders.

"This sword?" Darcy held it up. "I took it from a dead tsellodrin. He used it to kill Terra," she said softly. "Do you think it was foolish of me to take it?"

Tellius turned serious eyes on her. "No. If I could claim the weapons that took the lives of my parents, I would, and I would use them against every servant of Tselloch I could get my hands on . . . including Tselloch himself. But . . ." he picked up his doublet and brushed off the fabric, turning his gaze to it, "I suppose that's your job, isn't it? And Perry's, and Dean's, and . . . all the rest of you."

Darcy wondered if she imagined the note of bitterness in his voice, and she cleared her throat. "Yeah . . . I guess so."

"So, tomorrow morning then? Same time?" Tellius looked back up at her and whatever bitterness she had detected was gone.

"Definitely." Darcy turned to go and started in surprise. Rubidius was standing in the doorway watching them with his hands fingering his beard.

"It's a bit early for swordplay, don't you think?" he asked.

Tellius squared his shoulders. "I think Lady Darcy has a right to learn how to use a sword."

"Is that so?" Rubidius didn't look angry, only thoughtful. "And I suppose you are going to train her?"

"Yes," Tellius said. "Nobody else will."

"Hmmm . . ." Rubidius continued stroking his beard and studied them with shrewd eyes. Tellius held up under his gaze, his stature taking on the arrogant poise Darcy associated with his royal blood.

"Very well," Rubidius said. "Tellius, you will join Darcy and me after breakfast in my cottage. Darcy, a word." It was not a question. He motioned for her with a crooked finger and stepped aside so she could precede him into the hallway.

She went fearfully, clutching her sword to her chest with both hands. "You're not . . . angry?" she asked as soon as they were alone in the hall.

"Angry? Why would I be angry? What a foolish question." He waved her off. "Tellius wants to spend time with you and teach you a useful skill along the way . . . what is there to be angry about in that? No, I find it to be useful employment for you both."

"But I thought girls weren't allowed to learn how to use swords in Alitheia," Darcy said as they came to a halt at her door.

"A rule that I have come to disregard as dated," Rubidius said. "In these violent times, the more weapons one is skilled in, the better. No, I wanted to tell you something else." His eyes turned grave. "As you work with Tellius, be mindful that some scars run very deep. Yours are visible," he took her left hand and turned it over so the oval scar reflected the lamplight. "His are not."

Darcy's brow furrowed, but she nodded as though she understood.

He covered her scar with his other hand and then lowered it. "Dress for breakfast and come to my cottage afterward. And tell the others," he said, a little of his normal briskness returning. "I will have work for you all to do."

"Sam! You're . . . walking!" Darcy stood from Rubidius's table in excitement as Sam walked through the door. She was limping slightly, but other than that she seemed to be all patched up.

"Yeah, I know!" Sam beamed and jiggled her foot at them. "A healer came this morning and fixed it. Incredible, huh?"

"A healer?" Amelia turned the question on Rubidius. "Is that some kind of magician?"

"Yes," he answered. "It is a classification of master magician. I chose alchemy, but there are other areas of specialty into which master magicians may fall. Healers are increasingly rare, however."

"What does it take to be a healer?" Darcy asked as she watched Sam take her customary seat at the round table.

"One must be exceedingly gifted in the use of earth and water magic. The human body is so complex and those elements so tightly woven together within the body that it takes many years of study and practice to earn the title of healer."

"But once you become one, you can magically heal people?" Amelia asked, leaning forward.

"Healers can *accelerate* the healing process, perform surgeries, reduce pain, and help diagnose—all using magic, but they cannot magically erase a physical hurt. While most of us master magicians deal with the grandiose," he gestured widely, and Darcy recalled how he raised the wall of water in the cove the day before, "healers deal with the miniscule. It takes a great deal of concentration and control."

"That's why there are so few of them?" Darcy asked.

"That is one reason, yes. What healers we have in the land travel from place to place."

"So, Nurse Dembe isn't a healer?" Lewis asked. The light pouring in through Rubidius's cottage windows reflected off the new square spectacles he'd been given.

"No, she is a nurse. Nurse Dembe is capable of performing surgery and all the rest, but she does it without the aid of significant magic."

"She's brilliant, though," Tellius piped in from the corner. "She's brought more than one person back from the brink of death in the last couple years."

"She is, at that," Rubidius conceded, "but because she has only earth magic, she will never qualify as a master magician." Rubidius organized several stacks of parchment as he talked, and he brought them to the table. "I think you all know what this is," he said, placing one stack before each of them except Darcy.

"Great," Perry muttered, sneering down at Rubidius's idea of a review exam.

"Woo hoo," Dean said.

"You're short one," Amelia told Rubidius, nodding toward Darcy.

"Of course I'm not," Rubidius said, sounding annoyed. "She is working with Tellius and me for the morning."

"Lucky," Perry muttered at her, paging through his test. "Rubidius, how can you expect us to remember stuff like this? 'What color is the adromorphmagi fungus at each stage of its growth, and how do its colors indicate readiness for various stages of potion making?' Dean and I weren't even here for most of the lessons last year!"

"Well, it's a good thing *that* bit of information came from your first year," Rubidius said. "Now get to work, please!"

Her friends fell silent, poring over their pages, deep sighs issuing from several of them as Darcy scraped her chair back and joined Tellius at the table in the back corner. Rubidius joined them a moment later and tossed a piece of leather down on the table between them. On it was an ancient-looking painting of a man and a woman holding hands. A flaked golden circle surrounded the two figures, and on the edges of the image were the twisted faces and forms of monsters and foes in agony.

"The coroneia," Rubidius said, tapping on the image. "Tellius, you should recognize that word."

Tellius stared at the leather painting. He seemed to be fighting his sleep deprivation, so Darcy jumped in to help.

"What is it?" she asked.

Rubidius looked hard at Tellius a moment longer, as though hoping the young prince would speak up. When Tellius said nothing, Rubidius replied, "Although you have not heard the *word* before, Darcy, I suspect you recognize the illustration."

Darcy knit her brows and frowned as she looked back down at the painting. "Oh! That's the—uh—the—whatever it was that happened at the cove yesterday!"

"Thank you for that—*intelligent*—rendition of events," Rubidius said dryly.

I could do without the sarcasm, Darcy thought, but she said aloud, "So that's called a *coroneia*, then? What does it mean?"

"Oh," Tellius closed his eyes and rubbed them with his knuckles. "I think I remember this now." His voice came out somewhat muffled from behind his hands. He reappeared and blinked at Rubidius. "Doesn't it involve using the four elements all at the same time?"

"Exactly so," Rubidius said. "What Lady Darcy experienced for the first time yesterday was the phenomenon that occurs when all four elements are manipulated at precisely the same location at precisely the same time. As I wielded earth, fire, and water, you utilized your talent with wind," he addressed Darcy. "You added the fourth element to the equation and created the coroneia."

"So that golden burst, and the booming sound . . . that was the coroneia?"

"Yes," he tapped on the picture. "But it is more than that. How did you feel after the golden aura passed through you?"

"I felt . . ." Darcy cast back in her mind to the day before, "great! It was like I hadn't been using my magic at all; that's how rejuvenated I felt."

Rubidius seemed pleased. "That's part of the magic and mystery associated with it."

"It's like a power up," a voice said from across the room. "Like . . . in a video game!" Dean had turned around in his chair and was watching them, his quill dripping fat drops of black ink onto the edge of his parchment.

Darcy stifled the urge to giggle as Rubidius inflated like a mother hen. "What is this foolishness? You should be working on your test, not listening in on conversations that do not concern you!" With a flick of his wrist, Dean's quill smacked him in the face, leaving a large black splatter of ink across the bridge of his nose.

Perry burst out laughing. "Dude, your face!"

Dean flicked ink onto Perry's parchment. Perry raised his quill to retaliate but caught Rubidius's furious glare. He lowered his quill. "Whatever," he muttered as he and Dean went back to work.

As ridiculous as it had felt for Dean to use a videogame reference in Alitheia, Darcy understood his analogy. "So," she continued, "using all four elements together like that causes a magical—*reaction*—to occur, and this reaction makes magic revive. What else does it do?"

"It strengthens the existing magical connections. Your wind became stronger; my fire, water, and earth did as well."

"How long does the effect last?" Darcy asked.

"A magician is revived until using magic causes him or her to grow fatigued again. The strengthening of the existing connections, however, lasts as long as the magic holds."

"Does it happen over and over again? I mean, if I had stopped using my air talent and then started up again while you were still using your three talents, would the coroneia have occurred again?"

Rubidius shook his head. "No. It happens but once in any given circumstance. And now that it has occurred between you and me, it will not occur again unless we were to significantly use our talents together."

"So, if I made a little dust devil with my air and earth magic and you made a flame and a tiny water whirlpool right here, it wouldn't happen again?"

"Correct."

Rubidius sat back and studied Darcy. Tellius had fallen asleep on his hand again, and Darcy nudged him with her toe under the table. He opened his eyes sleepily.

"This brings me to why I wanted to discuss this with the two of you."

Darcy knew where this was going. She remembered a different session with Rubidius the year before, and a different drawing—a drawing with one element in each corner. She shot a look at Tellius, but his face had gone rigid, unreadable.

"When the two of you wed—"

"*If* we wed," Tellius said.

Darcy thought Rubidius would be angry, but he only inclined his head. "*If* the two of you wed," he amended, "and form your completion, you should, at the wedding ceremony, experience a powerful coroneia."

"Even if we're not using our magic at the time?" Darcy asked, confused.

Rubidius nodded. "Even so. Remember that in Alitheia marriage is more than a physical union, it is a magical one as well. The coming together of two people in marriage with opposite inverse talents is enough to form a coroneia. And, if my research can be trusted, this coroneia will be far stronger than what occurred between us yesterday, Lady Darcy. Your marriage coroneia will be the moment you begin to take on aspects of each other's talents. Think of it as a transfer of powers and a permanent rejuvenation. It is not that you will never grow weary again using your magic, but you will always have the other's strength to rely on, as well. Each successive coroneia you experience as a couplewill only make   you —"

A sudden pounding sounded on Rubidius's door, and all of them looked up.

"Stronger," Rubidius finished distractedly.

Rubidius stood and hurried to his cottage door. Sweeping it open, he faced a palace guard on the other side.

"Voitto Vesa has returned," the man said. "She requests an audience with Lady Darcy. She insists it must be at once!"

Rubidius turned to Darcy, a rare uncertainty reflected in his eyes.

CHAPTER 8
VOITTO'S PROMISE

Darcy stood, her hand going to her chest. "She wants to talk to . . . me?"
She could feel the eyes of each of her friends on her as she made her way to
the door. In the hall was a blue and gold clad palace guard. Darcy looked
from him to Rubidius. "Is it all right if I—"

"Yes, yes, go. I'm afraid you must." He held the door wider, allowing
Darcy to step past him into the hallway. The uncertainty had not left his
eyes and Darcy swallowed hard.

Rubidius closed the door in her face and the guard urged her to follow
him. She did so blindly, not paying attention to the doors they passed or the
direction they traveled as they wended their way through the castle. At last
he left her at a door leading to a short, shadowy downward staircase. "In
there, if you please," he said, nodding curtly.

Darcy took a few hesitant steps down into the darkness and then turned
around. "Are you sure—"

But the guard had already closed the door behind her. She took a deep
breath and descended the last two steps into the dimly lit room.

The room had no windows, and it stretched long and narrow into the
darkness. Black rectangular patches formed an irregular pattern along the
walls. She couldn't see where the room ended. Torch brackets lined both
walls, but the dim light in the room came from only one torch lit far ahead.
Sitting on a bench to the left of the torch, beneath a shadowy circle on the
wall, was the nark Voitto Vesa. Her blonde head was bent, her ears drooped,
and she appeared to be studying something in her hand.

"Vesa?" Darcy asked, using her day nark name since it was still morning. When she received no reply, she tried again with her full name. "Voitto Vesa?" She crept toward her, stepping gingerly across the flagstones.

Vesa gasped as though she had just realized she wasn't alone and sat up straight. "Lady Darcy!" She hurried from her seat and took Darcy's hand, drawing her back to the bench beneath the lit torch. "I am sorry for the secrecy, but I felt it best to speak where we would not be overheard."

Darcy sat down next to the female nark. Vesa had not yet let go of her hand, and it felt very odd; Darcy had never known Vesa to be particularly touchy-feely. "That's—that's okay."

Vesa nodded, her eyes dark and mysterious. She opened her fingers and released Darcy's hand, her own hand lying palm-up on her thigh. Darcy stared at her, but Vesa said nothing. Darcy looked down, her gaze drawn to Vesa's hand. Clear, shiny, new, and right in the middle of Vesa's left palm was an Oracle scar.

Darcy inhaled sharply and looked closer. "Vesa!" She looked up into the nark's eyes. "Why did you—when did you—*did you rescue him?*"

Vesa placed a hand on Darcy's arm, calming her. "I knew I could not rescue him, so I did not try. It has never been done."

Darcy's face fell. "But how could you go and not at least try?" she asked in a small voice, trying—and failing—not to sound accusatory.

"It has *never* been done," Vesa repeated. "The petitioner is under the enchantment of the Oracle and therefore at the mercy of it. For me to try would have been of no help to Yahto Veli and suicide for me." She shook her head, her blonde hair silvery in the flickering light. "I did not go to give myself the chance to rescue him, but to give *you* the chance."

Darcy stilled. "You asked the Oracle how Yahto Veli could be rescued, didn't you?"

Vesa inclined her head and smiled.

"But . . ." Darcy closed her eyes and tried to remember everything she had read in Batsal's *Histories* about invoking the Oracle. "I thought the Oracle would only answer a question if the petitioner was the person most concerned with the answer."

"I *am* the person most concerned with his rescue," Vesa said. "We were in the midst of our courtship when you left two years ago. Do you remember how upset I was when Veli hid from Yahto his intent to go on your journey? The last words I spoke to him were . . . *unkind*. Cruel, even."

"You and Yahto Veli?" Darcy asked. "But, you never gave any sign!"

Vesa shook her head. "It is you humans who are concerned with the outward affectations of love. Narks are deliberate and thoughtful in their courtships. Our courtship was slow, due to the odd nature of Yahto's personality. Voitto and Yahto were reluctant at first to accept each other as a candidate, but they were coming around to it in their own ways. We would not have wed for several years."

"If he's not rescued, will you never marry anyone else?"

"No. He is my match. So you see, I had a perfectly valid question for the Oracle."

"Still, I don't see how the Oracle could answer that! It would mean—well—it would mean losing one of its treasures. Unless . . ." There was one way the Oracle could answer Voitto Vesa's question without undermining its power. "Unless it made you pay with a promise not to tell anyone how to do it." Darcy looked sharply into Vesa's eyes.

Vesa stared at her. She opened her mouth to speak, but Darcy scrambled away and leapt to her feet.

"Don't! Oh, Vesa, I know what will happen if you tell me—if you break your promise to the Oracle. Rubidius told me . . . you'll die! You *can't* tell me! Veli wouldn't want you to do that for him; we'll find another way!"

"*Darcy!*" Vesa said. "Sit down, please. Let me explain."

Darcy stayed where she was. "I won't—not if you're going to do something stupid."

"Please?" Vesa asked. "You must at least give me a chance to explain the promise I made, and then you can decide whether to hear the Oracle's answer or not. There is no harm in that."

Darcy shivered and balled up her fists. She hated this. At every turn, her trip to see the Oracle returned to haunt her in different forms, and now Voitto Vesa's life was on the line, too.

Vesa waited while Darcy made up her mind. Finally, Darcy inched back to the bench, sitting rigidly, and Vesa sighed in relief.

"You are correct in guessing that the question I asked the Oracle was how Yahto Veli could be rescued," Vesa said. "You are also correct in assuming the payment required by the Oracle was the exaction of a promise that the information could never be revealed to any living creature, nor can *I* use it to attempt a rescue."

"And if you break that promise," Darcy said, "you'll die. Painfully, I'm told."

Vesa pursed her lips. "But you see, Lady Darcy, Voitto and I believe we have found a way around that curse. It's the only reason we attempted the question in the first place."

"What do you mean?" Darcy frowned at her.

"Voitto performed the invocation, and Voitto travelled down into the Oracle's lair to receive the answer and deliver the promise as payment."

"But—you're one and the same!" Darcy sputtered.

Vesa looked affronted. "We share the same body," she said, "but we are not one and the same."

"So, you think just because your night nark counterpart did all the actual work of the invocation, it will be safe for *you* to tell me the Oracle's response?"

Vesa shrugged. "I made no promise; Voitto did."

"But you still bear a scar!" Darcy pointed at her hand. "How do you know the Oracle didn't take your dual nature into consideration?"

Vesa studied her scar for a moment, rubbing it with her thumb. "I don't. But already we have gotten partially around it, for we did not die when Voitto let me see the answer in her mind."

"Or maybe that just shows the Oracle *did* take it into consideration," Darcy contradicted.

Vesa continued to rub her scar.

"And it's a risk you're willing to take?" Darcy asked sharply.

Vesa looked up then, her eyes fiery. "No matter how the Oracle portrays itself, it is not omniscient; it does not know the end of all things. It, too, is subject to laws and limitations. And so, yes, I am willing to take the risk. For my betrothed, I do so gladly, and if I die, I die."

Darcy couldn't remain seated any longer. She jumped to her feet and paced to the opposite wall and back, her mind reeling. "Did you at least see him? Do we even know that he's still alive?"

"He is alive, as are all the captives of the Oracle. But no, I did not see him."

Darcy stopped and stared at her. "How could you not have seen him? The gallery isn't very big, and the cells aren't deep!"

"Do you think the Oracle, after all these years, has only one gallery?" Vesa rejoined.

Darcy continued to pace. "He'll never let me go," she muttered. "Rubidius . . . he'll never let me go after him, even if you *do* tell me how."

"That is why I want to tell you, and only you, Darcy. You and Yahto Veli have a special relationship, a connection. Your love is strong, and I know you, more than anyone else, want to rescue him. I also know Rubidius. If given a way to rescue Yahto Veli, Rubidius *will* take it. And if you are the only person who knows the way to rescue him . . ."

"Then he'll have to take me," Darcy finished. Vesa's logic was sound, but Darcy still felt as though she was being led down a dark tunnel to an uncertain end. "But what if you're wrong, Vesa, and you *do* die? I want to rescue Yahto Veli more than anything else, but I can't have your death on my head, too!"

Vesa stood before Darcy. "I know the risk. Let my blood be on my own hands if my plan fails. But know this; I am giving you this chance first. If you do not let me tell you, I will take my information to Rubidius, and he will go to rescue Yahto Veli without you."

Darcy drew in her breath. "And you *really* think this will work?"

Vesa chuckled hollowly. "The Oracle cannot love, so it underestimates the power of love. It was foolish enough for it to believe the threat of death could prevent me from sharing information that could lead to the rescue of my betrothed. If the Oracle could err in that way, why could it not err in another?"

Darcy closed her eyes, feeling torn in two. She knew the choice she must make if she wanted any part in recalling Yahto Veli to life. "Okay. Tell me."

Vesa didn't wait a moment longer. She closed her eyes and chanted,

"With unraveled image, journey begins.
In error undone, destiny wins.
Pen of the Scribe shows the way.
Music, life-giving, holding sway
Held in the balance, the white thread reveals
The unseen path, through lily fields,
To serpent-eaters, down the hole,
First navigating the archipelago.
Breath of life, breath-ed once,
Broken bond of covenant."

Vesa breathed a deep, shuddery breath and opened her eyes.

"Are you . . . okay?" Darcy whispered.

Vesa smiled, pleased, but her eyes looked glazed. She inhaled, shuddering, her slender frame shaking, and her eyes rolled back into her head.

CHAPTER 9
THE UNFINISHED TAPESTRIES

Darcy lunged and caught at Vesa as she collapsed. Her weight was too great, though, and Darcy fell to her knees with Vesa's body slung across her lap.

Darcy finally found her breath. "Somebody *help me!*" she screamed. "*Help!* Please, oh please don't die. *HELP ME!*" Her screams echoed hopelessly against the walls of the underground chamber.

Vesa's frame shuddered again and she opened her eyes with a deep, throaty gasp, but all Darcy could see were the whites of her eyes. Vesa's hand seized up like a claw and grasped at a pocket on her jerkin. Darcy dug in the pocket, hoping to find some medicine or a remedy, but all she found was a crumpled piece of parchment.

"What—" she sobbed, smoothing the parchment out with one hand. Written on it was the oracle Vesa had just recited; she'd wanted to make sure Darcy wouldn't forget it.

Darcy moaned in frustration and thrust the parchment into the bodice of her dress. Vesa's eyes closed again, and she went rigid all over.

The door at the top of the short staircase burst open, and palace guards flooded into the chamber with a cacophony of sound.

Tick, tock, tick, tock, tick, tock . . . The grandfather clock in the corner of the room ticked off the time, sounding loud and unnatural in the tense stillness. Darcy and her five friends were waiting in what they had come to call the game room, or the lounge, of the west wing, but nobody spoke. Sam sat at the table with her head on her crossed arms, staring balefully out the window. Amelia played with her necklace, shooting odd, sharp glances at Darcy every time she adjusted in her chair. The boys huddled in the corner by the grandfather clock, making the only noise other than the ticking of the clock itself. They whispered together in hushed tones, and Darcy imagined they were discussing all the ways in which she was a horrible person who had murdered Voitto Vesa.

A door opened and closed down the hall, and Darcy jerked up straight. She couldn't hear any footsteps, but a moment later Rubidius, looking weary and strained, appeared at the door. "She's not dead," he said without preamble.

Darcy felt hot tears sting the backs of her eyes as Sam murmured inarticulately and reached across the table to squeeze Darcy's arm.

"She is very gravely ill. I do not know how long she will be able to hold out," Rubidius said.

"What *happened?*" Perry asked. "Darcy hasn't told us anything!" He shot a resentful look at her.

Rubidius opened his mouth, closed it again, and then looked at Darcy. "Let me speak with Darcy alone," he said. "The outcome of our conversation will determine whether the information concerning this incident will be passed on to you."

Darcy nodded and stood, avoiding everybody's eyes. She trailed in the wake of Rubidius's flowing robes, out the door, down the hall, and into his cottage.

"Rubidius, you know I didn't do anything to Vesa, don't you?" Darcy asked. "I would never hurt anyone like that!" She felt a desperate need to vindicate herself after the scene in the underground chamber. The guards who'd responded to her screams had suggested that Darcy had attacked the day nark. It had taken Lord Tullin himself sending Darcy away to the west wing—with an armed escort—for the accusations against her to cease. She was convinced that by now half the castle thought she was a murderer.

Rubidius raised both hands to stem the tide of her words. "Sit, please, Darcy. And don't be absurd! Of course I do not believe you could have done this thing to Voitto Vesa, and neither does anybody else."

Darcy collapsed into the closest chair and looked up at Rubidius as he drew his armchair close and sat down. "I knew full well where Voitto Vesa had been these months. I was one of the few, in fact, who were privy to the details of her journey."

"And you *let* her go?" Darcy asked incredulously.

Rubidius raised a hand. "How was I to prevent her from going? She is not a pupil of mine." He sniffed once. "I *did* counsel her against it, of course, but she would not be swayed."

"And she told you about her plan, for Voitto to do the invocation and receive the answer?"

"Yes. I thought it . . . an intriguing idea. But . . ." He sighed. "I feared it would end this way."

"But it hasn't ended yet!" Darcy cried. "You said she's still alive! If the Oracle really knew what she had done, wouldn't Voitto Vesa be dead right now?"

Rubidius stroked his beard. He looked tired and so very old. "I will admit she does appear to have had some measure of success in countering the enchantment," he allowed. "I examined her myself, with the healer, and we determined that we can do nothing for her, other than make her comfortable and see to her physical needs. It appears the Oracle is aware that *somehow* the promise has been broken, but the mysterious dual nature of narks is causing a problem for it. It could not detect when Voitto allowed Vesa to see the answer in her mind. Nor does its curse hold any sway over Vesa."

"Then . . . what is happening to her?"

"It is not what is happening to *Vesa* that concerns us. It's what is happening to *Voitto*."

"Oh . . . So, the Oracle detected that the promise was broken when Vesa spoke the answer aloud to me, and it tried to fulfill the curse by killing Voitto, but . . . it can't, because . . ."

Rubidius nodded. "We can only postulate, of course, but the healer was able to detect a battle between the elements in their shared body. Voitto is dying while Vesa is living. If Vesa is able to put up a strong enough fight, they will survive."

"But . . . wait . . ." Darcy shook her head and looked toward the window. "What about tonight? When the sun goes down and charge of the body returns to Voitto, won't that be the end of it? Won't she die?"

"That is the question that weighs heaviest on my mind," Rubidius said. "Let us hope that Vesa's soul will continue to struggle to live even while she sleeps."

Darcy stared hopelessly at the old alchemist, her mind reeling. She knew that if there was anything Rubidius could do to help her, he would have done it already. She hung her head.

"I suppose you want to know the answer the Oracle gave her," Darcy said after a moment. Rubidius didn't respond, and she looked up to find him watching her. "Don't you?"

"I do, of course, desire that information," Rubidius said. Darcy waited for his condescension, for him to bully her into telling him the oracle, but he only sat and watched her with mild interest.

All afternoon she'd mulled over why Vesa had revealed the oracle to her first, and she appreciated that Vesa tried to give Darcy what she wanted—

the means to rescue Yahto Veli. All Darcy had to do was hold back enough information from Rubidius to make her presence on the quest a necessity.

But Darcy didn't want to do that. She had kept enough secrets, strong-armed her way into enough situations, and acted selfishly enough to last her a lifetime already. She didn't want be that way anymore. She didn't *want* to withhold the oracle from Rubidius, not when it concerned the rescue of a dear friend. She could see that Rubidius expected her to use the information as leverage to gain a spot on the rescue team, but she'd had enough.

Darcy fumbled within her dress for the crumpled piece of parchment written in Vesa's flowing hand. She handed it to Rubidius before she could change her mind. "Here. It's all there, every word."

Rubidius raised an eyebrow at her and then looked down at the paper. "Thank you, Darcy," he said. He leaned forward and studied the words, reading them over and over. Finally he sat back and sighed. "Predictably cryptic," he said.

"Do you have any idea what any of it means?" Darcy asked.

"I have some ideas, yes, but nothing solid with which I can move forward. I will need to think on it." He handed the parchment back to Darcy, but she didn't take it.

"No, Rubidius, I gave it to you. I can't figure it out."

"You give yourself so little credit, Darcy," Rubidius said. "Vesa gave it to you, so it is yours. I have a good memory," he tapped his temple. "And I know where to find you should I have need to study it again."

Darcy took the parchment then, her fingers trembling. "We *are* going to do something about this, right?" she asked. "You *are* going to try to rescue Yahto Veli, now that we have this information?"

"Of course. I would not throw away the sacrifice Voitto Vesa has made. And . . . I begin to think that perhaps all roads lead to this destination anyway." He looked piercingly at her. "The populace is unhappy, as you know. I had thought it meant we must look to ways we could use you to actively fight Tselloch's forces this year, but now . . ." He shook his head. "Perhaps I was in error. Instead of forcing something to happen, I should have you take the door that has opened before you."

"Do you mean you'll let me come with you to rescue Yahto Veli?" Darcy asked, her heart racing.

He pointed at her hand where she held the piece of parchment. "Did you notice that Lewis is mentioned?"

Darcy's eyes widened. " 'The pen of the scribe,' " she recited.

"Lewis can only write that which Pateros gives to him. And if Lewis writes something that leads us to rescue Yahto Veli, perhaps that is Pateros's intent for you. Who am I to say you should not go? In fact, I have a feeling it may lead to a journey for all six of you, but let us wait to see what Lewis writes, eh?"

Darcy couldn't believe her ears. All year she had thought she would have to fight for the chance to try and rescue Yahto Veli, and now everything was falling smoothly into place for her. Well, she reminded herself, not *entirely* smoothly; Voitto Vesa was lying half-dead in the infirmary. But Darcy couldn't shake the optimistic feeling that everything would turn out okay.

Rubidius rose from his chair and began making tea at his counter. "I've sent a message across the bay to Eleanor. I imagine she will travel back with Cadmus immediately, in light of what has happened."

"Sure," Darcy said. "Rubidius . . . did Voitto Vesa tell you which direction the Oracle took her?"

"West, at first," he said. "Beyond that, I do not know."

"Do you think—"

"Do I think you were right to assume the Oracle itself does not move, but rather the magical entrance to it does?" Rubidius finished for her.

"Yeah."

He nodded. "Yes. I think you were accurate in that assumption. I have given it great thought over the year while you were absent, and the more I mull it over, the more logical it seems. The Oracle is a physical entity, so why wouldn't it have an established physical location? It would be a simple enough enchantment to move around the entrance to its lair." He gestured at his own door as a smile tugged on his beard. Rubidius took his door everywhere he went, even though he had forgotten where, exactly, he had left his cottage. "And," he continued, "now that we have the words of the Oracle itself confirming it can be found by following a set of directions, then it must, in fact, be findable.

"You may return to your friends, and you may also share with them any of this information that you would like to. But please send Lewis to me straightaway; I'd like to see if he has any . . . inspiration. The sooner we get to work on this, the better."

"I couldn't think of anything to write!" Lewis said, joining them later in the kitchen where they usually took meals when there was no banquet planned. He slumped into a chair and put his head in his hands. Sam nudged a plate of roasted potatoes toward him, but he ignored it. "And the sun is going to go down in a couple hours and Voitto Vesa is going to die, and it's going to be all my fault!"

"*What?*" Darcy almost spewed her potatoes out of her mouth. "Lewis, that's stupid. Whether or not she lives or dies has nothing to do with you."

"And we don't know that she *is* going to die," Sam said quickly.

"Well . . . okay then, but we'll never rescue Yahto Veli if I can't figure out what I'm supposed to write!"

"Don't push it, man," Perry said. "Don't you need to feel, like, inspired, or something?"

"Yes, and I don't. Rubidius went over and over the oracle with me, and I sat and meditated on every little bit of it, but . . . nothing."

"Well, you tried," Darcy said. "It's not like we have to know tonight. We couldn't start a journey right now even if we wanted to. Eleanor just got here, and she needs to talk with Rubidius, too, to make plans for us. So just . . . relax. Perry's right, you can't force it to come to you."

Lewis sighed and put a few potatoes on his plate, but he didn't look as though he had much of an appetite. They let him consider his food in silence. Most of them had already finished, and Perry and Dean were starting to look impatient.

"I think I'm going to head up to the weapons room," Perry said, pushing back his chair. "Dean, you want to come with me?"

"Yep," Dean said, standing up. "If we're going to be heading out on a journey, I should probably polish up my skills." He winked at Amelia.

"I'm coming too," Lewis said, shoving away his uneaten food. "Maybe you two can teach me something; that way at least I can feel *useful*."

Darcy, Sam, and Amelia watched the three boys disappear out the door. "He's too hard on himself," Sam. "It'll come to him. If the Oracle said 'the pen of the scribe' would show the way, then it will."

"Yeah," Darcy said.

"Let's go." Sam stood up. "We need to distract ourselves."

"You're right." Darcy stood too, followed by Amelia. If they didn't find something to occupy themselves, Darcy was going to spend the hours until sunset counting down the minutes to when Vesa would become Voitto and they would find out if she would live or die.

They exited the kitchen and wended their way through the ground floor corridors.

"This way," Amelia said, pointing down a side hall. "Shortcut."

They followed Amelia, passing several closed doors and branching hallways before Darcy recognized where they were. "Sam, Amelia, this is where it happened!" Darcy stopped at a door that was almost closed, the latch resting on the catch in the doorframe. It was a thick, old-fashioned door made of planked wood and black, wrought iron studs. The top of the door was curved to fit the arch of the doorframe.

"This is the door that was always locked last year," Amelia said, doubling back and looking at it with interest. "What's down there?"

"I honestly don't know. Vesa had only one torch lit and I couldn't get a good look around."

"Why did she want to talk to you there, of all places?" Sam wondered aloud, her arms crossed over her chest.

"I don't know. She said she didn't want to be overheard, and the room down there doesn't have any windows that I could see . . ." Darcy trailed off and shrugged. "Maybe it was just for the privacy."

"Or *maybe*," Sam said, her eyes gleaming, "she was already starting to work out the oracle and there's a clue down there!"

"Well, we can stand here talking about it, or we can go down there and check it out," Amelia said.

"Let's go!" Sam said eagerly.

Darcy chewed her lip. She'd not had a pleasant experience down there earlier and wasn't eager to revisit the gloomy underground chamber. But Sam could be right. There *might be* another reason why Vesa had wanted to meet her down there—a reason that could help shed some light on the oracle.

"Okay," she said.

The door made no sound as Amelia pushed it open. Darcy was surprised to see there was actually a good amount of light visible at the bottom of the short flight of stairs. *Somebody must have wanted to illuminate the scene of the crime*, she thought wryly.

They tiptoed down the stairs, Amelia first and Sam pulling the door shut behind them. Now that it was lit, Darcy could see it much clearer. The chamber was like a crypt beneath a gothic cathedral. The walls and floor were of flagged stone, but the ceiling rose above them with an even spacing of pointed arches. Terra-cotta ribs extended down from the arches at intervals to form embedded support pillars on which the torch brackets were hung. The room was very long; in fact, perhaps it wasn't a room at all, but a very long, wide passageway. It curved to the right far ahead of them so that they couldn't see where it ended.

The structure of the chamber wasn't even the most intriguing aspect of the space. Hanging between every embedded pillar on each long wall were tapestries—big ones, small ones, rectangular ones, square ones, and even the odd circular one. They looked old and dusty, and they hung rigidly on the walls, as though they had been superglued to the stonework behind them.

"Wow!" Sam went to the closest tapestry and touched it delicately. "Darcy, you didn't tell us these were down here!" Her finger came away smudged with dust and she rubbed it on her skirt.

"I didn't know these were down here," Darcy said, staring in fascination. "Vesa had only one torch lit, so most of this wasn't visible. And I wasn't really paying attention to my surroundings once I saw the scar on her hand."

"These are beautiful," Amelia said. "There must be hundreds of them. I wonder why they kept this place shut up last time we were here. Sam and I would have loved to come down here and look at these."

"Yeah," Sam agreed. "They should get someone down here to restore them, though. They're filthy!" She swiped her hand across one, revealing the colors beneath the grime to be quite bright.

Darcy stepped up close to a floor-to-ceiling tapestry that filled the entire space between two pillars. The thick layer of dust and cobwebs on it made it difficult to make out the picture, but Darcy felt sure that something was missing from the image. It didn't look . . . finished. She, like Sam, began to wipe the grime from the surface of the tapestry, revealing a landscape of mountains and forest beneath it. Everything she could make out looked oddly dark, and tiny gaps dotted the design. It was like one of those pixilation pictures Darcy had seen displayed around school by the art classes. When she stood back from the tapestry and viewed it as a whole, she could more easily make out the picture, but when she got very close, it became difficult to discern.

"Is it just me," she called to the others, "or do these all look unfinished?"

"Definitely," Amelia said. She was examining a small rectangular tapestry that seemed to have a portrait of a family on it. She stepped back from it and tilted her head to the side. "They look dark."

"I didn't even notice that," Sam said, "but you guys are right!"

"Darcy, where was Vesa sitting when you came in to meet her?" Amelia asked.

"Ummm . . . right over there, I think." Darcy pointed down the chamber and to the right. Several stone benches were spread throughout the space—likely meant for viewing the tapestries—but Darcy was almost certain she pointed to the correct one. She remembered that the shadowy shape above Vesa's head had been round, and there were very few round tapestries positioned above a bench.

They moved in unspoken agreement to the spot Darcy indicated and stopped before the bench, staring up.

"Wow, I can't make out anything of that picture!" Sam said. She hopped up on the bench and began to work away at the dust and cobwebs, getting thoroughly dirty in the process.

Darcy looked down at the front of her dress and Amelia's; they were all pretty filthy by now. She hoped they wouldn't pass any important nobles on their way back up to the west wing later.

The image Sam uncovered was mostly blue and, like the others, unfinished. The picture showed a sea or ocean, and where there should have been whitecaps on the waves, there were only blank spaces and tiny pinprick holes. Sam kept at it, and eventually blotches of green emerged.

"Islands, I think," Amelia said, squinting. She tilted her head. "I think this is supposed to be a birds-eye view of a portion of sea with a cluster of islands." She went rigid and gripped Darcy's arm. "*It's an archipelago!* A grouping of islands! It's in the oracle, and Vesa was sitting beneath an image of one—that can't be a coincidence!"

"No—you're right!" Darcy took several steps back to take in the entire image. "But . . . why wouldn't she say anything about it to me? How could she just assume I would figure it out?"

"Maybe she didn't want to jinx it, you know?" Amelia said, stepping back to stand with Darcy. "She didn't want to reveal any part of the oracle before she revealed the whole thing, because what if her plan didn't work and she died before getting the rest of it out?"

"I'm beginning to think Vesa assumed she *wouldn't* survive breaking the promise," Darcy said grimly.

"But she did it anyway," Amelia said, fingering her necklace. "That's love."

"How does it look so far?" Sam grunted. She stood on her very tiptoes but couldn't quite reach the upper portion of the tapestry. She settled back on her heels, breathing hard, and abruptly fell into a coughing and sneezing fit. "Oh . . . the dust!" She passed a hand over her face, leaving dark smudges across her forehead and the bridge of her nose.

Amelia laughed. "Sam, come on down. You can't get any more of that cleaned off with how dirty you are."

Sam hopped down and joined them. The dust even covered her hair, making her look like an old woman. "Oh, wow, you're right. That's an archipelago," she said. "I can see it clearly from out here. But how come there's no white in the entire picture?"

"I don't know. I guess they didn't finish it, like all the rest." Darcy gestured around them.

"We've got to tell Rubidius about this," Sam said eagerly.

"Yeah, I think you're right," Darcy said. She couldn't believe they had figured out something already that nobody else had . . . except possibly for Voitto Vesa.

"You need to take a bath, first," Amelia said to Sam.

"Uh uh, no way, there's no time. And besides, look at yourselves!"

Amelia looked down at her dress and her hands. "Yeah, I suppose you're right. You ready, Darcy?"

"Yeah," Darcy replied, dazed, but she shook her head to clear it. "Let's go."

CHAPTER 10
THE LAST OF THE LINE

Darcy, Sam, and Amelia went straight to Rubidius to tell him about the tapestry, but he wasn't in his cottage. They went next to Eleanor, who was still settling into her rooms after her quick journey back to Ormiskos Castle.

"Rubidius is in the sick ward with Voitto Vesa," Eleanor told them once they'd hugged her hello. "If you girls will give me a few minutes, I'll accompany you there.

"That's okay, Eleanor!" Sam waved as the three of them ran off down the hall.

"You really should clean yourselves up first, don't you think?" Eleanor called after them, her protest going unheard.

They piled into the infirmary just as twilight began turning to dusk. Rubidius and a man Darcy didn't know hovered over Vesa's bed, which was positioned precisely where Darcy had spent much of her convalescence at the end of her first year in Alitheia. The nark's hair had turned dark brown, her skin tanned, indicating that she was about to change. The girls held back against the wall, holding their breaths.

"That's the healer," Sam whispered, indicating the man Darcy didn't recognize, just as Eleanor glided into the room. She shot a reproachful look at the three of them before joining Rubidius and the healer.

Night fell within minutes, and Voitto's eyes flew open. Then, with a shallow groan like a deflating balloon, she sank into her bed. She made no further sound or movement, but her chest continued to rise and fall.

Darcy, Sam, and Amelia waited in silence against the wall. Rubidius and the healer exchanged pleased looks.

"She is stable," the healer declared. "For how long, I do not know, as she is still fighting the curse."

Nurse Dembe approached Voitto's bed to check on her patient, stopping in horror to stare at the three girls.

"You girls! You're filthy!" she shrieked. "How dare you enter this infirmary in such a state? Do you have no regard for the well-being of my patients?" With her arms flapping like a chicken, she chased them out of the room and slammed the door in their faces, even as they stammered their apologies.

Eleanor joined them a moment later, looking amused.

"Whatever information you have for Rubidius will have to wait until morning," she told them. "He will spend the night at Voitto's side, and he'll be quite preoccupied with magical deliberations regarding her care."

"But we think we found a clue to the oracle Vesa gave me," Darcy said.

"Even so, it will have to wait," Eleanor responded. "Now, please, return to your chambers and *bathe yourselves*."

They did as Eleanor directed. Later, Darcy lay in her bed staring up at the ceiling, smelling strongly of lavender soap from the lengthy bath she had taken. She knew she should have no trouble sleeping due to the early morning she'd had with Tellius, but she just couldn't make her brain relax.

There was so much to think about, and Vesa's oracle was only one aspect. In the crazy blur since they'd returned, Darcy hadn't found any time to tell Rubidius about the coldness in her hand or about the mysterious disappearance of Colin Mackaby in her world. She tried to push those things to the back of her mind as she turned Voitto's oracle over and over, using what very little she knew to explain the lot she didn't. In a way, it was nice to have another oracle to worry about, one that wasn't her own. She'd been over the last stanza of her own oracle so many times she could recite it in her sleep.

Vesa's oracle, though, was the only thing she could do anything about at the moment. And since it involved rescuing Yahto Veli, she knew she should feel happy, but Darcy couldn't conjure feelings of happiness any more than she could force herself to feel restful.

Darcy rolled out of bed and lit her gas lamp, squinting as the light hit her eyes. "I wonder if they'll let me downstairs," she mumbled, feeling as though she might as well *do* something if she was going to be awake anyway. She took her dressing gown from its hook by the door and shrugged it on. The deep scarlet, long-sleeved velvet cloak covered her nightgown and buttoned up the front with silver clasps, encasing her in a cocoon of warmth. She pulled her hair free of the collar and opened her door to peek down the hall. Two guards stood at each end of the long hallway, as usual. Darcy tucked her room key beneath the collar of her nightgown and exited her room, taking care to close the door quietly behind her.

Trying not to look guilty, although she had no reason to *feel* guilty, she approached the guards at the end near Rubidius's door. They immediately stood at attention.

"Can we help you with something, Lady Darcy?" the one on the left queried. He was very tall and his expression was kind.

"Um, yes. I was wondering if it would be all right for me to go downstairs for a bit."

"Now?" the other guard asked. "At this hour?"

Darcy shrugged, trying not to feel foolish. "I can't sleep, and there's a room that I'd like to . . . explore. The room with all the tapestries in it, do you know it?"

The first guard, the one with the kind face, nodded. "I know of it, but I cannot let you go alone. If you'll accept my escort, I will take you."

"Oh, okay. You don't mind, do you?"

He laughed. "Certainly not. It will be a nice change of pace. These night shifts do get long . . . not that I'm complaining, mind you! I consider it a great honor to guard the Six." He bowed deeply.

Darcy blushed. "Thank you."

The kindly guard then exchanged a few words with his fellow guard and proceeded down the staircase, instructing Darcy to follow in his wake.

They walked in silence for several minutes before Darcy said, "I'm surprised that they make you—a human, I mean—do the overnight shifts. Why don't they assign nark guards to those roles?"

"There aren't as many narks in Ormiskos as you might assume these days," he replied.

"Why's that?" Darcy preceded him through a door he held open for her.

"They are a declining race, didn't you know? There are fewer and fewer of them every year, and most stick to their own communities. There are some, like Voitto Vesa and Yahto Veli, who have dedicated themselves in service to us humans—and the royal line in particular. But it grows harder and harder to find replacements for those who fall."

Darcy remembered talking with the narks on her journey the year before about how narks reproduce, each couple having only two children. Such practice made their population growth static; actually, it made for negative growth. "Some of them die before they have two children, or before they even wed," she murmured.

The guard looked impressed. "Ah, so you know a thing or two about nark culture."

"Just a little."

"Hmm." He stopped beside the door to the tapestry hall. "There is an exit at the far end of the hall," he said, "but I will thank you to stay close to this exit. I will wait out here for you."

"Thank you." Darcy smiled at him and opened the door, relieved to see the torches were still lit, though burning low in their brackets. She descended the staircase into the half-lit gloom and made for the round tapestry of the archipelago.

She struggled onto the stone bench, tripping over the heavy velvet of her dressing gown, and stood upright before the tapestry. She had no desire to get filthy again, so she took care not to touch the tapestry, but Sam had done a pretty good job of clearing away most of the grime already. Darcy peered at the image of the archipelago. Her heart leapt as she noticed a few scrolling words on some of the islands.

The words were stitched in elaborate calligraphy that would be difficult to read in the best of circumstances. They were also written in Old Alitheian. Darcy sighed and rolled her eyes. She'd never gotten prolific at the Old Alitheian Eleanor had so dutifully taught them. She expected Sam, Amelia, and Lewis knew more than she did, but in the meantime there was no way Darcy would be able to discern any meaning in these words. She wished it were earlier and she could fetch Eleanor to complete the translation, but it was almost one in the morning and most of the castle was asleep.

A soft rustle echoed through the chamber, and she looked up, wondering if there could be bats. Darcy hopped down and took a few steps around the curvature of the wall, noticing a light at the other end of the corridor. Someone coughed. She cast a quick glance over her shoulder, remembering that the guard had told her to stay close but, curious as to whom her unseen companion was, she decided to proceed.

I'll be right back, she reasoned as she tiptoed further down the hall. Rounding the bend, she could see the end of the hall some hundred feet away. Sitting on a bench with his back to her, gazing up at an enormous, rectangular tapestry, was Tellius.

The torch next to the tapestry was newly lit and blazing brightly. He was alone, and he didn't appear to have heard Darcy's approach. Looking defeated and forlorn, he slumped forward with his elbows on his knees, his hands dangling between his spread legs. Darcy had seen her brother take that stance a million times since he had turned twelve, but Tellius's attitude appeared not indifferent like Roger's, but sorrowful; he looked weighed down with cares.

Darcy crept toward him. Tellius started and scrambled to his feet, raising his sword from its sheath at his side and taking a ready stance.

"Who is it? Who's there?"

Darcy took a frightened step back and raised her hands. "Tellius, it's just me!"

He stared at her in confusion for several moments, his sword held aloft. Darcy could see her pale and warped reflection in the blade, her gray eyes glinting in the flickering torchlight. He blinked and furrowed his brow, lowering his sword. "What are you doing down here at this hour?"

"I couldn't sleep—"

"So you thought you'd visit the Hall of Tapestries? Really?" He sounded incredulous. "It's after the breaking hour!"

"Well, I could say the same thing to you!" Darcy said, not wanting to be pushed around—and feeling a little betrayed, as well. Where was the polite Tellius who had volunteered to give her sword lessons the morning before?

"I'm to be king. I don't have to offer an explanation for being here." He sheathed his sword and crossed his arms over his chest. His eyes were red-rimmed as though he had been crying, and Darcy wondered what she had interrupted.

"Where are your guards?" she asked.

Tellius shifted his feet. "I came alone."

"Are you allowed to do that? Outside of the west wing, I mean?"

Tellius sighed and dropped his arms. "It doesn't matter if I am or not." He sat down heavily on the bench and resumed gazing at the tapestry. All the anger of a moment before seemed to have left him.

Darcy knew she should leave Tellius alone, that something was bothering him and she was intruding. Her guard would be mortified to know how far she had gone from the exit he was guarding. Still, she sat down at Tellius's side and looked up at the image on the tapestry. It was a portrait of a couple, a king and queen, for they were crowned and dressed in royal finery. They were painted half facing each other and half facing out of the image, their inside hands clasped. The king's free hand was raised from the elbow, his fingers pointing skyward. The hair at his temples was gray; he looked much older than his young wife, who was pregnant in the image. Someone had meticulously cleaned this tapestry already, for the colors were sharp, and Darcy could see clearly all of its flaws. Where she expected to see clouds in the sky, there were threadbare gaps. Darcy frowned and opened her mouth to draw this to Tellius's attention, when he spoke instead.

"I am the last of my line, you know."

"Huh?" Darcy said, wrenching her attention away from the tapestry. "Sorry, what was that?"

"The Ecclektos line, I'm the last of it. Well, I guess technically Cadmus is the last, but he has not been raised to rule as I have been."

Darcy wondered if this was what had been weighing so heavily on his mind. "What about Tullin? Isn't he an Ecclektos, too?"

"Yes, but he is old and childless. The rest of our family have been hunted down and killed, one by one, by Tselloch's servants." He looked at her, the torchlight casting deep shadows beneath his eyes. "Did you know my mother was only twenty-eight when they killed her? She wanted to have a large family, have more children . . . She died screaming in pain. Her blood ran through the—" He stopped and swallowed hard. "She was pregnant at the time. Nobody else knew, but I had overheard her telling my father. Not even Eleanor knew. I might have had a sister, or another brother, but instead I have a dead mother and a dead father, a single brother, and an elderly cousin. And still Tselloch seeks to kill us. What makes you think you can stop him from taking this castle again? From killing my brother or me? What makes you think you can set this right?"

"I—I *don't* think that! It's just—it's what the prophecy says. I didn't ask for any of this!" She leapt to her feet.

Tellius's expression seemed to soften from anger to dismay, as though a shadow lifted from him. "I'm—sorry," he said. "Please sit."

"I don't know . . . I think maybe I should go. My guard will be wondering —"

"Please," Tellius said. He looked again at the tapestry, avoiding her eyes.

Against her better judgment, Darcy sat, keeping as far from Tellius as she could.

"It's not that I am angry with you, really," he said after a moment. "I just wish *I* could do something. I've always hated feeling like my fate lies in other people's hands."

"Okay," Darcy said, not yet forgiving him for his verbal attack.

"Do you know who this is?" He gestured at the tapestry.

"No."

"It's Tellius the Fourth and his wife. She was pregnant with my grandfather, Tellius the Fifth, but she had the baby in hiding. This tapestry was completed and hung a month before Tselloch took Ormiskos. Tellius the Fourth was the last human to rule here, until you six came and helped us get the castle back."

Darcy forgot some of her anger and studied the portrait more closely. She could have been imagining it, but now that she knew this was Tellius's great grandfather, she could see a family resemblance. Although containing some gray, the rest of the king's hair was wavy and dark brown. His face had the same angles as Tellius's did—the same straight nose and strong chin.

"Why *are* you here in the middle of the night?" Darcy asked. "Just to stare at a picture of your great grandparents?"

Tellius looked down at his hands. "I told you earlier that I stay up most nights in councils and meetings. That is true only some of the time. The truth is, I have been having . . . bad dreams." He sounded embarrassed.

Darcy gripped her cold right hand in her left, images from her own nightmares coming unbidden to her mind.

"I've begun dreaming over and over of my parents' deaths," he continued. "I can't get the images out of my head." He gripped his hair as though to tear the aforementioned images from his mind. "Eleanor saved us, Cadmus and me, but I still heard . . . and saw . . . some *things*." He sighed and dropped his hands. Darcy held her breath. "I have no pictures of them because we lived in hiding my entire life, our identities kept a secret, and to create an image that could be misplaced and found by an enemy was too great a risk. This couple," he pointed to the tapestry, "reminds me of them. In my dreams they are always dead or dying. I come down here to remember what they were like when they were living."

Darcy felt desperately sad for him, but she had no idea what to say. She had always been terrible at consoling people, and she certainly felt no more comfortable with Tellius now than she ever had before. She wanted to express her sorrow for him and say something bracing and encouraging, but the words wouldn't come.

He didn't seem to expect it, anyway. He sat silently staring up at the tapestry and then said, "There, I have told you why I am here. If we truly are to be friends, you must now tell me why *you* are here."

"I . . . I told you. I couldn't sleep."

He raised a skeptical eyebrow.

"Really!" Darcy felt a stab of annoyance. "I couldn't sleep because I was thinking about Voitto Vesa and the oracle, and I wanted to come back here and look at the tapestry Sam and Amelia and I discovered."

Tellius frowned and looked over his shoulder. "Which one?"

"The big round one with all the islands on it," Darcy said. "Do you want to see it?"

Tellius shot one last look at the tapestry of his ancestors. "Sure." They stood, and he followed Darcy back up the passageway.

Darcy pointed it out as they came around the curve, telling him as they walked the words of the oracle Vesa had given her. He nodded, jumping up on the bench and looking closely at the tapestry as she told him her suspicions that it might be the archipelago from the oracle.

"Perhaps," he said, touching one of the islands.

"Hey!" Darcy felt a rush of excitement. "Can you read Old Alitheian? Can you read what's written on there?"

"Yes, but, these are just names . . . mostly."

"Oh." Darcy's excitement fell. "Well, do you recognize any of the names?"

"No. The person to ask would be Captain Boreas. He's explored a great deal of the Sea of Aspros. If this is out there, I'm certain he knows of it." Tellius looked closer at the image, leaning so close his nose almost touched it.

"What is it?" Darcy asked, standing on her tiptoes and craning her neck. When he didn't respond, she began to scramble onto the bench next to him, Tellius offering her a hand. Standing up, she brushed the dust off her hands and asked again, "What do you see?"

"It's just . . . something's odd," he said. "Everything white has been removed from this tapestry, too."

"What do you mean, 'removed'? I thought they were just unfinished." She leaned forward and looked as closely as Tellius was looking. There, at the edges of the tapestry, tiny tufts of white looked as though they had been cleanly cut.

Tellius shook his head. "No. Palace records indicate that the portrait of Tellius the Fourth, at least, *was* completed before it was affixed to the wall. Then an enchantment was placed on this room so that the tapestries could not be removed. It was done to prevent Tselloch from destroying them; they tell the story of our history and our heritage, you see."

"Why would Tselloch care about messing with that?"

"Because if you destroy a people's history," Tellius said, "they forget who they are and they lose their identity. Why would he want any Alitheians remembering freedoms they'd once held?" He shook his head again. "I think my ancestors were wise to enchant the room. Even if all the written records were destroyed, at least we would have our images. Tselloch did, however, counter with a spell of his own. He sealed off this room with an enchantment so powerful it took Rubidius most of the year to figure out how to lift it. We only got into this room a month ago; that's why everything is still so dirty."

"Okay, but why would Tselloch remove everything white?"

"I don't know. I'd assumed he'd done it to the portrait of Tellius the Fourth to obscure the image, out of spite because he couldn't actually remove the tapestry from the wall. But I don't know why he'd bother with this one," he gestured at the tapestry of the archipelago.

"But, Tellius, it's not just this one." Darcy hopped down and spread her arms, happy she knew something Tellius didn't. "*All* of the tapestries we looked at yesterday were missing their white thread—" Darcy stopped, covering her mouth with her hand and looking wide-eyed up at Tellius. "We're right! We're right about this tapestry!" She hopped up and down, her heart beating fast, feeling for a moment as though she were Sam. "The white thread! 'With unraveled image, journey begins!' All these images have been unraveled—partially, at least—and they're all missing the white thread. Vesa sat beneath *that* tapestry because she wanted me to figure out *which* unraveled image would begin our journey. All of this is stated in the oracle; it can't be a coincidence!"

Tellius jumped down and landed beside her. "But if the white thread is *missing*, how can it show us the path—or however that part goes?"

"In error undone . . ." Darcy murmured the second line of the oracle. "I don't know. But it's a start, isn't it? I mean, this is something we can work with!" She stomped her foot and balled her fists. "Oh, I *wish* I could tell Rubidius right now. I'm never going to be able to fall asleep tonight!"

Tellius, on the other hand, was beginning to look sleepy. He yawned hugely. "Well, we can't tell him right now. He's with Voitto, you know, and even *I* wouldn't fancy disturbing him when he's working on an enchantment like that." He stretched. "Perhaps we both should head to our chambers. We're meeting for sword lessons in only a couple of hours, after all."

Darcy groaned. "Maybe we shouldn't—"

"Do you want to learn or not?" Tellius raised an eyebrow.

Darcy deflated. "All right." She looked toward the door. "I have to go out that way. How did you come in?"

"I took . . . a different way," he said cryptically.

"Okay. I guess I'll see you in a few."

"Goodnight."

" 'Night." Darcy felt Tellius's eyes on her as she walked away. She looked back when she reached the foot of the stairs, but he was gone.

CHAPTER 11
THE COST

Three hours later Darcy dragged herself down the hall to the weapons practice room. She raised a weak hand of greeting to the kind guard who had escorted her to and from the Hall of Tapestries earlier and entered the room. She *had* fallen asleep, despite her protestations that she wouldn't, and waking up after so short a rest was almost more painful than being hit on the head with a frying pan.

Tellius was again asleep at the table, but he had at least changed his clothes this time. He wore a simple untucked tunic over brown linen pants and his feet were bare. His sword belt was on the table before him as he rested his head on his crossed arms.

Darcy sat down beside him and yawned. Tellius muttered something and turned his face the other way but slept on. Darcy hovered on the verge of poking him awake, but instead she lowered her hand.

"I'm just going to put my head down for a moment," Darcy whispered soundlessly, her eyes fluttering closed.

"Darcy? Tellius? What are you guys *doing?*"

Darcy sat bolt upright and blinked around, groggy from sleep and unsure whether she'd really just heard Perry's voice. Early morning light streamed through the windows, and Perry, Dean, and the weapons master Baran came through the door. Another door shut loudly above her head, and Cadmus descended the staircase from the balcony, a look of pure glee on his face.

"Lady Darcy." Cadmus bowed when he reached the bottom, and then he turned to smirk at Tellius. "Brother." He bowed again. Tellius made a quick movement, and Cadmus ducked away, afraid of his brother's retaliation.

Darcy turned to Perry. "I—we—"

"I'm teaching Lady Darcy to use a sword," Tellius said. "We both had a late night, though, and we fell asleep at the table."

"What were you doing that you had a late night?" Perry asked Darcy, his eyes narrowed.

Darcy blushed. "I couldn't sleep, so I went downstairs to check out a few things, that's all."

"Tellius was gone most of the night, too," Cadmus chirped. "Were you *together*?"

"That's none of your business, little brother," Tellius said as Perry's eyes narrowed further.

"Fascinating as this little interrogation is," Baran said dryly, "it has nothing to do with our morning forms. You can discuss it later, if it's so important to you. Let's begin." And without further ado, he turned to the boys.

Darcy shot an apologetic look at Tellius as Baran began to bark out instructions to each of the boys. Perry appeared angry and avoided her gaze. She sighed. Perry's jealousy seemed a bit much, considering he hadn't even told her he liked her yet. Still, she supposed it did look pretty bad, she and Tellius having fallen asleep together, even if it was sitting up at a table in a common room. She wasn't sorry, however, that she hadn't had to practice sword-fighting that morning. She felt much more refreshed after another hour of sleep, and she exited the room feeling confident she could explain everything to Perry later.

Darcy answered the knock on her chamber door thinking it was Sam wanting to walk with her down the hall to Rubidius's cottage. Instead she found Perry, and she let him in with some trepidation.

"*I* can teach you to use your sword, you know. You don't *have* to meet with Tellius every morning," he said as soon as her door was closed. "Unless you *want* to, that is."

"No, Perry, it's not like that. He volunteered to teach me; I just said yes."

"So you *do* want to meet with him?"

Darcy crossed her arms. "You're blowing this out of proportion."

"Why would he volunteer to teach you if he didn't like you?"

"What—you mean like, *like* like?"

He raised his eyebrows as though she were stupid.

"Oh come on, Perry! Think about what happened last year. If it hadn't been for Tellius freaking out over having to marry me someday, I would never have gotten caught up in all that Oracle stuff." That wasn't completely accurate, as Darcy well knew she'd had plenty of blame in the situation as well, but she pushed down that thought. This was about assuring Perry that she and Tellius had no interest in each other whatsoever. "Think about *why* I went to the Oracle," she said. "Do you really think it's likely that Tellius or I could change our minds so easily? We're friends, that's all!"

Perry visibly relaxed. "So you *don't* like him?"

"No! I like—" She stopped and bit her lip.

Perry took a step closer to her. "Me?"

Darcy rolled her eyes. "You know I do. Do *you* like *me?*"

His mouth turned up at the corner. "Of course I do."

Darcy's stomach performed a series of complicated acrobatics, and she broke into a silly grin. "Well—okay. Good. I'm glad—"

"I should probably go, Darcy. Dean already knows about—this—but we should be careful . . ." Perry looked meaningfully at Sam's door.

Darcy's elation evaporated. "Oh, right."

As if on cue, Sam called her name from the other room. "Darcy? Can you come and tie off my braid?"

Perry scrunched up his face and backed out the door. Just before closing it, he leaned forward and pecked a kiss on Darcy's cheek.

Darcy put a hand over the spot on her cheek, feeling dazed and giddy. Another knock sounded on the adjoining door, and Sam's voice came louder through the wood. "Darcy, did you hear me?"

"Yeah," Darcy sighed. "I'm coming, Sam."

Perry made no further attempt to engage in physical contact with Darcy over the next several days, but he liked to wink at her when no one else was watching, and he made a point of being at her side whenever possible. It seemed to annoy Dean, who was used to being Perry's right-hand man, but Darcy didn't care. As far as she was concerned, Dean could deal with it.

Neither did Perry make any further argument over her early morning lessons with Tellius, but he did remain rather stiff in the prince's presence. Darcy continued to marvel that Perry could ever imagine either of them developing any romantic affection for each other.

Sam remained oblivious to their flirtation, for which Darcy was grateful. Amelia, on the other hand, continued to watch with eagle eyes, and Darcy thus avoided being alone with Amelia. As for Lewis, things of a romantic nature were so far off his radar that Darcy sometimes wondered if he even noticed that she, Sam, and Amelia were girls.

Now that they were planning a journey likely to last several months, there was plenty to keep them all occupied. It was fair to say Rubidius had been astounded at what they'd discovered in the Hall of Tapestries, and Darcy had tried not to resent his tone of surprise that they could figure out something so crucial. Their discoveries had led to Rubidius's confident assertion that they must embark on a sea voyage to rescue Yahto Veli, though he was reluctant to start the journey without a clear message from Lewis's phoenix feather quill. As there were nearly endless preparations for such a journey, Lewis still had some time to ruminate.

Rubidius was busy most days, either with Voitto Vesa, who remained in a coma, or with the journey preparations. In the meantime, Eleanor had taken over the supervision and education of the princes and the Six.

"Really now!" Eleanor said. It was well into their third week in Alitheia, and they were gathered in the lounge for lessons, most of them having difficulty paying attention, their thoughts bent on the upcoming sea voyage and whether their mission would end in success.

Eleanor brought her hands together and, halfway across the room, Perry's book slammed closed. "You are acting as though you are children. I do not wish to waste my time."

"I was following along!" Perry threw up his hands in surrender.

"Your text is upside down," Eleanor informed him.

"I was trying to see if I could read upside down," Perry muttered, shrinking back under Eleanor's gaze. When she turned away, he grinned and winked at Darcy.

"Lewis is the only one attending to this lesson," Eleanor said. "I fail to understand why you still do not understand the importance of studying our history, our culture, our society."

"We're sorry, Eleanor," Sam said. She'd been twirling her braid for the last half hour and hadn't turned a page in her book. "We're just . . . distracted."

"And," Perry said, leaning forward, "aren't we supposed to be out there *doing* something? I mean, I thought the people were getting upset. I know we're getting ready to leave, but in the meantime couldn't we . . ." He trailed off, casting about for a suggested action.

"All I know is, everything of importance that I've learned in Alitheia, I've learned by *doing* it. By experience, you know?" Dean said.

Darcy cringed at the cruelty of insinuating Eleanor's lessons over the past few years had been obsolete, but Dean didn't seem to think he'd insulted her.

Eleanor sighed and sat back in her armchair. She was approaching her mid-seventies, and she looked frail, when she hadn't used to. She crossed her hands in her lap. "Very well," she said.

"Very well? Very well, what?" Perry asked.

She leveled her gaze on him. "Just that. Very well. If you would like to go and *do* something, perhaps it is time to take you into the city. Please return to your quarters." She stood, very slowly. "I will have the servants bring up plain clothes. If we go, we go in disguise. You will meet me at the stables in thirty minutes." She positioned herself by the door to the room.

"Really?" Sam asked, gaping at Eleanor in surprise.

"Go!" Eleanor said, and they jumped to their feet and hurried to their rooms.

Darcy sat astride Hippondus and watched Dean struggle to mount the small gray mare they'd chosen for him. She sniggered as he finally got into the saddle and almost slid off the other side.

Let's go help him out, Darcy said to Hippondus, using her ability to mind-speak with animals.

Hippondus snorted. *He sits astride Leiri as though she is a wooden barrel!*

Darcy laughed out loud. *Yeah, I see that. But still . . .* She nudged him with her heels, and he sidled up to the mare's side.

"Squeeze with your knees," she said to Dean. "Let go of the pommel and sit up straight. You don't need to hold on like that."

"I don't see why we can't just walk," he muttered, but he relaxed his grip on the pommel as instructed. Sam, Lewis, and Amelia had gotten riding lessons the year before while Darcy, Perry, and Dean had been off visiting the Oracle. Darcy felt lucky she already knew how to ride from years of summer camp before she'd started coming to Cedar Cove. And Perry, good at everything, seemed simply to take to it more naturally.

"What do I do with my hands?" Dean asked, still resting them on the pommel.

"Let your left hand rest on your leg," Darcy said, "and take the reins in your right hand, here . . ." Darcy leaned forward and retrieved the reins, which had fallen forward around the mare's ears. She handed them to Dean, and he held on as if they were a lifeline.

Darcy leaned forward again and looked Leiri in the eye, connecting with her. *Be gentle on him,* she said to her.

"What did you tell her?" Dean asked.

Darcy straightened and squinted at Dean. "I told her to buck you off if you tug on her reins too hard."

"Wha—?"

Darcy cantered away. "Don't forget, she can understand you!" she called back over her shoulder, Hippondus's laughter echoing in her head.

"What did you say to him? He looks terrified!" Perry laughed as she reined in beside him.

"Nothing." Darcy smiled.

"Urgh." Perry shifted in his saddle. "You actually enjoy doing this? I feel like I'm not going to be able to walk later. No offense," he said to his mount.

Eleanor cantered up side-saddle a moment later. "Are you all ready?" She looked them up and down. They were all dressed in sufficiently average clothes that any peasant on the streets might wear. Eleanor had gotten together an escort of palace guards, also dressed as commoners, but with heavier cloaks to hide their weapons.

Altogether they made up a party of twenty-five. Darcy spotted Tokala among the men and waved happily.

"We're going for a brief ride through the streets of Ormiskos Prime," Eleanor said. "Make no mention to anyone regarding your identities. In fact, try not to speak at all unless I give you leave."

"But, what are we doing, exactly?" Perry asked.

"We are going out. That's what you wanted, is it not?" Eleanor raised an eyebrow. "Follow me. We must not be seen exiting the main gate." Eleanor led them around behind the stables to a concealed entrance in the wall. Two posted guards opened the gate for them, revealing what looked like a wide game trail through the woods behind the castle grounds. Several guards cantered through first, followed by Eleanor, the six of them—Dean once again grasping his pommel in a death grip—and the rest of the guards.

They rode through the trees, often having to duck under low-hanging limbs. Eventually they came to what looked like a brush pile, and the front guards dismounted to move it out of the way. On closer inspection, Darcy saw it was a screen constructed to hide the trail. Once they were past it, they emerged into a field of grass. The old highway was visible on a rise a quarter mile further up.

"We are a couple miles south of the city now, having taken this way," Tokala said, sidling up next to her.

"That's wild!" Darcy said. "I never knew this trail was here."

He grinned. "That's the idea. Have you seen Badru?"

"Badru's here, too?" She swiveled her head to look around, excited to see her friend the young master magician.

"Yeah, he's . . . well he's over there." Tokala gestured to a group of men in heavy cloaks. "He's interested in seeing how your powers have grown since our journey last year. He's never stopped talking about that bit of magic you performed outside Fobos."

Darcy smiled, and she and Tokala rode side by side in silence across the field. When they reached the marble pavement of the old highway, he asked, "Sword lessons going okay with Tellius?"

"Yeah, they're great. Wait—you know about that?"

"Things get around the palace," he cast her a calculating, but not unkind, look out of the corner of his eye.

"What do you mean by that?" Darcy asked suspiciously.

"Nothing!" He kicked his horse into a faster canter and joined his comrades at the front of the line.

Darcy sighed. She supposed she should just get used to people assuming she and Tellius were an item. Most people still thought the prophecy meant she and Tellius had to get married someday. Only she and a select handful of people knew the prophecied king might not refer to Tellius at all. And only she knew that she would be *twice* wed. She cast her eyes toward Perry.

Before too long they were passing people of all sorts going to and from the city. As they passed the main castle gates Darcy looked to where, two years ago, men had been working on clearing the trees across from the castle to make room for new construction and rebuilding efforts. Now several structures had sprung up and side roads branched off in various directions. Darcy was impressed at how much was accomplished in just a few years.

The new construction made it feel as though they'd entered the city proper long before they actually passed beneath the arched gate. Darcy wondered whether Eleanor really intended for them to ride up and down the streets and then turn around and go back. It seemed rather . . . pointless.

They continued on the old highway, the press of people soon becoming so great they were forced to slow to a walk. Once they reached what felt like the center of the city, Eleanor gestured and they turned off into a side alley, the guards peeling off on side roads to make a wider net of protection.

Eleanor led them through the winding alley. Darcy heard a yell and looked back to see that Dean had almost gotten a soaking from slop thrown out of an upper window. Eleanor made several turns, taking them deeper into the heart of the poor sector of town, where they dodged barefoot children and mangy cats that skittered between the horses' hooves. People began to look at them oddly, and Darcy worried that even their plain clothes were too clean and new for this part of the city. An unsettling quiet permeated the area; the few sounds heard were the cries of children and angry shouts wafting out of open doorways and windows.

Eleanor drew in her mount and dismounted outside a house like any other in the neighborhood: tall and narrow and touching the one next to it. Whereas most dwellings in the area had open doors and windows to tempt in a breeze in the summer heat, this house was all shut up, and Darcy wondered if it was abandoned.

Eleanor said a few words to the remaining guards and then gathered the six of them close. Dean and Perry looked relieved to be on their feet once again.

"What's going on?" Sam whispered to Darcy.

Darcy shrugged and leaned in toward Eleanor.

"This house belongs to a friend of mine I'd like you to meet," Eleanor said. "It is safe to reveal yourselves to him." She turned and knocked three times on the door before pushing it open without waiting for an answer.

Darcy and the others advanced into the cool entryway of the dwelling. No lamps were lit, and darkness descended like a cloak when Eleanor closed the door behind them.

"Eleanor?" Sam asked, her voice trembling. "Are you sure he's home?"

"Oh yes," Eleanor responded, drawing her hood off her head. "He does not often leave. Come." She led them down the dark hallway into a sitting room at the back of the house.

A little more light shone in this part of the house, coming from a window high up on the wall. Sitting in an armchair in the single beam of light was a very old man with wispy white hair covering his pate.

"Eleanor?" he inquired without looking up.

"Albedos," Eleanor said, hurrying forward and placing a hand on his arm. "I have brought them to you. You wished to meet them, remember?"

"Yes," he answered, tilting an ear toward her, his neck craned awkwardly. The old man, Albedos, took Eleanor's hand in his and stood.

Eleanor turned him around, and all of them gasped. His eyes had been— *removed*—somehow, the sockets open and empty and the tissue within scarred shiny and red. His eyebrows, too, were gone.

Eleanor led him forward and introduced him to each of them in turn. With each introduction he bowed and reached up to touch their faces, tracing their features as if trying to see them through his hands. Darcy looked at him up close and saw that he wasn't as old as she had first thought. His hair seemed to have grayed prematurely, and his frailness seemed to come from a sense of loss rather than old age. Darcy guessed he could be even younger than Eleanor.

When they had finished with introductions, Albedos puttered off to the kitchen to make a pot of tea. Eleanor waited for one of them to speak.

Finally, Darcy asked, "How did he get like that? Who did that to his eyes?"

Eleanor indicated they should sit down before she answered. "Four years ago, Albedos had a wife, children, and grandchildren. He was one of our agents. He lived in a house in the more affluent part of the city under the rule of Tselloch, pretending also to be an agent for him, feigning his loyalty while passing information to us."

"So he was found out?" Perry asked.

"Yes, though he has never told me how. He does not like to speak of it." Eleanor looked down at her hands. "As you know, Tselloch's spies discovered your presence in Alitheia almost immediately after your first arrival, but you slipped away into hiding, and Tselloch was outraged. He ordered a kingdom-wide search, and it was during this time that Albedos was discovered. He was tortured, and he was forced to watch his wife, children, and grandchildren be killed before his eyes. When he still would not reveal your whereabouts, Tselloch put out his eyes with hot pokers and left him to die.

"But he survived, and he went into hiding until the city was retaken. The only thing that has kept him alive these past years has been the hope of someday meeting you, the bearers of the prophecy. You, the tools through which his vengeance will come. *You*, for whom he paid so high a cost."

They stared at Eleanor in dismayed silence.

"I can't believe he would sacrifice so much for us!" Sam gasped, wiping a tear off her cheek.

"It wasn't for us, really," Darcy said. "It was for Alitheia, for its future and its people."

Eleanor nodded. "When you scorn your education—even if you don't understand it—you scorn the sacrifice that people like Albedos have made."

"We'll try harder, Eleanor. We're sorry!" Sam said as the rest of them nodded solemnly.

Albedos reentered the room, carrying a large tray with several tea cups on it. The cups clinked together as he carried them, but he set his burden down without incident, capable of moving easily around his house despite his blindness.

Darcy's right hand began tingling, and she looked down at it in alarm.

"Tea!" Albedos announced. "I have sugar if anyone would like—"

Albedos's door crashed open, and Tokala rushed into the room followed by three other guards.

"Eleanor, they're coming! Badru says they've breached the magical barriers and are attacking the city. We must go at once."

Eleanor stood in alarm. "Tsellodrin?"

"Yes, and possibly tsellochim. Quickly, everyone, please! Badru is waiting to see us safely out, but he is eager to join the fight."

"Albedos—"

"Go. I will be fine." Albedos stretched his arms wide. "What more can they take from me?"

Eleanor nodded. "Children!"

They had already leapt to their feet and were crowding toward the door. Sam found Darcy's hand and clutched it tightly.

"It's okay, Sam, it's going to be okay," Darcy assured her, but she didn't feel so certain herself. The tsellodrin must be close, for her cold hand had not stopped tingling.

In a moment they were back out on the narrow street, and Darcy swung up into the saddle, her pulse racing. Distant screams echoed off rooftops. Badru was mounted on a steed at the end of the street, looking back and forth between them and something around the corner that Darcy couldn't see. Eleanor cantered over to him. "Can we get back out that way?"

"We have to try. They are coming in from the woods at the north end of the city. If we flee south, we may yet be able to beat them to the city gates. It's the crowds I'm worried about. Let's go!"

"Come on now, as fast as you can!" Eleanor called over her shoulder, and they took off.

In anticipation of the coming attack, the alleyways began to fill with people. Entire families fleeing for their lives crowded around their horses' flanks and, despite their best efforts, their mounts were forced to slow to a jerky walk.

They finally reached the old highway, and the palace guards shed their cloaks to reveal their colors, shouting, "Make way! Make way!" They pushed a track through the unrelenting crowd as the screaming got closer.

"Aren't you going the wrong way?" a townswoman asked frantically.

"Oy! The tsellodrin are back that way!" shouted a man wearing a white apron and covered in flour.

The guards ignored them, but Badru swung his mount around and rolled up his sleeves. "They're right!" he shouted to Eleanor. "These men will get you safely to the palace from here. I'm going back to fight!" he declared as he disappeared into the crowd.

They surged on, past streets leading out to private docks in the bay, and Darcy saw hundreds of people piling into boats of every kind. She wondered if they would cross the bay to Kenidros and if it was safe on the other side. The water would foil the tsellochim, but not the tsellodrin.

The guards finally succeeded in pushing them through the crowd, beyond the gate, and onto open road. They urged their horses into a gallop at the first opportunity, and before long they were turning into the castle grounds. The massive gate set in cedar trees embedded magically in the stone wall was already swung open to allow civilians to take refuge within, and a whole contingent of soldiers was preparing to exit as they entered.

"With me!" Eleanor called. She led them through the gathered crowd, over a wooden drawbridge, and to another gate set in the first courtyard wall. A guard was ready for them and quickly opened the gate to admit them to the palace grounds proper, closing it after them before any civilians could follow them through.

Several pages ran forward to take their horses' reins as the six slid from their saddles. Dean groaned as he hit the ground. "Never again," he muttered.

Darcy was too concerned about the city to worry about Dean's personal comfort. She gave Hippondus a quick pat farewell and rushed over to Eleanor. "What can we do?" she asked. "How can we help?"

Eleanor held a shaking hand to her forehead. "Nothing. You can do nothing to help them. Whatever the people may think, your job is not to fight their battles for them."

"I can help!" Perry stepped forward. "This *is* why I'm here, isn't it?"

Eleanor hesitated, but Tokala interceded. "We may need his sword," he said. "The clouds are heavy today; the tsellochim may have joined the fight. Only Perry can slay them by the sword. We could use him at our side."

Darcy felt a knot of fear that Eleanor could let Perry go, and Eleanor gave a reluctant nod. Tokala took Perry by the arm and led him off to join the other soldiers being fitted with armor and protective gear. Perry shot a quick look at Darcy, and then he melted into the company of men.

Sam gave a little sob and turned her face into Darcy's shoulder. Amelia patted her on the back. "He'll be okay, Sam," Amelia said. "He's been through battles before."

Dean, meanwhile, argued with Eleanor about going to fight as well, but she refused to give in to his pleas. "Perry is the warrior," she said. "You are the spy. We have no need of your abilities in this battle."

Dean scowled. "Come on, Dean." Darcy stepped up to him, Sam trailing behind her. "Let's go inside. We're just in the way out here."

Dean turned away and stared after the soldiers exiting the courtyard and taking Perry with them.

"Come on," Darcy said again.

"Just leave me alone, Darcy," Dean said.

"Hey!" Amelia looked indignant.

"It's okay, Amelia," Darcy said. "Let's head in."

"I'll stay here with Dean," Lewis said quietly so Dean wouldn't hear him.

Darcy looked to Eleanor for permission to leave the courtyard and enter the palace, but Eleanor was already addressing a group of pages who were readying some horses. Darcy sighed and Amelia shrugged. They walked together to one of the many side entrances and left the chaos of the courtyard for the relative peace of the sequestered castle passage beyond the door.

They stood in indecision, leaning against the walls and looking at each other. "I feel useless," Amelia said. "What are we *doing* here?"

"Amelia—the prophecy—"

"No, Darcy, I don't want to hear it. What good is a magical lyre going to do for the battle out there?"

"What if Perry dies?" Sam asked, her eyes welling with tears.

Darcy sighed and put a hand over her face. "He *won't*, Sam. I think we just need to trust that they—Eleanor, Rubidius, and the rest—know what they're doing."

Amelia snorted. "Really? If I've learned anything during our time here, it's that no one has any *idea* what they're doing. They don't even know what the prophecy means, or what any of the oracles mean, and they certainly didn't expect Pateros to send *kids* to fulfill their prophecy! I know Eleanor wanted to teach us a lesson today about—I don't know—how important we are to the people of Alitheia, I guess, but meanwhile the people of Alitheia are being *killed*. All this 'education' we're receiving is just stalling. They're trying to pass the time until we're old enough to hunt and destroy Tselloch's gateways without them having to feel guilty if we're killed."

"That's not—" Darcy protested.

"No?" Amelia sounded tired now. "Do you know what Sam and I did last year while you were gone? We took dance lessons, and etiquette lessons, and horseback riding lessons and . . . any number of other things to fill the time that had nothing to do with getting rid of Tselloch. The people are right to feel disappointed with us!"

"But that was *my fault*," Darcy insisted. "*I* was the one who invoked the Oracle and screwed everything up! Don't blame Rubidius and Eleanor."

Sam looked back and forth between them. She was no longer crying, but her eyes were very red, and she looked as though she were too afraid to say anything.

Amelia finally pushed off from the wall and began to walk up the passage. "Where are you going?" Sam called after her.

"Upstairs," she said, "to my room." She spread her arms. "What else can we do?"

"Amelia," Darcy said. "We're going to rescue Yahto Veli. We *are* going to do something useful."

"I hope so," Amelia said over her shoulder.

CHAPTER 12
AFTER THE BATTLE

Darcy and Sam trailed up the passageway after Amelia. Amelia and Sam turned to make their way up the grand staircase to the upper floors, but Darcy hesitated. The atmosphere wasn't as frenetic here as it had been in the courtyard, but there were still many people conferring in rapid voices, coming and going with purposeful strides. She could see Tellius's dark head visible over the shoulder of a palace guard.

His back was to her as he stood rigidly next to Lord Tullin, his father's cousin and the regent ruler. Tellius was dressed in a leather cuirass, his sword strapped around his waist, his bow and a quiver full of arrows over his shoulder. This attire, rather than making him look older, emphasized how small he was next to the fully grown castle guards and soldiers. Tullin shook his gray head, and she could tell by the set of Tellius's shoulders that he was upset.

"Darcy? Are you coming?" Amelia and Sam had started up the stairs and stopped to wait for her.

"No . . . you guys go ahead," Darcy said, turning back to look at the group amongst whom Tellius and Tullin stood.

"They're not going to let you do anything, Darcy," Amelia said impatiently.

"I know, just . . . just go ahead." She looked back to see them standing indecisively. "Maybe I can find out what Perry is doing, Sam," Darcy said to justify her actions.

Sam's raised her eyebrows. "Will you come and tell me if you do find out anything?"

"Of course! I'll see you guys in a few."

They continued up the stairs, but Darcy stayed where she was, observing the discourse in the entryway but mostly watching the conversation between Tellius and the men. Although she couldn't understand what was exchanged, she thought she knew what was going on. Tellius, like Dean, was not being permitted to join the fight, and Lord Tullin appeared quite frustrated with his young ward.

Two of the soldiers in the group were Tellius's nark bodyguards. They stood impassively observing the exchange, but their ears twitched here and there, belying that they were quite alert. If Tullin *did* allow Tellius to join the battle, those two narks would be right by his side the entire time.

Tullin turned away from Tellius as though to terminate the argument, and his eyes landed on Darcy, narrowing thoughtfully. He spoke to his young cousin, and Tellius jerked around and stared at her in surprise. Darcy felt her ears go red as Tellius turned back to his cousin and shook his head, but Tullin nodded, pointing to her. Tellius's nark bodyguards peeled away and indicated that Tellius should do likewise.

Tellius stomped toward her, his face stormy. "What are you doing here?" he asked when he reached the foot of the staircase. "Do you see any *other* women here? You're not needed."

Darcy swallowed hard. "I—"

Tellius didn't wait to hear her explanation, instead starting up the stairs. The two narks stayed close to Darcy, and Tellius soon realized none of them were following him. He stopped a moment later and turned around. "Well? Are you coming?" he asked impatiently.

Darcy kept her feet planted. "Are you saying I have no choice?"

"Why do you want to stay here?" Tellius asked. "So you can be in the way? If they're not going to let me fight, they certainly aren't going to let you!"

"I don't want to *fight*," Darcy said, keeping her voice steady even as her ire rose. "I'm worried about Perry. I wanted to find out if anybody knows whether or not he's okay."

"Well, he hasn't come back dead," Tellius said.

Darcy blanched.

Tellius ran a hand through his hair and looked away muttering. "I'm sorry," he said, not sounding sorry at all. "Will you please just come with me? I'm supposed to escort you to the west wing. It's not you they're trying to get rid of, it's me, okay? And the sooner I finish escorting you, the sooner I can get back down here."

Darcy sighed and started after him. "Fine." Tellius was so volatile she often didn't know how to feel about him. That morning during their sword lesson he had treated her with great deference, bordering on gentlemanly behavior. But as he'd shown that night in the Hall of Tapestries, he could turn the corner into bitter resentfulness without warning.

Darcy jogged up the steps to catch up to him; he was ascending as fast as he could without actually running. "I can take myself up to the west wing, you know. I didn't mean to cause a problem for you," she said, panting in his wake. "I understand wanting to help and not being allowed—*oof!*" Darcy tripped on the hem of her skirt and fell forward onto her hands.

"Highness," one of the narks said, a reproachful note in his voice. The other nark was beside Darcy in a moment, helping her to her feet. Tellius stopped and turned and, to his credit, looked a little ashamed.

He offered his hand to her, but as she was once again on her feet, she shook her head and avoided his gaze. He stepped down toward her. "At least take my arm," he said, something akin to penitence in his voice.

"Really," Darcy said through gritted teeth, "I *can* walk by myself. I *am* capable of it!"

Tellius exhaled. "I forget sometimes that you do not know all of our customs. If I am escorting you, you are *supposed* to take my arm."

"Then why didn't you offer it in the first place?" Darcy glared at him. His eyes darkened, the brown seeming to swallow up the green flecks as it often did when he was upset. "And I do know that custom. Eleanor has taught us a thing or two, you know," Darcy continued, her voice dripping with sarcasm.

Tellius's eyes darkened even further, and he looked as though he were deciding whether to apologize to her or shout at her. He did neither, instead turning on his heel and marching the rest of the way up the stairs without looking back.

They proceeded in silence all the way to the west wing. When they reached her door, Tellius turned to head back downstairs, but his nark bodyguards stood in his way.

"We're sorry, highness," one of them said. "We have orders to make certain you stay here until the battle is over."

Tellius gaped at them and Darcy, despite her annoyance, felt sorry for him. She expected him to proceed to his personal apartments on the next floor, but he didn't. Muttering under his breath, he turned his back on his guards, brushing past Darcy on his way to the weapons practice room.

Darcy watched him go. She knew he wasn't really angry with her, but rather he was angry with Tullin. She wished, without knowing why, that she could somehow make things better for him. She remembered her promise to go see Sam, but her feet carried her instead to the weapons practice room door.

Inside, Tellius had removed his heavy leather cuirass and his bow and arrows. They lay scattered on the floor, where she imagined he had thrown them in anger. He sat at the table with his head in his hands, the narks standing inconspicuously in separate corners of the room. Darcy stood and stared at him, contemplating her next move.

Tellius stood at last and turned around. "What are you—why are you looking at me like that?" he sputtered in surprise, all the fight seeming to have left him.

Darcy blushed. "I wasn't looking at you like *anything*, I just . . . was wondering if I could help you feel better, that's all."

Tellius ran his hand through his hair, leaving it sticking up. "There's nothing you can do."

"What if . . ." Darcy cast her eyes around the room. "What if we distract ourselves?"

"How?"

"What about a little practice? I could use some more work on that combination you showed me this morning."

Tellius looked unconvinced. "I suppose that we could do that," he said, but then his eyes lit up. "Why don't you go and get your real sword?"

"Really?" Darcy grinned. So far he hadn't let them use anything but the wooden practice swords. "Okay, I'll be right back!"

She hurried from the room, looking forward to the distraction from worrying about Perry. As she left, she heard one of the narks mutter something to Tellius, to which he gave an angry reply. She didn't catch what it was, and she didn't care.

While in her room, she pulled off her skirt and shimmied instead into her single pair of linen pants. She held her sword—bound in its leather scabbard—under one arm as she tucked her shirt into her pants with the other hand and hobbled awkwardly back down the hall to the practice room.

"Where are you going, Darcy?" Sam's voice echoed down the hall behind her, and Darcy turned to see Sam popping her blonde head out her door.

"Sword practice with Tellius." Darcy waggled her sword at her friend.

"Now?" Sam frowned. "Don't you usually do that in the morning?"

"We need a distraction," Darcy said. "No word yet about Perry, by the way," she said, heading off Sam's next question.

Sam let out a relieved breath. "Well, I won't feel good until he gets back."

"Do you want to come and watch us?" Darcy asked. "It could take your mind off things."

Sam brightened. "Sure!"

They entered the practice room together, and Tellius looked questioningly at Sam.

"Just watching," she said and took a seat at the table.

Tellius shrugged. "Okay," he addressed Darcy. "You'll notice a weight difference between your real sword and the practice swords, so why don't you unsheathe it and take a few swings to get the feel of it."

Darcy did as he instructed. Her sword was smaller than his, so while she noticed a difference in the swing, it had more to do with how the weight was distributed than how heavy it was. Tellius, meanwhile, swung his broadsword back and forth in a few of the forms exercises. Darcy tried to imitate him without feeling foolish under the eyes of the two narks and Sam.

"How does it feel?" Tellius asked after a few minutes. "Are you ready to try that combination?"

"Sure," Darcy said. She stood in the ready stance with her sword above her head, as this particular combination dictated, and waited for Tellius to engage her. He raised his sword up next to hers.

"Slowly," he said, and he began to count through the numbers he'd given to the various stages of the combination of moves. They barely touched their swords together the first go through, and Tellius seemed pleased she had forgotten only one move. They went through it again, and Tellius counted faster. This time their swords clanged lightly as they came together, and Darcy made it through without a bobble.

"Excellent," Tellius said. "Let's try it this time without counting, same speed." When Darcy performed the round without error, he said, "Again like that, but match my speed and force this time."

Darcy nodded. They had gone through this combination with the wooden swords before, but it made her adrenaline pump to do it with a real sword. If either of them slipped up, the consequences could be far graver than a bruised hand. But Darcy once again made it through, their swords now making loud clangs that rang out through the room.

Sam clapped when they were finished, but Tellius said, "Again!"

He came at her fast, and Darcy countered through the combination. As Darcy straightened into her ending stance, Tellius threw in an extra move. "Ouch!" she gasped as his blade slipped through her grip and sent her sword clanging to the floor.

Darcy clutched her right hand in her left, staring at the deep cut on her palm between her forefinger and thumb, the numbness already there somewhat diminishing the pain. Tellius stared dumbly at her, as though he couldn't believe what he had just done, and Sam ran to her side, asking if she was all right. Darcy looked at the floor where her blood was dripping all over and she turned, horrified, to Sam.

Sam's eyes widened as she caught onto what Darcy was thinking, and she pursed her lips. Placing her body in front of Darcy's, she examined the cut while blocking Tellius and the advancing nark so they couldn't see. Darcy uncurled her fingers, and running through the blood flowing from the gash was a thin thread of black—it was only a *thread*, but it was definite. She and Sam exchanged a serious look, and Sam reached down to tear a strip of cloth from the bottom of her skirt to dress the wound.

Tellius shook himself out of his shock. "Darcy! I—I'm sorry! I didn't mean to do that! Let me see—"

He dropped his sword and took a jerky step toward her, but Darcy threw up her left hand to stop him. "It's okay! Just—just leave it alone. Sam's gonna take care of it."

He stopped as her fingertips brushed his chest. "I'm sorry, I'm so sorry," he said again. "I was trying to add the combination we worked on yesterday. It was a test to see if you could put the two of them together without being told—we've done that sort of thing before!"

Darcy nodded and closed her eyes. The pain was intensifying, and the throbbing made it difficult to listen to Tellius. She bit her tongue to keep from pointing out that, yes, they'd done that sort of thing with *wooden* swords, but she didn't want to make him feel any worse than he already did.

Tellius continued to sputter in the background as Sam wrapped Darcy's hand tightly with the long strip of linen. Darcy stepped her foot in the blood on the floor and tried to smear it around without anybody noticing, sure that the small trace of black would disappear within the red.

"You should go to the infirmary, Lady Darcy," the nark said.

Darcy shook her head and smiled weakly as Sam tied off the strip of linen. "No, really, it's fine. It's not that deep."

The nark looked at the smear of blood on the floor.

"I know it bled a lot," Darcy said, "but it's just a scratch."

"He's right, you should go," Tellius said, looking very pale, his freckles visible beneath his tan.

"I'm not going," Darcy said. "They'll have plenty to do with the battle going on—"

The door burst open, and Dean and Lewis appeared. Lewis doubled over, clutching at a stitch in his side as Dean said, "Here you are! You should come—quickly!"

Sam raised a hand over her mouth and looked faint.

"Is it Perry?" Darcy asked, her voice squeaking.

"I don't know—maybe!"

Darcy and Sam looked once at each other and then ran out of the room after Dean and Lewis. Tellius disregarded his bodyguards and followed behind them. As they ran down the hall, Amelia appeared at her door, looking alarmed.

"What's wrong?" she asked. "Where are you going?"

"It's Perry!" Sam called back at her.

Amelia gave a sharp gasp and joined them. They pounded down the stairs, through a broad corridor, down another set of stairs, and through a short passage between rooms, arriving at the main landing above the grand staircase. In the entryway beneath them, a group of men stood gathered around a kneeling Perry and another man lying on the floor before him, both of them covered in blood.

A breeze ruffled behind them as Rubidius swept past crying, "Make way!" The old alchemist practically flew down the stairs and interposed himself into the center of the circle.

Darcy rushed behind Rubidius, not looking back to see who else was following her. She fought her way through the crowd that had closed around Rubidius and dropped to her knees next to Perry.

"Are you okay?" She put a hand on his arm.

Perry looked dully up at her. His hair was matted with blood and sweat and an ugly bruise bloomed on his left cheek. Darcy looked him over but, although he was covered in blood, some of it black, he appeared to be uninjured.

Perry caught her hand. "It's not my blood," he said. "It's—" his voice caught and he looked down.

Darcy followed his gaze to the figure on the floor. It was Badru, the young master magician.

Badru's pale hair stuck to his face in bloody strands, and his hands were covered so thickly in blood that it looked as though he had submerged them in red paint. Several puncture wounds rounded a gaping hole beneath his heart, and his garments, too, were soaked with blood. With every beat of his heart, blood spurted out through the hole as though a mighty hand within his chest was wringing out his life like a sponge.

The spurts came slower and slower despite Rubidius's frantic muttering and magical concentration. Badru turned his eyes on Darcy. His spectacles were missing, and without them he looked very young.

"Where's the healer?" Darcy cried, kneeling in the ever-expanding puddle of Badru's blood, but Rubidius ignored her.

Tellius's voice sounded in her ear, and she looked up to see him kneeling beside her. "He's been sent for, but he's busy with another—" Like Perry, Tellius halted as his voice broke and cleared his throat. "He won't make it," he whispered.

Rubidius's hands stilled and his voice silenced. Badru reached up and grasped Rubidius's hand, pulling the old magician close.

"The—wards—are . . . back up," he said with great effort, blood coating his lips and dribbling down his chin.

Rubidius nodded, a sheen in his eyes.

"It's—over," Badru gasped, and his hand went slack. The blood ceased pumping from his chest.

CHAPTER 13

BREAKING AND ENTERING

Everyone stared in silence at the dead magician.

"I tried to protect him," Perry gasped. "But I couldn't do it. There were—too many of them. He was repairing the wards. He didn't have a weapon! They drew me away on purpose, I think, and—and they cut him down. But he got those wards back up just before they did. And then . . . they fled. I tried to get him back—to carry him—but I was so tired—"

Rubidius reached forward and closed Badru's blankly staring eyes. "Perry," he said, "you did what you could do. You did well; you protected him long enough." He looked up at the guards, soldiers, and nobles standing around them. "The attack is over," he said. "Please notify Lord Tullin and see to the injured. Have someone bring a funeral cloth." He looked down once again at Badru. "Perry," he said after a moment, "please go to the infirmary."

Perry swallowed hard and nodded. He got slowly to his feet, wincing and holding his thigh.

"You *are* hurt," Sam said. "I thought you said you were okay!" The remainder of their friends had gathered around them, visible now that most of the soldiers had gone off to complete Rubidius's orders.

"It's just a minor stab wound," Perry gasped, still sounding shocked. He took a step and stumbled.

Darcy hopped up to help him, but Dean got there first, shooting her a look of resentment. "I got you, man. Let's go." Lewis hurried forward and took

Perry's other arm across his shoulders, and together they hobbled toward the staircase, Sam and Amelia hurrying along in their wake.

Darcy watched them go, a dark sense of unreality curling in the pit of her stomach. Perry was okay; he was only hurt in the leg. But Badru was . . . *dead*. He had saved their lives multiple times the year before, and now he was gone, just like that.

Darcy held her hands to the sides of her head, as though she could hold her emotions in if she squeezed hard enough. Her right hand felt sticky, and she looked down to see her blood seeping through the makeshift bandage Sam had wrapped around her injured hand. She pulled it away and stared stupidly at it, balling her fingers into a fist.

She looked back down at Badru's lifeless form. A man arrived with a large, thick cloth, and the soldiers laid it out neatly on the floor a short distance away. They began to move Badru's body to the cloth, where they'd wrap it and place it in the morgue with the other fallen soldiers from the day. Darcy's throat closed up as she wondered whether he had any family.

Tellius rose and stood beside her, his knees, too, covered in Badru's blood. He watched the cloth preparations, looking lost and a little afraid. He glanced next at Darcy, and she turned her head to catch his gaze. He seemed fragile, about to break, and deeply grieved. Darcy, moved by compassion and her own need for comfort, awkwardly put an arm about him.

He leaned into her hug and wrapped his arms around her. Her head came only to his chin, which he rested on the top of her head. Although he looked fragile, he felt taut and rigid. Darcy wondered if he wished he could have fought to protect Badru as Perry had done—if he wondered if he could have made a difference. She wanted to tell him he was just a boy, but it was becoming more and more difficult to think of Tellius as a child. In a few short weeks they would be the same age, and Darcy didn't think of *herself* as a child anymore.

Tellius's chest rose and fell beneath Darcy's forehead. She'd expected him to cry—even wanted him to—so that she could feel as though she were comforting him. But really he was comforting her. She screwed up her face against her torrent of tears, glad it was hidden against his chest, and let him hold her tightly until they subsided.

He finally set her back from him and caught her right wrist as she dropped her arms. "You're still bleeding," he said, his voice strained.

Darcy sniffed and yanked her hand away, surprised to see hurt flash across Tellius's face. "I—I can't stay here anymore," she whispered. "Thank you for—" She stopped, wanting to say, *for helping me feel better,* but it seemed such a trite thing to say. She turned on her heel and fled up the stairs.

The west wing was deserted. Even the usual guards were not at their posts, and Dean, Lewis, Sam, and Amelia were all with Perry in the sick ward. Darcy stumbled down the hall, her hand sending jabs of pain up her arm, and she knew she had to dress it properly if she wanted to avoid the infirmary. She looked up and down the hall to affirm its deserted state and did something she would never have done were she not so desperate.

She ran to Rubidius's door and tried the knob. It was open. With a quick twist and yank, she was in his cottage and closing the door behind her.

"Okay, Rubidius," she muttered under her breath. "Let's see if I can remember how to make a healing poultice."

It was a basic remedy, something Rubidius had taught them very early in their first year, but Darcy still had a difficult time remembering exactly what herbs went into the mixture. She stared at the dried bunches hanging from his rafters and took a few of them down to smell them, finally giving up and looking for the giant book of herbal remedies she knew he kept around his cottage somewhere.

She found it on a shelf behind a jar of what looked like pickled salamanders and paged through it, looking for the picture she had seen before. After finding the instructions, she laid the book open and began to pound and mash the herbs she had taken down, feeling pleased she had remembered *something* of the remedy. The strip of linen Sam had used to wrap her palm was almost completely soaked through now, so once she had everything mixed together into a paste, she unwound her hand and discarded the strip for a clean one that she found in a wooden box beneath Rubidius's bed.

She laid her hand out on the table and stopped for a moment to study the wound. It was a clean, straight gash, deep enough to bleed profusely and cause her great discomfort, but not deep enough to have severed the tendon. About to apply the poultice, the voice of her mother intruded in the back of her mind, telling her to wash it first. She went to Rubidius's hand pump and worked the water into a stream.

"If you paid closer attention in lessons, you would not have had to use the book," Rubidius said from behind her. Darcy spun around as he entered his cottage and snapped the door closed behind him. He walked around his table to her side and began to wash his hands without another look at her.

The basin filled with red as he scrubbed his hands clean of blood, and Darcy watched him with wide eyes, wondering if he was angry with her. Of course he must be; she had entered his cottage without permission and while he wasn't at home.

Rubidius finished washing and dried his hands. "You may wash it," he said calmly.

Darcy did as he instructed, wincing as the cold water entered the wound. She turned around to find him holding out a towel with which he gently patted her hand dry.

"Come. Sit," he said, leading her to the table where the poultice was prepared. He examined it expertly. "More sage than I would usually advise," he said after a moment, "and you should try to make it less runny in the future, but I think it will suffice." He held out his hand for hers and began to apply the poultice.

"Aren't you going to ask me why?" Darcy asked softly.

"Oh, I know why. I've known for some time," Rubidius said matter-of-factly. "You are hiding your coldness."

Darcy gasped. "How could you know?"

Rubidius was quiet for so long Darcy thought he might not answer at all. But finally he said, "While you were recovering from your time in the dungeon, Nurse Dembe commented to me that the fingertips of your right hand were always cold. It puzzled her, but it did not take me a great deal of mental discourse to figure out why. Stronger people than you have been turned by much less."

"So you've known . . . all this time!"

"It's been an interesting observation, I will admit. I thought at first that perhaps it would consume you and the prophecy would be lost. But it has not done that, has it?"

Darcy shook her head. "I barely touched him," she whispered. "I only reached out because I didn't want—I didn't want to die."

"Quite understandable," Rubidius said.

"I didn't know what it would make me."

"Well, it hasn't made you anything . . . yet."

"You don't think I'll become a tsellodrin?"

"That I do not know. For most people the change is immediate. For others, very slow, but never as slow as this." Rubidius finished tying off her new bandage and sat back to stroke his beard.

"Do you think it's because I travel back to my world every year?"

"Is the coldness dormant in your world?" Rubidius asked.

Darcy's stomach dropped and tears stung her eyes. "No. It's actually . . . *spreading*, now."

Rubidius nodded, and his fingers stilled. "We can only wait and see."

Darcy felt a surge of hopelessness. "Is there nothing we can do? Is there no remedy?"

Rubidius shook his head. "I have already done for you everything I can."

Which is what? Darcy thought, but she held the words back.

"Had you thought of it at the time, it would have made a much more profitable question to ask of the Oracle," he said, "for no one who has elected to become a tsellodrin has ever turned back to human."

The Oracle. "You also said nobody has ever rescued someone from the Oracle before, but we're about to do that."

"We're about to *attempt* to do that," Rubidius said. "I am not saying there is no hope for you, Darcy, I am saying we must wait to see how it unfolds. Perhaps this is all part of the prophecy."

Darcy thought ruefully that they could add it to the long list of other things they didn't know, remembering Amelia's complaint from earlier that day.

"You should visit Master Perry in the infirmary," Rubidius said, dismissing her. "He has been asking to see you."

Darcy stood and made her way to the door.

"Darcy, do make certain always to wear your ring," Rubidius said, almost as an afterthought.

She turned back to him and frowned. "My Ecclektos ring? Why is that important?"

Rubidius smiled. "No reason other than the usual." He stood and turned his back to her as she confusedly fingered the ring. "And Lady Darcy," he said, "my door will be locked in the future, although I doubt a lock will remain a barrier should you be thoroughly determined to break and enter."

"I understand," she replied, though she wasn't quite certain what he meant.

Darcy awoke in the middle of the night to a strange light. She sat bolt upright in bed and stared at the orange glow pouring through her window casements. A low roaring sounded came muffled through the glass and curtains, not loud enough to have woken her under usual circumstances, but she had only just fallen asleep after returning from several hours in the infirmary with Perry.

She slid from the bed, threw her dressing robe about her shoulders against the chill, and ran to her window seat. Pulling the curtains wide open, she looked down. The roar grew louder, sounding almost like a battle. The orange glow flickered like fire, though she couldn't see the source, for it came from the other side of the castle. She reasoned frantically that the castle couldn't be under attack; Badru had restored the wards!

She hopped down from her window seat and rushed to her door. At the end of the hall the guards shifted and muttered in low voices, shooting furtive looks over their shoulders. Darcy hurried to them.

"There's something going on outside!" she said. "I think we're under attack!"

"We can't be," one of them said, though his eyes belied that same suspicion.

"You should return to your bed," the other guard said in a very deep voice. "Whatever it is, it will be dealt with."

"No! I want to go see. If we're under attack, maybe I can help."

The guards exchanged an amused look. "We cannot allow you to leave the west wing if there is any threat to the castle," the deep-voiced guard said.

"So there *is* a threat!"

The guards remained impassive. Darcy huffed and turned the other way, intending to try the guards at the other end of the hallway but detouring into the library instead. She turned up the gas to the chandelier, its growing light gleaming off gold script on leather spines, and then turned a sharp left to find her way to the staircase.

She mounted the stairs two at a time and flipped the hidden latch to gain entrance to Tellius's balcony. She hesitated at the door to his room and then knocked loudly. No response came for several moments, and she raised her hand to knock again just as Tellius yanked open the door. He wore his nightclothes, but he looked wide awake.

"What are you—"

"The castle's under attack!" she said, pushing her way past him into the room.

"I know," he said.

"We need to—wait—did you say *you know?*"

"Yes. My bodyguards are in the hall and my door has been secured from the outside. I know what that means." He looked pale in the light of the single lamp on his table, but he didn't look at all surprised.

"How come this door wasn't locked?" Darcy pointed at the one through which she had come.

"It was," he said. "It only locks from the inside, and I will be in a great deal of trouble if they find out I opened it."

"Then why did you?"

"I figured it was you."

"Oh." Darcy stood dumbfounded in his room, her adrenaline starting to slow. She wondered what she had expected them to be able to do. Charge out into battle? Now that she was thinking more clearly, she didn't know why she had come. "I just—I just wanted to know what was going on," she said.

"It's a riot, I think. I was listening at the door to my guards talking in the hall when you knocked."

"A *riot?* Like—of the people of Ormiskos?"

He nodded.

"*Why?*"

"They're upset about the attack today. A lot of people lost their lives. I think they want Tullin to make you six do something about it. And they're mad at me, too." Tellius sighed.

Darcy reeled. "That doesn't make any sense! What do they expect us to do? And why would they be mad at you?"

"They expect you to do what the prophecy says you will do, and they want it done *now*. As for me," Tellius rubbed his face with both hands, "they think I'm a distraction and that I'm weak. They don't understand why we are moving forward with coronation plans in two years. They think everything would get better if my cousin would just focus on ruling and on the threat at hand. At least, that's what I'm *assuming* they're angry about. I didn't hear much through the door, but it's a sentiment I've heard often enough."

"Badru *died* today to save them! How can they march on the castle? It's not fair!" Darcy said angrily.

"Who said it has to be fair?" Tellius asked. "I feel as though I could sway them if my cousin would let me *talk* to them. But he won't, especially not when things get like this. 'It's too *dangerous*,' he says."

"What? This has happened before?"

A movement in the corner of the dim room drew their attention. Emerging from behind a tapestry was a sooty-faced, grime-covered man holding a long sword in one hand and a dagger in the other.

His eyes were fixed upon Tellius.

CHAPTER 14
THE VEIL BETWEEN THE WORLDS

Tellius acted quickly and pushed Darcy behind him.

"What do you want?" he challenged the man, confronting him instead of calling for his guards.

"I expected to find you sleeping, little prince." Beneath the soot, the man's face flushed very red.

"I do not sleep when my people are in distress," Tellius said as Darcy peered around him, amazed at his calm, articulate speech.

The man's eyes bulged in rage. "We," he said, seething with wrath, "are not *your* people. If we were your people, you would be *protecting us!* If we were your people, my daughter would not have *died* today!"

Tellius edged Darcy toward the door. "I am sorry—"

The man snarled and dove across the bed toward the two of them. Darcy screamed for the guards as Tellius motioned with his hands, gathering the flame from his lamp into his palms. He tossed the fire into the man's face as he advanced on him with his sword. The door crashed open, and the two narks breezed in with the speed of their kind, diverting the blade plunging toward Tellius's chest and slamming the man into the far wall. After a brief struggle, the man was disarmed and incapacitated.

The man sobbed and shook his fire-singed head as more guards hurried in to take him away to the dungeons. The two narks lit the other lamps and faced Tellius and Darcy, registering Darcy's presence and the open balcony door. They looked thunderous as they returned their gazes to Tellius.

Darcy stood with her hands over her mouth. Tellius straightened up, and Darcy moved closer to his side.

"What were you *thinking*, highness?" one of the narks asked.

"He didn't come in through the library door," Darcy said, hoping to exonerate Tellius.

The bodyguard furrowed his brow as he asked, "Then where did he come from?"

"Over there." Darcy pointed across the room. "He came from behind the tapestry."

The other nark went to the tapestry and pulled it aside. A door opened outwardly into a dark hole behind it.

Darcy turned shocked eyes on Tellius. "A secret passageway?"

Tellius said nothing.

"I'm going in to investigate," said the nark holding the tapestry. "Lock it behind me."

The other nark did as instructed, then turned to stare daggers at Tellius. "You were not to use this door," he said. "You promised to keep it locked."

Tellius pursed his lips and folded his arms.

"And now you see why," the nark concluded. "Lord Tullin will be notified of this. And I will ask Rubidius to have this doorway magically sealed."

Tellius made a noise of protest, but the nark held up his hand.

"How will the other nark get out?" Darcy asked.

"The other side, of course," Tellius muttered.

"But how did that guy even get into the castle? How did he know about this?"

"You didn't recognize him?" Tellius asked, looking at her. "He was one of those staying with you at Sanditha your first year. He must have studied the map Amelia found—the one that showed the tunnels and secret entrances. He was there when she found it, and he relocated with us to Paradeisos. He must have been one of those who studied it in preparation for the final battle."

The nark nodded. "An astute observation, majesty," he said, his voice kinder. "But Lady Darcy must return to her quarters. I do not know why she is here, but if Lord Tullin discovers you were alone in your chambers with a girl—"

"We weren't doing anything!" Darcy felt her ears blush horribly. "I came up here because I heard the riot and I was scared and wanted to see if Tellius knew about it."

"The riot is over," the nark said. "Lord Tullin has pacified the people . . . for now. I will have a guard escort you to your chamber."

Darcy nodded, defeated, and waited for a guard to take her back to her room.

Darcy woke the next morning after a very restless night full of dreams of assassins entering her room through secret panels and trapdoors. She evaded each of them only to find herself kneeling in a pool of Badru's blood over and over again. She groaned and pulled her hair over her face, trying to shut out the images and gain a few more minutes of sleep, but it was no use; she was awake.

She hadn't bothered to remove her dressing gown before falling into bed the night before, so she felt uncharacteristically warm as she rose from the bed and walked to her bathroom. After freshening up and failing to erase the deep circles beneath her eyes, Darcy walked back out to the center of her room. Placing her hands on her hips, she looked around, wondering if her chamber, too, had a secret tunnel leading to it.

The thought that a stranger might be able to gain access to her room while she slept sent a shiver down her spine. She went to the window and walked the circumference of the room, trailing her fingers along the walls. Her chamber had no floor-to-ceiling tapestries like the one in Tellius's room, but a door might still be hidden in the cracks between the stones. She rapped her knuckles on a few spots, but all she gained was sore knuckles. She tried pulling on books and candlesticks as she'd seen characters do in movies, but nothing happened. She got down on her hands and knees and peered beneath her bed.

"What are you doing?" Sam asked from above her, having let herself in through the adjoining door they kept unlocked.

Darcy looked up, still holding her coverlet. "I'm . . . never mind." She stood and brushed off her skirt, feeling foolish.

"I knocked, but you didn't answer," Sam said. "Really, though, what were you doing?"

"Didn't you hear the noise last night?" Darcy asked.

Sam shook her head. "What noise?"

"There was some sort of riot, and I went up to Tellius's room to see if he knew about it." Darcy went on to tell Sam about the encounter with the assassin and the secret tunnel that led from his room.

Sam covered her mouth and stared at Darcy with wide eyes. "That's—wow! You guys could have been killed!"

"Yeah, well, Tellius handled himself pretty well, actually," Darcy said. "And the narks—you know how fast and strong they are. I don't think the assassin ever had a chance."

"I can't believe how upset people are with us." Sam sat down on Darcy's bed and worried a thread in the coverlet. "What can we do? Really? We don't know where the gateways are, we don't know how to get rid of

Tselloch, and we don't know how all of our talents are supposed to work together to make this happen. Add to that the coldness in your hand—"

"Which, by the way, Rubidius knows about now," Darcy said.

Sam blinked at her. "Good! So add to that your hand, our voyage to rescue Yahto Veli, and Colin Mackaby's disappearance off the face of the earth, and we have a few unsolvable riddles before us!"

"You could say that."

Amelia joined them, and they sat staring morosely at, but not really seeing, each other. Finally a knock sounded on the hallway door, and Darcy trudged over and opened the door to find Eleanor on the other side. The old woman was dressed in a high-necked black gown, her silver hair tied back in a tight bun. She looked like a caricature of a Victorian governess.

"Breakfast in the lounge," she said. "I have some announcements for you."

"I still need to get dressed," Darcy said, looking down at her dressing gown. "I'll meet you down there."

Darcy pulled on a dark dress, taking her cue from Eleanor's attire. She had a feeling they would be attending a funeral for Badru that day.

She wasn't wrong. She entered the lounge to find everyone gathered around a table covered with a pleasant spread of muffins, fruit, and tea, but only Dean was munching. Perry leaned on a crutch against the far wall, though he looked mostly recovered. The bruise on his face had already faded to a green tint. He looked up and acknowledged Darcy's presence with a glance, even if he didn't smile. She understood.

Darcy inconspicuously made her way to stand at Perry's side, and when Eleanor started speaking and all eyes were on her, Perry reached over and squeezed her fingers lightly.

"Badru's funeral will be at noon," Eleanor said. "He will be laid to rest in the royal plot, and you all will be in attendance. You should know, also, that our plans are almost finalized for your embarkation."

"You mean you aren't coming with us?" Sam asked.

Eleanor smiled weakly. "I am far too old for such a journey. I will remain behind with Cadmus and Lord Tullin. Tellius, however, will be journeying with you."

"What? Why?" Perry asked. "Isn't he needed around here?"

"After the attempt on his life last night, Rubidius has reconsidered Tellius's safety in the castle. He feels it might be best for the people, too, if Tellius is out of sight for a while," Eleanor said.

Amelia frowned at Darcy and whispered, *"What* attempt on his life?"

"I'll tell you in a minute," Darcy said as Lewis, Dean, and Perry also looked questioningly at her.

"Please meet me in the west courtyard at a quarter to noon. Dress appropriately for the funeral. Darcy, what you have on is fine. You may have the rest of the morning to yourselves. Rubidius and I have too much work to complete, what with the attack and riot yesterday and the preparations that still need to be made for your journey."

"When do you think we'll be ready to go?" Lewis asked. He turned a muffin over and over in his hands, but he hadn't brought it to his mouth yet.

"We can be ready in a week, but Rubidius is still hesitant to set out without—"

"Without a clear message from me. Yeah, yeah, I get it," Lewis mumbled. "Well, I guess I know what I'm doing with *my* morning."

Eleanor looked at them for a moment with pity in her eyes, which soon became strength and resolve. "I know this is difficult for you, ripped from your own world and uncertain how to fulfill your purpose here. Just . . . take it step by step; do the next right thing." She folded her hands before her and nodded. "I will see you in a few hours," she said, and she exited the room.

Lewis threw the muffin down on the table in disgust and slumped into a chair. "I've got to get some inspiration, here!" He yanked his phoenix feather quill out of his bag and pulled a couple of pieces of parchment toward him. He began making frantic marks on the first page.

"What happened to Tellius last night?" Amelia asked Darcy. "Did Eleanor say someone tried to *assassinate* him?"

Darcy nodded. "Yeah." She told them of the events the night before. Sam stood next to Lewis and watched him.

When Darcy was finished, Sam asked Lewis, "What are you writing?"

"The alphabet," he answered gruffly.

"Lewis, you can't force it."

"I know."

Darcy put a hand on Sam's arm, but Amelia stepped forward. "Would it help if I played something, do you think?"

Lewis looked up at her and blinked behind his Alitheian spectacles. "It might."

"Okay, I'll go get my lyre." Amelia hurried from the room.

Perry hobbled over to the table and picked up a muffin.

"I'm not hungry." Darcy sighed, looking at Sam watching Perry.

"Me neither," Sam replied.

"Do you want to go down to the tapestry room? I hear they're copying the archipelago tapestry onto a piece of parchment so we can take it with us as a map, but I'd like to get a look at some of the other tapestries down there, too."

"Yeah, okay." Sam perked up a little.

"Do you guys want to come?" Darcy asked Perry and Dean.

"All the way downstairs?" Perry winced and tapped his crutch on the floor. "Nah, I'd rather stay here."

Dean, unsurprisingly, agreed to stay with Perry, so Darcy and Sam made their way down the hall to the staircase alone. They heard Amelia start to play on her lyre back in the lounge as they began their descent. The guards didn't seem to care where they went during the day, as the castle was usually abuzz with people—extra eyes everywhere to keep them out of trouble.

They entered the Hall of Tapestries to find people on ladders all over the cavernous space, cleaning away the grime and dust covering the tapestries. A special team had set up a table by the bench beneath the archipelago, and was meticulously copying every detail of the picture onto a huge piece of leather, even going so far as to use paints to convey the colors. A fussy-looking man with tiny round spectacles perched on his nose hovered over the artist, pointing out fine details from time to time.

Darcy and Sam watched for several minutes without drawing any attention to themselves, and then they began to explore the other work being done around the room. Darcy meandered to an enormous tapestry that covered the whole wall just inside the room and stepped back to admire the progress. It was a map of Alitheia, she discovered, although it appeared very old. She could see in the southern quadrant the twin bays, side by side, that framed Ormiskos and Kenidros, but only the gray edifice of Ormiskos Castle was represented on the map. Kenidros Keep had not yet been built.

Darcy traced on the map her oracle journey from Ormiskos. Although they had not followed any established road, she knew they had moved east through Ormiskos Prime and across the inlet into the wilderness. From there they had traveled due north for several weeks, finally coming upon the valley of Fobos. This part of the map was near the top, and Darcy dragged over an abandoned stepladder so she could get up high enough to look at it.

"There it is," she murmured. "The valley. And those are the mountains." She traced her finger over the path she was sure they had taken up the mountainside to the lair of Archaios the dragon, the watcher of the valley. She frowned as she moved her finger back down, tracing her way back to the valley where she found marked on the tapestry a dot that read—in runes she could barely sound out—*Fobos*. The village must have been very old, old enough to be depicted on this map before Kenidros had even been built. If the village was that old, then perhaps the darkness—the spell of fear that had ensnared them—was that old too. Darcy searched the trees just south of the village, but she couldn't make out any depiction of darkness at all. If the spell had been in existence then, the artist must not have known about it.

Darcy returned her gaze to the mountains. She thought about her time with Archaios. He'd known how to destroy the gateways . . . and he hadn't told her. Even now she shook her head in frustration. How could he have called himself a servant of Pateros and have refused to tell her that very crucial bit of information? Hadn't he known they were at war?

She reminded herself that of course he had known. He'd known a lot of things; he'd even known something about the bone whistle, although she'd never gotten a chance to ask him what.

Darcy's eyes flew wide. *The bone whistle!* She'd barely given it a thought since leaving Archaios's cave. Where was it now, she wondered. She traced her path through the mountains, imagining as she did Perry carrying the whistle around his neck. The map didn't show the sinkhole through which she'd been transported to the Oracle; it must have been a newer geological feature, younger than this map. *The trees had been young*, she reminded herself, closing her eyes and leaning her forehead against the rough fabric.

She fought to remember what had happened to the bone whistle once they'd gotten to the sinkhole. Maybe Perry had kept it . . . *No*, she recalled. He'd been playing with it, but Yahto had gotten upset and taken it from him.

That meant Yahto had it with him—down in the Oracle's lair. Surely that had to mean something. She ran through Voitto Vesa's oracle in her head once more.

" 'The white thread,' " she murmured. No, that had already been worked out; the white thread was missing from the tapestries. " 'Breath of life,' " she continued. "Breath of life! That could be it!" She thought through the ways the whistle had aided them. It had saved them from the fear spell and the wolves. Was it too great a stretch to say it had given "life" to them? Darcy thought it was worth mentioning to Rubidius, though she wondered why, if the bone whistle was to help him, Yahto Veli wouldn't have tried to blow on it by now.

"What did you find? You have that look on your face," Sam said from beneath her.

Darcy backed down the ladder. "It's not what I found, it's what I remembered."

Darcy and Sam returned to the west wing to find the others had gone off to their separate quarters to dress for the funeral. While Sam went to her chambers to do the same, Darcy hurried down the hall to Rubidius's cottage and knocked on the door. When he didn't answer, she asked a passing servant where the old alchemist might be.

"In the infirmary checking on Voitto Vesa, my lady," the servant answered. "And then I believe he will be preparing for the funeral."

Darcy accepted that she wouldn't have an opportunity to tell Rubidius about the bone whistle until after the funeral, and she headed back to her chamber. A door opened down the hall and she turned to see Lewis walking toward her, tugging uncomfortably on his sleeves.

"How come the only black clothes they've given us are long sleeved?" he grumbled. "It's going to be sweltering out there."

"I don't know. Maybe it's inappropriate to show too much skin at a funeral."

He grunted. "Yeah, maybe. I suppose it's that way back home, too."

"How did it go with Amelia?" Darcy asked. "Any luck?"

"No."

"That would explain your bad mood," Darcy mumbled under her breath.

Lewis continued. "It was actually really distracting to have her play. All I could think about was *old* stuff I'd written—scribbles and notes from hours of lessons with Rubidius last year. Nothing new at all."

"Don't worry about it. When it's time, it will come to you."

"Sure," Lewis said, unconvinced.

They gathered in the west courtyard at the appointed time to meet Eleanor for the walk out to the royal burial plot. Tellius and Cadmus joined them, along with Lord Tullin, Rubidius, and a coterie of guards. As they made their way, Tellius walked up beside her.

He wore a heavily brocaded black velvet jacket over black pants and boots. It was hot outside and beads of sweat already stood out on his brow, but he didn't seem to notice. They approached a very ornate wrought-iron gate that looked heavy enough to squash a horse. "It's called the Gate of Passage," Tellius said to Darcy, his eyes taking in the arched top.

Darcy's gaze followed his to find words engraved in swirling Old Alitheian at the top of the arch. She struggled to make them out, but Tellius translated them for her.

" 'For none of us lives to himself alone and none of us dies to himself alone. If we live, we live unto Pateros; and if we die, we die unto Pateros. Whether we live or die, we belong to Pateros.' "

Darcy studied Tellius as he read the words with such longing in his voice, and she wondered if he was thinking of his parents . . . and if he believed them. She didn't even know if *she* believed those words, or if she understood them. How much more difficult it must be for someone who'd already lost so much.

"Are they buried in this plot?" Darcy asked. "Your parents, I mean."

Tellius turned to her. "No. They died far from here. And all this land was under Tselloch's control, remember?" He gestured widely. "We did not even know this gate was here until the vines were cleared away. Even the graveyard itself had been overrun with his . . . *foulness*. It's been cleaned up now."

"Where *are* your parents buried?"

"In the woods somewhere. Their bodies were recovered by our supporters and buried, but I don't know that I could find their graves anymore. It was a long time ago."

Darcy bit her lip, feeling again the uncharacteristic urge to hug him as she had the day before. But Rubidius stepped away to draw the crowd's attention.

Rubidius came forward, and they all fell into two lines, forming a gauntlet. He passed through to the gate, muttering, and the gate's many locks undid themselves with creaks and groans. Rubidius stepped back and said loudly, "The dead pass first."

Pallbearers marched forward with Badru's wrapped body on a litter between them. They carried him through the gate, and the rest of the mourners fell in line behind them. The path wound up a slight incline through the trees, and Darcy recognized that, in their world at Cedar Cove, this was the path to the volleyball clearing.

She mused how odd it was that so many things were the same. *"The veil between the worlds is thin,"* Rubidius had said, *"in the vicinity of an open gateway."*

They emerged from the trees into a clearing much larger than the volleyball court in her own world. Scattered throughout in neat rows were myriad headstones, and growing next to each headstone were bunches of white lilies. A fresh grave had been dug, and beside it Badru's body was brought to rest as Rubidius began his eulogy.

Darcy heard little of what he said, as she stared unfeelingly at the hole. Sam sniffled beside her, and Tellius went rigid, but Darcy felt as though her grief was spent. Movement near the grave caught her attention; a few high animals had come down to pay their respects. A small red squirrel perched solemnly nearby, and she wondered if it might be the same one that had nodded at her in her own world not too far from here, when Darcy was new to Cedar Cove and had no idea the adventures that awaited her.

The veil between the worlds, Darcy thought again, *is thin . . .*

As the pallbearers lowered Badru's body into the grave, Eleanor and Rubidius magically filled it with dirt.

Darcy's knew now was not the right time, but she couldn't tear her mind from the squirrel and the similarities between worlds. In her mind, she heard Sam's voice saying Colin had *"disappeared off the face of the earth"* . . . recalled the village of Fobos and the fear spell no one could lift . . . felt the cold darkness in the woods behind East Mooring . . . and felt the fear, the unfathomable fear. *"They complained of phantom voices and inexplicable terror. The villagers gradually moved away from Baskania's gateway,"* Eleanor had said. *"We do not know where it is."* Darcy clapped her hands to her ears to stop the deluge of thoughts.

"It's okay, Darcy," Perry said, having interposed himself between her and Tellius. "I know; I'm upset, too."

"It's not that!" Darcy gasped, seeking his eyes, then Sam's, then the others'. She trembled with shock.

"Then what is it?" Perry frowned.

"I know where one of Tselloch's gateways is!"

CHAPTER 15

THE PEN OF THE SCRIBE

"Rubidius!" Darcy fought her way to Rubidius's side and clutched at his sleeve. "I have to talk to you—*now!*"

The old alchemist stood beside the newly filled grave, his head bowed and his eyes closed, as a couple of men from the palace guard transplanted white lilies to the mound of dirt at his feet. He looked up at the urgency in her voice. "Wait, Darcy. Wait until we have passed back through the gate."

"But this is important—*really, really* important!"

He lowered his bushy eyebrows. "So important that it cannot wait until Badru's ceremony is complete?"

Darcy exhaled and bit her lip hard. She hated that he was making her wait, but he was right; now wasn't the time. She nodded.

"Thank you." He directed his attention back to the grave, and with raised hands, he magically carved into the headstone Badru's name, the dates of his birth and death, and an epitaph describing the bravery of his passing.

By the time Rubidius had finished, Darcy was fairly dancing with impatience. Perry and Sam shot her questioning looks, but she ignored them.

Finally Rubidius said his parting words, and the procession began to make its way back down the path to the Gate of Passage. Darcy followed in Rubidius's wake, determined not to be parted from him. Soon they were once again within the castle courtyard, and Rubidius had shut and sealed the gate. The crowd began to disperse, except her five friends who crowded around her to hear her explanation.

Rubidius turned wearily to her. "Yes, Darcy?"

"I know where a gateway is." she said without preamble. "I *know where one is!*"

Rubidius blinked once, taken aback. "You know where a gateway is," he repeated. "Explain."

"Okay." Darcy waved her hands excitedly. "In our world, Colin Mackaby —you remember us telling you about him, yes?" Rubidius nodded. "Well, he's disappeared. At camp we looked all around his cabin and we found a spot that felt a little bit—just a *little* bit—like the fear spell we encountered outside of Fobos." She looked at Dean and Perry, on whose faces realization was beginning to dawn. "Well, it got me to thinking about the veil between the worlds and about how you told us things can leak through in the vicinity of an open gateway."

"Darcy," Amelia said, "are you saying you think there's a gateway to Alitheia behind East Mooring?"

"No, not to Alitheia. Eleanor taught us in history about Baskania's journey through to Tselloch's world—well, what's known about it, at least —and Tselloch's world is supposed to be really dark and scary, right? I think Tselloch is opening a gateway from *his* world to our world, and Colin is *there*, not here." Darcy paused to let her words take effect. "It would explain why we experienced something in our world that we also experienced outside of Fobos. And it would explain why the villagers didn't know how to get rid of the darkness; because it's *not a spell!* I would bet anything that there's a gateway to Tselloch's world in the midst of that darkness, and that it's not only open, but active, causing elements from his home world to leak through into Alitheia around Fobos."

"Holy cow!" Perry exclaimed. "I bet you're right, Darcy! Boitheia said they had a means of very quickly transporting tsellochim to their valley. It's got to be because they're coming directly through the gateway from his world!"

"And remember how sad the whole valley looked?" Darcy asked. "Everybody was so scared and worn out, even the livestock. What if it's not just any gateway, but Baskania's gateway? What if the villagers who lived back in Baskania's time moved away, but not *far* away because they couldn't pass through the mountains with all the dragons and giants and centaurs, and the forest to the south was too impenetrable to settle?" Darcy hopped up and down on the balls of her feet. "What do you think, Rubidius?"

Rubidius stroked his beard. "It is a very probable hypothesis," he said, "very well worth looking into." He dropped his hands.

Darcy blinked and took a step back, incredulous there were no shouts of joy, no pat on the back, no "Great Scott, you're right!"

"Well?" she asked expectantly.

Rubidius looked down his nose at her. "Well, what?"

"*Well* let's look into it, then. Let's go!"

Rubidius sighed. "You cannot simply run off to Fobos. I must investigate the area, send scouts, gather information . . . it will take a great deal of time to organize and execute."

"Besides, Darcy, we have to go and rescue Yahto Veli," Sam said.

"If you send scouts up there, they'll just get caught," Perry said. "We did —all of us. Not even Badru could do anything against the darkness that trapped us. We're the only ones who stand a chance."

Darcy wondered if Perry had really forgotten or if he was obscuring the facts because he wanted to get out and do something proactive.

"No . . ." she said, "that's not entirely accurate." She shot an apologetic look to Perry. "*We* don't stand a chance either, not if we don't know how to fight it. The only reason we didn't die was because the Oracle called me out. And because we blew on the bone whistle."

Rubidius looked sharply at her. "And where is this bone whistle now?" he asked.

Darcy shook her head, amazed. "Yahto Veli has it. He took it down to the Oracle with him."

"So the only weapon we have against the darkness that *may or may not* be coming through a gateway from Tselloch's world into Alitheia is a musical instrument lost in the Oracle's lair?" Amelia said.

Rubidius remained passive, but Darcy could tell by the sharpness in his eyes that he was excited. "It does appear, as I said before, that all roads for you seem to lead to rescuing Yahto Veli. We must rescue him, recover the whistle, and tackle the mystery outside of Fobos . . . in that order."

"But, Rubidius, what do we do if Tselloch is creating a gateway into *our* world?" Amelia asked. "Magic doesn't exist there!"

Rubidius looked very troubled. "That is . . . a very good question. I must assume Tselloch would create a gateway to your world only if he believed it to be necessary for his survival, although I cannot see what effect it would have on his conquest of Alitheia."

"Unless he wants to try and kill us in our home world," Perry said. "We don't have magical abilities there; we'd be ripe for the picking."

"Oh, Rubidius! Could he do that?" Sam gasped.

"That may be his objective, but do not forget—we must first establish whether Darcy's theory is correct. *If* there is a gateway outside of Fobos, and *if* your experiences at this camp of yours are indicators of the same sort of magic coming through to your world from his world, then we will address the issue."

"What do we do until then?" Dean asked.

"We ready ourselves for our first step. We leave in three days to rescue Yahto Veli." He drew himself up and looked at Lewis. "With or without a new message."

Much later that day, Darcy knocked on Lewis's door. The others were in the lounge enjoying some games after dinner, but Lewis had sequestered himself in his room with his quill, trying to force some sort of revelation. Sam had urged Darcy to leave him alone, but Darcy had had a few thoughts about their conversation earlier that day, and she wanted to talk through them. She left the laughter of the game room behind and meandered down the dim hallway to his door.

He answered quickly, as though looking for an excuse to be distracted. "Oh, hey, Darcy." He peered out at her. "What do you want?"

"I want to talk to you about what you told me earlier. Can I come in?"

"Okay." He opened his door wide, and Darcy entered his chamber. The floor plan of his room was the same as Darcy's, but flipped. He had a spacious area with a bed, wardrobe, fireplace, and sitting area, and a separate bathroom. The color scheme was much more masculine, and instead of frilly ruffles, he had deerskin pelts.

Shelves and shelves of books covered his walls, and Darcy eyed them enviously, wishing she had as many in her room. She turned her attention back to Lewis, who had sat down in an armchair next to a small table. He held his head in his hands, looking miserable, his glasses on the table before him.

Darcy approached him and delicately picked up the phoenix feather quill. Lewis made no sound of protest, so she continued to study it. It was very long, about the length of her forearm, and brilliantly colored. The large red feather had orange and yellow stripes, and strands of the feather were gold —not the yellowish color that sometimes passed for gold—real, metallic *gold*. She turned it over once or twice and then let it rest flat on her palm.

Lewis looked up at last. "You don't need to tell me I'm not worthy to have it."

Darcy rolled her eyes in exasperation. "Lewis, get over yourself!"

"Well, I'm not!"

"If you hadn't written what you had the first year, I would have died in the dungeon here, or—" she stopped herself. She wasn't ready for everyone else to know about what she'd done in the dungeon. "And last year you wrote that great poem telling the others to wait for me to come back from the Oracle, I just couldn't see what it meant in time."

"Then what *are* you thinking?" Lewis put his glasses back on.

"I'm thinking about Voitto Vesa's oracle and what it means for you. The Oracle's answers are always tricky. They seem to mean one thing, but they really mean another." Darcy closed her fingers over the feather. "You said this morning that you were distracted when Amelia played, that all you could think about was old stuff you'd written."

Lewis nodded.

"Well, what if that's it? Maybe you're not supposed to write something new at all. Maybe Amelia's music was pointing you back to something you'd already written."

"I would agree with you, except that what I kept thinking of was worthless."

Darcy dragged a heavy armchair closer to the table. "Show me."

Lewis sighed and reached into his bag and began sorting through a stack of old parchment. "Rubidius makes me keep it all," he muttered. "I know it's here somewhere . . . Here." He pulled out a single page and spread it before them.

Darcy put down the quill and looked at the page full of Lewis's cramped script.

Known also as the Resurrection Bird, the phoenix is characterized by brilliant red and gold plumage that changes colors as it undergoes its yearly cycle. The phoenix stands about two and a half feet tall at the high point of its cycle, but its height and general beauty diminish from this point until the winter solstice. At sunset on the winter solstice, the phoenix is consumed by its own fire, dies, and is reborn from the ashes, hence the moniker "Resurrection Bird."

"What is this?" Darcy asked, looking up. "Were you copying something? It doesn't sound like you."

"I was copying what Rubidius was telling me. He thought it might be useful for me to learn something about the bird my feather quill comes from. It was interesting, but, really, what was the point of it?"

Darcy frowned and continued reading.

It is very rare to see a phoenix in the wild, as they are elusive and secretive. It has been said that a phoenix can be seen only when it wants to be seen, usually when it has a gift to purvey. The gifts of the phoenix generally consist of tail feathers, which they may shed at will. Tail feathers are highly useful, as they never wear out and are easily enchanted. Other gifts of the phoenix may include, but are not limited to, tears, talons, songs, or even blood. The uses of many of these are unknown as they so rarely are given as gifts.

Phoenixes are thought to migrate south every winter to the Island of the Sun, upon which they complete their burning and are protected during their rebirth and fledglinghood. The location of this island is unknown, but it is rumored to be found only by the phoenixes themselves.

Darcy looked up. "Lewis, do you know what this says? It says phoenixes travel to an island every winter!"

"So, what, you think the 'Island of the Sun' is part of our archipelago?" Lewis asked. "Even if it is, this doesn't tell us how *we* can find it because *we* are not phoenixes." He scratched his nose. "Captain Boreas has never even seen that archipelago from the tapestry, and he has no idea how to get there."

"Well, he *wouldn't* if the rest of the islands are like the Island of the Sun and can only be found under special circumstances." Darcy picked up the quill again and stroked it. "Maybe the oracle is meant to be taken *literally*." She held up the quill and stared hard at it. "If it never wears out, it has to be magical. And if it's magical, then it might have other properties nobody knows about yet."

Lewis watched Darcy intently. "What are you getting at?"

"Follow me," Darcy said, jumping to her feet. "But we'll need to get an escort."

Rubidius himself accompanied them downstairs. Together they trooped all the way down to the grand receiving hall of the castle—a room Darcy usually avoided, as it prompted bad memories from her first encounter with Tselloch. The receiving hall had enormous floor-to-ceiling glass windows that opened out to a veranda overlooking the beach and docks, and it was the easiest place for Darcy to test her theory.

It was cool out on the terrace as evening fell, and the bay was lit up with lanterns on the ends of docks and in the bowsprits of boats. Ornate gas lamps lit the veranda itself and, standing in the light of one of them, Darcy once again placed the spine of the quill flat on her palm so the curved ends stuck up. She was afraid it might blow away on the breeze, but it seemed to stick to her palm as though weighed down in the middle. For several moments nothing happened, but then a strong breeze caught against it, shivering through the fibers of the feather. They rippled unnaturally, and the feather spun around, the shaft pointing out to sea and glowing as if it were suffused with golden ink.

Darcy grinned from ear to ear and looked up at Rubidius, who was staring at the quill, astonished.

" 'The pen of the scribe shows the way,' " Darcy said.

"Indeed," Rubidius murmured.

"It's—it's a compass?" Lewis stammered.

"Of sorts." Rubidius took the quill from Darcy, and its golden glow faded away. He placed it on his own palm as Darcy had done, but nothing happened even as the wind caressed it. He frowned and handed it back to her.

Darcy repeated the positioning of the quill, and the moment the wind touched it, it once again glowed and pointed the way out to sea.

"Why does it only like Darcy?" Lewis asked.

"Wind," Rubidius muttered. "The magic of the phoenix must be tied to the wind. Of course, it being a bird . . . Darcy can channel the magic because of her elemental air magic," Rubidius said almost breathlessly.

"That's it, then, isn't it?" Darcy closed her hand over the feather quill and handed it reverently back to Lewis. "That's the last thing we need!"

"It is not the *last* thing we need, but we now have what we need to begin, and I freely admit I am relieved to have discerned that portion of the oracle." Rubidius smiled down at them. "You two should get some rest. Once we have embarked, rest may be difficult to come by." He placed a hand on each of their shoulders and led them back into the castle.

Darcy, Sam, and Amelia watched the men gear up to leave for the valley of Fobos. Darcy felt a deep sense of trepidation and couldn't help but wonder if she ought to be travelling with them instead of on the quest to rescue Yahto Veli. She told herself that was crazy, that she'd wanted to rescue Yahto Veli for over a year and should be relieved. Besides, she knew she couldn't help them, but these thoughts didn't make her feel any better about watching some of her old companions head out on what was certain to be a very perilous quest.

It had been decided that the soldiers Tormod, Daylan, and Tokala would travel north with the wolf Lupidor and the nark Borna Fero to scout out the possibility of a gateway outside of Fobos. Rubidius had chosen them because they knew the way and what to expect, having travelled with Darcy to the Oracle the year before. Rubidius had instructed them not to engage with the darkness, so as not to be caught, but to camp there for some time and observe. He hoped that by the time they returned from their sea voyage, the scouts would also have returned with their findings.

Keep an eye out for Lykos, would you? Darcy asked Lupidor as the crew made ready. *I would bet he's still out there somewhere.*

I will, Lady Darcy. And you be safe on your journey, as well. Remember, no talking with any unfamiliar animals, yes?

Darcy knew he was ribbing her for her foolish engagement of forest animals on their journey together the year before, but she couldn't smile. Instead she threw her arms about his neck, wished him and the others goodbye, and stood back with Sam and Amelia as the men finished donning their gear and exited the castle gates.

"They're off," Amelia said quietly as the massive gate creaked closed behind the small band of men. "And soon we will be, too."

Their own crew was loading their gear onto the *Cal Meridian* and storing it below deck alongside crates of salted meats, rounds of cheese, bags of dried fruits, and barrels of wine. Darcy had no doubt that before too long they would crave some variety in their diet on board, and she hoped some of the sailors were also prolific fishermen.

"It's time." The soft voice came from behind them, and they turned to find Eleanor waiting. She held a small valise in hand and wore travelling clothes.

"Eleanor!" Sam said, surprised. "I thought you weren't coming with us."

"I am not. Cadmus and I are riding across the bay with you, to be let off at Kenidros. You will then start your journey out to sea." She held out her hand, and Sam took it genially. "Come."

They walked together across the front courtyard and through a gate giving passage to the beach and the docks. Darcy spotted movement through a cluster of trees near the shore, and she stopped to look closer. She waved on Eleanor and the girls to walk ahead of her and detoured to approach the trees.

"It's him." Her breathing sped up as she got closer. Colin Mackaby was taller than she remembered, and his hair was long, belying blond roots the color of his father's hair. He wore winter clothes—a heavy jacket and jeans tucked into army-style boots. He stood with arms crossed over his chest, watching the sailors loading the *Cal Meridian* down at the docks.

Colin's form flickered on the breeze, the tree trunks visible through his chest. Darcy approached him without fear, but he ignored her until she stood just before him. Finally he turned his gaze on her; both of his eyes were brown, and far more hostile than they had ever looked when he'd worn his single blue contact. Darcy wondered why their departure on the *Cal Meridian* was making him so upset. Surely the rescue of one nark couldn't be of any consequence to Colin Mackaby, no matter where he was or what he was mixed up in. Could he even know the purpose of their journey in the first place?

"Colin?" Darcy asked. "Can you hear me?"

His eyelids twitched, but his mouth didn't move.

"Where are you? How can I help you?" Darcy knew she had only moments before her friends noticed her absence and started looking for her. "Are you in . . . *his* world?"

Colin ignored her, his angry gaze returning to the ship.

Frustrated, Darcy swiped her hand through his misty form, and a sharp jab of pain shot through her cold right hand. She gasped and snatched it back, her heart racing as though she'd received an electric shock. He looked at her, then, and his eyes deepened to darkest black as he smiled maliciously. He flickered once and vanished.

Darcy stood clutching her right hand to her chest and breathing hard. She heard the caw of crows and looked up to see several of them circling the *Cal Meridian*. Crows in Alitheia, like wolves, were split in their loyalties, some loyal to Tselloch and acting as his spies, others loyal to the monarchy. She didn't have special powers of discernment like Sam, but her unease suggested the crows circling the ship were acting as his spies.

Darcy jogged from the copse of trees and down to meet her friends.

"There you are," Sam said, relieved. "Where have you been?" She rubbed the head of Pinello, the badger who was bonded to her as Hippondus was bonded to Darcy. Despite pleas from Sam, Amelia, Dean, and Lewis, who all had small animals, Captain Boreas had refused to allow any animals on board, barking that they'd enough mouths to feed without seeing to the special diets of animals.

"It's . . . difficult to explain," Darcy said, shaking out her right hand. Sam raised an eyebrow but didn't comment.

"Come along, please!" A voice rang out from the docks. The six of them shouldered their personal bags and said final farewells to their animals. They made their way out to the dock, and Darcy double-checked that her sword was strapped around her waist.

They climbed into one of the small coracles and found their balance as it bobbed wildly beneath them. When they were settled, Darcy pointed skyward. "Look at the crows. Do they look friendly to you?"

Sam frowned. "Not exactly."

"They look to me like Tselloch's spies. I think he knows we're leaving, and he's not happy about it." Darcy went on to tell Sam and Amelia about seeing Colin's apparition in the trees.

"I don't get the connection, though," Amelia said. "What do Colin and the crows have to do with each other? And why would Tselloch even care that we're going to rescue Yahto Veli?"

Darcy sighed. "I don't know."

CHAPTER 16

A FAIR WIND

Tselloch may have been angry about their departure, but he didn't seem able to stop it. They boarded the ship and weighed anchor without any difficulties. The crows tailed them to Kenidros where a very solemn Eleanor and a not-so-solemn Cadmus disembarked with two narks and Torrin. While the coming separation from his brother didn't seem to bother Cadmus, Tellius said farewell and watched his little brother and Eleanor go with very serious eyes and then disappeared below deck.

Rubidius instructed Darcy to stand on the top deck beside the impressive figure of Captain Boreas who—with his golden curls, sharp blue eyes, and deep tan over rippling muscles—still reminded Darcy of the Greek god Apollo. She took the phoenix feather quill with her and placed it on her palm. With the first breath of wind, the quill turned rigid and golden and spun to show them the way.

Boreas whistled as he watched the magic. "That's our heading, all right. Bayard!"

The freckle-faced redhead, who now no longer could be called a youth, snapped to attention beside his captain. "Yes, sir!"

"Take the wheel. I'm going to map our heading on the charts."

"Yes, Cap'n!" Bayard said. He shouted a few orders down to the men on deck and took Boreas's place as the captain disappeared below deck.

Darcy, Sam, and Amelia had supplanted the captain's place in the ship's only cabin, despite their protests that they could manage very well below deck and didn't need any special treatment. Still, he had set up a nice berth for himself, complete with a table for his charts, and he didn't seem to mind.

Darcy remained beside Bayard. "You have a lot of responsibility now, don't you?" she said after a moment, once it seemed as though the *Cal Meridian* was well on its way. They'd left the bay and entered deeper waters, the bow rising and falling with heavy splashes as the wind picked up.

Bayard chuckled, but his blush belied his pleasure. "You could say that. I'm first mate now."

"Wow! You must have made quite an impression." Darcy's arm was getting tired from holding the quill, and she glanced at her palm. "Umm . . . can I put this away now, or do you still need it?"

He looked down in surprise. "Oh, sorry, you can put it away. I've got a really good bearing. You've pointed us straight out to the beacon, see?" He nodded ahead, and his red hair parted over his forehead in the stiff breeze.

Darcy lowered her arm and squinted. "That tiny blinking light out there?"

"Yes."

"Hey—that's in our world, too! At our camp . . . at night you can see a red blinking light on the horizon. Sam told me it's a lighthouse. Yours is white, though."

"That beacon marks the southernmost boundary of Alitheian waters. All of this," Bayard looked around, "is considered Alitheian waters up until that point. It's enchanted to shine as long as the proper line of kings prevails in Ormiskos. It was dark for a very long time while Tselloch sat on the throne, as you can imagine."

"Sure," Darcy said, mesmerized.

"I like it. After a long voyage, it welcomes me home," Bayard said, gazing out at it.

Darcy tore her eyes from the beacon. They were fast approaching an island that was visible from shore, and Darcy could make out the ruins of an old fortress scattered amongst the trees. "I never knew that was there."

"It's called Rodo Pelekanos!" The wind picked up even more and Bayard had to shout over the snapping of the sails and the scurrying sounds of the sailors at work. "Named in the Old Alitheian for the pelicans that roost on the island; it was an old military fortress long ago. It's said to be good luck if we see a white pelican as we pass by!"

Just then, a whole flock of white pelicans rose en masse from the island's trees and took flight above them, scattering the few remaining black crows, which screeched and winged back toward land. Darcy didn't believe in luck, but she couldn't help grinning, and she saw Sam wave merrily at the birds from the deck beneath her.

"Beautiful, aren't they?" asked a familiar voice.

Darcy turned swiftly. "Wal Wyn! I didn't know you were on board!"

"Aye." The nark, fairer than most, grinned at her. "Rubidius asked me to accompany you. Well, I'm actually here with His Majesty."

"With Tellius?"

Wyn nodded. "It is time for my trial period."

"What do you mean by—"

Rubidius waved her down from the top deck. She shot an apologetic smile at the nark and descended the staircase. "Session," Rubidius said. He held open the door to the captain's quarters, which would also serve as a classroom in addition to sleeping quarters for the girls.

"Here?" Darcy scowled. "Now?"

"What better time is there?" Rubidius asked. "We are well on our way. Captain Boreas will not need a new heading from you until we pass the beacon, and there is nothing you can do on deck to help the sailors."

"If I close my eyes," Amelia said, ignoring Rubidius and leaning against the railing, "I can almost imagine I'm out for a sail at Cedar Cove."

"Come along," Rubidius said sharply.

Amelia sighed and followed the rest of them into the cabin that suddenly felt very cramped. Rubidius took the only chair, and the boys found seats on the floor as Darcy, Sam, and Amelia squeezed side by side onto the bed.

"Rubidius, didn't you bring your front door?" Sam asked, looking a little green. The schooner went up a large swell and down the other side, and she gripped the edges of the bed. "It would be nice to—you know—get off the ship for a while."

"Sam, we just got on board!" Perry said, aghast. "You've never had trouble sailing at camp before."

"This is farther out than we ever went at camp," Sam said. "The swells are a lot bigger out here!"

"I did, in fact, bring my front door," Rubidius said, "but we cannot use it on board the *Cal Meridian*."

"Why not?" Sam asked, sounding supremely disappointed.

"It needs a fixed location for the charm to work. As long as we are in motion, I cannot use it."

"So why even bother bringing it?" Amelia said.

"It is always helpful to have one's front door close at hand," Rubidius said, as if it should be obvious.

"What are we going to be studying?" Lewis asked.

"I would like to review survival techniques. We are, after all, on a journey, and one never knows what may happen. We may wreck on an island. We may be lost at sea. Do you know what you would do?"

"That's optimistic," Perry muttered to Darcy. "Only an hour at sea and he's already pointing out everything that could go wrong!"

Darcy didn't want to seem off-putting to Perry, so she smiled and raised her eyebrow as though she agreed with him, even though she silently agreed with Rubidius. It would be nice to know how to handle themselves should the worst happen, and it would also give them something to occupy their time. Since Captain Boreas had never set eyes on the archipelago before, they were in for a long journey.

Sam was earnestly sick by the middle of the night, and Darcy couldn't wait to get out of the cabin and away from the sounds of retching and the stink of vomit.

Captain Boreas had brought in two hammocks, and Sam insisted on taking one of them and leaving the single bed for Darcy or Amelia. After playing rock-paper-scissors for it, Darcy won the bed, which turned out to be a grave mistake. Sam took the hammock closest to Darcy, and when she first got sick, it splattered on the floor beside the head of Darcy's bed. Even after she cleaned it up, Darcy couldn't get the smell out of her nose.

Through the rest of the night Sam got sick at odd intervals and then cried because she felt so horrible. Darcy and Amelia took turns holding a bucket for her and assuring her that it was all right, even though it was making them miserable, too.

Finally, Darcy insisted Sam take the bed, and once she was no longer in the swinging hammock, Sam dozed off, followed by Amelia. Darcy, though, was fully awake and didn't feel like climbing into the vacated hammock, so she sat in the corner and studied Voitto's oracle by the light of a single candle.

" 'With unraveled image, journey begins' . . . check. 'In error undone, destiny wins.' " She paused, still unsure of what that part meant. " 'Pen of the Scribe shows the way.' Got it . . . 'Music, life-giving, holding sway.' Probably has something to do with Amelia."

Darcy tapped a finger to her temple and squinted in the dim candlelight. " 'Held in the balance, the white thread reveals.' That's the tapestries. But does it mean we won't be able to find the path because it was all unraveled? Or was it just meant to point us to the archipelago tapestry . . ."

Amelia groaned and rolled over in the hammock, and Darcy froze, afraid she'd been mumbling too loudly. With a great sigh, Amelia's breathing returned to normal, and Darcy began again, quieter.

" 'The unseen path, through lily fields, to serpent-eaters, down the hole, first navigating the archipelago.' " She sighed, thinking of all they didn't know about yet. " 'Breath of life, breath-ed once.' Possibly the bone whistle, but——" She scratched her head, wondering why Yahto wouldn't have blown it already if it could save him.

" 'Broken bond of covenant.' " Darcy raked her fingers through her hair, and then she started again from the top.

When she determined it was around dawn and it wouldn't seem strange for her to exit the cabin, she left the room and closed the door behind her, breathing in the fresh, salty air, particularly refreshing after the sickness in their cabin. The sky was still quite dark, but it looked as though the sun would break over the horizon at any moment. Wal stood against the main mast next to a nark Darcy didn't know. They both yawned mightily; it was just about time for them to turn.

Darcy looked around and saw Tellius standing at the railing not far from the two narks. She walked toward him, and he gave a sudden lurch and vomited over the edge.

Darcy halted and tried to back away, but Wal spotted her and hailed her a good morning. Tellius turned around, and Darcy thought it would be rude now to avoid him, so it was with great reserve that she approached.

"Seasick?" she asked by way of greeting, surprised when he shook his head. "No? Then what—"

He leaned forward and rested his forearms on the gilded railing, closing his eyes as though in pain. She studied his profile, noting that his cheeks were flushed and his hair was matted back from his forehead, not with salt spray, but with sweat.

"Oh," Darcy said, feeling sorry for him. "Bad dream?"

He looked at her, his eyes bloodshot. "I'd rather not talk about it."

"Okay. Sorry."

They stood together in silence. Tellius seemed to recover some vigor as time passed, but Darcy felt increasingly uncomfortable in the awkward silence. They watched the sun break the horizon in the east, the spectacle obscured by the heavy mist that hung over the Sea of Aspros.

Tellius seemed to revive even further with the arrival of the sun, and he turned to her and said, "We should be having lessons right now!"

"Oh! I hadn't thought of doing them on board."

His eyes turned quizzical. "Why not? You'll never get good if you don't practice."

"But—*here*, with everyone watching?" Darcy looked around at the busy sailors and blushed. "I'd feel stupid."

"Do you think everyone will just look away when you have a real opportunity to use your sword?"

Darcy thought frantically for another excuse. It was one thing to practice swordplay alone in the weapons room or with a couple of observers, but in front of a bunch of strange men was another story. She landed on an excuse that might have been rather cruel, but she thought it would work.

She held up her right hand, still bandaged from where he had cut her. "I'm a little nervous practicing with real swords after, you know . . ."

Tellius glanced at her bandage and blanched. "Right. I'd forgotten about that. Sorry . . . I won't ask again." He returned his gaze out to sea.

Darcy kicked herself inwardly for making him feel bad. "Well . . . maybe we could just wait until this heals," she said. "I still want to learn."

That seemed to brighten Tellius's expression a little, and he agreed.

Darcy smiled, feeling much better, and continued to watch the sunrise. The silence that fell between them this time didn't feel awkward at all.

The fog lifted off the water in stages, and once it had cleared, they found they were well and truly out to sea. Darcy was both fascinated by and scared of the deep, dark water all around them. There was no sign of green trees or mist-shrouded shoreline anywhere around them; they had left all land far behind. The beacon lay before them, and it looked much nearer than before.

A bell rang somewhere below deck, and the sailors passed off their tasks to the fresh crew coming up from below.

"That'll be breakfast, too," Wyn said, coming up behind them.

"Sure," Darcy said, her attention caught on a vision in the air beside them. She tried to find it again, wondering whether her sleepless night had caught up to her and she was hallucinating.

She saw it again. "Tellius! Do you see that?"

"What?" He had made no move to go down for breakfast, seemingly content standing beside her.

"There! I think I see a face on the wind." Darcy pointed, and Tellius squinted. About twenty feet off the railing, a human face and female figure made up of nearly transparent wisps of cloud, flew along beside them. Darcy pointed and exclaimed, and the figure disappeared, only to reappear several feet from where she had been.

"See?" Darcy asked. Now that she had gotten a clear view of the wind-girl's form, she could see her easily without trying.

"I don't see—"

Darcy grabbed his hand and pointed with it, forcing him to look down his own finger. The wind-girl stared curiously back at them.

"Oh . . . I *think* I see something now . . ." Tellius muttered. "But what—"

"It's a zephyr!" the nark Darcy didn't know said in surprise, looking over their shoulders.

"A zephy*ra*," Wyn said, correcting his fellow. "It's a female, see? I never thought I'd see one; I've only ever heard stories. Most people don't even believe they exist."

Darcy couldn't tear her eyes off the wind-girl—the *zephyra*. "What's a zephyra?"

"A wind spirit—rather like a nymph of the air, but different. It is extremely good luck to see a zephyr or zephyra on a journey, for they bring fair wind with them," Wyn said. "I can't imagine why she has chosen us, however."

"She seems curious about Darcy," Tellius said. "Maybe it's because of your wind magic. She feels some sort of bond with you."

As soon as Tellius said it, Darcy knew it to be true; she grinned, feeling the same bond to the zephyra. "What does that mean, 'she brings a fair wind with her'?"

"It means she is pledging to help us on our journey. As long as she is able, she will give us aid."

The zephyra nodded and smiled, showing sparkly white teeth. She *poofed* away in a shower of white mist, and a sudden gust of air caught their sails and urged the *Cal Meridian* forward.

"It's a fair wind, Captain!" Bayard called down from the wheel.

Darcy lowered her hand, still unwittingly holding Tellius's since pointing out the zephyra. She threw her head back and laughed, basking in the morning sunlight as her hair whipped about her face.

"What are you doing with my *girlfriend?*" Perry asked from behind them.

CHAPTER 17

BEYOND THE BEACON

Darcy looked up sharply. She glanced down in horror to see she and Tellius were still clasping hands. She shook off Tellius's grasp and leapt forward to intercept Perry as he strode toward them, looking like he was going to punch Tellius in the face.

The two narks got to him first and stopped his progress with firm hands on both of his shoulders. Tellius tried to back up but he was already against the railing. He and Wyn shot questioning looks at Darcy.

"It's okay!" Darcy held up her hands. "Really! Perry, I was just showing Tellius something, and I was holding his hand to help him see it."

Perry was breathing deeply in and out of his nostrils. "*Why* did that require holding hands?"

"No reason, it was . . . silly. Trust me!" Darcy entreated, mindful of the looks the sailors were giving them.

Perry continued to struggle, and the narks kept their hold on his shoulders.

"What does this term mean—*girlfriend?*" Wyn asked. "You are, of course, a girl, and Master Perry is, indeed, your friend . . . so why has it made him so upset?"

"It doesn't mean anything—that is—it means just that. I am a *girl* and a *friend* of Perry's. Perry just thought that Tellius was trying to . . ." she searched for an explanation that wouldn't offend anybody present. She shot a sharp glance at Perry, willing him to calm down and figure out what she was trying to do.

Perry shook himself out of his anger. "Yeah . . . I, uh, I thought Tellius was taking Darcy's hand to—to—to take her someplace she didn't want to go," he said lamely. He looked apologetically at Darcy and then at Tellius. "I'm sorry, man. No offense, right? I get a little worked up if I think one of my girl *friends* is in trouble."

The two narks released Perry, but Tellius narrowed his eyes at him, unconvinced. He took a step or two away from the railing. "I'm going to get breakfast," he muttered and strode away.

Darcy breathed a deep sigh of relief as Wal Wyn and the other nark followed Tellius down into the hold. Then she rounded on Perry.

"Why did you do that?" she hissed at him. "You thought he was trying to 'take me someplace I didn't want to go'? Honestly, that was such a lame excuse I'm surprised they bought it at all!"

"I'm sorry." He put his hands on the railing and hung his head. "I guess I have a little problem with jealousy."

Darcy turned her back on the ship so they both were staring out to sea. "I already told you. The idea of Tellius and me *liking* each other is completely ridiculous, remember?" she said in a low voice.

"Yeah . . . I know. It's just that I like you so much, and we never get to spend any real time together—*alone*, that is." He reached a hand up to tuck a strand of her hair behind her ear.

"Stop it!" she said, slapping his hand away. "We're hardly alone now."

He chuckled. "True."

Darcy sighed, but then she smiled. "Girlfriend?" she asked. "You've never called me that before. I thought we just *liked* each other."

Perry grinned down at her. "But I think of you as my girlfriend. Do you have a problem with that?"

Darcy shook her head, failing to hide her spreading smile. "No more jealousy, okay?"

"Deal," Perry shook her hand.

They turned around to head down for breakfast and found Amelia standing behind them, looking tired and ill-tempered.

"We need to talk," she said.

Amelia led them to the farthest corner of the supplies hold. It was beneath the sleeping berths and next to the small holding cells, and it smelled strongly of salted meat. She didn't say a word until they were alone, and then she rounded on them with surprising vehemence.

"How *dare* you start dating? Do you want to break Sam's heart? Because that's what this will do to her!" She spoke primarily to Darcy.

"Of course I—we—don't want to hurt Sam." Darcy said. "But what are we supposed to do? We like each other, so shoot us!"

"It's not like we're doing anything wrong, Amelia," Perry reasoned, though he looked guilty. "Darcy and I have been through a lot together and now we want to date. I know Sam's had this—*thing*—for me for a long time, but she really needs to get over that!"

Amelia shook her head and Darcy was startled to see tears in her eyes. "You just don't get it, Perry; you never have. Sam *invests* in people, and once she makes up her mind about something important, she sticks to it. That's why I was so happy when you finally became friends with her, Darcy, because then she could stop going on about this girl named *Darcy* 'who lives down the street and really needs a friend.' She'd made up her mind that you were going to be friends *long* before you ever came to Cedar Cove. So when I say this will break her heart, I mean it! If she finds out you betrayed her, she will be destroyed. It would have been the same thing if *I* dated Perry, and even *I* liked him a couple years back. But I got over it because it wasn't right."

"Really? You liked me?" Perry said.

"Shut *up*, Perry!" Amelia snapped. "Do you see?" She looked earnestly at Darcy.

"But, Amelia, Perry doesn't like Sam . . . he likes me."

"And what am I supposed to do?" Perry sounded irritated. "Not date anyone because my old friend Samantha Palm likes me?"

"No. It just means you can't date someone she's so close with. It's cruel. And she doesn't just like you, Perry . . . she's in love with you."

Perry crossed his arms and sniffed in disbelief. "This is ridiculous," he said. "I'm finished."

Perry walked away, but Darcy stayed in the shadows where she was, keeping her face down. The ship gave a sudden pitch and she put out her hands to steady herself against the barrels. "I don't know what to do," she said quietly.

"Do the right thing. Break it off with him."

"Amelia—what if I told you to break it off with Simon?"

"That's different."

"Is it?"

"Yes! Simon and I aren't hurting anybody."

"And neither are we! Nobody except for you and Dean know about this, and that's the way it will stay."

"How can you possibly keep this a secret?" Amelia asked with a humorless chuckle. "It's going to come out."

"Not if we're careful and we don't tell anyone." Darcy twisted her mouth, feeling the sudden hot urge to do what she wanted to do, without regard for anybody else's feelings. Who was Amelia to tell her she was wrong? Wouldn't Sam want her to be happy? Darcy'd never had a real boyfriend before. She deserved this.

She tried to step around Amelia, but Amelia stopped her with a hand on her arm. "What about the prophecy, Darcy? You're supposed to marry Tellius—you know that."

"No I'm *not!* You know as well as I do that I might not have to. And why does everything in my life have to be decided for me? Am I supposed to go through life like a zombie, just waiting for the next prophesied event to happen to me? No! I refuse! And you don't know the half of it! You don't know the rest—" She broke off, aware she'd been about to spill the beans about the rest of her oracle, the part she'd never told anybody about.

Amelia's eyes widened. "The rest of what?"

"Nothing." Darcy pushed past her and fled for the ladder out of the hold.

"Darcy! The rest of *what?*" Amelia called after her, but Darcy didn't turn back.

Darcy and Perry, despite feeling that Amelia had been way out of line, had felt guilty enough to avoid each other for a few days. Amelia, instead of continuing to be angry with Darcy, had begun following her about with worried eyes. Darcy kicked herself inwardly for making her suspect there was more to her oracle.

Three days passed, and Perry avoided Darcy so assiduously that she began to wonder if he *had* changed his mind about dating her after all. She'd wanted to ask him, but it was nearly impossible to find time alone on the cramped schooner.

They'd continued on at a clipped rate, and the weather had stayed pleasant, so Darcy assumed the zephyra still aided them. They had seen only one speck on the horizon in three days, which Captain Boreas had confirmed with his seeing scope was a Celmian vessel, whose trade routes sometimes crossed into Alitheian waters.

On the third day, Sam emerged from the cabin, looking pale and thinner, but well at last. That same afternoon, they passed the beacon. Captain Boreas gave the *Cal Meridian* a wide margin around its bright light, and Darcy and the others stared in awe as they passed. The brilliant star of light sat atop a pinnacle of rock that jutted up from the sea. It blinked a slow and even pattern, and once they were beyond it, Darcy felt a sense of loss.

"We're out of Alitheia well and proper now," Bayard said. "These are dangerous waters."

"Why are they dangerous?" Sam asked, her voice weak.

"Ah, pay no attention to him," Captain Boreas said. "He's just parroting what the old sailors say. Lady Darcy?"

"Yes?" Darcy looked up.

"A new heading, if you will."

"Right!"

Darcy retrieved the phoenix feather quill from Lewis and went to stand on the top deck. She set the quill on her palm, and the zephyra reappeared and watched her curiously. The sun was beginning to set and the wind on their faces was getting cool. As it caught the feather, the gold lit up the palm of her hand.

"Bearing nine degrees west, fellows!" Captain Boreas shouted down to his men, eyeing the quill and then looking up at the newly risen moon.

The zephyra shook her silvery head and frowned, but Darcy shrugged at her and closed her hand over the feather. "That's the heading," she murmured, as if the wind spirit could hear her. "There's nothing I can do about it."

The zephyra blinked away, and Darcy thought she felt the ship slow.

"Something's been bothering me," Darcy said, tapping a finger on the archipelago map spread out before her and her friends. Captain Boreas let them look through his maps and charts in his space below deck, as long as they didn't mess anything up. "We know the phoenix feather is leading us straight to this 'Island of the Sun,' and that it's probably one of the unnamed islands in *this* archipelago, but we still don't know what the white thread would have shown us if it had still been in the tapestry. Voitto Vesa's oracle said that the white thread would reveal the path. I feel like we're missing something."

"Well, obviously we're missing something." Dean rolled his eyes. "We're missing the white thread!"

"Thank you, Captain Obvious." Perry sat up and dug his hands into his hair, grown longer over the last month at sea. He was thinner than he'd been a month previous, as he, too, had at last succumbed to seasickness. In fact, Darcy and Tellius remained the only ones of the seven teenagers not to have gotten sick from the rise and fall of the ship these last four weeks. They all were getting a little peaky, though, as their diet was limited to what they had on board and what the sailors could pull from the sea. Rubidius refused to transform their supplies into more appealing food, deeming it a waste of his energy when they had perfectly good rations to eat as it was.

"We can't do anything about the white thread," Amelia said. "It's gone. Drop it, okay? Aren't you more concerned about our lack of progress?"

Darcy rolled her eyes; she was just trying to stay occupied. Being on a ship for so long with the same company made her feel as though she were in a cage. "Yes, but that's my point. Maybe we're lacking in our progress because we're missing something the white thread would have shown us."

"Captain Boreas is worried," Sam said. "He won't stop talking about it. I think there's an old superstition about this archipelago."

"What—like a Bermuda Triangle type thing?" Dean asked.

"Something like that. I overheard him talking with Rubidius about it a couple nights ago. He seems torn—like he wants us to find it but, at the same time, he doesn't. He said we should have gotten somewhere by now."

"Every time I get a new heading, it's to find we've somehow gotten off the *last* course the feather gave us," Darcy said.

"I think we're going in circles, personally," Perry said, resting his head back on his arms. "And I'm getting tired of being on board this ship. There are always people everywhere; there's no place to be alone." He looked up at Darcy with searching eyes, and her heart beat faster. Amelia cleared her throat and Darcy broke off the gaze.

"I'm going topside," she said, and she swung down from the hammock. "I need some air. Where's Rubidius, anyway? We haven't had a lesson in days."

"Up with the captain, I think," Sam answered. "I bet they're getting worried about supplies."

Up on the deck, Darcy found Rubidius and Boreas arguing in low voices, and she edged closer to eavesdrop as inconspicuously as possible.

"—tell you there *is no* archipelago anywhere nearby!"

"We must have faith in the phoenix feather," Rubidius insisted. "It cannot lead us falsely."

"Aye, perhaps not, but the fates are against us! Ever since we took our first bearing beyond the beacon, that zephyra of Lady Darcy's has been pushing against us. Darcy gives us one heading, and the zephyra pushes us the opposite direction. I have to fight simply to stay on course, and still it's no use."

Rubidius was silent for a moment. "And you think it has something to do with these *stories*."

"All I know is that my men are talking, and they're getting worried. There is a place in this vastness, a place that ensnares ships. They say this spot on the map, so far from anything else, is protected by magic. Any ship that tries to approach it is shunted off in a different direction. The only ships to have penetrated it have done so by accident—blowing in on a gale or a storm. Our magical phoenix feather charts a direct course toward this mysterious void, and the zephyra just as assiduously directs us away from it. What would you have me think?" Boreas gripped the wheel until his knuckles turned white. "More importantly, what would you have me *do?* We are almost out of supplies and are no closer to rescuing Yahto Veli than we were when we left."

Rubidius sighed. "What do you suggest?"

"We must land somewhere and restock," Boreas said. "Then we can continue this quest, however futile I might consider it to be."

Rubidius nodded. "Very well."

"If we bear east, in four days' time we can make land on a small chain of islands I know of. There we can restock and reevaluate our progress."

Rubidius nodded again and turned to find Darcy watching them. He smiled wryly.

Captain Boreas gave the order to come about and as the ship swung around to the east, the wind picked up.

"Apparently your zephyra approves of our going off course," Rubidius said, placing a hand on Darcy's shoulder and gazing out to sea. "She's been fighting us these four weeks."

"I can't imagine why," Darcy responded. The wind was chilly, and she shivered. "We're just trying to find a group of islands."

Rubidius looked quizzically at her. "Surely you don't think it is just any group of islands. I am sure you heard, the archipelago we seek will not be easily found, nor will it be easily left once we are within it. The zephyra fears for your life; she has a peculiar bond with you, air worker."

Darcy snorted. "Air worker? That sounds so impressive."

"An Alitheian who can work air magic is an impressive phenomenon."

"I'm not an Alitheian, remember? Just a visitor."

"Perhaps."

"What did you mean about it being difficult to leave the archipelago?" Darcy asked as she watched a group of sailors teaching Tellius how to climb the ropes hanging from the sails. He slipped down once, then twice, but his jaw was set and his eyes determined.

"Have you not thought at all about the return journey?" Rubidius shook his beard. "I should not be surprised. Youth is so myopic."

"Your *whatsit?*" Darcy wrinkled her nose.

"Nearsighted," he said, "lacking in foresight. That feather will get us in to the archipelago, but what will lead us out?"

"Is that a rhetorical question?" Darcy tried to stay lighthearted even as her stomach clenched. She hadn't, in fact, thought about the return journey. "I guess I figured we would just leave the way we got in."

"Hmmm . . ." Rubidius said. "Perhaps the most obvious answer will turn out to be logical, in the end."

Darcy made a face as he looked away, not appreciating another riddle to worry about. She turned back to watch Tellius and gasped as he lost his grip and fell six feet to the deck.

Rubidius heard her and narrowed his eyes. "He's fifteen today," he said. "Did you know that?"

"Who—Tellius? Today's his birthday?" Darcy asked. "No, he didn't say anything!"

"Indeed. Will you resume swordplay with him soon?" Rubidius asked.

Darcy squinted, but his expression held only innocent curiosity. She held up her hand and examined it. She'd removed the bandage several days ago, and the wound had healed into a long, red scar. "Yeah, I suppose I should. I just don't want to get cut again."

"I'm certain Captain Boreas could dig up some practice swords," Rubidius said.

"Do you think it's right for us to go off course like this?" Darcy asked abruptly.

"It's difficult to say. I worry about Voitto's state back home, and I am anxious to rescue Yahto Veli," Rubidius answered. "Any time lost is of concern to me, but the captain is correct about one thing: If we run out of supplies, we will not be able to complete a rescue of any sort."

"What about those stories?" Darcy asked, and she hugged her chest. "About the archipelago, I mean. Is it possible those stories are true? Do ships get lost there?"

"Those stories are as old as the Sea of Aspros itself."

Darcy expected him to go on, but he didn't. "It doesn't mean they aren't true, though," she pressed.

"No, it does not."

Darcy continued to stare at him, but he seemed disinclined to say anything else. She rolled her eyes and looked away. Tellius laughed with the sailors, and the pleasant sound drifted up to her ears.

"How is your coldness?" Rubidius asked unexpectedly.

The question was like a splash of icy water over her pleasant feelings. Darcy released her chest and waggled her right hand, frowning. "Fine. In fact, it doesn't feel like it's spread any more since I got to Alitheia. That's strange . . . I would have thought it would spread here and be dormant at home."

Rubidius quickly concealed his pleased smile. "I'm going to catch a rest," he said, turning from her. "Perhaps you should wish Tellius a happy birthday."

Darcy made another face at his retreating back and headed to the main deck.

"You didn't tell us it was your birthday!" Darcy called up to Tellius. He was dangling ten feet above her, holding on to three different ropes.

He glanced down at her. "Why would I? It's not a big deal!" he shouted down.

"Highness, please be careful," Bayard cautioned, perched above him on a peg of the main mast. "Maybe you should head down if you would like to talk with Lady Darcy."

Tellius wrapped one of the ropes around his left arm and let go of the other two, sliding down the single rope in a fluid motion to land squarely on the deck. "Ha! Finally did it without falling!"

He looked as though he desired praise, but she didn't give any. "Doesn't it feel weird?"

Tellius scowled and began examining his hands for calluses. "Sliding down a rope? It's a little strange, but I'm getting used—"

"Not *that.*" Darcy stomped her foot. "Your birthday! We're the same age now."

He shrugged and looked at her. "I suppose we are. It's probably weirder for you than it is for me. You're the one who has to live every year twice."

Darcy trailed after Tellius as he went to get a drink from a barrel of fresh water.

"We're running low," he said, eyeing the skimpy ration the burly mess officer gave him.

"Yeah, Boreas is concerned about that. That's why we're taking a detour. He says he knows of a chain of islands nearby where we can restock a few things."

"Really?" Tellius perked up. "Great! I'd love to get off this ship for a while."

"Sure, it will be great. Um, Tellius—I'm ready to start sword training again, whenever you are," Darcy said before she could change her mind, "but I'd like to find some practice swords, if that's all right. Rubidius said Captain Boreas probably has a few on board."

Tellius sobered and took up her right hand. He stroked his thumb along the new scar, sending a shiver down Darcy's spine. She snatched her hand away before he could notice how cold it was.

"You'll probably have that scar for the rest of your life," Tellius said. "I really am sorry. It was stupid of me to want to practice with real swords so soon into your training. I was just frustrated about not being allowed to fight in the battle, and I took it out on you."

"Really, Tellius, it's okay." Darcy blushed furiously without knowing why.

"Everyone insists on treating me like a child," he went on. "But I'm not a child anymore. I don't think I've been a child since I heard my parents being murdered."

"Are you still having nightmares?" Darcy asked tentatively.

Tellius stiffened and looked away. He didn't say anything for a long time.

"Tomorrow morning at dawn," he said. "I'll find us the practice swords."

The zephyra continued to be pleased with their detour, and she appeared often as they made their way to the chain of islands. Darcy enjoyed seeing her, but she couldn't shake her sense of unease about the route. She attributed the nervousness to her connection with the magic of the phoenix feather. Lewis, who also had a connection with it, complained of the same feelings of insecurity and said that the feather itself had begun to weigh heavily in his pocket.

"It's a feather," he said in exasperation on the fourth day, "how can it *want* to do anything?"

"I don't know," Darcy responded. "It's like we started a magical chain reaction that it wants to complete."

"Or maybe the Oracle is drawing us in," Dean said ominously.

"That doesn't make any sense," Darcy said. "We didn't invoke it; we're going to *take* something from it. It certainly doesn't *want* to be found."

"Well, whatever the heck is going on with the feather, I'll just be happy to stretch my legs on solid ground again," Perry said.

"Hear hear!" Sam agreed.

A bell rang above their heads, and they all piled out on deck to see what was happening.

"Land ho!" The sailor in the crow's nest pointed. "Due east . . . land ho!"

The atmosphere on deck charged with excited energy as the sailors picked up the pace. They had spotted a large green island far out on the horizon and, even squinting, Darcy couldn't make out any details. Despite her uneasiness, she couldn't deny the sight of green trees and solid ground made her heart pound in happiness. She and the others ran up to the top deck for a better view.

The only person who didn't seem excited about the sight of land was Rubidius. He confronted Boreas and scowled deeply.

"You're saying you've never actually landed on this island?"

Boreas set his jaw. "No, I have not, but I've passed it several times before. It is unknown territory, but we have no choice but to land. We *need* supplies!"

"I don't like it," Rubidius said. "Anything could be there."

"Chances are it is uninhabited," Bayard said, standing close at his captain's elbow. "But if you're concerned, Captain, I volunteer to lead an advance party to shore. We can signal you if there's trouble or if it's all clear."

Captain Boreas nodded his approval, and Sam piped up. "If—if Rubidius would be willing to come along, you should take me, too."

Darcy blinked, shocked at Sam's bravery.

Sam's cheeks were flushed with the light of adventure. "Really. If there are any islanders, you'll need me."

"Sam—what are you *thinking?*" Darcy dropped her head into her hands as Rubidius and Boreas consulted over Sam's suggestion.

"I have to get off this ship, Darcy," Sam whispered back. "Even if only for a few minutes. I know I haven't been getting sick like I did the first couple of days, but I haven't felt well for *four weeks*."

"And you're not afraid?"

Sam shrugged. "That's why I asked Rubidius to come, too. Like Bayard said, it's probably uninhabited, but they could use my talents if they run into anybody."

It was twilight before they drew close enough to the island to weigh anchor. Rubidius had agreed to Sam's suggestion of going ashore with Bayard's advance team, but not until morning. Darcy usually watched the sunset, but this evening she set her back to it and watched the island instead. Radiant streaks of red and purple illuminated a lengthy stretch of beach and the tree-covered crags that rose up beyond it. She stayed at the railing until the waters around them grew dark and peaceful, and the moon threw its reflection across the glassy surface.

"Darcy, are you coming to bed?" Sam called from the door of the captain's quarters.

"Coming," Darcy said, and she turned away from the island and joined Sam and Amelia in their cabin.

CHAPTER 18

THE SONG OF THEANISI

Perry twined his fingers through Darcy's as they stood at the railing of the ship. Sam and Rubidius were one hundred yards away in a coracle bobbing toward shore. Amelia, Dean, and Lewis on her other side were blocked from seeing the gesture. But Darcy was still aware of the sailors' eyes and, after a quick squeeze, she gently removed her hand from his grasp.

The early morning sunlight rising behind the island made it difficult to stare after the coracles for too long, and Darcy had to drop her gaze periodically.

"They'll be all right, don't you think?" she asked Perry, holding her hand like a visor across her forehead.

He shrugged. "There's no chance of tsellodrin or tsellochim out here, and what could be worse than that?"

"Gee, I don't know . . . vicious natives? Cannibals? Monsters?" Darcy pondered the possibilities and Perry laughed.

"She's right. Any of those things are possible."

Perry looked surprised to find Tellius standing nearby. "Oh come on, don't be so pessimistic!"

"I want breakfast," Dean said, pushing away from the railing. "Who's coming?"

"I don't know how you can eat at a time like this," Amelia said darkly.

"At a time like *what?*" Dean asked, exasperated. "There's no danger! They're just going to scout things out."

"I can't wait to get on shore," Perry said, staring wistfully toward the beach.

"Right, well, I'm getting food." Dean stomped away.

"*You're* probably hungry, Darcy. Exercise always makes me hungry," Perry said, referring to the sword practice she'd had with Tellius that morning. She was still rather sweaty and hadn't changed her clothes because she'd wanted to see Sam off.

"I can't eat right now," she said. "I want to wait here for their signal."

Perry and Lewis joined Dean for breakfast, but Amelia and Tellius remained at the railing with Darcy. They saw the small party of sailors disembark onto the beach; Sam looked small and dainty in their midst, and she stood uncertainly off to the side as the men circled up. After a few minutes' conference, they headed en masse up the beach and disappeared into the forest.

Darcy let out a sigh and dropped her gaze. "And now . . . we wait."

Two hours later, Perry brought Darcy a drink of water and a bowl of porridge. "You have to eat *something*," he said.

Darcy wrinkled her nose and glanced over at Tellius, her sole remaining companion at the railing—aside from Wal Wyn and Selini Elafi, the two narks who always hovered close to him. "Thanks. You didn't bring Tellius anything," she said.

"Yeah, well, he's a dude. He can take care of himself."

"I don't know what you mean by *dude*," Tellius interjected, "but I am not hungry."

Neither was Darcy, but she choked down a few bites of porridge to make Perry happy and swallowed the water thankfully. Finished, she handed the bowl and cup back to him.

"Anything yet?" he asked, squinting toward shore.

"No signals, but we think we saw some smoke up on the mountain a while back."

There was movement at the tree line just off the beach, and they all leaned forward in expectation. It was Rubidius and Sam, and with them were a handful of people. The two men and two women were tanned, though not dark skinned, and wore simple, modest garments.

Rubidius raised a hand and beckoned to them, and Sam waved, her excitement clear even from across the distance.

"All right!" Perry jumped up. "We can go ashore!"

"Captain?" Tellius turned and looked up at Boreas, deferring to the ship's authority.

Boreas looked through his seeing glass and smiled. "It does seem to be safe," he said. "Crew, ready the remaining coracles. We'll have to make a few trips." He rattled off the names of the few sailors who would be staying on board to tend to the vessel, and there followed a great flurry of activity.

Darcy returned to the cabin to change her clothes and notify Amelia. She shoved a few things into a pack for them, including Amelia's lyre. An impatient knock sounded on the door, and she and Amelia hurried out to join the first party to go ashore. Soon she was knee to knee with Tellius in a coracle heading toward the island.

"We think of ourselves as Alitheian settlers, still, after all this time," their host said, handing each of them a piece of some foreign fruit and a stick with roasted meat speared on it. He chuckled and wiped his hands on his apron. "I guess old blood runs thick."

They were seated around a campfire in the center of a very civilized, but rather small, village. The islanders had darker skin, their deep tan the result of years spent living largely outdoors. In most respects, the islanders looked and sounded like the average Alitheian, just with a slight lilt to their accent.

"So you left Alitheia when Tselloch first came?" Darcy leaned forward to clarify. The fruit in her hand was very ripe, and the juice began to run down her arm. "I mean, your ancestors did?" She took a bite of the strange fruit to stop the running, and it tasted sweet and mild and almost . . . flowery, like Darcy imagined nectar would taste. She took another bite.

"Yes," said their host; he'd called himself Apeti. Others had gathered around them, but most seemed too shy to engage in conversation. "We have their records and the stories they passed down. It was known that the shadow creatures could not abide water, and so to the water they took."

"Their answer was to run away?" Tellius asked, a note of disapproval in his voice. "They left the problem for others to deal with?"

"Tellius," Rubidius said in a warning tone.

But Apeti smiled. "It is okay. We know our ancestors' ways were not for everyone. But we do not regret their decision to come here to Theanisi. We have a new society unto ourselves, free from the cares of the shadow creatures, free from any cares at all."

"From *any* cares?" Boreas asked in disbelief. "Every society has its cares, however great or small." The burly captain scanned the quaint village. "It seems to me as though your numbers are few. After so many years, surely you would have populated this entire island!"

Their host nodded. "Perhaps I spoke too quickly. We have not been blessed with the fruit of many children throughout the ages, and we lose some to illness. But as to outward aggressors, there have been none.

Theanisi is far off the usual trade routes. By your own admission, Captain Boreas, even such an experienced sailor as yourself has never set foot on our island!"

"And you've never thought of leaving?" Darcy asked, finding it unusual that they would be content with such a limited existence. "Don't you have ships, or anything?"

"What need have we to leave? Theanisi provides everything we need to survive. We are self-sufficient, and we are happy. Look around. We live in a veritable paradise." He grinned from ear to ear and opened his arms wide.

Darcy ate her meat and studied the trees and the surroundings as he'd urged them to do. It was pleasant enough, that was true, but it wasn't her idea of paradise. The landscape looked much the same as in Ormiskos, but some of the flowers were different, and instead of ferns carpeting the ground, there were myriad broad-leafed plants and clumps of bushes heavy with yellow fruit. There were fairies, too, but something was different about them that Darcy couldn't quite put her finger on.

She turned her attention to the villagers surrounding them and watching silently. The man and the two women who had accompanied them from the beach up the rocky trail to the village had melted into the crowd. All the villagers dressed the same. Their garments, simple tunic dresses for the women and pants and shirts for the men, were made of a burlap-type material, and everyone was clean and shod. They wore necklaces, bracelets, and anklets of what looked like pieces of white shells, and the jewelry made soft rattling noises as they moved. Although quiet, none of the villagers seemed unhappy. In fact, there was a great deal of smiling and whispering going on. It seemed to Darcy that she, Sam, and Amelia were attracting the most attention, particularly from the young male villagers. She scooted closer to Sam.

Because of Sam, at least they knew these people—although oddly happy —meant them no ill will. Sam had assured her on their hike that everything was fine, the people perfectly trustworthy.

Darcy went about finishing her food, vaguely aware that Boreas, Rubidius, and Apeti were discussing re-provisioning the ship. She glanced over to a nearby bush, where several fairies lolled about on the flowers, lackadaisically watching the humans. That, Darcy finally pinpointed, was what made them different. Fairies usually had a frenetic energy and insatiable curiosity.

Must be island life, Darcy thought. "They say everything moves slower on an island," she mumbled and popped the last of her fruit into her mouth.

She was offered seconds, which she gladly accepted. All these new tastes were wonderful after a month on board the ship. She hoped Boreas would bring along some of the strange, yellow fruit when they left.

"Did you see that Rubidius set up his door?" Sam asked, polishing off the last of her meal.

"Where?" Darcy looked for a place to wipe her fingers and, finding none, she tried to wipe them discreetly on her skirt.

Sam pointed. "Back in the woods over there . . . between two trees. He didn't seem to want anybody to know where he was putting it, but I saw him sneaking off. Well, actually . . ." She laughed lightly. "I sensed he was doing something he didn't want our hosts to know about, and it drew my attention to him."

"I thought that he trusted them," Darcy said.

"Oh, he does. I think he's just being careful about his cottage. It *is* a rather impressive spell, and I bet he just doesn't want to explain it to everyone."

"And don't forget, it's a portal straight back into Alitheia," Tellius said in a low voice. "If anybody were to get in there and exit through the rear door, the spell on his cottage would be broken and we all could be in jeopardy. *Anything* could pass through from there to here."

"I hadn't thought of it like that," Sam gasped.

Darcy yawned and stretched. Her full belly and the solid ground beneath her feet made her feel very sleepy. "I wonder if we're staying the night here."

"Surely we are," Amelia said. "It's already late afternoon, and they still have to pack the ship with new provisions. I doubt Boreas would want us to leave at night."

"We *are* staying the night. We've just settled it with Apeti," Bayard said, and they craned their necks to gaze up at him. The redheaded first mate tended to find his way to Amelia's side whenever possible, his infatuation with her unabated over the years. "He says they have plenty of empty cottages for our use. Apeti actually invited us to stay for as long as we have need, but I'm certain we will depart tomorrow."

"It sure would be nice to have a longer break," Amelia said wistfully. "It's so peaceful here."

"But, Amelia, think about Yahto Veli," Darcy responded quietly and yawned again.

"I think I'm ready for bed," Sam admitted. "Or at least for a nap. I'd like to do some exploring after that."

"I'm with you on that nap," Darcy agreed.

"I'll join you," Amelia said.

"Follow me." Bayard offered a hand to help Amelia to her feet. "I'll take you to Apeti and we'll find you a cottage to rest in."

Darcy woke up feeling cold and confused. Their room was very dark, and Amelia's soft snores and Sam's heavy breathing told her they were still fast asleep. She sat up and dangled her feet over the edge of her cot, the world tilting unevenly as she came upright. For a moment she thought she was back onboard the *Cal Meridian*, but the chirping of the night insects in the forest suggested otherwise. She rested her head in her hands, her fingers still sticky from the fruit she'd eaten that afternoon.

She raised her head and peered around the space, but it was too dark to see much. Sharp, silvery light, the only source of illumination, filtered in through the cracks around the door.

Darcy felt wide awake as if someone had dumped a bucket of ice water on her head. She closed her eyes and struggled to remember what had woken her. Images from a dream began to flicker through her mind of someone who was trapped, who needed their help. She started when the face of Pateros the bear filled her mind's eye. *"WAKE UP."*

Darcy opened her eyes again, slowly this time. She shivered in the cold, unseasonable for a September night, but who knew what the weather was like on Theanisi? Darcy set her feet on the floor, noticing that she was wearing soft, pliable shoes of the same burlap material worn by the islanders. As she stood, she made a soft, tinkly rattling sound, and she felt around to find she wore a necklace, a bracelet, and an anklet, all made of island shells. She fingered her long-sleeved tunic dress in confusion and reached up to find she even had bits of shell braided into her hair. She couldn't remember even changing her clothes.

Darcy walked to the door in the dark, thoughtlessly avoiding the pesky lump in the earth floor next to the washbasin. She paused, glancing back at the lump and wondering how she'd known it was there. Frowning, she shook her head and deftly swerved around the one wood beam that hung lower than all the others. She cracked open the door to let in a little more moonlight, and as it fell across her sleeping companions, she noticed they too were dressed as she was. Sam's hand dangled over the edge of her cot, a half-eaten fruit on the floor just beneath her limp fingers.

Darcy frowned and looked outside. The village was arranged in concentric circles on the slope of the mountain. In the center of the circles lay the fire pit they'd eaten around earlier that day, a village well, and other common-use booths and structures. *There's the baker's booth,* Darcy thought. *The one beside it is the tanner's. The seamstress works over there . . .* Darcy swallowed, her breath exiting her mouth in a frosty puff.

A glimmer of light caught her attention, and she ducked behind her doorframe as a brilliantly lit figure glided down the mountain.

A spectacularly beautiful woman garbed in sleeveless robes of shining silver appeared. She was barefoot, and her long, blonde hair hung loose and flowing about her shoulders, bare even on this cold night. She was singing, although Darcy couldn't see her mouth move. Her wordless song pulsed in tandem with the light emanating from her, throwing soft illumination upon the dark cottages she passed. Darcy felt a thrill of terror. Her breath caught in her throat and her heart pounded painfully in her chest.

The woman continued to walk, looking neither left nor right, and came to a stop before a cottage across the village center. Her song grew louder, and the door of the cottage opened to reveal an elderly man. He stepped into the corona of her light and stared at her, entranced. With neither word nor gesture, the woman turned and began to walk back up the mountain, the man following closely on her heels.

Darcy breathed in shallow gasps, torn between following them and hiding beneath her bedcovers. With a quick look over her shoulder at Sam and Amelia, she darted out the door after the lighted pair.

"This is none of my business," she grumbled to herself. "We're leaving in the morning!" But her feet compelled her upward. The woman's song continued unabated, and the old man made no noise other than the fall of his feet upon the ground. Darcy kept well back, far outside the reaches of the light. She stuck to the shadows and followed only as closely as necessary to keep them in her sight.

Before long they exited the village and were climbing a rocky path through the dark trees. Darcy struggled to keep up, while the woman and man walked unflaggingly on. The beacon of light was now far away as the path grew steeper, and soon Darcy was progressing on hands and feet, stopping frequently to hold her breath when she sent cascades of pebbles tumbling noisily down the trail. The shining lady and her companion never seemed to hear her, and Darcy continued on.

The higher they climbed, the more severe the cold became. Tree limbs were frosted over, and the only spots of color were the yellow orbs of the fruit plants, the low shrubs seeming almost to give off their own light in the darkness.

They must have climbed for over an hour before the terrain leveled out into a well-manicured trail stretching like a tunnel through evergreen trees, recently dusted with snow. *Isn't it too early for snow?* Darcy thought, shivering.

Now that the path was easier to follow, Darcy felt the pull of the woman's song, compelling her to walk closer than she should. Darcy shook her head hard and pinched herself on the arm, reminding herself to be quieter and stay hidden.

Her mind a little clearer, Darcy saw they were approaching a grotto near the summit of the small mountain. The sky was clear above them and the scent of salt air wafted in from the ocean. The space at the top was sheltered by a half-circle of rock, and a waterfall shimmered over the top of the rock face, running in cascades over several protrusions into a mirror-like pool and down the side of the mountain. Next to the pool a stone chair sat atop a stone dais, and the lady glided toward it and sat down gracefully.

Darcy ducked behind a clump of bushes off the path and watched the man follow the shining lady into the grotto. He stayed within her circle of light and, once seated, she finally turned to look at him. Her eyes were fierce like a hawk's, her visage beautiful and ageless, old and young at the same time, but difficult to look at because of the light that emanated from it. She was not human; she was *other*, whatever that might be, and Darcy felt simultaneously attracted and repulsed. She didn't need Sam to tell her this was a being not to be trusted.

The elderly man showed none of Darcy's repulsion; he lurched toward the woman on his knees, his arms stretched wide in supplication. He opened his mouth. "Thea . . . Thea . . ."

Darcy held her breath, desperate yet horrified to find out why this entity, this *Thea*, had brought an old man to her sanctuary in the dead of night.

Thea gazed down upon the man, and her face softened. She reached out and stroked his wrinkled cheeks with both hands as though he were a small child. Murmuring words Darcy couldn't hear, she reached out to a bush growing near her throne and plucked one of the yellow fruits from it. After breaking it in two with her hands, she gave both halves to the old man. He grasped them gratefully and began to eat, the juice running down his forearms to the ground.

Thea gently grasped him by the shoulders and turned him away from her. Darcy could see his face now, his wide old innocent eyes and satisfied smile. Thea caressed his cheek, and Darcy began to breathe easier, feeling foolish at her earlier unease. Thea bent over, her glowing mouth nearing the old man's throat, her lips parted as though she were going to kiss him. He continued to eat, his eyes closing in purest ecstasy.

And then, in a motion both fluid and vicious, Thea tore out his throat with her teeth.

CHAPTER 19
THE SONG OF THE MUSICIAN

Darcy pressed her hands to her mouth to keep from screaming. She bit her fingers until she tasted her own salty blood, but she couldn't tear her eyes from the horrific scene before her, the scream she dared not release resounding in her head.

Thea was no longer beautiful. Her song had ceased as she feasted on the flesh of the old man, crouching over his fallen body like a vulture over its prey. Her face, so perfect and peaceful a moment before, had transformed into a hideous mask, white eyes and fangs almost glowing. Her fingers, too, had grown into long claws, which she used to grip the old man's body. Blood ran down her chin, stark against the silvery whiteness of her skin, and her hair undulated about her shoulders like living snakes.

The man made no utterance of pain. His face was mildly surprised, like he'd been caught in a practical joke. The fruit he'd been eating fell from his grip and lay forgotten at his side, like the fruit lying beneath Sam's fingers by her bed.

Oh no, oh no, oh no . . . Darcy forcefully swallowed the bile forcing its way up her throat and gritted her teeth hard. A deep trembling began in her stomach and spread throughout her arms and legs until she could barely keep her teeth from chattering.

The horrible creature swiftly severed the man's head, consuming everything. Too petrified to move, Darcy watched in horror until she finally managed to squeeze her eyes shut and pray that Pateros would make her invisible. *Please, if you are able, if you can hear me!* she prayed. *Please, if you are able, if you can hear me!*

Darcy heard a rustle and a soft splash, and she wondered how long she'd been cowering there. She opened her eyes to see Thea standing in her pool beneath the waterfall, fully dressed, letting the water cascade over her hair and shoulders. The man was gone, even his bones. All that was left to show anybody else had been in the grotto was a wide red stain in the snow and a half-eaten piece of fruit.

The entire front of Thea's silvery robes was stained crimson, and blood reddened her chin and hands. Her eyes were closed and she began, once again, to hum.

Darcy's chest rose and fell rapidly. She held her breath, hoping the rushing water would keep Thea from hearing her escape. She willed herself to move, but her feet were frozen to the ground.

"Come on!" she hissed, wrenching one foot from its place, then the other. Her body had been in a crouch for so long she was unable to walk, or even stand. Instead she lowered herself to all fours and backed away through the underbrush as quietly as she could, keeping her eyes on the monster in the waterfall. Thea's eyes remained closed and her new song never faltered. Darcy made it out of sight and far enough away that she could no longer hear it.

With a half sob, Darcy made her way out to the path, having no choice but to take it if she didn't want to get lost. Standing at last on legs that would barely hold her, Darcy stumbled blindly. After a few feet, she lurched against a tree and finally lost her battle against the bile that had been threatening her. She felt no better after emptying the contents of her stomach, the horrible scene replaying in her mind. Wiping her mouth with a shaking hand, she continued as quickly down the mountain as her shaky legs would take her.

She reached the steepest portion of the path, sat down hard, and flipped over onto her stomach. She began to slide herself down feet-first amid a shower of rocks, wincing as protrusions scraped across her skin and jabbed into her stomach. She felt certain her dress would be in shreds by the time she reached the bottom, but when the path leveled out and she scrambled to her feet, her clothes were remarkably intact, having suffered only minor tears.

She dodged off the side of the path, listening hard for any sound of pursuit from above, but all she could hear was the pounding of her own heart in her ears.

"I made it." Feeling a rush of adrenaline that lent strength to her exhausted limbs, Darcy picked up her skirt and raced down the path toward the village.

The sun was cresting as Darcy careened into the village, an ethereal red glow reflecting off the circular huts. No snow dusted the ground this far down the mountain, but a heavy frost covered the plants and cottages, the sun's radience refracting off of it in sugary sparkles. A few people had awoken and begun working outside their cottages, but nobody paid any attention to Darcy as she raced, with that uncanny sense of familiarity, between the huts to her own.

Sam and Amelia were still asleep, and they didn't stir even when Darcy banged open the door. Darcy went straight for Sam's bed and kicked the half-eaten fruit under the cot. She yanked the animal pelts off of her and shook her violently. "*Sam!* Sam, wake up!"

Sam opened her eyes groggily, and she blinked up at Darcy.

"Sam, come on, we have to get out of here!"

"Darcy?" Amelia asked from her other side, her voice muffled with sleep. "What's all the commotion?"

Darcy spun around. "We're in danger; we have to leave!"

"Nonsense," Amelia said. "If we were in danger, Sam would have sensed it. Now go back to sleep." To Darcy's dismay, Amelia lay back down and closed her eyes.

She turned back to Sam, but she was already sleeping again, the corners of her mouth turned up in a smile.

"They're enchanted," Darcy whispered in horror.

Leaving the cottage and her sleeping companions behind, Darcy ducked outside and scanned the village. A door opened across from her in the very same hut from which the elderly man had exited the night before. Darcy held her breath, waiting for the searching looks and concerned faces, but the woman who'd opened the door stepped outside looked perfectly at ease as she shook out her morning laundry. Darcy recoiled, wondering how it was possible that she didn't know, that she could have failed to notice that a member of her family was missing. She shivered.

"Why is it *so cold?*" Darcy asked desperately to no one.

She picked her way along the inner circle of huts, once again knowing exactly where she was going. The village was coming to life around her, laughter and happy voices floating all about on the breeze. Just before Darcy reached the cottage, its door opened and Boreas and Bayard stepped out, followed by Wal Wyn, Selini Elafi, and Tellius. They were dressed as the other men in the village, and Darcy's heart stopped when she saw their vacant, relaxed expressions.

"Captain! Captain Boreas, wait!"

Boreas turned toward her. "Ah, Lady Darcy. Fine morning to you."

"Yeah, sure . . . We—we *are* leaving today, yes?"

"Leaving?" He frowned. "I thought we might stay another day, actually."

"*Why?*"

"We're still gathering provisions, you know," Boreas answered lightly.

"Don't we have enough supplies to last us a while yet?" Darcy asked. She felt like screaming, but she kept her voice even.

"Relax, Darcy." Wyn put a warm hand on her shoulder. "You should enjoy the break from being at sea."

The men and narks migrated toward the central fire pit, and Darcy watched them go. "I'm the only one," she mumbled incredulously. "I'm the only one who's not enchanted."

She heard familiar laughter behind her and turned to find Dean, Perry, and Lewis approaching, looking strange in their burlap garb and shell jewelry.

"Perry?" she asked, stepping into his path. He looked down at her, mildly surprised.

"Good morning," he said.

"Perry," she said again, searching his eyes. She took his hand and pressed his palm to her cheek, but his fingers were limp and unresponsive. She dropped his hand and touched his face. "Do you know who I am?"

"You're Darcy." He sounded amused. "Coming to breakfast?"

"I—okay," Darcy said. She trailed after him to the fire pit like a lost pet, and a whole host of villagers gathered around for a communal meal. She took a seat between Tellius and Perry, and her other companions spread about them. She watched the cheerful chatter and felt like the only person awake in what everyone thought was a good dream, but was actually a nightmare.

As she looked around at the crowd, Darcy spotted almost no old people. The man she'd seen last night, if he were here now, would have been the oldest person around. Everybody else ranged from very young to about middle aged, with only a few approaching silver-haired maturity.

"Rubidius." Darcy leapt to her feet and looked around but could see no sign of the aged alchemist.

"Fruit?" Somebody thrust a fruit in her face, and she took it mechanically.

"What are you looking for?" Perry asked, bringing a piece of fruit to his mouth.

"Rubidius!" she shouted.

Perry took a bite and closed his eyes. "He's having a lie-in," he said.

"He's having a *lie-in?*" Darcy shrieked, exasperated at Perry's use of the unfamiliar term. "You mean—you mean he's still sleeping?"

Perry nodded.

"You *saw* him sleeping?"

He smiled up at her. "Yes, of course!"

Darcy exhaled in relief and put her hand over her heart, her legs feeling wobbly beneath her. She collapsed back onto the wooden bench between the two boys, searching her brain for something she could do to break the spell, to get a response . . . to get their attention.

Darcy reached over and pinched Perry hard on the arm. He made no reaction, as though pain didn't register. She removed herself from the bench, knelt in front of him, and slapped him across the face hard enough to leave a red handprint. This time he looked down at her with placid surprise, his face still registering no pain response. He raised his fruit to his mouth and kept eating.

Darcy's insides churned as she thought of the one thing she knew would illicit a negative response. She dropped the fruit she'd still been holding and grabbed Perry's face. "Watch me," she instructed him. Leaning over, heart thumping, she grabbed Tellius on either side of his face and kissed him directly on the lips.

She pressed her lips hard to his, but too quickly for him to react. It was more a matter of mashing faces together—but that wasn't the point. The point was to make Perry jealous, preferably enough for him to fly into a jealous rage. Darcy pulled away from Tellius, and, grimacing, looked back at Perry.

He watched her with interest, but with nothing resembling jealousy *or* rage, and then smiled at her and went back to his breakfast.

Darcy's heart plummeted, and she shot a look at Tellius. He was touching his fingers to his lips—*some* response, at least—but then he dropped them and looked down at the food in his hand.

"We're dead," Darcy said. "We're all dead." She scrambled to her feet and ran back to her hut, bumping into people who made no sounds of protest and pushing between others who only smiled and called after her cheerfully.

Darcy stopped short outside her cottage where Sam and Amelia had just emerged, holding the yellow fruit in their hands. Darcy eyed the fruit, narrowing her eyes.

"Don't eat that!" Darcy knocked the fruit out of Sam's hand, certain it carried the enchantment. She turned to Amelia next and swatted her fruit onto the ground.

"Darcy," Amelia said in a tone of mild reproach. She was the only person who sounded remotely displeased about anything. She leaned over to retrieve her fruit, but Darcy kicked it away.

"Don't eat the fruit—it's enchanted!"

"Enchanted? How lovely!" Sam said.

"No! Not *lovely*, not lovely at all! Bad—very, very bad!" Darcy insisted. She shook Sam's shoulders and then turned to Amelia. "Do you understand?"

Amelia looked wary for a moment before the calm returned. "Oh, Darcy, you're so dramatic." She linked arms with Sam and drew her away toward the crowd.

"Amelia, I'm serious!" Darcy jogged after them and hissed in Amelia's ear. "Look around you. Look at all the people; there's nobody *old* here!"

"There's nobody old here?" Amelia smirked. "Really, Darcy, you need to get some sleep. Sam and I had a lovely rest."

Darcy ran her hands through her hair and tugged hard to keep from screaming. Sam and Amelia melted into the crowd, and soon Darcy noticed the familiar faces of the sailors, chatting and laughing as though they had known the villagers their entire lives.

"Good morning to you." Darcy jumped as a voice sounded in her ear. She turned to find Apeti standing at her elbow, smiling and holding out a fresh piece of fruit.

"No thank you," she said.

"You look disturbed in spirit," the man said. "This will help."

"I said, no thank you!" Darcy shouted, but then she bit her lip. "I'm sorry —"

"No apology necessary." He smiled at her again and tucked the fruit out of sight.

Darcy thought about how Sam had said the people were trustworthy. Rubidius had trusted them as well. Sam couldn't have been wrong, which meant she had to be right—that the people must mean them well. Maybe they really didn't know what Thea did . . . if they even knew about her at all.

"Who's Thea?" she asked abruptly.

"Thea?" Apeti's smile grew broader and his eyes took on a dreamy quality. "Why, she's our benefactress—the giver of all good gifts and the goddess of the island. It was she who taught our ancestors the secrets of life on this island, and she who gave us the fruit. We must eat it daily, for it contains all the nutrients necessary for our health and survival. It grows throughout the year, even in the winter." He gestured at their surroundings, glistening with frost.

Darcy's blood seemed to run cold as the air around them. "Apeti—what time of the year is it?"

"It is a week before the winter solstice," he answered.

"What?" she whispered, closing her eyes.

It was December. She'd been enchanted, too. Pateros hadn't wanted her simply to wake up out of her sleep; he'd wanted her to wake up out of her enchantment.

"Indeed, and we are so pleased you all decided to join our village," Apeti continued, oblivious to her alarm. "In one week you will see Thea for yourself when she comes down to bless us during our solstice celebration."

"I—I—don't know what to say . . ."

"You will be able to thank her for sustaining your life and welcoming you among us. No thanks are necessary until that time."

Darcy huffed, changing tactics. "What does Thea do with your old people?"

"Oh, it is a most glorious passing!" Apeti said, his eyes glazing. "When we are ready to die, she comes for us and bears us peacefully away. It is said that she ushers us into our eternal resting place herself, caring for us until the end and closing our eyes as a mother to a child."

"That's one way to put it," Darcy muttered under her breath.

"No Theanisian ever feels any pain in the passing," he continued. "It is her greatest gift to us."

Darcy looked around, remembering what Boreas had said the day before —or, three months ago—about the small population of the island. "But Thea doesn't take just the old people, does she?"

If she'd expected this to alarm Apeti, she'd have been disappointed. He merely looked thoughtful.

"There are too few of you here," Darcy continued. "Tselloch came to Alitheia five hundred years ago; your island should be so full of people there hardly would be space for them all, but look at you! How many of you live here? A hundred and fifty? Two hundred?"

"As I once told your captain, our numbers *are* small. Our women do not bear many children, and illness takes some—"

"But I thought you said the fruit keeps you healthy! No, that's not it," Darcy shook her head. "Thea gets greedy sometimes, doesn't she? She takes the young when there are no old ones to take, *doesn't* she?"

"She takes the ill—"

Darcy stomped her foot. "You're contradicting yourself! You're not supposed to *get* ill. And you think it's this great, peaceful passing, but it's not. It's—"

"Fruit?" Apeti held up the yellow fruit once again.

Darcy stepped back in alarm, shaking her head in disbelief. "You really don't know . . ." She turned her back on Apeti and entered her hut.

Darcy sat on the edge of her cot in the cold, dark interior of the hut. She ordered herself to calm down, reminded herself that Rubidius had said all roads seemed to lead to this journey. Surely there was a reason why Pateros woke her; he must have known there was something she could do. She held her head in her hands, trying to recall the last three months, but they were blank, as though erased from time. So she thought instead back to her last memory: leaving the ship and coming to the village.

She and Amelia had packed a few things and gotten into a coracle. They had disembarked on the beach, met Apeti and his companions, and then hiked there, to the village. They ate a meal, they went to bed . . . She repeated this as a mantra, searching for meaning and finding none.

She stood up and paced the room, starting over again. She and Amelia had packed a few things . . .

"The pack." She stopped, and her eyes shot wide as she thought of the oracle and of Amelia's lyre, tucked away somewhere in the pack. *Music, life-giving, holding sway.* "Holding sway over what?" she asked the empty room. "Over enchantment?" Her heart leapt with hope, and she ran out of the hut.

Darcy pushed her way through the crowd, searching for Amelia. She found the girl lounging against Bayard's shoulder, laughing at something he'd said. "Amelia." Darcy gripped her by the shoulders and turned her away from Bayard. "Where's our pack?"

A faint line knit between Amelia's eyebrows. "Our pack?"

"Yes, the pack that we brought from the ship; where is it? What did you do with it?"

"Oh, that. I gave it to Rubidius as soon as we arrived."

"You gave it to Rubidius?" Darcy repeated.

"Yes, but I don't know what he did with it." Amelia brushed Darcy off and snuggled up to Bayard again.

Darcy searched the crowd for the flash of red at the bottom of Rubidius's long beard, and she spotted him at last, awake and eating a . . . *Drat!* He wasn't going to be of any use to her.

She looked away in frustration and closed her eyes, puzzling out where Rubidius would put the pack. He would have known Amelia's lyre was in it and would have wanted to keep it safe. Darcy could think of only one place: his cottage. *"Did you see that Rubidius set up his door?"* Sam had said. *"In the woods over there . . . between two trees."*

Darcy jumped up and headed for the woods.

It took her a good hour to find Rubidius's door, for it had sat unused and forgotten since the day he first set it up. It was far enough from the village that the only sounds she could hear were the loudest of laughs, but she still felt exposed and frightened, wondering if the villagers would turn on her if they knew what she was trying to do, or worse, if Thea ever walked the woods by day.

The door to Rubidius's cottage was indeed set up between two sturdy trees. It seemed very odd that there was nothing behind it and she could walk a full circle and view it from all sides. Fruit-laden bushes had grown up around it and sent vines curling over the curved top of the old wood as though trying to obscure it from sight. Darcy pulled at the resistant vines and stomped them down until her hands and forearms were badly scratched and the front of her dress was stained with yellow juice. Darcy wiped her hands on a clean corner of her skirt and mopped the sweat from her brow, careful not to get any of the juice into her mouth.

She tried the handle, but it was locked. "Of course," she said and let her forehead fall against the door with a weary thump, remembering he had told her months ago that he wouldn't be leaving his door unlocked anymore. " . . . *although I doubt a lock would remain a barrier should you be thoroughly determined to break and enter.*"

She stood back and regarded the door with her hands on her hips. Reaching out, she caressed it and tried the handle again. Finding it unyielding, Darcy huffed and crossed her arms over her chest, wondering if Rubidius had thought she could just *will* it to open.

"Oh." She dropped her arms and stepped up to the door again.

She placed her hands on the wood near the curved wrought-iron handle. This time she closed her eyes and felt inside the fibers of the wood with her earth magic, but she was tired, and the effort felt like pulling apart the tightly wound fibers of a thick rope.

She slowed her breathing and concentrated harder. She began to see the wood in her mind. She moved her hands toward the doorframe and felt where the iron bar penetrated the wood. Continuing to focus, she searched for the inside of the lock, and found it. There was the tumbler, too, and if she pushed hard enough with her mind . . .

A soft click sounded beneath her hands, and Darcy opened her eyes. She exhaled in amazement and removed her hands from the door. Hardly daring to breathe, she grasped the handle and turned it, joyous as the door creaked open.

In a moment, she was inside Rubidius's cottage, the bright morning sunlight of Alitheia reflecting through his windows off the heavy snow outside them. Familiar smells assaulted her with a force that brought tears to her eyes. She closed the door on Theanisi and felt her mind become perfectly clear.

Darcy didn't want to go back out there; she was afraid to—just being out there had been enough to cloud her mind even without the fruit. But sitting in the middle of the table was the pack containing Amelia's lyre, and she knew what she had to do.

"Where are we going?" Amelia whined. "I want to go back with the others!"

"We will, in just a minute," Darcy said gently, leading Amelia by the hand. "I need to show you something, and then we can go back, okay? It's really cool, I promise."

"Oh, fine," Amelia said. "But you're being so strange, Darcy!"

Darcy scoffed inwardly, but she feigned a laugh, which wasn't too difficult because her nerves were making her rather jittery.

The sounds of the village faded away behind them, and Darcy brought Amelia to a halt in front of Rubidius's door.

"Ooh, fruit!" Amelia said, reaching to grab one of the half-trampled vines Darcy had beaten down earlier.

"Not right now," Darcy said, trying to keep the edge out of her voice. "We need to do something first." She reached out and swung open Rubidius's door. Warmth emanated from the open doorway but Amelia recoiled as though it burned her.

"No, I don't want to go in there!"

"Please, Amelia, just for a moment—I promise!" Darcy stood behind her and tried to coax her forward, keeping a firm grip on her arm.

"I won't go in there," she said, panicked. "You can't make me!" She twisted wildly like a mad dog on a leash.

Darcy was ready for this. She yanked Amelia toward her and grabbed her shoulders with both hands. Amelia, jerked her arms up, spun around, and struck Darcy solidly across the face.

"Ow!" Darcy shouted, staggering back. Amelia made to run back to the village, but Darcy lunged and football-tackled her over the threshold. Holding her down with the weight of her body, Darcy searched for the door with her foot and kicked it shut.

Amelia continued to struggle, her tone changing from panic to anger.

"Ouch! Darcy! What are you *doing?* Get *off* me!" Amelia put both of her hands on Darcy's chest and shoved.

Darcy rolled and slammed into Rubidius's cupboards, raising herself on wobbly arms. Amelia rose shakily to her feet, stumbling in the process like a drunkard. She staggered over to Rubidius's table and put her hands on the back of a chair for support, breathing rapidly. "What happened to me?" she gasped. "I—I don't feel right—I don't understand . . ."

Darcy winced with the effort of pulling herself to a sitting position, and she leaned back against the cupboards. "You've been enchanted," she said. "I told you this morning."

Amelia breathed a humorless laugh. "Enchanted? But that's impossible, Sam said—"

Darcy closed her eyes and nodded. "I know, and she wasn't wrong. It's not the people who are against us; it's this *creature* they worship."

"Thea." Amelia looked alarmed. "Wait, how do I know that?"

"Because we've been here for three months," Darcy responded tiredly.

"That's impossible!" Amelia repeated. "We arrived *yesterday.*"

"No." Darcy stood and limped over to the window, pulling the drapes wide open. "It's been *three months.*"

Amelia stared out the window, her fingers working frenetically at the hem of her sleeve. "Snow," she said. "Lots of it."

Darcy sighed and let the drapes drop.

"How can this *be?*" Amelia turned and collapsed into a chair at the table.

"It's the fruit," Darcy said, joining her. "It must be. Eating it makes all your cares go away—"

"That doesn't sound so bad," Amelia said.

"It makes people forget . . . bad things, and important things you should be doing."

"Like . . . rescuing Yahto Veli. Like getting back to Ormiskos. And going . . . home."

"Yes."

Amelia worried her sleeve again. "You called Thea a creature," she said. "What did you mean by that?"

Darcy shivered and leaned forward. "The Theanisians worship her like she's a goddess—she's their great benefactress, so they believe. They think she does all this wonderful stuff for them, but it's a lie, and they don't know it." Darcy swallowed hard. "I saw her. Last night. Amelia she—she *ate* a human being . . . an old man. It was *horrible!* If she's a goddess, she's the worst sort—a demon . . . some sort of siren, or something."

Amelia covered her mouth with her hand. "A siren?" she repeated, her voice muffled.

"Yeah, like in *The Odyssey*—do you know *The Odyssey?*"

Amelia nodded.

"Well, it was kind of like that. She sang this song that entranced the man and he followed her all the way up the mountain. I followed close behind —"

"How did you get disenchanted?" Amelia interrupted.

"I don't know exactly, but I think Pateros woke me up. Anyway, I followed them, and she led him to this grotto high up in the mountain, and there she—she—" Darcy's throat closed up and she tried to express without words what she had seen by gesticulating wildly.

Amelia held up her hand. "Okay . . . I get it. Where are the others? How many have you saved?"

Darcy shook her head. "They're all still enchanted. I've only gotten you out."

"What? *All* of them? Even Rubidius and the narks?" Amelia gaped like a fish, her eyes wide.

"Yes, all of them."

"And you chose to wake *me* up? Are you crazy? I'm just—I can't—why didn't you get one of the others?"

"Because it had to be you, Amelia. It's been foretold. Here we've been thinking that we took a detour—that we went off course to this island to restock—but the Oracle knew the path we would take all along."

"What are you talking about?"

"Voitto's oracle, Amelia. 'Music, life-giving, holding sway.' "

"That could mean anything," Amelia said, beginning to sound panicked again.

"Listen," Darcy leaned forward. "We can't rescue them one by one without the villagers figuring out what's going on. We're not strong enough to force the men in here, nor do we have the time. What if Thea takes another victim tonight? What if it's Rubidius? We don't have a choice, Amelia, and this is the only plan I have. You have to play." Darcy reached for the pack and pulled out Amelia's lyre.

Amelia took her instrument in trembling fingers. "I'm afraid, Darcy. What if I go back out there and I fall under the enchantment again?"

Darcy sighed. "Just, don't eat any more fruit, okay?"

Amelia closed her eyes and cradled her small lyre to her chest. She sat in silence until Darcy said, "Um, Amelia?"

"Give me a minute, Darcy, it's coming to me."

Finally she placed her fingers on the strings and began to strum a simple tune. Darcy felt her senses refresh, her mind awake and alive.

"This is it," Amelia said, opening her eyes. "This is the song I have to play. Open the door, Darcy."

The Theanisians flinched as the music struck their ears, their faces a mixture of anger at the intrusive sound, and shock at the unfamiliar feeling of anger. The sailors, though, shook their heads and rubbed their eyes as though waking up. They looked not angry, but alarmed and confused, as they began to examine their clothing and look at each other with questioning expressions.

Darcy hurried to those she recognized. "You've been enchanted, but we're making our escape. Come on!"

A general sense of alarm spread through the village, and soon Darcy was pushing through a crowd of angry villagers and confused sailors to reach everyone in their crew. Strong hands grasped her from behind and swung her around.

"Is it true what they're saying?" Perry asked, standing with Dean and Lewis, who had his arm around Sam.

"Yes!" Darcy said. "And if we don't escape soon, the *goddess* they worship will come down here and kill us all. We have to hurry!" She led them toward Amelia, who now had the two narks and Tellius at her side. The narks protected her from the crush of the angry crowd. Others were fighting their way toward the music, and the crowd became increasingly violent.

"You've ruined everything!" Apeti screamed at Amelia, tears running down his cheeks. "*Everything!*" He covered his ears to shut out the music.

Somebody grabbed Darcy's hair and pulled her to the ground, and she cried out as Perry and Dean pushed a man off her and pulled her to her feet.

Villagers everywhere were lashing out, the angry mob pressing in around them.

The earth began shaking beneath them, and the people around them tumbled to the ground, wailing and moaning, while Darcy and her friends kept their footing. Terrified that Thea had come, Darcy lifted her eyes, but it wasn't the demon. It was Rubidius.

He looked wild and angry, like his old self. He held out his arms, keeping the people flat on their backs while the *Cal Meridian* crew surged toward Amelia.

"Your cottage, Rubidius! Did you get your front door?"

"I did indeed," he growled. "Let's move!"

He held the spell over the people while their crew began a quick descent down the path to the beach. Once they were out of sight, he dropped his arms in exhaustion. "Time to run!" he shouted.

Shouts and cries echoed behind them as the villagers gave chase, but it wasn't the villagers Darcy was afraid of. She wondered frantically how long it would be until Thea recognized what was happening.

They broke out onto the beach and looked around. Mercifully, the coracles were still tied there, though overturned and crusted with sand and mussels. The *Cal Meridian* floated far out beyond the breakers, but its rich blue sails now hung in tatters on the masts.

Several sailors dove into the sea and began to swim out to the vessel. Darcy and the other six teenagers ran to the coracles and turned them over, brushing off the sand and pushing them toward the waves. Rubidius made sand devils that engulfed some of their aggressors, and the men and narks grappled hand and foot, weaponless as they were, with the enraged villagers.

Wyn and Elafi broke away from the fight as soon as they saw the young people had gotten the coracles in the water. They slung Darcy, Sam, and Amelia into one of the vessels with ease. Tellius, Dean, and Lewis took another coracle while Perry readied a third. Wyn boarded with the girls, Elafi with the boys, and both narks took up the oars. Faster than any human could row, they propelled the small vessels through the water toward the waiting ship.

A great wailing broke out on the shore, and Darcy looked up in horror to see a shining beacon had risen from the top of the mountain. Thea sprouted enormous leathery wings like a dragon and let out a shrill shriek as she flew through the air and descended upon them. Her fangs glistening and her claws bared, she swooped and snatched a sailor from the deck of the *Cal Meridian*, snapping his body in two and flinging the halves into the sea.

"Look out!" Darcy screamed as Thea swooped around again and aimed herself at their small vessels. Wyn rowed even faster as Darcy tried to harness the wind to blow Thea off course, but she might as well have been an ant pushing against an elephant. Thea dove between the two coracles and hit the water like a boulder, the resulting wave overturning them. Darcy heard Sam shriek before the water closed over her head and she was tossed about in the bubbling, churning waves.

She felt a hand grasp the back of her dress and drag her to the surface. Wyn had a grip on all three of them, and he kicked mightily toward the *Cal Meridian,* closer now than it had been before. Darcy coughed and sputtered and saw through hazy, waterlogged eyes the few men on board tossing down rope ladders.

A terrible keening filled her ears. She grasped one of the ladders and looked back to see Selini Elafi grappling with Thea just above the waves. She pierced the nark through with her talons, but he continued striking out at her with his fists and kicking at her. Beneath them, Tellius and the boys struggled to swim for the vessel.

"Get—on—board!" Wal Wyn ordered the girls, the three of them clinging to each other and the ropes. With a flip, he surged back toward his embattled kin.

"Go, Sam!" Darcy urged, pushing Sam toward the ladder. Sam grabbed on to it, her arms shaking and her shoulders sagging. She tried to move her foot to the next rung but could barely lift it.

"Let go," a sailor called down to Darcy and Amelia. "We'll pull you up one at a time!" They did as instructed, treading water as Sam was pulled up and away.

The keening shrieks stopped, and Wyn reappeared, dragging Tellius, Dean, and Lewis. "Don't look!" he cried, but Darcy had already glanced out over the sea.

Elafi's lifeless body floated facedown in the swells, his blood spreading about him in a red sheen. Another shriek pierced the air, and the great beast fell upon Rubidius. He stood in the third coracle as Boreas rowed. Perry was cowering against its side and Bayard took up a ready stance. Rubidius raised his hands and shot water up at Thea like a fire hose, pelting her mercilessly. She tried to dodge to the side, and he raised a wall of water to block her path, his jaw set but his trembling arms belying his waning strength.

A thick, white cloud formed in the air before Thea and exploded, a heavy mist raining down upon them. Darcy's zephyra emerged from the fog and heaved an immense whirlwind hard against Thea. The goddess's wings beat feebly against it, the membranes ripping and tearing in her struggle. Thea's enraged shrieks became alarmed, and she tumbled head over heels, backward in the ferocious wind.

The remaining sailors in the waves ducked as Thea and the wind blew over their heads. Thea alighted among the villagers on the beach, screaming her fury but making no further attempt to assault the *Cal Meridian* as long as the zephyra hovered over their ship.

"Your turn, Darcy," Wyn said, and Darcy grasped the rope ladder. The sailors began to pull her upward, and she looked back toward the beach. Thea was glowing and beautiful once again. Like a shepherdess leading her sheep to the slaughterhouse, she led her people—her *prisoners*—back up the path to their village.

CHAPTER 20
THE KISS

The extreme coldness of the waters in December didn't sink in until Darcy was well on board and coming down from her adrenaline rush. She huddled against the railing, shivering madly and staring at her blue fingers. Disgusted at the sight of the shell jewelry, she yanked off the bracelets and tossed them over the side, Sam and Amelia doing the same.

"W-w-what h-happened t-t-to the s-s-s-sailors we l-left on b-b-board?" Sam managed to ask through chattering teeth.

Darcy shook her head and closed her eyes. Three months had passed since they'd left the sailors with the ship. Had the sailors been able to, Darcy thought they would have attempted a rescue of some kind. But they hadn't—at least not one that she could remember. Darcy could only assume Thea had taken care of them. She looked up at the shredded sails and had no trouble imagining Thea's claws slashing though them.

Boreas was busy barking orders to his men to remove the tattered sails and install the backups. "Quickly, men, quickly!" he shouted. "Before that she-devil returns!"

Perry, Dean, Lewis, and Tellius stumbled over to where the girls huddled against the railing and collapsed before them. "You're okay? All of you?" Perry asked breathlessly. He and Tellius looked the most concerned with their welfare. Lewis—who had managed to keep his glasses on his face—stared into space, his teeth chattering behind blue lips, while Dean busied himself removing all the shell jewelry from his body.

Tellius touched Sam's shoulder, then Darcy's, then Amelia's, as if to check that they were really there. "We sh-should get in-in-side," he chattered. "Get dry."

He helped Sam to rise and then offered a hand to Darcy, but Perry got to her first. Amelia took Tellius's offered arm and clung to her lyre with her other hand. They stumbled on weak legs, the girls to their cabin, and the boys to their berths.

Darcy, Sam, and Amelia stripped off their sodden garments and found the warmer clothes that had been packed away in a trunk in case the journey lasted through winter. They helped each other pick the bits of shell out of their braided hair, their numb fingers fumbling and slipping. Darcy lit the gas lamps, but they gave off little heat, so they huddled together in a heap on the bed, wrapped up in the thick blankets, and tried to keep each other warm.

"I d-don't understand why this h-happened," Sam said. "I thought they were *trustworthy!*"

"They w-were, Sam." Darcy closed her eyes and vigorously rubbed her hands together, even as she knew she would never warm the right one. "It wasn't a p-problem with your m-magic."

"You s-s-saved us all, d-didn't you, Darcy?" Sam's asked. "I led us in, and you led us out."

Darcy shook her head. "N-no . . . it was Pateros. And Amelia."

Amelia snorted. "No, Darcy, Pateros may have w-woken you up, but the rest was all y-you."

Darcy sighed, too tired to argue. Her eyelids grew heavier as she grew warmer, and before long she was fast asleep.

Darcy awoke to the sound of waves slapping against the hull and the familiar rocking sensation of the *Cal Meridian*. Suddenly aware she wasn't alone, she sat up straight and looked around. Perry was perched on the edge of her bed, watching her with a small smile.

"What time is it?" Darcy blurted.

"It's . . . oh, I guess around noon," Perry said.

"Theanisi?"

"Far behind," Perry said. He wore a heavy woolen jacket and his long, clean hair was brushed back from his face.

"Where are we going? I haven't given a heading!" Darcy swung her feet around, struggling against the blankets Perry had trapped under his weight. He stood so she could free her legs and then sat again once she hung them over the edge of the bed.

"I think the general consensus was *away,*" he said. "They said we'd worry about a heading once you woke up."

"Oh . . . okay. Why are you here—I mean, why are we alone?" Darcy blushed.

He smiled sideways at her. "I told them I'd come and see if you wanted any lunch."

"And Amelia didn't stop you?"

"Bayard's got her distracted."

"Oh." Darcy's face itched, and she reached up to scratch beside her eye, feeling an abnormal puffiness and tenderness. "What the—do I have a mark here?"

She turned her face to Perry, and he gingerly touched the spot. "Yeah. You have an impressive black eye, actually. Did it happen in the crowd?"

Darcy laughed. "No . . . actually, I think Amelia gave it to me."

Perry grinned, bemused, and Darcy told him how she'd had to fight Amelia to get her into Rubidius's cottage.

"That's just—you're just—just amazing. Did you know that?"

Darcy brushed off the compliment with a shrug. "Nah, it wasn't anything anybody else wouldn't have done."

Perry looked at her very seriously. "No," he said. "It was amazing. I don't think I ever would have thought of rescuing us like you did."

Darcy wanted to reply, but Perry's face was very close to hers and her stomach was doing somersaults.

"You saved us all, Darcy," he said, repeating the words Sam had spoken the day before.

"Donberidiclus," Darcy mumbled, her tongue not working properly. She swallowed and tried to say it again, without mumbling this time, but her mind had shut out every thought but one. *He's going to kiss me.* She closed her eyes a moment before he touched his lips to hers.

His lips were soft as they pressed against hers, but she felt rather surprised by their squishy wetness. She kissed him back and waited —waited for the fireworks and tingles she'd always assumed she would feel when she got kissed for the first time. Her brow furrowed as the butterflies in her stomach hardened into a knot, and when he pulled away, she winced and looked down. *This is wrong,* she thought. *This is very wrong.*

"I've wanted to do that for a long time," Perry said, sounding so pleased that Darcy forced herself to look up and smile at him.

"Mm hmm."

She gritted her teeth as he leaned toward her again, but a movement in her periphery caught her attention and she jumped guiltily.

Perry pulled back with a frown and sprang to his feet, looking around. Standing in the doorway was Tellius, staring at them, his mouth open and his eyebrows raised. Darcy wanted to hide her face, for she knew she was blushing so deeply she could probably light up the ship at night, but she stared transfixed at Tellius's face. There was no way he hadn't seen the kiss.

He and Perry stared at each other for a good, long moment before Tellius looked to her. His expression hardened though he blushed almost as furiously as she did.

"I—Lady Sam asked me to come and check on you. She would have come herself, but she was engaged in conversation with Lewis, and—" He swallowed. "Shall I tell them you're not coming to lunch?"

"No!" Darcy scrambled to her feet and straightened her skirts. "You can tell them I'm coming . . . I'm coming."

"Very well." Tellius turned to leave, but then he stopped and turned back, pointing a finger at Perry. "You should not be here with her—*alone*, like this."

"You're one to talk," Perry said, sneering. "I seem to remember coming upon you two asleep together in the weapons practice room not too long ago."

Tellius gritted his teeth and stuck out his jaw, looking much older than he was. "That was—"

"Don't say different," Perry said. "I don't see how that was any different!"

"I wasn't—we weren't . . ." Tellius trailed off and shook his head, and Darcy closed her eyes in mortification.

"I only kissed her," Perry said. "That's all. And since you two worked out that you don't actually *have* to get married someday, *and* you don't *like* her, I don't see how this is any of your business, really."

Darcy gaped at him, and Tellius gritted his teeth even harder. He nodded, turned on his heel, and disappeared out the door.

Later that day, Darcy stood nose to nose with Captain Boreas, arguing fiercely. "But we *can't* just give up and go home! Rubidius—say something!"

"We didn't get the supplies we needed," Boreas insisted again. "We cannot go on. If we do not turn back now, we will starve to death."

"There's always fish, isn't there? *And* water!" She gestured toward the rain barrels which were full to the brim, though frozen over.

"It's the middle of winter, Darcy," Rubidius said. "We've lost much time and many men. Perhaps it would be best to head for home, restock, and try again in the spring."

"But . . ." Tears sprang to Darcy's eyes and she wiped them away angrily. "What about Yahto Veli? What about Voitto's oracle? We've already come so far! I'm ready to go on; *we're* ready to go on."

"And what if we do rescue him," Boreas asked, "and we run out of water on the way back? A lot of use we will be to him then."

Darcy held up the feather, resting it on her hand to spin out its direction, but Boreas ignored it. He peered over the railing to where the zephyra floated. She watched their arguing with interest.

"What do you want?" Darcy shouted at the wind spirit. "If it weren't for you, we'd be in the archipelago already, and we *certainly* wouldn't have ended up on Theanisi!"

The zephyra shook her head sadly, but Darcy ignored her, suppressing the nagging thought that the zephyra had saved them from Thea in the end. "Just go away," she grumbled.

With a shimmer and a flutter, the zephyra disappeared.

Darcy lowered the feather, feeling bad about shouting at the zephyra now that she was gone. She noticed the feather was still glowing, though it usually lost its luster after she finished giving the bearing.

"Lewis?" Darcy called, looking around, knowing he liked to stay close to his quill. He appeared at her elbow a second later.

"Yes?"

"Does it usually do this?" she held up the quill for inspection.

He frowned. "No. Let me see." He took it, and once it touched his fingers, his eyes lit up. "I need a piece of parchment, please!"

Rubidius drew a scrap out of a pocket of his robe and handed it to Lewis, who snatched it up and began scribbling. When he'd finished, the quill ceased glowing.

Darcy took up the scrap of parchment, but her heart sank as she read the combinations of letters and numbers with no actual words.

"What is this?" she asked.

"I don't know, I just write it down."

"Give it to Boreas," Rubidius said quietly.

Darcy handed it to the captain, who took it reluctantly. He scanned the paper and muttered a curse under his breath.

"What is it?" Darcy asked again.

"Coordinates," he said. "Coordinates for my chart of the Sea of Aspros."

"We must follow them," Rubidius said.

"It's not the direction the feather points us to," Boreas said.

"It does not matter. If this is where Pateros is leading us, then we must follow."

Boreas handed the wheel over to Bayard and stomped down the stairs. At the bottom he turned and jabbed a finger up at Rubidius. "This better lead us somewhere we can resupply, because if it doesn't, I'm taking this ship home with or without approval from you."

"I understand perfectly," Rubidius said, a small smile on his lips.

Darcy's heart thumped and she wanted to leap for joy. They *would* rescue Yahto Veli, she was sure of it now. Pateros wanted them to keep going.

A shout and scuffle down on deck caught her attention, and her smile faded. She glanced down to see Tellius grappling with a young sailor—a blonde Darcy thought was Perry until he turned around to reveal his face. He looked familiar to her, as all the sailors did now, but she didn't know his name.

Tellius lunged at the sailor, who stepped expertly aside as the *Cal Meridian* gave a sudden roll, and punched Tellius right in the nose. Tellius went down with a moan and clutched his bleeding face as a blur flew across the deck. Wyn threw the young sailor up against the main mast, holding him there by his neck.

"What is the meaning of this?" Boreas emerged from the hatch clutching a roll of charts. He took in the bleeding prince and the nark pinning his sailor to the mast. "Into the hold with you," he said, glaring over at his sailor. "Do you think you can attack the future king of Alitheia with impunity? A night in the brig should straighten you out!"

Wyn dragged the sailor to his captain, as the young man shouted, "He hit me first, sir, he hit me first!"

Boreas took the young man by the scruff of his neck and shoved him down into the hold, following ill temperedly behind him.

Darcy rushed down the stairs to Tellius's side, but he was already shaking off Wyn's ministrations and dragging himself to the railing. He leaned over it with a groan and spit out a mouthful of blood as Darcy approached.

"Are you okay?" she asked.

He grimaced and avoided her gaze. "Why should you care?" He shook his head and let his nose drip blood into the waves.

Darcy recoiled as if he had slapped her. "Because you're my friend, Tellius."

"Friend." He clenched his jaw. "I'm not sure you know what that means."

Darcy's heart sank, but her eyes flashed. "*Did* you hit him first? Do you like picking fights, now?"

He laughed ruefully and spit out another mouthful of blood. "You don't know—"

"Then tell me!"

He turned his face toward her, holding his hand beneath his nose. Speckles of blood mingled grotesquely with his freckles. "I was defending *your* honor."

All the fight left her in a whoosh. "*What?*"

Tellius gestured toward the entrance to the hold. "Sailors have colorful imaginations, all right? And they like to gossip. Did you really think nobody saw Perry going into your cabin today?" He shook his head and looked back out to sea. "I overheard a couple of them talking about it, and you wouldn't have liked what they were saying. But—I'd seen you two, and I knew all Perry had done was *kiss* you." Tellius blushed and hung his head. "I confronted them, and the one sailor turned *belligerent* about it. He called you a name and . . . and I hit him."

Darcy put a hand out to touch his arm, but he stepped away. "I'm so sorry; I didn't know," she whispered.

"We're on a ship, Darcy," Tellius said. "People see things, and they talk about them. If you are any friend to Sam, you will tell her what is between you and Perry, and you will do it before she hears of it from somebody else."

"Does *everyone* know that Sam likes Perry?" Darcy asked in exasperation to no one in particular. She closed her eyes. "What a mess—"

"Did I imagine it or did you kiss *me* on Theanisi?"

Darcy opened her eyes as Tellius angrily tore up strips of linen to shove up his nostrils.

"That was—you don't understand—that was different! I was trying to break the enchantment, so I was doing things that might make people react."

"And did I?"

"Well, sort of. I was actually trying to make Perry jealous . . ." She bit her lip as an angry grimace crossed Tellius's face. "Don't worry," she said. "It wasn't a real kiss. You didn't even kiss me back—not like I *wanted* you to! Like I said, it was just—"

"I get it. You can stop."

Darcy put a weary hand to her head. "You know, I don't get it . . . you used to *like* Perry! What happened?"

Tellius finished cleaning up his nose, and when he spoke, he sounded as though he had a strong head cold. "Things change. He's become arrogant and conceited, and he treats other people's feelings with indifference."

"Well, that's rather harsh," Darcy said but decided she'd better not fight Tellius on it, under the circumstances. Instead she went silent and stood beside him, watching the waves.

"I think it would be best if we stayed away from each other, Darcy," Tellius said after several silent minutes.

"W—what?" She looked at him wide-eyed, but he wouldn't look back at her.

"No more sword lessons, no more anything. I wouldn't want to ruin things between you and Perry and . . . whoever else you run around kissing."

Darcy staggered back, stung, as Tellius turned and walked away. She stayed at the railing for a long time, tears running in tracks down her cheeks into the sea.

Lewis's coordinates led them to a stock of supplies, and Boreas laughed out loud when he saw where they landed. He sent several sailors ashore with the coracles and some shovels. It didn't look like much to Darcy, just a spit of sand with a couple of low shrubs growing, covered with ice. The sailors reached the shore and trudged around with the shovels, searching for something along the ground.

"What are they looking for?" Dean asked the captain.

"The marker that will tell them where to dig." Boreas chuckled again and crossed his arms over his chest.

"Dig for what?" Amelia asked.

"Supplies, of course!"

Amelia raised her eyebrows and Boreas pointed. "It's a Celmian supply dump, see?" They followed the line of his finger and saw a red flag tied to a limb of one of the shrubs. "The Celmians dig cellars on tiny island spits like this one and leave barrels of supplies, in case they ever find themselves in need."

"So we're going to *steal* their supplies?" Sam asked in alarm.

Boreas waved off her concern. "Eh, I'll refill what we take the next time I pass this way. Besides, nobody has been here for months; I can tell by the wear on that flag. They always tie a new one after a visit. I wouldn't be surprised if they forgot this location. It is rather close to *her* island. Perhaps they felt her evil and have stayed away."

"Captain Boreas, does this mean you'll agree to us continuing on to the archipelago?" Darcy asked. Her friends perked up with interest.

Boreas continued to stare out at the tiny island, chewing his cheek. "Aye. We must go on, I fear." He sighed deeply.

"Why are you so afraid to find this archipelago?" Amelia asked.

"I'm not afraid of *finding* it," Boreas said. "I'm afraid of being unable to find our way *back*. I've a spirit as adventurous as the most hardened seadog, but this journey forebodes ill with me."

"Relax!" Perry clapped him on the back. "You're with us, and Pateros has to draw *us* back, doesn't he?"

Boreas shot a glance at Perry and sniffed ruefully. He returned his gaze to the sailors as they dug for the supplies.

"What? I'm right, aren't I?" Perry looked around for support.

Darcy studied him, Tellius's words echoing in her mind. *"He treats other people's feelings with indifference . . ."* Perry might have been correct about Pateros drawing them back, but what about the rest of the people on the ship? Boreas's fears were not unfounded.

But it was also clear they were supposed to rescue Yahto Veli. Darcy swallowed hard. "How about I give you that heading now so you can be ready to go when the sailors return?"

Boreas agreed, and Darcy retrieved the phoenix quill from Lewis.

Their heading pointed straight out to the remotest part of the Sea of Aspros, the spot on Boreas's maps where no islands were charted and where ships had mysteriously disappeared. Darcy's zephyra had not returned, so they no longer bucked her resistance to their heading in that direction, but Darcy noticed that the closer they got to the empty part of the map, the less the wind seemed to blow. Boreas called for coming about with much greater frequency than his normal wont, and all attempts to head directly along the phoenix feather's course resulted in dead sails.

After three days, Boreas called the crew to the oars, and the sailors descended, grumbling, down into the hold to the rowing deck. The sails were lowered and tied to the booms, the jibs pulled in as well.

"It's just as well," Boreas grumbled as he watched his orders carried out. "Look ahead."

Storm clouds gathered on the horizon, and Darcy felt a thrill of foreboding. They'd endured many soaking rains onboard the *Cal Meridian*, but this looked much more severe.

"A storm?" she asked, licking her dry lips. "In December?"

"Weather is unpredictable on the Sea of Aspros, regardless of the season, and we're a fair deal further south than we started out. This looks to be a violent gale, to be sure, no gentle rain or snowfall!"

"Great," Darcy said, less than thrilled about Sam blowing chunks again.

She still hadn't told Sam about Perry, and she'd avoided Perry as much as possible since their dreadful first kiss. She knew he noticed, but she was too cowardly to face him, and she wondered now if it were even necessary to tell Sam anything.

She closed her eyes and pictured Perry's face. She was still attracted to him, but it felt more like the attraction of an observer to a beautiful vase in a museum, admiring of its beauty but without any desire to take it home and be responsible for it. After three days of examining her feelings inside her head, she'd decided officially that she no longer *like* liked Perry Marks. Definitely not in the romantic sense, and she wondered how much she even liked him as a friend.

Tellius's words about Perry's character had lodged inside her brain like a cancer, and the more she replayed them, the more she had to admit he was right. All her fantasies about Perry and their dating had fallen flat, culminating in a kiss that felt awkward and forced. They simply weren't right for each other, and hiding the relationship from her best friend in the world was killing Darcy inside. Perry would get over it, but she didn't know if Sam ever would.

"Perhaps you should go below, Lady Darcy, or at least into your cabin," Boreas advised. The wind had picked up already, and the sails made wild flapping noises against the booms as the sailors cursed and struggled to finish their tasks. "This is not going to be pleasant."

Darcy nodded and hurried to do as he instructed. She thought her friends would be down below, so she headed toward the hatch. As she reached the top step, a curious song pierced the wind, and Darcy looked to the sky to see a large bird with brilliant red, yellow, and gold plumage streaking overhead. She watched it in awe as the phoenix flew straight into the heart of the storm and disappeared with a flash of light.

Darcy ducked through the hatch, smiling to herself in confidence that they were headed the right direction, the phoenix song still resonating in her head.

CHAPTER 21
THE ARCHIPELAGO

Sam wasn't the only one to blow chunks during the storm. After over twenty-four hours of being tossed about on the sea like a toy in a toddler's bathtub, Darcy and Tellius were once again the only two to remain unaffected by the turbulence.

At least taking care of all their sick comrades gave Darcy something to think about other than her conflicted love life, and required Tellius to bury the hatchet for the time being as well. They had no help from the adults, for all hands were either at the oars or following Boreas's orders. Rubidius spent most of his time at the wheel beside the captain, and Darcy suspected the main reason they hadn't yet been pummeled to the bottom of the sea was because Rubidius held them together with his magic.

All of the teenagers were miserable together, and they had a front-row seat to the rowing action on the deck just above them. The *Cal Meridian* creaked and groaned with the dipping and splashing of oars, and Darcy prayed Rubidius would be able to hold them together and the crew's strength wouldn't fail for as long as it took to ride out the storm.

Sam retched again, and Darcy held a bowl under her chin, but there was nothing left to come up.

Sam groaned and sat back. "How much longer, Darcy?" she asked. "How much longer?" Darcy could barely hear her over the roaring din.

Darcy didn't answer. Instead she wiped a sweaty arm across her brow and looked up, catching Tellius's eye. He'd been helping the boys, and he'd been very caring toward all of them . . . even Perry. He looked away after a moment, and Darcy glanced back at Sam. Breathing very shallowly, Sam began to calm as her eyes narrowed to slits. Perhaps, mercifully, she would fall asleep as Amelia had about an hour before.

"You look terrible!" Tellius shouted in Darcy's ear over the howling wind.

Darcy jumped and turned to find him leaning over her, bracing himself on the support beam against which she was leaning.

"You should try to get some sleep!"

"Speak for yourself!" Darcy shouted back.

"I'm fine!"

"Oh yeah? Well you look like death warmed over!"

Tellius stumbled against her legs as the ship groaned and keeled to the side. "*What?*"

Darcy pushed off him. "Never mind!" She looked down at Sam to check that she was okay after the violent roll, but Sam's chest was rising and falling peacefully. She glanced over at the boys, and they were also, at long last, sleeping. Darcy closed her eyes but didn't feel sleepy at all.

"I don't think I could sleep right now!" she called to Tellius.

"Me neither!"

"Do you know what I *really* need? Some fresh air!" Darcy stank of vomit all over, and she worried that if she didn't get away from it all for a few minutes at least, she would soon join the ranks of the sick.

Tellius squinted at her and then looked over his shoulder toward the ladder. "Follow me!" he said, pulling her up by the arms.

They climbed together, past the rowers and up to the main hatch, against which Tellius rammed his shoulder. He grimaced in pain as he tried to force it open against the wind, but he soon gave up, panting, "It's no use; I'm too tired!"

"Let me help!" Darcy climbed up beside him, knee to knee, and pressed her hands against the wood. Tellius gathered himself and once again dug his shoulder into it.

"Yaaaarrrggghhh!" Tellius cried as it creaked, cracked open, and flew out of their grasps to slam open against the deck as the wind took it. He laughed, relieved, as he poked his head out, and Darcy joined in, half-hysterically. Together, they squinted against the violent, salty spray. It was dark out and everything tilted and whirled about them, lighting strikes illuminating the driving rain and churning sea.

"This is *incredible!*" Darcy shouted, closing her eyes. The spray stung her skin, but it still felt wonderful after the long hours of confinement in the hold. She reached up and pushed away dank strands of her hair that had been blown across her face by the gale-force winds.

The *Cal Meridian* rolled again to the side, and Darcy lost her footing on the ladder. Tellius grabbed her around the middle and held her steady until the ship righted itself. "Here!" he called, offering his shoulder for her knee. "I'll boost you up!"

She took it gladly, pushing off and pulling herself up to sit on the rim with her legs dangling into the hatch. She offered a hand to Tellius, and he hoisted himself up and sat across from her.

"Better?" he shouted, and she nodded and gave him a thumbs-up.

They sat and enjoyed the fresh, if turbulent, air, and Darcy was quickly soaked through and freezing, but it felt like a much needed bath, and she didn't mind.

Without warning, the *Cal Meridian* pitched to the side over a massive swell, and the deck tilted at a forty-five degree angle. Darcy shrieked as she lost her grip on the edge of the hatch and tumbled backward down the slick deck, glimpsing Tellius's horrified face as he shouted, "*Darcy!*" He disappeared from view and the railing rushed up to meet her.

She crashed into the railing and her vision momentarily went black. She threw her arms out to grab onto the wooden bars, but her hands fell through the slats and she hung, face down, over waves that boiled eight feet below her . . . six feet . . . four . . . as the ship tilted further.

"We're going to tip over!" she screamed in vain. A blur slid down the deck and landed beside her on the railing, a firm hand gripping her arm, keeping her from tumbling to the depths.

Wal held her steady until the *Cal Meridian*, with a groan and a splash, righted itself on the waves. Quick as lightning, he yanked her back toward the hatch, intercepting Tellius, who was scrambling toward her.

"Are—you—*mad?*" Wal hollered. "Get below deck, *now!*" He grabbed Tellius by the shoulder of his soaking-wet tunic and shoved him unceremoniously through the hatch. He dumped Darcy in after him and slammed the hatch closed, cutting off the wind and rain with an immediacy that made Darcy's ears pop.

Darcy landed on top of Tellius at the foot of the ladder, and she struggled to right herself as she trembled from her near brush with a watery death. Tellius wriggled out from underneath her and held her by the shoulders. He was shaking almost as badly as she was.

"Are you okay?" he shouted.

Darcy couldn't answer through her chattering teeth.

Tellius yanked her to him in a fierce hug, pressing her head to his chest, and she could hear his heart racing in his ribcage. She was too tired to protest, too tired to move, so she let her eyes close and enjoyed the secure feeling of being held.

"Come on!" Tellius said after a moment, and he peeled her away and helped her descend to the next deck. He yanked a blanket from an unoccupied hammock and threw it around her shoulders. Pulling her down next to him by the sputtering, swinging oil lamp that threw light over the faces of their sleeping companions, he leaned back against the wall and tucked her under his arm. He rubbed her shoulders with both hands, trying to help warm her, and the wind died down to almost quiet.

"I would have gone in after you."

A crash of thunder resounded and the ship tilted again, but feelings warmer than the blanket engulfed her, and she felt an almost unnerving sense of *rightness*. Closing her eyes and letting her head fall against his shoulder, she let herself drift off to sleep.

The storm had abated by the morning, and gone with it was Darcy's sense of rightness. She opened her eyes, thinking for a moment that she had gone deaf, but discovering that the quiet came from clear skies and calm seas.

She groaned and pushed herself up from the spot where she'd fallen asleep against Tellius, but he was gone and Perry sat next to her instead, watching her with concerned and tired eyes.

"Hmm," Darcy said, clearing her throat. "Hi. Feeling better?"

"Yeah. Was it really bad—taking care of all of us while we puked everywhere?"

Darcy laughed without humor. "It doesn't rank in my top ten list of favorite experiences." She straightened and leaned back against the hull of the ship, drawing her knees up to her chest. "It was impressive, though," she continued, trying to keep the mood light. "I didn't know you could turn that shade of green."

"Yeah." Perry grimaced and rubbed his face. "Well, I don't think I'll ever be able to eat salted fish again . . . not that I ever eat salted fish back home . . ." He reached out to tuck Darcy's hair behind her ear, but she pulled back.

"Perry . . ."

He sighed and looked away, draping his hands over his knees. "What?"

"This isn't . . . right."

He stared at a spot on a beam, his jaw working. "Because of Sam?" he asked after a moment.

"No . . . well, partially . . . but mostly no."

"Because you had to clean up my puke?"

Darcy felt a glimmer of encouragement; he wasn't as angry as she'd expected him to be. "Tellius cleaned up your puke. And . . . no."

He sighed again and shook his head, twiddling his fingers and staring at them.

"I'm sorry," Darcy said in a small voice. "I just don't like you like that anymore. It didn't feel right. Do you know what I mean?"

"Yeah, I do actually." Perry fell silent for a moment. "I mean, I really enjoyed kissing you, don't get me wrong, but afterward . . ."

Darcy searched his face. "It felt wrong, right?"

"Yeah." He looked at her. "It felt like I was taking something that didn't belong to me."

Darcy swallowed hard and blinked.

"I still think you're an amazing girl, Darcy," Perry said.

"You're pretty cool, too." Darcy smiled.

He smiled back and leaned over to kiss her cheek. "Friends?" he said, drawing away and offering his hand.

"Friends." Darcy shook on it.

Her smile fell as she saw his face turn pale. A clunk and a clatter sounded behind her, and she turned around to see Sam standing at the foot of the ladder. A bowl of porridge lay spilled at her feet, and her eyes welled up with tears. Without a word, she spun around and clambered up through the hatch.

"*Sam!*" Darcy scrambled out of the hatch and slipped on the slick deck. She picked herself up and stared around in wonder, her mouth hanging open. The water around them was preternaturally blue and the sky was the crystal clear that only follows a terrible storm. The *Cal Meridian* was resting in calm seas, and dotted all around them were little green islands. They had reached the archipelago.

None of the islands were close enough to see clearly yet, and for miles around they were enclosed in the high circle of a fog bank, as though the ship and the islands lay in the hole of an enormous donut made of mist. Boreas stomped about growling orders to his crew, and the sailors scrambled to put everything to rights.

Darcy reached up to pull her hair off her neck, fanning herself to keep from breaking a sweat. She furrowed her brow in confusion over such unseasonably warm December weather, but she shook herself out of it and considered where to find Sam. There was only one place Sam could go to be alone, so she turned for the captain's cabin.

"Sam!" Darcy pounded on the door. She could hear Sam sobbing inside the cabin, but she'd locked the door to keep Darcy out. "Sam, please. Will you let me in? I need to talk to you."

Finally the door cracked open, and Amelia's bright hazel eyes glared out. "I hope you're happy."

"No, I'm *not* happy. Please . . . can you convince her to let me talk to her?" Darcy pleaded.

Amelia let out an angry breath like a snake and glanced over her shoulder.

"I don't want to talk to her!" Sam wailed from the recesses of the room. "Make her go away!"

"Amelia, I was *breaking up* with Perry. That's what she saw—she just doesn't understand!"

"I'll let you know," Amelia said and shut the door, throwing the lock with a loud click.

Darcy let her forehead fall against the door with a clunk and stared at her feet. Sam had never treated Darcy like this before—had never been this *angry* with her before—and it made Darcy cold inside that Sam was her best friend and Darcy'd acted like an idiot over a boy.

Darcy felt someone watching her and she lifted her head and turned to see the sailors shooting glances at her, standing dejected at the cabin door. She remembered Tellius's warning that the sailors liked to gossip, and she wondered what sort of stories they'd make up about her now.

It had grown so warm that many of the sailors had removed their shirts, and she saw Tellius among them, shirtless as well. He looked thin and wiry next to the strapping sailors, but there was potential in his frame for a well-muscled build. Darcy looked away quickly, hoping he wouldn't think she was checking him out.

Amelia finally opened the door, wide this time, and stepped out. "You can go in," she said. "She wants to talk to you alone."

"*Thank* you," Darcy whispered and slipped inside the cabin.

Sam sat on the bed with her back very straight. Her eyes were bloodshot and red-rimmed, but she was no longer crying, though every other breath caused her frame to shudder. Darcy opened her mouth to speak, and the corner of Sam's lips twitched as she looked away.

"Sam, I'm *so* sorry," Darcy said. "I know I'm the worst friend ever, but you have to believe me that what you saw wasn't what you thought—"

"So you *haven't* been dating him?" Sam asked, using the sharp tone she usually reserved for Colin Mackaby.

"Well—uh—no . . . I mean, yes, but that's not what I meant." Darcy chewed her lip. She took a deep breath and tried again. "Perry and I have been . . . *together* . . ." Sam's eyes welled up with tears again, and Darcy said quickly, "But I was breaking up with him—*that's* what you saw!"

Sam wiped at her tears with both hands, her quiet sorrow cutting through Darcy far more painfully than any bitter words. Darcy felt tears spring to her own eyes.

"How long?" Sam whispered. "Since before we came to Alitheia this year?"

Darcy sniffed. "Sort of. We—we kept in touch through the school year. But we didn't actually *say* anything about it until we got here. We just kind of . . . slid into it . . ."

Sam's face crumpled and she looked away. "I've—been able to—tell that you've been hiding—something from me—for a while—you know, with my talent," Sam hiccupped. "And Perry—too—but I told—myself—that you wouldn't—that you would never—*do* that to me!"

"I'm *sorry!*" Darcy cried. "I'm really, really sorry! We liked each other —"

"Why didn't you *tell* me? I would have understood!" Sam wiped tears off her cheeks. "I would have been hurt, but it would have been better than this—than finding out you've been *lying* to me!"

"I know, Sam, I know . . . I was scared, and—" *selfish.* Darcy swallowed the last word. "Please, please forgive me, Sam. I don't like him anymore. It was . . . beyond stupid of me to date him behind your back. I know how long you've liked him."

"But he doesn't like me, and he never has, and he never will," Sam said bitterly. "It's not about him. This is about me and you."

"I know you feel like you can't trust me anymore—"

"Can I?" Sam challenged. She looked devastated. "I *know* there's more you're hiding from me, and it doesn't have anything to do with Perry."

Darcy shuddered and stepped back, the last stanza of her oracle flashing through her mind.

"Now here's something more to help you understand
The words of the prophecy you now have at hand.
There shall be a wedding, not one, but two,
With the deepest color defining you.
Lady Darcy, intended, you must look ahead,
Twice wed,
Twice dead,
Twice stained red."

"Sam . . . if you promise to forgive me—I—I'll tell you—everything!" Darcy said. "Just—please forgive me, Sam."

Sam shook her head. "I want to know your secret, Darcy, but not like this—not as some sort of *bribe* to get me to forgive you."

"*Do* you, though?" Darcy was desperate.

Sam's mouth worked for a moment. "I—I *will*, Darcy, but . . . it's too soon. Give me some time . . ."

Darcy nodded and swallowed hard, and silence descended between them. "Do you want me to go?"

"Yes, please." Sam avoided her eyes. "And please send Amelia back in."

"Okay." Darcy opened the door and stepped aside for Amelia, who had been listening against the wood. Amelia brushed coldly past her and shut the door in her face.

Darcy stood outside the door and tried hard not to cry again. Sam hated her. Amelia hated her. Perry wasn't exactly happy with her right now; it never felt good to get dumped, no matter what the circumstances. Dean, she was sure, would be happy enough that he had his best friend back now.

Tellius brushed past her carrying a large coil of rope without saying anything or acknowledging her presence in any way. She sighed. Perhaps Lewis would still be her friend. She assumed he'd been oblivious to everything that had been going on the whole time anyway.

Darcy meandered over to the railing and climbed the steps to the top deck with feet that felt as though they weighed a ton each. She went to the bowsprit and watched as the sailors shimmied up and down the lines, reattaching the jibs and patching tears. Droplets of water rained down on her as the canvas triangles were unwrapped, and she ducked to stand in a safer spot.

They were so close; she could feel it as she gazed out at the islands. The Oracle was there somewhere; they only had to find it. Darcy tried not to panic at the enormity of the task before them. She counted at least twenty islands within immediate sight, and more lay farther on toward the other end of the fog bank.

The phoenix feather quill had served its purpose in getting them to the archipelago and would be of no further use now, for it was not the Island of the Sun they desired to find, but an island far more sinister, if the Oracle's "personality" were any indicator. Now what would they do? Search each island one by one?

" 'Held in the balance, the white thread reveals, the unseen path, through lily fields . . .' " Darcy repeated for what felt like the millionth time. So, that brought them at last to the elusive white thread. Darcy exhaled and raised her eyes to the sky. "Well, Pateros, you've gotten us this far. Will you take us the rest of the way?"

As if in answer, a phoenix song filled the sky as another of the spectacular birds winged its way over her head and disappeared toward an island on the horizon. Darcy thought idly that she wished they were going to the phoenix island, for it would be far nicer than where they were headed. She tried to imagine what it would be like, but she couldn't suppress a sudden and curious desire.

She had to go see the captain.

CHAPTER 22
THE WHITE THREAD

Darcy found Boreas in his berth beneath the rowing deck, where he had rigged up a long table upon which to spread his charts. An overturned barrel against the hull served as a support, and he had the map of the archipelago spread out with debris strewn haphazardly around and on top of it—metal compasses, half-melted candle stubs, a set of scales for weighing coins, several spools of coarse white string the crew used to mend the sails, bits of charcoal, a magnifying glass, and several other items the purposes for which Darcy didn't know.

She eyed the spools of string with interest and waited for Boreas to finish speaking with a sailor about repairs to the main mast. When he finally turned to her, she felt a bit foolish. She didn't actually know why she'd come to speak with him.

"So," Boreas said, "Rubidius tells me the phoenix feather is of no use to us now that we're within the archipelago. He says we're not going to the phoenix island."

"Yes, sir," Darcy responded.

"So where *do* we go next?" Boreas sounded exhausted and irritable, and Darcy wondered if he'd slept at all since the storm.

"I was wondering if maybe you had any ideas," Darcy said.

Boreas laughed. "Me? You've been telling me where to go and what to do since this journey began, and now you want my opinion?"

"Well, can we at least study the archipelago together? Maybe we can find something."

Boreas exhaled. "I've been over this map countless times, my lady, and I've not seen one thing that relates to that oracle you received."

"Still . . . now that we're within the archipelago, maybe something will reveal itself," Darcy suggested.

"Lady Darcy, you said all of the white thread had been removed from the tapestry, so what good will it do to study an image that is missing the one thing we need?"

Darcy bit her lip. "How long would it take us to search each island one by one?"

"More time than we have, that is for certain."

"We have to try *something*," she said.

"Did you ever think maybe the Oracle lied to you, eh? Or gave you a hint that's impossible to follow because it doesn't want to be found?"

Darcy shook her head. "It can't do that. It's part of its magic code—Rubidius called it 'covenantal magic.' It gives one true response in exchange for one item of payment. To break its own covenant is to risk losing its power. So, what it told Voitto *has* to be true and it *has* to be follow-able."

Boreas sighed. "Very well," he said, stepping over to the countertop and beginning to push things off the map. He smoothed out the rolled edges and placed his paperweights on the corners to hold it down. A spool of thread rolled back over the image, its string uncoiling, followed by another. With a grumble, Boreas grabbed them up and dumped them on top of the scale that had been pushed back against the hull.

A strand of thread from one of the spools trailed over the edge of the scale and remained draped over the map. Boreas went to brush it away with an exasperated grunt, but Darcy, heart pounding, flung out her arm to stop him.

"Captain Boreas," she said. "Look!"

He withdrew his hand and scowled at her. "What am I supposed to be looking at?"

"The white thread." Darcy pointed at the spools resting on his scales, perfectly balanced on each side. " 'Held in the balance the white thread reveals, the unseen path . . .' " She pointed to the single strand that was draped over the image, the frayed tip of the thread resting on a nameless island near the center of the archipelago.

"You think the thread—*that* thread?" Boreas guffawed. "Impossible."

"But it's pointing to an island, and the spool is balanced on your scales!" Darcy cried.

"Coincidence only! It's too simple and cannot possibly be the answer."

"But that's how the Oracle *works*," Darcy insisted. "It gives us answers we think mean one thing but really mean another. It foretells things—not always huge events—just enough to make us puzzle over them, because that's what the Oracle wants us to do. It knew we would look for something grandiose, so it foretold something really mundane and obvious, something that we could easily overlook."

"You are telling me the Oracle *knew* I would pile up those spools on those scales and this thread would uncoil and land directly on its island?" Boreas asked, incredulous. "That's an awful leap of faith, Lady Darcy."

"That's exactly what I'm saying. Why not? You said it yourself; you don't have any better ideas."

Boreas mumbled something under his breath that sounded like "lunacy," but he nonetheless circled the island with a lump of charcoal. "I will consult Rubidius when he wakes. If he agrees, then we will begin our search for this island. But first we must determine where we *are* in this forsaken archipelago. My compass isn't working," he said, tossing it into the pile of odds and ends, "and the sun follows an unpredictable path through the sky. Heavy magic lies over this entire archipelago. I wouldn't be surprised to find that another three months have passed once we find our way out—*if* we find our way out."

Darcy wished he wouldn't be such a buzzkill, but she was too cowardly to say it out loud. Her ears buzzed with excitement, and she couldn't wait to run upstairs and tell Amelia and Sam, until she remembered they were not exactly on speaking terms at the moment. She'd have to find Lewis; he would be happy to hear about it. She excused herself from Boreas's presence.

She found Lewis at the railing. He was winding up a coil of rope, getting it twisted and muttering under his breath. Perry and Dean were helping the sailors alongside Tellius, and Dean smirked at her while Perry avoided looking at her at all.

"What did you do to Sam?" Lewis asked without preamble before Darcy could get a word out.

"Really? You want to talk about *that?*" Darcy sighed and rolled her eyes.

"Of course I do!" Lewis adjusted his glasses up the bridge of his sweaty nose. "She won't come out of your cabin and Amelia said you broke her heart."

"I thought you stayed above all the drama," Darcy said. "Blissfully oblivious . . . isn't that how you like it?"

"Well, sure, but maybe I can help. Plus," he said, rolling up his sleeves, "I think it's important that Sam trusts you, you know? 'Cause her role is to be the companion, and that means you need her as *your* companion, because all of this seems to hinge around you somehow."

Darcy puffed out her cheeks in resignation. "Okay, fine. Sam found out that Perry and I were dating, and . . . well, you know how long she's liked Perry."

Lewis looked exasperated. "That's it? That's all she's mad about?"

"It's a big deal to her, Lewis!"

He shook his head. "Girls. I mean, you said '*were* dating,' so you're obviously not together anymore, right?"

"Not as of this morning."

"Then Sam just needs to get over it."

"She's mad that I lied to her."

"Oh. Well, I guess that's a little worse. Still, I'll talk to her. I've known her long enough to make her see reason."

"Lewis . . ." Darcy said, unconvinced. "When a girl is upset about something, the last thing she wants is a *guy* to show up and tell her she just needs to get over it."

"Girls," Lewis grumbled again, shaking his head. He turned toward the captain's cabin, but Darcy stopped him with an iron grip on his arm.

"Seriously, bad idea. I mean it. Just give her time. I think—I *hope*—she'll forgive me soon, and we can put all of this behind us. Anyway, that wasn't what I wanted to talk to you ab—"

"Perry's such an idiot," Lewis said, cutting her off. "I don't know why he doesn't see how great Sam is. She's the coolest, sweetest girl I've ever known!"

Darcy squinted at him. "Lewis . . ."

"Sorry," Lewis said. "What was it you wanted to talk to me about?"

He stepped aside as a sailor with bulging muscles took over the rope he'd been attempting to coil, and Darcy drew him away from any curious ears.

"I think I found the white thread! In Boreas's berth." She told Lewis what had happened and he listened, his eyes getting wider.

"I *suppose* that could be it," he said slowly when she was finished.

"Of course that's it! It's so obvious!" Darcy was more convinced than ever that she had figured out the riddle.

"It just seems too simple. How can it be that the tapestry, with all the white thread meticulously removed from it, has no connection while some accident with the thread spools *does?*"

Darcy shook her head. "The complexity is in the simplicity."

"Don't speak nonsense, Darcy."

She shoved him, annoyed. "You'll see."

"I hope you're right."

Darcy had hoped Sam would have forgiven her by that night so she could tell her about what she'd discovered, but she was disappointed. Sam avoided her and Amelia stuck to her side. When it came to be bedtime, she and Amelia grabbed blankets and took hammocks down below with the boys, leaving the tiny captain's cabin—feeling much larger in its emptiness—to Darcy. A part of Darcy wanted to stomp down to the lower deck and yell at Sam for dragging it out, but she remembered the advice she'd given Lewis that afternoon: just give her time.

As Darcy settled down on the bed—alone and depressed—the one bright spot in her mind was that Rubidius had agreed wholeheartedly with Darcy's assumption about the white thread. His agreement had brought Lewis over to her side as well, and she figured the rest of her estranged friends had at least heard about it by the time night fell, even if she hadn't gotten to tell them herself.

Darcy expected to fall asleep much quicker than usual without the snores and heavy breathing to contend with, but instead she tossed and turned. The ship was very quiet as the seas were so calm—unnaturally calm, and Darcy remembered Boreas mentioning that the archipelago was blanketed in magic.

Finally Darcy fell asleep, but almost immediately she found herself awake—in a different bed. She was huddled in a small room in a cottage that looked cozy in the dim light. The wall beside her bed was made of cut logs and a curtained window on the far wall let in the weak very late—or very early—sunlight. An old woman sat reading a book in a rocking chair beside her bed. A second bed sat on the other side of her rocking chair, where a tiny boy with curly brown hair lay fast asleep.

The woman turned a page in her book, reading by the light of a dim candle on the end table beside her, and Darcy sat up and looked at her. "Eleanor?" Her voice came to her ears as if from over a great distance. Eleanor ignored her.

Placing her book down in her lap, Eleanor frowned. She appeared much younger than when Darcy had last seen her. She stood gingerly from her chair and went to the window, pulling the blinds open infinitesimally and staring out into the dusky light. She seemed to be listening for something. The door to the bedroom banged open beside her. Eleanor spun to face the door but didn't jump in surprise.

The tiny boy in the other bed rolled over and murmured, but slept on. Standing in the doorway was a pretty woman with long dark hair, dark eyes, and a familiar face. The woman cast Darcy a glance of love and tenderness, even as her eyes contained fear.

"They are coming," she whispered to Eleanor, who had gone to stand before her. "They are almost here. He's gone outside with Yeriel; they're going to try and lead them off. But you must go—*now!* Take the boys." The woman's voice cracked as she looked to Darcy and pressed a hand to her lips to keep from crying.

A sound pierced the woods outside—a sound Darcy knew only too well
—the deep animalistic snarl of a tsellodrin. One snarl was answered with
two, and then the cottage was surrounded by them. The woman dashed to
Darcy and whispered urgently.

"Be brave, like your father. I love you!" She pressed Darcy to her chest in
a hug that was over too soon. She handed Darcy over to Eleanor and
tenderly gathered up the small boy from the other bed. After pressing a
single kiss to his forehead, she allowed Eleanor to take him from her arms.

"Come with us," Eleanor urged the woman. "There is still time."

"There is no time!" she replied. "I must bar the way for you."

"Then you take them, and I will bar the way," Eleanor said. "They need
you!"

"I will not leave my husband, nor can I protect them as you can. If
Pateros spares us, we will find you. Now *go!*" The woman pushed them
toward the corner.

A loud thud resounded against the heavy wooden planks of the cottage,
and the snarls of the tsellodrin became haunting, foghorn-like cries. A
man's voice shouted at them from outside as the woman ran from the room.
She slammed the door behind her and threw a heavy bolt on the other side.

"Come, Tellius!" Eleanor looked at Darcy and motioned that she should
follow her. With her free hand, she concentrated her magic on the
floorboards and they lifted up to reveal a dark tunnel. "Go!" Eleanor
pushed Darcy into the hole and slid down after her, the limp form of the
smaller boy slung over her shoulder. Eleanor handed Darcy the child and
worked her magic to bring the boards once again down over the hole. Darcy
cradled the boy to her chest, amazed that he could still be sleeping.

Darkness as black as pitch descended on them, and the crash of
splintering wood sounded from above. A piercing cry of pain followed, and
Eleanor placed a warning hand on Darcy's shoulder, but Darcy didn't need
to be told to stay quiet. The smaller child began to stir, and Darcy said,
"Ssshhhh . . ." as quietly as she could.

Eleanor muttered something over the boy's head and he drifted
immediately back to sleep. Heavy footsteps stomped above them, and
crashes, as first one bed and then the other were overturned. The
floorboards shuddered only inches above their heads, and dust rained down
on them, but Darcy didn't move. The tsellodrin snarled back and forth to
each other.

"They are long gone from this place. You will never find them!" said the
woman, their mother, triumph in her voice instead of sadness. Darcy felt a
surge of pride.

A violent shuffling followed, and the woman cried out in pain, as though
the sound had been ripped from her throat. There was a sound like a sack of
potatoes hitting the boards above them, and the snarls of the tsellodrin
receded from the room. Darcy felt something warm and sticky dripping on

her face and reached up a trembling hand to feel it trickling through a crack in the floorboards. It smelled coppery, like—

Darcy awoke with a start, twisting in her sheets and thrashing about with her arms. She sat bolt upright and let out a shuddering cry. Covering her face with her hands, she wasn't surprised to find tears pouring down her cheeks.

Feeling claustrophobic and nauseated, Darcy kicked free of the blankets and got to her feet. She grabbed a cloak from a peg on the wall, yanked open the door, and stumbled out into the fresh air. Afraid she might be sick, she went to the railing, the gold glinting in the moonlight. She hung her head over the edge, taking great gulps of air, and shuddered. She knew exactly what she'd just seen.

Trying to calm her shaking body and empty her mind of the horrific dream, Darcy listened to the soft conversations of the sailors and the gentle creaks and groans of the *Cal Meridian* as it drifted along. A scrambling noise sounded behind her, and a moment later Tellius appeared at the railing, shaking and sweating as she was. He, too, hung his head, breathing hard with his eyes closed and grasping the railing.

It was a moment before he noticed her there, and he looked up with confusion and apprehension in his eyes. They gaped at each other, and Darcy wondered if she should reveal what she had just dreamed—wondered if he *knew* what she had just dreamed. Perhaps he had been there, too, and had seen her intrude upon his memory.

"Why do you dream of becoming a tsellodrin?"

Darcy's jaw dropped in horror. "You—you saw *that*? My nightmare?"

"I didn't *see* it; I *was* it—you, that is. I think I was you in the dream. I—I cut my foot and there was black blood everywhere—coming out of me. And my eyes . . ." He shuddered and closed his fists. "I was in some strange dwelling, and your mother was calling—*your* name . . . I was so cold!"

Darcy closed her eyes and forced her breathing to slow.

"Why?" Tellius asked again. "Why *that* nightmare?"

"I—I don't know!" Darcy lied. "It's just . . . something I've been afraid of since I first saw the tsellodrin."

Tellius stared at her, his mouth twisting.

"It *is* a scary idea, isn't it?" Darcy prodded him to believe her.

He sighed and lowered his gaze. "Yeah, it sure is." Then he frowned at her. "Why are you up? Were you woken by the same dream?"

Darcy bit her lip. "No . . . ah . . . I think we traded dreams tonight."

She watched as the words sank in and Tellius's face transformed from confused, to frightened, to angry. "You saw *that* night? You *experienced* it?"

"I didn't want to be there, trust me!" Darcy backed away.

His face crumpled, and he swiftly turned away from her. She watched his shoulders rise and fall as he worked to regain control of himself. When he turned back, his face was calm, but his eyes were blank and vacant.

"Was that really how it happened?" Darcy whispered before she could stop herself. "It was *horrible!*"

Tellius's jaw clenched beneath his cheeks, but he said nothing.

"I'm so sorry, Tellius," Darcy said. "When you told me about your nightmares, I could only imagine how bad they must be, but now I know —"

"You don't know anything." Tellius glared at her. "You only saw it as an observer. *I* experienced the real thing. That was my *mother* and my *father* dying . . . you can't know what that felt like!"

Darcy knew it would do no good to tell him of the emotions she'd felt during the dream—emotions she was certain were his—and how his mother and Eleanor had thought she was him.

"How often do you have your nightmare?" Tellius asked abruptly.

"Often enough, I guess. But it's different versions of the dream every time. When I'm dreaming it, I never remember—that is—I never realize I'm dreaming until I wake up."

"Yeah . . ." Tellius said. "That was how it was for me just now, too. That's what made it so terrifying, I guess."

"Nothing like yours, though," Darcy said. "Yours was far worse, Tellius."

He hung his head, clenching his jaw for a long time, and Darcy grew worried that she'd angered him again. But he didn't move away, and he didn't speak harshly to her again.

"Why do you think this happened to us?" Darcy asked. "Why did we enter each other's dreams?"

Tellius looked up and stared off into the star-spangled sky. "I think it must be the magic of this place. It's turned everything on its end; perhaps it can make people enter each others' minds, as well."

Darcy smiled, glad to have Tellius speaking pleasantly. "Boreas said the sun is not in the proper place, but what else is weird around here?" she asked.

"Winter is summer," Tellius said, holding his hand up as if to touch the air. "And the stars are confused."

"Really?" Darcy squinted upward, searching for the big dipper or Orion's belt . . . any constellation she was familiar with, but she couldn't find any.

"Of course! Haven't you studied astronomy?"

"It's not exactly a required class where I come from," Darcy responded dryly.

"How do you know where you are when you're on a journey?" Tellius asked, incredulous.

"GPS?" Darcy suggested. "But—never mind about that," she said, taking in Tellius's blank expression. "I can't explain how it works. It's—it's kind of like my world's version of magic. Tell me about the stars."

Tellius hesitated. "It won't make any sense to you if you've never studied them before."

"At least tell me what's wrong with them now. Are they flipped, or something?"

"No, they're not flipped, they're completely different. The North Star is missing and none of the constellations are familiar. I'm sure Boreas and Bayard are at their wits' end trying to navigate through here."

"At least they have the map of the archipelago," Darcy said. "We know the island we're heading for; certainly we can find out where we are."

"I'm glad you're so . . . optimistic," Tellius said, sounding exactly the opposite. "Meanwhile, I would like it if we could keep our own dreams to ourselves."

"I doubt there's anything we can do about that," Darcy said.

"If we continue to share dreams, it's going to make it difficult to stay away from each other."

"Is that such a bad thing?" Darcy rolled her eyes inwardly. "Perry and I —"

"I hope you don't experience any more of my memories." Tellius bowed and walked stiffly back to the hatch.

CHAPTER 23
THROUGH LILY FIELDS

The following afternoon, Rubidius carried the map up to the top deck and barked at a couple of sailors to hold the edges down while he studied it with Boreas. Darcy and the other six teenagers hung around nearby; Sam allowed herself to be in Darcy's presence, though she hadn't greeted her that morning, and she kept her eyes cast down to the side. Perry glanced back and forth between Darcy and Sam and looked, for once, a little penitent.

Growing bored watching Rubidius and Boreas pore over the map, Darcy scooted closer to Lewis. Curious whether she and Tellius were the only ones to share dreams, she whispered, "Did you have any strange dreams last night?"

Lewis wrinkled his nose at her and scratched his head. "Yeah, actually, I did . . . I, uh, dreamed of *cheese*. Like, I was obsessed with it! All I wanted was cheese, cheese, and more cheese . . . and everything around me was huge!"

"Oh, Lewis!" Darcy snorted, finding it uproarious that he had exchanged dreams with a mouse onboard the ship.

"What?" he asked.

"Nothing . . . nothing." Darcy waved him off, trying not to laugh too hard and disrupt the map perusing. Sam glanced piercingly at her, as though curious about what the joke was, but she looked away when she caught Darcy's eyes.

"As I thought!" Rubidius stated, drawing all of their attention. "It is not named on our map, but I think it must be this one, here." Rubidius jabbed a bony finger at an island on the map.

"What are you looking for?" Amelia asked, nosing her way in.

"The Island of the Sun," Rubidius replied.

"But I thought we weren't going there," Dean said.

"We're not," Rubidius said, "but do use your brains, Master Dean. What day is it today?"

"It's the winter solstice, burning day for the phoenixes—the whole reason they come here," Darcy said; she'd been thinking about it ever since they left Theanisi and she'd seen the phoenixes migrating.

"That's right," Rubidius said, gentler this time. "Lewis, what did I tell you is said to happen on winter solstice when the burning occurs?"

Lewis scrunched up his face. "At sunset, when they burn, their simultaneous . . . combustion, I guess you could call it, sends a flash of light into the sky. It's supposed to be visible for miles. Then, at sunup the next morning, they rise from the ashes."

"So you think we'll see this flash of light?" Dean caught onto Rubidius's thought.

"I do." He fingered his beard. "And if we can tell the origin of the flash, and link it to an island on our map, then we should be able to figure out where we are and navigate to the Oracle's island from there."

"What makes you think this is the Island of the Sun?" Boreas pointed to the map. "As you said, it is unlabeled."

"It has no *name* on the map, but it is marked with two runes . . . here and here," Rubidius said, pointing them out.

Leaning over the table to look, Darcy could hardly make out any runes; they looked to her like unintelligible dark squiggles, but Rubidius seemed confident.

"Death . . . and Life," he said. "Side by side. Surely it must indicate the death and rebirth of the phoenixes. I would stake my life on it!"

Boreas sighed. "So we must wait until sunset?"

"Sunset," Rubidius confirmed. "And then, Pateros willing, we will be shown the way."

Sunset took forever to arrive. Sam and Amelia stayed to themselves in the captain's cabin, Dean and Perry helped the sailors and held mock battles with wooden practice swords, Tellius disappeared below deck to take a nap, and Lewis hovered up in the bowsprit reading a book. Darcy sat on the top step of one of the staircases with her chin in her hands, bored and keyed up for the arrival of sunset. She kept her eyes peeled for more phoenixes overhead, but it seemed as though all had migrated already.

Sunset did come, descending rather quickly as it was the shortest day of the year. Though it felt as if it were summer in the archipelago, the calendar appeared still to follow the rest of Orodreos. The impending sunset brought everybody out onto the deck; Sam and Amelia emerged from the cabin, and Tellius, Wyn, and a coterie of sailors came from the hatch. Wyn's skin and hair were darkening, his eyes looking sleepy. They all stood together in silent expectation, looking all around for the light.

The sun dipped below the horizon, turning the waters from deep scarlet to purple. Wyn closed his eyes as Wal took over and, just as darkness descended, a flash of light erupted from an island on the horizon to the west.

The burning flash of the phoenixes shot up straight into the night sky like a column, undulating red, yellow, orange, and gold. Darcy gasped and stumbled forward, feeling as though something precious had been ripped from the world, but as the column shrank and eventually disappeared, that feeling dissipated as well.

Boreas held his looking glass, and Bayard stood close at his elbow, ready with a lantern and a piece of charcoal. "Okay." Boreas seized the charcoal from Bayard. "The Island of the Sun is *there*, and if it is the island we marked on the map earlier, then . . ." He paced over to the map, Bayard trotting in his wake and holding the lantern high. "That places us *here*." He marked the map with the charcoal and pulled a compass out of his pocket, the kind used in geometry to draw circles and find angles. "I judged that flash of light to be about twenty furlongs away, so . . ." He opened his compass wide and measured the distance from the mark he'd just made to the Island of the Sun and then muttered as he calculated in his head. He used the same spacing on the compass to measure the distance from their current position to the island indicated by the white thread. It was in almost exactly the opposite direction.

"Sixty-five furlongs," Boreas muttered and looked up at Rubidius. "If we had wind, we could make the island in an hour or two, but in these dead waters . . ." He shook his head. "With rowers we will need the night."

The night. The words sent a chill of anticipation through Darcy. In the morning they would land on the island where Yahto Veli was held captive. In the morning she would have to face the Oracle again. Darcy swallowed hard and rubbed at the oval scar in the center of her left palm.

"Let us make it happen," Rubidius said, and Boreas gave instructions to the sailors who would have to row.

"Hungry?" Lewis asked, appearing at Darcy's elbow.

"What? Oh, yeah, I suppose. I didn't have lunch."

"Let's go get some food."

"Okay." Darcy appreciated Lewis acting normal around her while everybody else avoided her. "Hopefully it'll keep my mind off what's coming."

"Is the Oracle really so horrible?" Lewis asked as they descended the stairs and got in line before the cook pot.

"Yes," Darcy asserted. "Only I don't know what to expect this time around. Like you said months ago back home—this time I'm coming as an aggressor, not a petitioner. I have no idea how the Oracle will respond."

Lewis stepped aside and allowed Darcy to get her food first. The cook had put together a boiling concoction of what smelled like fish stew. Darcy sighed and accepted a bowl and a hunk of crusty bread. She tried to gnaw on the bread while Lewis got his food, but it proved impenetrable to human teeth, so she discreetly tossed it overboard when nobody was looking.

Darcy and Lewis looked around for a place to sit, but all available barrels and spots against the railing were taken up by sailors getting a quick meal before heading either to their bunks for a nap before their shift or directly to the oars.

"Wanna go to my cabin?" Darcy suggested.

"Sure."

They navigated between legs and coils of rope over to the door of the cabin. Darcy swung it open, but came up short. Inside were Sam and Amelia, both with tears streaking their cheeks.

"I . . . uh . . . yyyeaah," Lewis said, swiftly backing out. "I'm gonna go."

Darcy jerked around to follow him, but Sam called out, "Darcy! Don't go . . . please. Come inside and shut the door."

Darcy sighed and did as requested. Once within, she remained backed against the door, hugging her bowl to her chest like a shield. "I didn't realize you had come back in here . . . sorry," she mumbled.

"No—Darcy, we're sorry," Sam gasped. She opened her quivering hands to reveal an engraved metallic square.

"My compact!" Darcy started forward, but stopped herself.

"I was moving a few things around and it—it fell out of your pack," Sam said tearfully. "I picked it up and looked in it, and I . . . I looked *horrible!* Like a hag, or something! I gave it to Amelia, and she saw the same of herself. We've been acting . . . just . . . cruel and unforgiving toward you and we're sorry. Being angry with you doesn't mean I have to be bitter. And, I know why you didn't tell me about Perry . . . you didn't want to hurt me."

"Well, yeah, but Sam, I was also being selfish. You were right about me lying to you; it was wrong, and I'm sorry, too." Darcy set her bowl on an upturned barrel and went to kneel on the floor near Sam and Amelia.

"You don't have to apologize again, Darcy. It's okay, I forgive you," Sam said, smiling through her tears. "Will you forgive me?"

"And me?" Amelia asked quietly.

"Yes and yes." Darcy grinned at them. She took the compact from Sam and tucked it away in her pack again. As she set down the pack, Sam blindsided her with a crushing hug, which Darcy returned, casting pleading eyes upon Amelia.

"Don't worry; I'm not going to hug you!" Amelia said, smirking.

Sam and Amelia went to get their own bowls of stew, and they all picked at it together in a circle on the floor of the cabin.

Sam lifted her spoon and let some of the grayish goop drip back into her bowl. "Yurgh. So, what do you think we can expect in the morning?"

"I don't know," Darcy said, forcing herself to take a bite.

"I guess we should try and get some sleep tonight," Amelia said.

"That's going to be difficult," Darcy said. "Here I've been dreaming about this day all year long, and now it's finally here. I don't know *how* I'm going to be able to sleep. Speaking of which . . . did you guys have funny dreams last night?"

Sam scrunched up her face. "Yeah. I dreamed about Simon and Amelia dreamed about Perry." She laughed. "And I've never even *met* Simon!"

"That's because you actually *entered* each other's dreams," Darcy said. "Tellius and I think it has something to do with the magic over this place. It causes reversals and swaps and stuff."

"Tellius and you?" Amelia raised her eyebrows.

"Oh . . . yeah. Well, I had Tellius's nightmare last night, and he had mine. We both woke up and ended up on the deck and talked about it." Darcy looked down, remembering the dream and wanting even less to go back to sleep.

"You had Tellius's nightmare," Sam repeated. "You mean you saw his parents being murdered?"

"Heard it, actually. He didn't really see it, he was hidden, but it was . . . I'd rather not talk about it."

"That bad, huh?" Sam asked softly.

Darcy nodded, shoving a spoonful of stew in her mouth while Amelia and Sam exchanged pitying glances.

Darcy swallowed. "Guess who Lewis exchanged dreams with," she said, seeking to ease the tension. "A *mouse!*"

Sam snorted in laughter, spraying stew out of her mouth as Amelia squeaked and scooted away.

"No, really?" Amelia asked, her face splitting into a grin.

"The poor mouse!" Sam wheezed, clutching her side. "It must have been scared out of its mind!"

The three of them dissolved into laughter and then stayed up talking until their eyelids began to droop.

The shouts of the sailors awoke Darcy from a troubled slumber. She jerked awake from Tellius's dream and looked toward the hammocks. Sam and Amelia were struggling to sit up, their faces looking frightened in the dim light.

"What's going on?" Sam asked in a quavering voice.

Amelia had freed herself of her hammock and was dressing quickly. "It feels as though we're moving a lot faster now, doesn't it? Maybe we picked up a wind."

"It doesn't feel like a wind," Darcy said. "It feels like we're on a conveyor belt, or something." She stood and helped Sam down. "Let's go see."

Darcy and Sam got dressed and opened the cabin door to peer outside. The sky was still very dark and the *Cal Meridian* was indeed moving rapidly, though the air was just as dead and windless as ever and the rowers had even stopped rowing. Sailors up and down the vessel had abandoned their posts and were peering over the railing into the water.

"We must be caught in a current!" Darcy led the way to a free spot on the railing and poked her head over the side, but all she could see was smooth black water sliding past.

"It's getting shallow, Cap'n!" a sailor called from the bowsprit overhead.

Darcy, Sam, and Amelia abandoned their post to climb the stairs to the top deck, where they found the boys, Tellius, Wal, Rubidius, the captain, and a sailor taking soundings with a weighted rope. He tossed it in and pulled it up rapidly.

"Shallower still!"

Boreas ran a hand through his hair. "Sailors!" he shouted. "Back to your posts! All hands to the oars. Row in reverse!"

The sailors scrambled to do his bidding and Rubidius stepped up to the bowsprit. "I'll do what I can," he said, placing his hands on the banisters and closing his eyes.

The ship's forward momentum began to slow as the rowers set about rowing backward and Rubidius set about his magic.

"Look!" Sam pointed into the water.

The rest of them crowded to the railing to find they were now sliding between patches of white.

"Water lilies! Huge ones!" Amelia shouted.

"They're the size of basketballs!" Sam stared in excitement.

Each enormous lily sat on a lily pad the size of a trashcan lid, and they soon surrounded them, the sea appearing as a floating garden.

"They're beautiful!" Amelia said dreamily.

The lilies stretched on ahead of them into the darkness, illuminated only by the light of the moon and the swinging lantern hanging from the bowsprit of the *Cal Meridian*. Darcy noticed a black smudge on the horizon and said, "We're coming up on the island."

"Through lily fields," Lewis said meaningfully.

The light of the lantern illuminated a few feet beneath the surface, revealing tangles of vines undulating and swaying in the current.

"Sir!" A sailor came panting up the stairs and approached Boreas. "Sir, the rowers can't row anymore. The oars keep getting befouled by the vines!"

"Tell them to keep trying. We're approaching land. If we don't reverse our momentum, we'll run aground!"

"Yes, sir!" The sailor ducked out of sight.

"Rubidius!" Boreas swung around, but the old alchemist merely shook his bent head. Sweat stood out in beads on his forehead.

Darcy's eyes slid from Rubidius back to the water beneath the swinging lantern, and she watched as a thick vine lying atop a lily pad twitched and slid into the water at their approach. Darcy's mouth popped open and she looked harder at the vines just beneath the surface. "Snakes," she whispered.

Sam looked at her. "What?"

"They're snakes, look!"

Swimming through the vines with bead-black eyes were hundreds of water snakes. Sam gave a shudder of horror and dug her nails into Darcy's arm as Amelia paled and stepped back from the railing.

"I don't do snakes," she whispered hoarsely.

The sailor taking the soundings gave a shout as a black, oily-looking serpent slithered up his rope. He dropped it as if it was on fire, and rope and snake disappeared beneath the surface. "Sorry, Cap'n," he said nervously.

Boreas swung his head from side to side. "It's no use. We're going to crash." He strode to look down at the main deck. "Pull in the keel!"

Their momentum had increased with the failure of the rowers to continue fighting against the current. At Boreas's words, Rubidius slumped forward against the railing and would have slid to the deck had Wal not sped to his side to support him.

The alchemist's face was pale, and he murmured as Wal helped him to stand, "There is some magic implicit in this. It's too strong; I can't fight it any longer."

The speed of the *Cal Meridian* increased even more, and the darkness loomed closer than ever. Tellius strode to the bowsprit and stretched out his hand, the fire in the lantern flaring brighter at his command. The expanded halo of light revealed that the dark chunk of land was about to flank them. The bottom of the ship scraped against land, and the hull shuddered as they were shot into a channel filled so thickly with water lilies that the water looked white.

"Brace yourselves!" Boreas shouted as the ship bottomed out yet again.

Darcy and the rest of them crouched against the railing. The sky was beginning to turn gray with morning light, illuminating that they had been pulled into a broad river by the current that sucked in rather than spewed out.

The *Cal Meridian* shuddered and groaned as it slid over a sandbar, its momentum carrying them another hundred yards before the ship fishtailed to the side with a loud crunch. The current continued to push until the ship swung around backward and slammed into another barrier of rocks. With a final groan and quiver, the vessel came to a stop, keeled over at a twenty-degree angle and stuck solidly in the bed of the river.

The current ceased, and the lily-filled waters stilled like the rest of the sea within the archipelago. Darcy had the horrible sensation of being caught around the ankle like a baited animal, yanked into a cage and secured for the hunter to find.

Her body recoiled as she watched the first snake slide up and over the side.

CHAPTER 24
CORONEIA

Amelia whimpered and clung to Lewis as Sam shrieked and attempted to scale Darcy's shoulders. Darcy, uncertain and disoriented after the beating the ship had taken, began sliding down the tilted deck toward the lower end, where the snakes were growing in number.

"Stop, Sam! *Get off!*" Darcy scrambled to catch her feet under her and stop her slide down the deck.

Chaos erupted, swords and knives flying, as the sailors began to stomp and beat at the snakes that were sliding up through the railings in an ever-increasing wave. Darcy freed herself from Sam, who promptly scrambled up on the platform by the wheel. Darcy snagged a hanging rope to pull herself to her feet, and she kicked out at a black serpent hissing its way toward her foot, managing to knock it back down the deck into the teeming masses of its kin. Darcy used the rope to pull herself to stand on the railing between the wheel and the drop to the main deck below. Offering a hand to Sam, she hefted the girl to stand beside her and shouted at her to hold onto the rope, too.

Darcy eyed the chaos from her new vantage point, thinking frantically that their ship would be overcome in minutes. Some of the sailors were flicking their hands, causing snakes to fly away back to the bottom of the ship, and she gasped.

"Earth magic," Darcy whispered as she glanced to the bowsprit, looking for Rubidius, but the alchemist was slung unconscious over Wal's shoulder. It was almost changing time for Wal, but he continued stomping at the snakes around his feet, even as he shot wary glances to the horizon. Darcy spotted Tellius standing atop the railing, clinging to a jib and staring at the mass of snakes, his mouth twisting violently.

"Tellius!" she screamed. "Fire!"

He looked up, searching for her voice, and she waved at him, catching his attention. "*Fire!*" she screamed again.

His eyes went wide and he shot his hand out toward the dangling lantern. The flames flickered toward him, beating against their glass cage. Darcy concentrated hard on the cage. She felt the catch release with a click, and the flames flew into Tellius's outstretched hand. He waved toward the water below, pushing it shoreward and dragging many of the serpents with it. Darcy flicked her fingers, deflecting the serpents now climbing toward her and Sam's feet as she generated a wind, swinging it above her head. The shimmery particles of air danced to life before her eyes, and she blew into them, sending them toward Tellius to lend oxygen to his fire, his flames leaping higher.

A circlet of bright golden light cracked and flashed about them, encircling Darcy and Tellius as it had Darcy and Rubidius so many months ago. The coroneia pulsed against their chests, contracting into a golden disc and then expanding with a soft sonic boom, golden light rippling like a still pond disrupted by a pebble.

Darcy's fatigue vanished. She hopped down from the railing and advanced on the wave of serpents, many of them now lying stunned or mangled on the deck. She seized on them again and again with her earth magic, forcing the tenacious few that remained to retreat back into the river. Tellius descended to the lower deck, blasting with fireballs anything that wriggled, and Darcy watched him in admiration. She had never seen him so powerful.

Darcy gasped as she felt a sting of pain at her ankle. A tiny black snake slithered over her foot and she shook her leg violently to detach it. The snake went flying through the air and over the deck, leaving two bloody pinpricks on her ankle.

Tellius formed a lasso of fire in the air and called everyone to his side.

"We have to get off the ship!" he shouted. "I can hold the fire around us until we get to shore, but we must hurry!" He expanded the loop of fire to encompass the whole crew of fifty people, and Darcy joined them on the lower deck. The deck was badly listing to the side, but Tellius managed to lower the lasso and let it drop to the water as sailors began to clamber over the railing. Although the *Cal Meridian* had grounded, the water was too deep to stand, and the two coracles hanging off the side of the ship were lowered for Darcy and the rest of the teenagers.

Tellius sat in the coracle with Darcy, concentrating on his fire as the sailors treading water around them began to push them toward shore. The snakes fled from the flames as they hissed along the water. Darcy sagged back against the edge of the coracle, suddenly dizzy. All the strength that had come to her through the coroneia seemed to have fled. She gasped to catch her breath, and her aching arms dropped useless to her lap.

As they gained shallower water, the sailors splashed ashore in disorganized chaos. The coracles ground into the riverbed, and Darcy and the others sprang out and hurried the several feet to shore. Darcy's legs wobbled, and she leaned against Sam as they ran, but she pressed on. They didn't stop until they were well up the bank, away from the snake-infested waters.

Once everyone was ashore, Tellius let his fire flicker out, and he collapsed, exhausted, to the bank. Darcy watched, horrified and spellbound, as a fresh tide of black snakes swept up and over the *Cal Meridian*, carpeting the ship in an undulating mass.

Darcy's vision blurred and she wondered if she was crying. She touched her face, but her cheeks were dry. Unable to hold herself upright any longer, she listed to the side and then keeled over backward, dimly aware of her head hitting the grassy slope. The early morning sky flickered into darkness.

"She should not be alive . . ."

"—cursed by the gods."

Darcy struggled to place the strange accents through the buzzing in her ears.

"Erpeto is angry . . ."

"All the others have died."

" . . . how much longer?"

She was burning up. She couldn't move. Hands pulled and prodded at her.

"No way to know . . ."

She drifted again into a black, dreamless night.

"She's coming out of it again. Go fetch Rubidius!"

A starburst of light exploded in her head. Pain—excruciating—radiated from her ankle. She raked in a hoarse breath that burned her lungs and made her cough spastically. Her vision was blurred, and she shook as she cracked open her eyes. The colors swam together above her. She was inside . . . a tent, it looked like a red tent. She closed her eyes and the light went out.

A flutter of movement sent a breeze wafting over her face. She flinched; it was bitterly cold against her burning skin. She opened her eyes again. Rubidius's skewed face swam into view. His mouth moved, forming her name, but the sound came to her ears as through a swimming pool. He placed an icy hand against her forehead. She moaned and shifted away from him, her body going limp with the effort. She was dying. She could feel her spirit leaving her body.

"Leeeave . . . ussshhh," Rubidius's soupy voice sounded again in her ears.

She closed her eyes to shut out the colorful glare of the room. Rubidius picked up her hand, and needles of pain shot through it. He muttered something in another language, and her ankle seared in pain. She gasped, her eyes flying open again. Rubidius knelt at her side, clasping her left hand and rocking back and forth, muttering under his breath. Darcy tried to wheeze out a protest, to tell him to stop, that he was hurting her, but she couldn't make a sound.

Rubidius muttered louder and more insistently, and then he collapsed to the floor beside her. Darcy's insides wrenched and twisted, feeling as though she were being tugged from the inside out. She groaned, arched her back, and then lost consciousness.

Darcy sat bolt upright in bed and then lowered herself back down, her head swimming. "I'm thirsty," she croaked.

"Darcy!" Sam fumbled for Darcy's hand, lifting her wrist to check her pulse. Sam dropped her wrist, and a breeze blew in as Sam raised the tent flap and called, "Amelia! Lewis! Tellius! She's up!" The tent flap fell, and Sam's shadow sped away.

Darcy licked her dry lips and turned her head to the other side. Lying on a bed beside her was Rubidius, unconscious or sleeping, his face tinged green. He was breathing in very shallow breaths.

Darcy struggled to sit up again. She didn't want to be flat on her back if a bunch of people were coming to see her. She managed to hoist herself into an elevated position with her back against the headboard, and then she stopped to catch her breath and calm her heart rate, waiting for Sam to reappear with everybody else. She looked down at her foot. Tossing aside the blanket that had been thrown over her, she could see a baseball-sized ring of greenish flesh around the two puncture wounds left by the snake's fangs on her ankle, spidery black veins radiating out from the spot. Darcy dropped her head back against the headboard, holding back the heaving of her stomach.

The tent flap opened wide, letting in a ray of sunlight. Tellius entered first, his face very grim, and Perry jogged in on his heels, out of breath. He started toward her side, but stopped as Sam ducked in with Amelia, Lewis, and a man that Darcy didn't know who was dressed in a grass skirt, his skin caramel-colored and sunkissed, his hair in tight dark curls.

"Darcy, this is Therapi; he's the village healer," Sam said. "He's going to take a look at you, okay?"

Therapi drew closer, an intense expression in his almond-shaped blue eyes. He leaned over Darcy's foot and gently squeezed her ankle in several places. The scent of sweet hibiscus flowers and sun-baked clay washed over her.

"Okay, yes? Pain?" His accent was thick.

"No . . . not a lot," Darcy said. "It feels a little . . . stiff and sore, but not really painful."

"Ahhh!" Therapi smiled, showing a wide mouth full of yellowed teeth.

"Good!" He gestured behind him. "She may have water. Only a little bit." He stepped aside to allow Sam to come forward with a wooden cup of water, chuckling to himself and looking at Darcy in awe.

Darcy took a sip of the cool water and let it flow down her throat, puzzled as to what was going on. She knew she had almost died, and she remembered Rubidius doing something to bring her back . . . She shot another troubled gaze at the alchemist lying prone in the next bed. She wondered how long they had been on the island. She could see the islanders were friendly . . . of course, that didn't mean much; the Theanisians had been friendly, too.

Darcy lowered the cup and looked at her friends. They were watching her with tense expressions, as though they expected her to fall over dead at any minute. "Where are we?" she rasped.

Sam looked at Therapi, who had moved to Rubidius's side and was checking the old man's pulse and listening to his heart by laying his head on Rubidius's chest. "This island is called Nofaronisi."

"Nisi?" Darcy raised her eyebrows.

"Nisi is the Old Alitheian word for *island*," Tellius said. "These islanders, too, have Old Alitheian stock. Some even speak our language," he gestured to Therapi, "but it's a secondary tongue for them."

Darcy cleared her throat. "You seem to know a lot about this place."

Tellius exchanged looks with the others. "We've been here for three and a half weeks," he said.

Darcy had half-expected that, but hearing it out loud still gave her pause. Therapi made a clicking noise with his tongue and came back over to her. He looked inside her cup and said, "Drink! I will be back," before ducking out of the tent.

"Three and a half weeks," Darcy said, taking another swallow of water and licking her lips. "And I've been sick this whole time?"

"You should have died," Sam said. "Nobody knows why you didn't."

"Rubidius knew something," Amelia said.

Darcy's face contorted. "*Knew* something? He's not dead," she said, looking over at him again. "He saved my life. Do any of you know how?"

"No," Sam answered. "The last time you woke up—a few days ago—he made us all leave the tent. All we know is one moment you were almost dead, and then the next, *he* was found on the floor by your bed, and you were sleeping peacefully. Your fever had broken and everything! It's like . . . it's like he took your sickness into himself, or something." Sam swallowed hard.

"He'd been working on something for several days," Tellius said. "He'd shut himself up in his cottage, brewing potions. I think he drank one of them before he did—*this,*" he gestured to Rubidius.

Darcy looked up. "How did he get his cottage here? Was somebody able to go back to the *Cal Meridian?*"

"The ship is . . . well, let's just say we can't reach it," Sam said. "Captain Boreas has been searching for a way, but the snakes are everywhere. Even at a distance you can see they've infested it, and he's not willing to risk any more of his men." She shook her head. "We don't know how we're going to get out of here. I'm just thankful the islanders have been welcoming to us."

"But, his cottage—"

"He keeps his front door in a pouch at his waist when he's travelling," Tellius said.

Darcy closed her eyes and pinched the bridge of her nose, trying to recall half-remembered images. "I heard them say all the *others* were dead . . . and the gods being angry—or—or cursing me, or something."

"The others were the sailors who were bitten. We—we lost ten men, I think. They all died within twenty-four hours, and we expected you to do the same," Amelia said.

Darcy blinked at them. "Where's Dean?" she asked, finally coherent enough to note his absence.

"He's fine, don't worry!" Sam said. "He's using his talent and scouting out the island. We think we might know where the Oracle is, based on the islanders' old superstitions. Dean went to check it out with Bayard and a couple of the sailors; they've been gone for a few days."

"Aren't you worried that the Oracle might trap them? He shouldn't have gone without me!"

Amelia snorted. "And what could you have done to help them? Even if you weren't lying here half-dead . . ."

"At least I know what to expect from the Oracle!"

"So does Rubidius," Amelia said. "But he didn't have a problem sending Dean to scout it out. He didn't think the Oracle would reveal itself unless forced to, and Dean and Bayard promised to be careful."

"So . . . what else do we know about these islanders?" Darcy asked.

"They're really superstitious," Sam said. "They've said over and over that *nobody* has ever survived a bite from the echidnas—the water serpents. They . . . how would you put it?" Sam looked to the others for help.

"They both revere them and fear them," Tellius supplied.

"They worship a whole host of gods," Lewis said, "but their chief god—goddess, actually—is a representation of the echidnas. They call her Erpeto, the Great Echidna."

Amelia shuddered. "I don't know *how* they can worship these horrible snakes!"

"I think they believe worshipping them keeps them from swarming the island," Lewis said.

"Erpeto actually demands a sacrifice of one hundred echidnas every year at the winter solstice," Sam said.

"Let me guess," Darcy said. "After they sacrifice them, they eat them?"

"Yep."

" 'To serpent-eaters,' " Lewis quoted from the oracle.

"Well, at least we know we're in the right place," Darcy said.

They all nodded.

"That's how they found us, actually," Perry said. "They hold their festival down by the water, and they were sleeping off the feast when they heard our commotion. They saw Tellius's fire," he nodded at the prince, "and thought at first he was a god. Rubidius had to explain about elemental magic and everything—"

"It's odd," Sam said. "Because all of them *should* have innate magical talents, too, but it's like they've forgotten. They explain everything supernatural as having come from a god or goddess. I don't think they believe Rubidius about the elements, because they treat Tellius like he's really special, and now that you've survived the echidna bite . . ."

"They might think you're a goddess, too," Tellius finished. "At first there was a great quarrel in the village over whether we were cursed by the gods or blessed by them, because a lot of us died, but a lot of us escaped being bitten. I think many of them had been waiting to see if you lived or died before they made up their minds."

"So, they don't practice magic at all?" Darcy asked. "But you said that Therapi was a healer."

"He is—but not the Alitheian kind. He's the local medicine man," Perry said. "He deals in herbal remedies and whatnot. He was really excited to meet Rubidius, because they were able to share with each other different herbs and stuff."

As if called on, Therapi reappeared in the tent carrying some broad leaves, a bowl of some kind of paste, and a length of fibrous rope.

"Good," he said, taking Darcy's empty cup from her. He handed it to the female islander who followed him in. She, too, was dressed in a grass skirt, and she wore a woven top and several strands of colorful beads around her neck. She stared at Darcy with wide, awe-filled eyes, and Darcy shifted uncomfortably.

Therapi handed the woman the leaves and the rope and then smeared some of the paste on Darcy's ankle. He took several leaves and wrapped them around her ankle, tying it all tight with the length of rope. "Now, you must sleep," he said when he was finished.

Darcy didn't feel tired at all. She felt alert now that she had spoken with her friends. Weakness from lack of nutrition was the only thing keeping her from climbing right out of the bed. She shook her head at Therapi. "I'm not tired," she insisted. "I've *been* sleeping!"

"Sleep," he insisted again, shooing her friends out of the tent.

They went with apologetic looks on their faces, except for Sam.

"Let me stay. I won't keep her up; I promise."

"Fine, fine," Therapi said. "The rest of you—out!"

Sam took a seat in the chair by Darcy's side and waited until Therapi, the islander woman, and all the others had filed out. Darcy shimmied down in her bed, resting her head on her arm and looking up at Sam.

"What's the deal, Sam?" Darcy asked after everybody had left. "Can we trust these people?"

"As far as I can tell, yes. I know I said the same thing on Theanisi, but this place is different," Sam whispered back. "Like I said, they're really superstitious and they were wary of us at first . . . which I prefer to the sort of welcome we received on Theanisi. Things were *too* perfect there; we should've known something was up. These people are genuine, and they *fear* their gods like they fear the snakes."

"Tell me about this place that Dean's gone to check out," Darcy said.

"Well, the Nofaronisians worship a lot of gods, right? And they believe there is a god that lives in the center of the island—which is pretty big, by the way. Their legends say that when this god came to the island several hundred years ago, he brought the snakes with him. The lily pads surround the entire island, and the snakes that live in them basically cut Nofaronisi off from the rest of the world. When the god came, the archipelago became —like it is—a sort of magical vortex where everything is confused and flipped."

"Several hundred years ago . . . But, the Oracle is older than that."

"Maybe it could move around at one time?" Sam suggested.

"It's a pillar of stone, Sam." But Darcy knew the Oracle was something much more complicated than that.

Sam shrugged. "I'm just telling you my theory. The islanders sure are afraid of it, whatever it is. They call him the Magus. In Old Alitheian it means the Wise Man—"

"But *the Oracle is not a man,* Sam!"

Sam threw up her hands. "Again, I'm just telling you what I've heard. The only time the Magus ever revealed himself to the people was when he first came, and he instructed them to leave him alone and stay away from the center of the island. Instead of wanting to be worshipped, he wanted to be shunned. He promised dire curses on them and their descendants if they disobeyed him, and nobody has seen him since."

"So how do they know this wasn't just some crazy old man who has long since died?"

"They don't. But the magic that came with him is still in place. That, and they're way too afraid to go and check. The whole center of the island is marked off with warning signs and talismans."

"But they're okay with Dean and Bayard going to scope it out?"

Sam smiled. "We didn't exactly tell them where they were going. They're supposed to be heading around the coast, looking for a way through the lily pads."

Despite Darcy's firm determination to stay awake, she was overcome by a huge yawn.

"Take a nap, Darcy," Sam said, patting her on the arm as a mother would. "I promised I wouldn't keep you up."

"I need to get better—*fast*," Darcy insisted, her eyelids drooping.

"Well, resting will help you do that. I'll wake you up in a few hours for some soup."

Darcy watched Sam settle back in her chair and let her eyes drift closed.

CHAPTER 25

BEHIND THE CURTAIN

Four days felt like four months to Darcy as she lay in bed, waiting for Dean's company to return with their report. At long last, Dean returned with Bayard and the sailors to tell everyone about what he had found.

Heading due east from the village's shrine of Erpeto had led them to the first barrier. Overcoming the barrier and continuing inland, they'd found several more talisman warnings, but no people. They'd penetrated to the interior of the island, which sloped gently upward to a low volcanic peak. The terrain was covered in tall, bristly grass and palm-like trees with heavy limbs covered in knots and scissor-like fronds. Several hours' hiking had brought them within sight of a strange dwelling that was heavily warded. All their attempts to gain access to it had left them disoriented; they'd never managed to get closer than two hundred yards before being involuntarily turned around.

"So, we just hung out for a few days and observed," Dean said. "Nobody ever showed themselves, so we eventually came on back."

"Wow," Sam said, her mouth hanging open.

"Good to have you back, man," Perry said, clapping Dean on the shoulder and grinning.

Darcy listened, taking care to appear merely curious, though her mind began to reel.

Three days after Dean's report, Darcy was strong enough to walk. She tested her leg carefully and, aside from the lingering stiffness, it felt okay. She dressed herself in the linen shirt and pants that had been left for her— clothes that must be reserved for the infirm, as Rubidius had been changed into similar attire. She cast a last look at him, lying in his bed, and stepped outside the tent.

She knew roughly where she was headed, as Sam had given her a lesson in the layout of the village, but she nonetheless stood and stared about her in wonder. The early morning air was cool and some of the nighttime insects were still chirping. All of the village tents were a salmon-red color —the same color as the volcanic rocks strewn as far as she could see. They were far enough from the river inlet that it looked to Darcy like a twinkling silver ribbon far off down the hillside, the wreckage of the *Cal Meridian* invisible from the village.

Darcy hoped she had risen early enough. Sam and Amelia should still have been sleeping, and she felt confident enough that she'd beaten the boys to waking as well. The only people she could see were some women outside who looked to be preparing food. Those nearest looked up at her, some with a hint of fear, but they didn't engage her. There was something reverential in the way they looked at her and, had Darcy had the time, she would have told them to save their deference.

Darcy counted the tents to her right and found the one Sam had told her was Rubidius's. She loped that direction and ducked inside the tent flap, relaxing as it fell closed behind her.

Aside from an unused bed, the only thing in Rubidius's tent was his door, which he'd set up between two support posts. Darcy crossed to it, unlocking it as she had on Theanisi, much faster now that she knew what she was doing.

The inside of his cottage was freezing cold, the temperature outside in Alitheia typical for late-January. Darcy looked around, feeling suddenly lost. She closed her eyes and forced herself to think.

"Survival gear," she told herself, concentrating on scanning the room for anything that might help her rescue Yahto Veli and survive the Oracle.

A leather pack sat in the middle of the table, and Darcy snatched it up, thinking it was rather convenient to find one there, empty and ready for her.

But the pack wasn't empty. Darcy dug around in it to find the items within were familiar.

"What the—this is *my* pack!" She upended it, and a note fell out along with two books, her compact, her throwing knife, and a comb. Darcy picked up the note written in Rubidius's handwriting. She pulled a chair out, sat down, and read.

I have no doubt concerning the course of action you have chosen to take, and while I would discourage you from doing it alone, I begin to think that alone may be the only chance of success that you have.

If you are reading this, I have successfully performed the enchantment which allowed me to draw your illness into myself ~ or enough of it that you were able to recover fully. I took pains to prepare myself with a potent batch of strength potion to give my body a chance to fight off the infection. I would be much appreciative if you would leave the bottle, which you will find beside my washbasin, with instructions to administer it to me three times daily while I am convalescing.

Now to the matter at hand, I am sure by this time you have gained from the scouts the location of the anomaly at the center of this island. It is, I am certain, the entrance to the Oracle's lair, and I have further concluded that only you may have success of breaching the wards and entering the Oracle's presence. Know this:

The bond formed with the Oracle in the exchange of payment for answer is a magical covenant, and such covenants have rules. Voitto's oracle tells us of a 'broken bond of covenant,' and you, Darcy, are the one against whom the covenant has been broken. The Oracle has committed a magical offense. Your need for justice shall pull you through the wards, and Yahto Veli, too, will be freed by his need for satisfaction. This magic abides deeper than anything the Oracle can manipulate.

I leave you with your pack. Take the knife, as well as anything practical you think you could use. Should you desire it, you will find your sword on top of the hearth. I pray for your success and hope that we shall meet again.

Consider the bone whistle Yahto took with him into the lair, and use what you know to your advantage.

~R.

Darcy folded the note carefully and tucked it away in her pack. Rubidius had known what she would do, and he had not forbidden her from doing it. In fact, he had completed the puzzle and confirmed she was the only one who *could* do it—if his theories were correct. And they usually were.

She left the compact, books, and comb on his table, knowing they would be safe. She strapped the knife to her ankle and pulled her linen pant leg down to cover it. Then she filled a canteen with water from his pump and put the canteen in her pack. From the rafters she grabbed a few herbs that she knew to be restoratives and found a hunk of cheese and some nuts in the cupboard. She caught a glimpse of a large spool of string on a shelf, and she tossed it in her pack as well.

Once everything was shoved haphazardly in her bag, she found a piece of parchment and scribbled a note to Sam, explaining where she had gone and asking her to administer the strength potion to Rubidius three times a day. Lastly, she removed her sword from the mantelpiece and strapped it around her waist.

Darcy exited the cottage and locked the door behind her. She dumped the note and the bottle of potion onto the unused cot in Rubidius's tent, certain they would find it when they searched the village for her. After peeking out of the tent and finding the coast clear, she jogged to the tree line at the outskirts of the village and began to edge her way around to the shrine of Erpeto—visible in the distance beneath a tall statue of a rearing snake. Reaching the shrine in about ten minutes' time, Darcy took her bearing from the rising sun and plunged into the forest, heading due east.

The first barrier was a hedge of thorns, and though Darcy hacked away at it with her sword, the limbs were thick as young saplings, and she couldn't force an entrance point. Giving up, she tossed her pack up and over the hedge and climbed a tree that stood close to the briars—a sort of cross between a palm tree and an oak with stout, spreading branches and pointed, fan-like leaves. Once she clambered into the upper limbs, she edged out onto one that hung over the briars. After getting shakily to her knees, she let her legs drop as she caught the limb in her armpits. Her feet still about five feet off the ground, she let her arms slide down until she was hanging on with her fingers, and then she pumped her legs to swing herself forward and dropped.

She hit the ground and fell to her knees. Her ankle protested weakly, but she stood, grinning, thankful for the adrenaline flowing through her. From the position of the sun, she could tell it was well into the morning now, and she expected to hear shouts of pursuit from her friends at any moment. Dean, at least, would know exactly where she'd gone.

She brushed herself off, retrieved her pack, and continued trudging east. On a tree just past the thorn barrier was nailed a sign painted with an abstract face grimacing grotesquely, and words in a language Darcy couldn't understand, although she was sure they said to stay away. Darcy smiled grimly and continued on.

The forest was sparse, and she frequently found herself walking through exposed clearings of the tall, spiky grass Dean had mentioned. In the open spaces she could make out the gentle slope of the volcanic hillside, and she often had to correct her course to continue walking due east. The forest was teeming with exotic birds and insects—enormous creepy, crawly things, some of them bigger than her hand, that scattered before her heavy, purposeful strides.

Darcy decided not to stop for lunch as the sun climbed to the center of the sky. She had no desire to sit down with all the bugs, and she was still nervous about being caught and taken back to the village. Instead, she grabbed a handful of the nuts she'd taken from Rubidius's cottage and took a swig of water from her canteen.

She approached another talisman warning, this one a cross made out of old snake skeletons, the bones bleached white long ago by the sun. Beyond it stood a post covered in red paint with another dire warning scrawled in Nofaronisian. A snicker burst out of her, but she quickly suppressed it and picked up her pace. With as many horrors as she'd seen on this journey, a few scary signs weren't going to spook her.

About mid-afternoon Darcy arrived at the edge of the sparse forest. Before her the hillside stretched up toward the low summit in a field of grass. She stopped for the first time and dropped to her knee. Resting there, she took a look around for the dwelling Dean had mentioned, but she couldn't see anything matching its description and knew she must have wandered off course.

Still crouching, she ran her hand over the rocks and reddish shards of clay around her feet and scooped up a handful. She sifted through them, looking for one that might be of use to her. Finding none, she continued to search as she worked her way along the edge of the tree line.

Just inside the trees about a quarter mile north of where she'd come out of the forest, she came upon an area of ground that had been cleared of the tufty grass. Glimpsing the clear remains of a fire pit, she knew this must have been the scouts' camp.

"Back on track." Relieved, she tromped over to the fire pit. They had lined it with smooth white stones, and Darcy quickly spotted one that was long and narrow and looked sturdy enough. She opened her pack and removed the large spool of string. After tying the end around the narrowest part of the rock, she yanked the knot tight so it wouldn't slide off. She swung the little contraption around to test its durability and, satisfied, reached up to catch the rock in mid-arc. She put the spool back in her pack and tucked the rock into the waist of her pants, so it looked as though she had a string attaching the pack to her waist.

Feeling confident, Darcy returned to the edge of the trees and faced the summit. She looked around, spinning in a complete circle, still unable to see anything that resembled the dwelling Dean had described. She bit her lip, squinting in the distance, her heart beginning to pound.

"Where is it?" She stomped her foot and turning her gaze to the sky. A gorgeously colorful exotic forest bird flew over her head, winging toward the mountain. Nearly at the summit, it recoiled like a bird who has flown into a window, and flapped away, shedding feathers and shrieking.

As the air echoed with the bird's distressed caws, the invisible thing it had struck flickered into view.

Darcy smirked, thinking this guy should have taken a lesson from Rubidius on how to properly cloak a building.

It was formed like an igloo of stones, with no windows or doors that Darcy could see from her angle. It rested about two hundred and fifty yards further up the mountain, close to the summit. The only thing betraying that someone actually lived there was a narrow chimney poking out the top through which a thin stream of smoke was billowing.

Darcy took a deep breath and let it out slowly. It was time to find out who —or what—this "Magus" was and what he had to do with the Oracle. Darcy checked that she still had her string-tied stone tucked at her waist and then began her hike to the structure.

She'd taken twenty or thirty steps when she found herself facing the other direction. She froze, her eyebrows furrowed and her heart pounding. She hadn't felt herself get turned about. She turned on the spot to face the dwelling, and once again began her approach, taking long, determined strides. As her fifth footfall hit the ground, she found herself striding determinedly back toward the forest. She stopped and huffed a strand of hair out of her face. Putting her hands on her hips, she closed her eyes and tried to concentrate on what Rubidius had written to her.

Darcy turned once again to face the dwelling and held up her left palm, showing her scar.

"I've come to correct the wrong done against me! The covenantal magic was broken, and I am here for what is mine!" She smiled to herself, proud of how she phrased these words, rather like Tellius surely would have. She waited for something to happen, for the earth to move or a clap of thunder to sound, but everything remained still. The chimney continued trickling smoke, undisturbed, only the chirp of a bird puncturing the silence.

She sighed, stepping toward the structure again, and the world tilted upside down. She hung by her feet from the grassy slope, the sky a cavernous hole beneath her dangling head. Before she could let out a scream, her momentum carried her forward and the world righted itself. She gasped for air with her feet planted firmly on solid ground, two steps closer to the dwelling than she'd been before.

Darcy slapped a palm to her chest, as if she could slow her racing heart merely by pushing on it. She had made it through the wards.

Taking another hesitant step forward, fearful of finding herself once again dangling over a void of air and sky, Darcy advanced on the dwelling. The ground remained beneath her feet, and Darcy picked up the pace of her hike, soon reaching the dwelling.

The igloo-like structure was about the size of a small one-bedroom house, and the thin stream of smoke continued to curl upward from the narrow chimney. Darcy walked around to the far side and found a stoop and an arched stone frame of a doorway, but the door itself had been walled in with stones. She wondered if she should knock but then felt foolish for the thought. If this Magus fellow had walled in his doorway, he didn't want any visitors. Still, it seemed uncivilized not to announce her presence. She raised her hand and rapped her knuckles against the hard stones.

There was no response—not that Darcy had anticipated one.

She began to pull at the stones in the doorframe, digging her fingers between the cracks and prying them loose. She got a few to wiggle out, barely a start against the possible several feet of stones that stood before her. Her fingernails chipped and her knuckles raw, she dropped her arms to her sides.

She hadn't wanted to resort to magic. She'd wanted to save her full strength for the battle ahead. But, feeling it was the only way, she raised her hands and began pulling the rocks free with her magic. Watching them tumble into a pile at her feet, she continued until a dark open doorway stood before her.

The flickering light of a small fire within gave off little illumination, pale compared to the blazing sun outside. Darcy took a deep breath, pulled the stone from her waistband and held it in her hand, and ducked inside.

Thick, hot air hit her in the face, and she wiped a hand across her brow, already breaking a sweat. The stifling atmosphere was filled with the pungent aroma of burning herbs, and as her eyes adjusted to the dim interior, she saw the fire beneath the chimney hole in the center of the stone igloo. Above it hung a metal censer full of twigs and herbs, but no furniture decorated the space to indicate anyone might live here. Only a pile of rags lay close to the fire.

Darcy approached the heap and unsheathed her sword to poke at it. Her hand trembling, she raised her arm, holding her breath as she brought the sword point near the pile. She nudged the rags, and a sharp hiss issued from within as they shifted as though something moved beneath them.

Darcy jumped back, startled, ready for a snake to come slithering out. Instead, the rags shifted again and hunched up, looking almost like a small child moving into a sitting position. The folds of fabric slid down, and Darcy made out a mouth, grumbling, twisting, and snarling. Above it a nose appeared with nostrils flared. Finally, a pair of eyelids flipped open to reveal blank eyes, snowy white in blindness. She was looking at neither a pile of rags nor a sitting child, but an impossibly old man. His skin was stretched so tightly over his facial bones that he looked like a skeleton grinning up at her. His arms and legs were twigs upon which his loose skin hung, and tufts of white hair stood out atop his crown. His garb was a knotted toga of the dirty rags.

Darcy stared, wide-eyed and horrified.

"You—you're the Magus, yes?" She held her sword steady.

The old man turned his face from her. He raised a bony arm and wafted the fumes of the censer toward his nose, breathing deeply. "Yeeeessssss," he hissed. "How did yooouuuu get paasssst my wardssss?"

Darcy squared her shoulders and raised her chin. "I'm looking for the Oracle. It owes me something, and I know you have something to do with it."

"Yeeessssss . . ."

"Well . . . I demand to see it, then. Are you, like, its doorkeeper, or something?"

"Noooo."

"Then what—who—are you?"

"I am the Oooldeeessst, I am the Wiiissseeeesssst, I am the Mooossst Powwweeerfuuul. I am the Maguuussss."

Darcy snorted. This decrepit old man, alone in an igloo of rocks, wasn't exactly her idea of what the oldest, wisest, most powerful being in Orodreos should look like.

"I once met a dragon who was over three thousand years old. You can't be older than him," she said.

"Arrrchaaaiooossss . . . yeeessssss. I am ooooldeeer than himmm."

Some of Darcy's mirth disappeared, her smirk melting into a thin line. "So you've been around a while. What about Pateros? I *know* you're not older than he is."

The Magus pursed what was left of his lips and hissed again like one of his echidnas. He stood and hobbled away, facing the wall. Darcy assumed she'd made him upset, but it was his own fault. He wasn't older than Pateros—or wiser, or more powerful—and he knew it.

"How can I get to the Oracle's lair?" Darcy asked, though his back was still turned.

"Would yooouuuu like to sssspeeeaaaak with it?"

"Yes!"

"Ooone moment . . ."

Darcy looked around and waited, chewing on the inside of her cheek.

"What do you want, Darcy Pennington? Why have you disturbed my sanctuary?"

Darcy's heart rate shot up like a geyser, and she peered wildly around as the Oracle's voice boomed throughout the dwelling.

"Y—you know what I want . . . and why I have a right to be here!" she said. She spun around, but she couldn't tell from which direction the voice had come. The Magus gave a sickly cough, his face still to the wall.

"Tell me," the Oracle said. *"Give me a reason not to kill you where you stand."*

"Really?" Darcy forced a laugh. "You can't do that. You have no magical hold on me at all! I'm not one of your petitioners. I found your dwelling without the aid of your enchantment, and I've come back to get what is mine. You broke the covenantal magic, and you know it."

Darcy thought of the letter Rubidius had left her and what he'd said about Yahto Veli, and she took a deep breath.

"It seems curious that you required Yahto Veli to stay as payment when an object so powerfully magic as the bone whistle was within your grasp, doesn't it? But you didn't want Yahto Veli at all, did you? You wanted the whistle. You knew he had it, and to get it you deceived me into thinking you wanted the nark. Do you deny it?"

"*No.*" The Oracle's voice sounded matter-of-fact and not at all shocked as Darcy had expected it to.

"Then you must know what that means!" she insisted, throwing her hands up as she stood in the near-empty room. "You took two payments for one question, breaking the covenant and rendering your claim to Yahto Veli—*and* the bone whistle—null and void."

Darcy took a deep breath to steady herself. "In addition, you have violated the rights of Yahto Veli by holding him as payment in this invalid covenant. You must not only release him, but compensate him as well." *Satisfaction*, Rubidius had called it.

"*Must I?*" the Oracle teased, sounding genuinely amused.

"Yes. Because if you don't . . . I know what will happen to you. You *use* covenantal magic to your own advantage, but you did not *invent* it; it's part of the magical laws that hold all of Orodreos together. If you don't make this right, your power will fade."

Silence. Darcy held her breath.

"*You have shown great tenacity in coming so far.*"

"Don't flatter me." Darcy clenched her jaw. "I came for my friend, and I'm taking the bone whistle, too." She frowned. "Why did you do it? You had to know it would destroy you."

"*I am the oldest; nothing will destroy me!*" the Oracle shouted, enraged. Darcy flinched, but when she wasn't immediately struck dead, she smiled, knowing he couldn't hurt her.

"You two really have a bad case of megalomania, do you know that?" Darcy said, exasperated. "The Magus also said—"

"*Pay no attention to the Magus!*" The Oracle's voice shook. "*He is inconsequential.*"

Darcy stepped back as though physically struck, her head snapping to gawk at the Magus.

"No way . . ." she said. "This isn't—you're not—this is *The Wizard of Oz!*"

"*What is this foolishness you speak?*"

"I can't believe I didn't see it before." Darcy laughed out loud. "He's the man behind the curtain! *He's* the Oracle—*You're* him!" She raised her sword into the ready position and advanced on the Magus, pointing it at his back. "You're flesh and blood," she said to him. "You can be killed."

The Magus turned around, his milk-white eyes staring directly at her.

"Give me back what is mine, or I will kill you," Darcy said. "Goodness knows the world would be better off without you."

His mouth split into a malicious grin, and she hoped he couldn't sense that she was bluffing, that she could never kill an old man in cold blood, even a very wicked one.

The Magus opened his mouth to speak, and the voice of the Oracle poured forth. *"If you can find what you seek, it is yours to take."* With a gesture of his bony hand, the ground opened like a trapdoor beneath Darcy's feet and swallowed her up.

CHAPTER 26
THROUGH THE LABYRINTH

Darcy was ready. As the ground fell away beneath her, she chucked the rock she'd been clutching as hard as she could toward the far wall of the dwelling and let the string unravel on the spool as she fell.

With no magical transportation this time, she tumbled through a very real, very dirty, narrow, earthen chute. She hit the ground, rolled, and came to a halt as quickly as she could. Springing up and breathing hard, she checked the string emerging from the pack on her back. It stretched up above her head into the blackness of the hole through which she'd fallen. She tugged lightly on it, and it held firm. The hole had sealed itself off with her rock— her anchor—still on the other side.

"It worked." She silently thanked the mythological Ariadne, her inspiration for using the spool of thread to find her way back out. Brushing the dust from her hair and her clothes, she recalled Voitto Vesa's oracle. " 'Down the hole' . . . check," Darcy said, satisfied.

She shook her head, still reeling that for all these years people had speculated what the Oracle was, never imagining it was an old man sitting out in the middle of an island in a mysterious archipelago. But he couldn't be just a regular old man, or he would have been dead long ago . . .

Darcy ran a hand through her hair, shaking herself from the thought. She didn't know how much time the Oracle would give her to find Yahto Veli, and she didn't want to waste any of it. The last time she'd been here, seven months had passed topside in the span of Darcy's hour in the Oracle's lair.

How much time would pass for her this time? She didn't have seven months to spare.

"One thing at a time," she told herself. "Find Yahto Veli."

She turned a full circle. The hole had dumped her into a crossroads, and four tunnels stretched away into murky, yellowish light. Darcy ran through the words of the oracle again in her mind, but could find nothing further to guide her steps, *"Breath of life, breath-ed once"* being no help to her until she found the whistle.

"So, find the whistle first," Darcy reasoned. "It was probably *taken* from Yahto, which would explain why he never blew on it." She breathed a little easier as she pieced things together aloud; her courage renewed, she sheathed her sword, which she'd still been grasping in her right hand. "Eeney, Meeney, Miney, Mo," she muttered under her breath, turning another slow circle. Choosing a tunnel at random, she started down it at a jog.

Darcy hoped her string would last, finding quickly that the Oracle's galleries were far more vast than she'd guessed. Twenty feet down her chosen tunnel, it branched again, this time three ways, and she chose another one at random, still trailing the string behind her.

Several hundred feet down her selected path, Darcy noticed deep grooves on the walls of the tunnel, as though made by claws. A heavy and unpleasant smell wafted toward her, and she slowed to a stop, her heart beating fast. Perhaps not all of the Oracle's acquisitions were caged.

Darcy retraced her steps to the last junction, re-spooling her string as she went and choosing a different path. Down this new tunnel were shelves of books, ancient and musty with rotting spines and gilded titles in languages Darcy didn't understand. The rows of books continued without end for several hundred more feet, and Darcy stopped and began to retrace her steps again.

"This is ridiculous," she grumbled, returning to her last intersection and pausing to straighten the string on her spool. She couldn't search every branch of the maze. There had to be a way to go about it logically, but the murky silence of the cave system mocked her frustration.

"Think!" she ordered herself, pursing her lips. She considered where the Oracle would store the bone whistle—something it had wanted bad enough to risk its power. "If it were me, I'd keep it close," Darcy reasoned and began heading back the way she'd come. The epicenter of the Oracle's power, she figured, had to be near the center of the labyrinth; where better to put the heart of the labyrinth than right beneath the core of the volcanic peak? Going back to where she'd started would give her a point of reference for her location within the mountain.

She picked up the pace, winding faster, and reached the point where the end of her string disappeared into the ceiling. She positioned herself as she'd stood in the dwelling above, closed her eyes, and pictured what direction she'd be facing outside on the mountain.

"I had my back to the door," she reasoned, "and the door faced the summit. That means the tunnel to take should be . . ." She looked over her shoulder behind her. "That one."

Confident she was about to make progress, Darcy took off running. Her new passage branched almost immediately, and she chose the branch that kept closest to the direction of the summit. Down that corridor, the walls were filled with small cubbies fitted with bars, each of them containing a tiny, trapped creature: fairies staring listlessly, goblins raking their fingernails over the stone walls, sprites, gnomes, and a multitude of others Darcy couldn't discern for her rapid pace. Her eyes stung and she wiped a tear from her cheek, desperate to aid them but knowing she had no power to break their curses. Someone, at some point, had given them over as payment.

The tunnel branched again, and this time the branch she wanted proceeded down a few steps through a low arch where Darcy had to duck her head. At the bottom of the steps lay piles of gemstones, some of them as big as Darcy's fist, discarded and unwanted. The Oracle valued the obscure and the living much more highly than treasures; after all, what could the Magus do with treasure other than make miserable the people who had once owned it?

Past the piles of gems, the tunnel narrowed and veered away from the center of the mountain. Darcy stopped and bit her lip, wondering if she had chosen the wrong way and should turn back. With a hesitant glance over her shoulder, she kept on moving forward, slowing as the tunnel began turning in a wide spiral. Hoping it would terminate at the center of the labyrinth, she ignored all further branches in the tunnel and continued forward at a run.

The tunnel passed through a gallery of animals, and Darcy continued jogging, trying not to look into their doleful eyes. She inadvertently made eye contact with a dog lying just inside the bars, and she slowed to reach a hand out and brush its head. With a desperate snarl, the dog reared back and bared its teeth before releasing a piercing howl.

"*Hurry, oh brave one.*" The voice of the Oracle sounded throughout the cavern, taunting her. "*Your time above runs out, and there are beasts in my gallery who freely roam.*"

"Yeah?" Darcy tried to infuse bravado into her voice even as it quaked. "How about a little help? You need me to take my friend and the whistle off your hands just as badly as I need them back!"

The Oracle remained silent. Huffing under her breath, Darcy continued past the rows of animals.

"How far does this go?" she mumbled aloud after trudging along another few hundred yards of tunnel.

"*It is vast,*" the Oracle answered. "*It is the greatest treasure ever amassed.*"

"You call this treasure?" Darcy snorted and kicked at a goblet that had fallen from its shelf. "I call it pathetic!"

The walls around her rumbled, a few small rocks falling from the ceiling and pelting her on the head. Darcy bit her lip. "Sensitive, aren't you?" she muttered under her breath.

"You know," she said aloud, "if you wanted to, you could use your power for good. I'll bet you know *exactly* how to get rid of Tselloch."

The Oracle gave a hollow laugh. *"If you wanted to know that, you should have asked. I am not the only selfish one."*

Darcy scowled. That was not the direction she'd intended the conversation to go.

The tunnel widened and she sped up, bursting out into the cavernous chamber housing the rune-engraved stone pillar she'd once *thought* was the Oracle. It glowed with a weak yellow light between its cracks, giving the impression that it lit the entire tunnel system, but now that she'd seen how vast it was, she knew that was impossible.

She approached the stone with a satisfied smirk at having at least found *something* in this labyrinth. More than ten tunnels branched off from the chamber, but she felt certain the Oracle would have placed the whistle in the tunnel through which she'd entered when she'd come here the first time . . . if she could only remember which one that was.

Darcy jerked her head around at a slobbering, slurping sound coming from an opening on the far wall. Her jaw dropped as she eyed the creature that emerged. It had reptilian front legs, and a lizard-like tail sprouting above the rear legs of a lion. Long, humanoid arms and a muscular human chest gave way to the toothy grimacing face of a crocodile. Its eyes skittered to Darcy and it gave a piercing howl.

Darcy stumbled backward and dropped the spool of string. She was still scrambling to unsheathe her sword when, with three bounds of its powerful hind legs, the beast was upon her. Knocking her flat on her back, it raked its razor-sharp claws down her shoulders, pressing the air from her lungs as it sat on her chest. Its jaws opened wide as it lunged for her face, and Darcy squinted her eyes and let out a frantic shriek.

Air rushed into her lungs as the beast was plucked from her chest, and she stared, blinking, as it hung suspended by a gigantic black hand and then was whisked away down one of the far tunnels.

Darcy coughed and wheezed, heaving more air into her lungs as she sat upright and hugged her chest.

"Why—did you—save me?" she gasped.

"You already know," the Oracle responded, its voice silky and smooth. *"I had hoped for an entertaining fight, but you proved yourself to be . . . pathetic."*

Darcy winced at his use of the word she'd chosen just a short while ago to describe the Oracle's treasure trove.

"So you're just playing with me?" she asked bitterly. "I suppose this is really funny for you."

"*If I am to lose my treasures, I deserve some compensation, do I not?*"

"That's debatable," Darcy muttered, picking herself up. She winced and clutched at her bloody left shoulder and retrieved her spool of string.

"*You think you are very clever, don't you, Darcy Pennington?*"

"I don't know . . . a little, I guess." She shrugged.

"*The string. It is an old trick, and it is not yours.*"

Darcy froze, afraid the Oracle was insinuating that she was cheating. "Yeah, well I didn't want to spend half my life wandering around down here."

"*I have allowed it.*"

"Gee, thanks," Darcy grumbled. "Now if you don't mind . . ." She marched across the chamber and peered down each side tunnel, listening for a sound she knew she'd recognize when she heard it.

She lost count of how many tunnels she'd checked when she finally heard it: the low moans and deep sighs of regret. Darcy quickened her steps as she headed down the corridor, where on either side were large holding cells full of old, grizzled humans with oozing, dripping sores on their left palms. "*Those who would not pay,*" Darcy remembered, and she shivered, averting her eyes as the prisoners became aware of her.

They began throwing themselves against the bars, wailing and pleading with her to speak to the Oracle for them, to reason with it, that they would pay, that they had learned their lesson, that they were sorry . . . Darcy swallowed the lump in her throat. The smell coming off their sores made her nauseous. She walked down the middle of the passageway, just out of reach of the prisoners' grasping hands, finally reaching the end of their gallery and clambering into the next.

She hurried through the display of glass bottles containing rolled bits of parchment—the collected promises—giving them hardly a second glance, her mind only on finding the bone whistle.

Beyond the last bottled promise was the final portion of the gallery, where the Oracle stored the oddments and creatures and disfigured beasts it had collected. Darcy began approaching each cell, grabbing the bars and peering inside, her eyes peeled for the small bone whistle on its leather thong. Her heart pounded harder with each cage she searched, and as her eyes raked over a creature in a cell halfway down the corridor, she stopped short with a gasp.

Sitting just feet from her, on a stone bench in a cell no bigger than a bathroom stall, was Yahto Veli.

CHAPTER 27

THE OATH OF SERVICE

Darcy fell to her knees before Yahto Veli's cage. He sat with his arms resting listlessly at his sides and his chin against his chest. His light blond hair hung lank and matted down around his shoulders; it must be daytime up above—whatever day it was.

"Veli!" Darcy stretched her arm through the bars and reached for him, but he made no movement or sound, frozen in a state of enchanted dejectedness.

She thought he would at least recognize her voice, and her eyes stung as she wondered if maybe he hated her. She was the one who had done this to him.

"Veli, *please*, look at me. It's me—Darcy," she tried again. Her hand brushed his leg and he shifted his head ever so slightly to look down at it.

Darcy pulled her arm back and grasped the bars with both her hands, trying to shake them, but they were immovable. "If I can—get—you—*out of here*," she gasped, pounding her fists against the bars, "you'll be okay; I know it!"

Veli made no move, only continued to look down.

Darcy beat at the bars once more and then collapsed to the floor, exhausted and desperate, tears streaming down her cheeks.

"Amused now?" she asked the Oracle.

"*Quite*," he responded immediately.

Veli looked up at the sound of the Oracle's voice, his long pointed ears remaining droopy. Darcy straightened, alert for a sign of recognition, but still he gave none. She leaned closer to peer at his face, and he looked . . . older . . . *years* older. Crow's feet radiated from the corners of his eyes, and lines creased skin that now looked dull, lacking the elasticity of youth. Silver threads, barely visible in the blond, ran through his hair.

As she watched him, his skin and hair darkened, as if he'd stepped into a shadow. "What—" Darcy choked as he changed from day nark to night nark, from Veli to Yahto, right before her eyes.

She supposed it could be nighttime already, as she'd no idea how quickly time was passing outside of this enchanted place. She sobbed as she took in Yahto's appearance, his aging even more apparent with the coarse silver streaks radiating from his temples back through his pitch-black hair.

"How long has it *been?*" Darcy whispered. "It's only been two years . . ."

"*I do not follow your rules of timekeeping,*" the Oracle replied haughtily. "*Minutes to my petitioners may pass as years for my pets.*"

Darcy's stomach heaved and she clapped a hand over her mouth to keep from vomiting. It hadn't just *felt* like so many years to Yahto Veli, she thought; it had actually *been* so many years.

"Why?" she whispered. "Why do you do this? So they can die more quickly?"

"*They do not die,*" the Oracle responded. "*They age forever and never pass on.*"

"Like you?" Darcy asked, imagining the Magus's decrepit old body.

The tunnel echoed with the Oracle's silence.

Darcy rocked back on her heels and stared at her dear friend who had offered up his life to save hers. "I have to get you out of there," she murmured, brushing tears from her cheeks. Yahto's eyelids flickered, his hair lightening in an instant, and she was looking back at Veli. She hiccupped back a sob.

"I'll *be right back,*" she said, getting to her feet. She didn't expect a response. Leaving her pack and the spool of string on the floor before his cage, she hurried further into the tunnel and began again to search the piles for the bone whistle.

"Please be here; please be here," she whispered over and over as she pored over the piles of bits and bobs, some of it neatly displayed on shelves and in alcoves, some of it tossed haphazardly in heaps. She'd thought surely the Oracle would display such a valuable treasure. "But not if he wanted to make it difficult for me."

Darcy closed her eyes and put her hands on her hips, trying to slow her pounding heart and think. Her eyes flew open and her nostrils flared. "Earth magic."

But she'd never tried anything like that before—not when she couldn't see the object and didn't even know if it was there. But she had gotten stronger, and she knew it was possible. She'd seen Rubidius summon things out of his cupboards countless times.

Squinting her eyes shut, Darcy imagined the bone whistle, feeling its contours and smoothness and its rough leather strap. She felt around the cavern with her mind, her earth sense searching for the familiar particles, for anything she could grasp onto.

Her subconscious brushed against the known shape—the smooth, flattened curve. Opening her eyes slowly, so as not to break her concentration, Darcy held out her hand in the direction of the familiar touch and pulled. A loud clanging rattle disturbed the silence in the tunnel as the whistle lifted from the center of a pile of metal objects and soared directly into her hand.

"Yes!" Darcy grasped the whistle in her shaking hand and hurried back to the cage, finding Yahto once again.

" 'Breath of life,' " she quoted, " 'breath-ed once.' Okay, I guess I've got one shot." She put the whistle to her lips, took a deep breath, and blew, hard.

The whistle reached a pitch almost outside her hearing range but well within the range of a nark. Yahto flinched, a stronger reaction than he'd shown to any of her pleas, and he covered his ears with his hands. Life flickered in the depths of his eyes, yet he still he looked at her without recognition. With a great crunching sound, the bars of his cage crumbled and dissolved into powder, the walls of the tunnel shaking violently.

"*Enough!*" The voice of the Oracle roared through the chamber, and Darcy yanked the whistle from her mouth, her lungs devoid of air. The shaking stopped, the dust settled, and still Yahto Veli sat.

Darcy slung the leather thong of the whistle around her neck and tucked it out of sight down her shirt before moving hesitantly into the cell. She placed a gentle hand on Yahto Veli's shoulder, and he looked at it, and then up at her.

"Yahto?" she murmured. "Do you know me?"

His eyebrows furrowed in confusion, and his whole body trembled. He opened his mouth, and his lips parted tackily, as though he hadn't spoken in years. He tried to form a word, but he made no sound.

"Come on," Darcy said, sighing. "Let's get you out of here."

She offered her hand to him, and he stared at it before placing his hand in hers and allowing her to haul him to his feet. He stumbled against her, and she slung his arm about her shoulder, feeling strange and awkward helping him to stand and walk; Yahto Veli had always been the strong one, so capable and wise.

Darcy took two laborious steps out of the cell, and Yahto imitated her movements, holding himself up on shaking legs. Darcy's injured shoulders screamed out in protest as she bent to retrieve her pack while supporting Yahto's weight. She left the spool behind on the stone floor and began to follow it out.

Darcy moved very slowly to match Yahto's crawling pace—Veli now, as she watched him transition again. The prisoners they passed screamed out as they saw one of their own being freed. Darcy kept her arms locked around Veli's waist, tightening her hold as a prisoner reached out and grasped his leg. She yanked him free, and once liberated, he stared at Darcy, opening his mouth again and closing it sadly, still unable to say a word.

Painstakingly they plodded back through the main chamber beneath the summit of the mountain, working their way along until Darcy stumbled to a halt beneath her dangling string. Peering up at the ceiling where the string disappeared, she wondered how she was supposed to get them out.

She pinched the bridge of her nose and took a breath, readying her strength to force a hole with her earth magic. But before she could raise her hands, the hole opened above her and earthen stairs descended.

"That's awfully friendly," Darcy muttered ruefully.

Fresh air wafted toward them, and Yahto's ears perked, his back straightening. A shiver set his hair to blond as he abruptly changed to Veli; it had to be daytime. Darcy steered them toward the stairs, and he pushed himself up after her.

Emerging at last into the igloo dwelling of the Magus, Darcy supported Veli to the wall and leaned him against it while she lowered herself into a crouch, panting. The hole to the labyrinth contracted with a loud cracking and rumbling before closing up before their eyes. The old Magus sat at the fire, breathing over his censer, turning his blind eyes to them.

"Goooo noooowww," he rasped. "Beee gooone. I haaavvve done with yooouuuu."

"No," Darcy said. "You owe Yahto Veli some sort of gift—something to compensate for all the time you unjustly took from him."

"I haaaavvvve alreeeaaady givvveeen him a giiiifffft . . . in hissss pockeeet," the Magus replied.

"What is it?" Darcy was losing patience.

"It isss sssooomething far more vaaaaaluable than yooouuu deeessserrrve!" The Magus's voice deepened into a demonic rumble. "BEEEE GOOOONE!"

Darcy straightened from her crouch and stumbled back, scrambling to distance herself from the Magus and nearly tripping over her feet. She offered her shoulder to Veli once more, and they hobbled through the destroyed doorway as quickly as Veli's weak legs would allow. Darcy breathed the fresh air outside the confines of the igloo, and she looked back over her shoulder to see the stones she'd torn down were back in place, as if untouched.

"Come on." Darcy gave Veli a tug. "We're almost there."

She felt the thrill of euphoria rush through her as her body buzzed with adrenaline. She had done it.

She came around the dwelling with Veli in tow and spotted a few familiar forms silhouetted against the tree line. "Hey!" she called, waving her free arm wildly. "*Hey!*"

The forms pointed at her and waved back. She could hear their shouts of joyful disbelief and she grinned. They rushed toward her but couldn't approach beyond the wards, so she and Yahto Veli struggled the last of the distance on their own.

She passed beyond the edge of the wards and, with a groan of gratitude, let Boreas and Bayard take Veli off her shoulder. Shaking all over, she collapsed into Sam's embrace with weary relief.

"You're alive!" Sam sobbed. "I knew it! I knew you had to be alive! Why did you go alone? Why didn't you bring me?"

"Sam," Darcy said, "I'm sorry, but I just couldn't risk losing another friend to the Oracle!"

"You're so stupid, Darcy!" Sam continued to sob, holding onto her tightly.

"You did it," Tellius said, staring awestruck at Veli. "I can't believe you did it!" The young prince approached the nark and embraced him, but Veli merely stared at him, hopelessly confused. "What's wrong with him?" Tellius pulled away and gaped at him. "He looks so . . ."

"Old," Darcy said as Boreas and Bayard helped Veli to one of the tents they'd erected and they disappeared inside it. "It's part of the Oracle's cruelty. Speaking of which," Darcy pried herself out of Sam's grasp and examined her long, curling nails, "how long was *I* gone?"

"About four months," Lewis answered, approaching her and giving her a rare hug.

"You were right, Sam," Darcy said. "Time is not a constant. It doesn't at all match up with the time difference last time."

"Why does the Oracle play around with time like that?" Sam wondered aloud.

"Because he can," Darcy answered. She wanted desperately to sit down and eat a real meal, but instead she dug into her pack for the cheese she'd brought from Rubidius's cottage. Finding it moldy after four months away, she chucked it off into the grass.

"He?" Tellius raised an eyebrow. "Not *it?*"

Darcy sighed and ran weary hands through her greasy, unkempt hair. "It's a long story."

The looks on her friends' faces was worth the telling of the story, even tired as Darcy was. They brought her some food and drink and let her lie down on the only bed in Tellius's tent as she spoke, and soon she was full and sleepy. The crew decided to spend the night at the camp and Darcy was relieved to make her way to her bed in the girls' tent where she let her eyes close and soon drifted off.

In the morning, Darcy emerged from Sam's and Amelia's tent to find Veli sitting on a log by the fire. He looked up as she approached and raised his eyebrows, a glimmer of recognition in his eyes. He stood and faced her, and a hush fell among those who were awake around camp as they stopped to watch.

She drew close to him and stopped to give him space, but he reached out his hands and cupped her face. "I've been . . . coming awake," he said in a very thin, slow voice, long out of use. "I begin to . . . remember." He searched her face, and tears began pouring down his cheeks. "My *friend,*" he said. "You have . . . recalled me . . ." He bent and kissed the top of her head.

Darcy fell to her knees and clasped her hands in front of her. "I'm—so—*sorry*—Veli! Can you ever—forgive me? Can—*Yahto*—forgive me? It was —my fault, all—my—fault!"

Veli dropped to his knee before her and gave her, for the first time in too long, a smile. "Forgiveness is . . . unnecessary. What . . . we did . . . we did out of love . . . for you."

Darcy hung her head and continued to cry, filled with remorse.

Veli lifted her chin gently. "What's done . . . is done. Forgive . . . yourself, Darcy."

"But when I see what's been *done* to you—"

"It is over," he said, his voice growing stronger with each word he spoke. "And I am . . . thankful . . . for you." He stood laboriously, as if he were much older than he even appeared, and drew her up with him. "And now . . . there is something . . . I must do. I need . . . a sword." He smiled over Darcy's shoulder, and she glanced around to find Tellius watching them.

Tellius unsheathed his sword and gave it to Veli, hilt up. Veli nodded his thanks and pushed the tip of the sword into the ground. He knelt over the sword, grasping it with both hands, and bowed his head over it. Tellius inhaled sharply from behind Darcy.

"We vow to you . . . Lady Darcy Pennington," Veli said, "our lives and . . . swords. With every breath . . . we will defend you; with every step . . . we will follow you; and with every moment . . . we will pray for you. We vow these terms until death . . . takes us . . . and never shall a foe oppose you . . . that has not first opposed us. We are yours . . . without qualification . . . and never to be revoked . . . Do you accept this solemn oath?"

Darcy's mouth fell open and she looked to Tellius for help.

"You're supposed to say yes," Tellius said, sounding strangled. "In order to complete the enchantment, you have to say yes."

"Don't you need to discuss this with Yahto first?" Darcy asked weakly.

"It has been . . . discussed. We are of one mind," Veli answered.

"Okay . . . yes! I accept." She felt a pull from inside her, as though a knot had formed between them, and she took a step backward in amazement.

"*That* is covenantal magic *properly* utilized," a gravelly voice declared.

Darcy spun around. "*Rubidius!* You're alive!"

Rubidius grunted. He was leaning on a cane and looked almost as sickly as Veli, but he appeared strong. "Of course I'm alive," he said. "*I* wasn't bitten, after all." He dissolved into a fit of coughing.

"I'm just glad you're okay," Darcy said. "You saved my life."

"There seems to be a lot of that going on lately," Boreas said, joining them. "And now a pledge to save a life in the future . . ." He looked at Veli.

"Can you explain—" Darcy began.

"I defer . . . to Tellius," Veli said, getting to his feet and returning the sword. "I fear that I need . . . rest."

Tellius took Darcy by the elbow and drew her away from the adults. "I can't believe he did that," he muttered. "It's—unheard of!"

"Did what?" Darcy asked him once they were well away. "What was that oath about?"

Tellius pursed his lips as he stopped walking and released her elbow. He shifted his feet and put his hands on his hips. "It's called the Oath of Service. Royals in Alitheia receive two nark bodyguards for life at the moment they come of age. Up until that time, bodyguards rotate as compatibility is tested between them and their assigned royal."

Darcy nodded. "So that's what Wal Wyn meant when he said it was his trial period with you!"

Tellius nodded, looking troubled.

"So . . . what's the big deal, Tellius? You look like somebody died!"

He clenched his jaw. "The *big deal* is that the Oath of Service is *only* supposed to be taken with a *royal* who is *of age,* and the magic is binding until death. *You* are not of age, nor are you—" he stopped himself and looked away.

"Royal," Darcy supplied.

He nodded curtly.

"So you think this means—*again*—that we have to get married." Darcy felt her stomach tighten. "Tellius—"

"You don't understand!" He glared at her. "You *kissed* someone else . . . someone to whom you are not engaged!"

"So what?" Darcy clenched her fingers into fists. "That relationship is over now! I broke it off!"

"It matters because I felt . . ."

"What? You felt what?"

"Betrayed!" he snapped.

Darcy took a step back. "But . . . you don't even like me like that. You don't *want* to like me like that!"

"I know!" he shouted.

Others in the camp were beginning to stare, and Darcy shot a furtive look at Sam and Amelia, who had emerged from their tent and were gawking open-mouthed.

Darcy raised her hands in frustration and returned her attention to him. "You're not making any sense," she hissed, hoping he would take the hint and lower his voice as well. "And I've been through a *lot* in the past twenty-four hours."

"I know," he snapped. "And I'm glad that you're okay. I'm glad that you rescued Yahto Veli. I just wish you had brought me along!"

"Is that what this is about?"

"Maybe! I don't know . . . No!" He shook his head and put his hands on his hips.

"Tellius," Darcy said wearily, "can't we have this conversation some other time?"

He nodded, rather harder than was necessary, and said, "Fine." Without another glance at her, he stalked back to his tent.

Darcy exhaled and looked up at the sky.

"What was *that* all about?" Sam asked as she and Amelia approached.

"Honestly . . . I have no idea," Darcy responded.

"Oh . . . I think *I* know," Amelia said, smirking.

"Amelia." Darcy rolled her eyes. "No. You don't understand. Tellius is under way more stress than anyone realizes. And he's confused about . . . well, a lot of things."

"Uh huh," Amelia said, eyeing Darcy coyly.

"Oh, come on!" Darcy said. "Can we talk about more important things? Like . . . how the heck are we going to get off this island?"

"They're working on it now," Sam said, while Amelia continued to grin. "There's a window of opportunity while the echidna are spawning . . . but I'm not sure what the plan is."

"Well, at least we have *some* plan," Darcy said. "I'd hate to have rescued Yahto Veli only to be stuck here forever."

"*We* wouldn't be stuck here, at least," Sam said. "Rubidius thinks Pateros would draw us back regardless of where we were."

"Well, maybe Pateros will help us navigate out of this archipelago, too," Darcy said.

CHAPTER 28
ORMISKOS BURNING

The echidna retreated out to sea to spawn for two weeks every June, although the Nofaronisians had been reluctant to divulge that information. They thought it might anger Erpeto for the strange foreigners to escape her serpents, but after the amazing Rubidius and the astounding Darcy insisted that they leave the island, the Nofaronisians finally agreed.

That meant once the serpents were out to sea, they had only two weeks to repair the breach in the hull of the *Cal Meridian* and portage her over the rapids on the far side of the inlet which would carry them back out to sea. Boreas was nervous about meeting the deadline, but Rubidius was confident that the Nofaronisians would help them get it done.

Darcy spent most of their last weeks hiding in her tent from the villagers who insisted on bringing her wreaths of flowers and bowing before her as she walked by, despite her many protests that she was not a goddess. Tellius had reverted to shunning her, once again, and she didn't press him. Perry remained rather stiff around her, but she thought he got a little friendlier every day.

A week after they'd returned to the village, she sat with Veli as he guarded the opening of her tent.

"I found this in my pocket," he said, drawing out a green-tinted glass bottle about six inches tall with a cork stopper in the top and a tiny scroll of parchment on the inside. He held it out to Darcy and she took it with a puzzled frown as disappointment washed through her.

"Why would the Oracle give you one of his promises? What *possible* use could this be?" She fingered the top, but the stopper refused to budge, seemingly fused to the bottle. "*And* it's sealed off with magic, so we can't even read the scroll!"

"Some usage will present itself in due course," Veli replied, tucking it away in his pocket once again.

Darcy shook her head and looked away. "The Oracle said it was 'more valuable than we deserved.' That looks like garbage to me."

Veli patted her hand, drawing her gaze back to him. "Just because we cannot see the value in it now does not mean it is not valuable. Give it time." He chucked her chin, and Darcy smiled in spite of herself.

Veli felt like a breath of fresh air to her now that his physical recovery was well underway. Darcy spent much of her free time talking with him about it, but she always stopped pressing when his eyes took on a far-off look and the muscles around his mouth began to tighten.

"The Oracle did not anticipate my dual nature, you know," Veli said, once the bottled promise was out of sight. "Most prisoners go insane, because the loneliness is . . . unbearable. But narks are never alone. I was always cognizant of Yahto's presence, as he was of mine. We spoke often, in the transitions between days. You said the transitions appeared to happen very quickly, but it was not so for us. What you felt as only a few hours in his lair, we felt as many days. Though we couldn't break through the enchantment to speak to you—or even to recognize who you were—we did know *something* was happening."

"How long was it for you, Veli?" Darcy whispered, her eyes raking through his silver-threaded hair.

He smiled grimly. "Years and years," was all he would say. "I am . . . past my prime now, but not elderly."

"Did the Oracle feed you? How could you stay alive all that time?"

"He had no need to feed us; the enchantment sustains his prisoners in a state of limbo. Rather, *he* fed off us."

Darcy's face contorted in horror. "*What?*"

"Why else the accelerated aging . . . but no death? For what other purpose could he desire to have living trophies? His enchantment draws the life out of others and into himself."

"Narks seem to cause him a lot of trouble," Darcy said. "Voitto Vesa got around his curse with her double nature, and you were able to stay sane."

Veli's eyelids flickered at the mention of Voitto Vesa, and he smiled. "Perhaps, in his original form, he was from a time before the narks."

"But I thought narks came to Alitheia before humans did."

"Perhaps he is not, in fact, human."

The June spawning season finally arrived, and Darcy, Sam, and Amelia headed down the hillside to watch the crew splash into the water to begin the ship's repairs. Darcy shivered watching them go, imagining the snakes that had swarmed over the vessel and the agony of the bite she'd received.

"Are they *really* sure the snakes have gone out to sea?" she asked the others.

"I think so," Sam replied. "They're so afraid of them I don't think they'd get anywhere near that water unless they were absolutely *sure* it was safe."

"If you say so."

Days passed without incident, and the repair work was completed in a week and a half, leaving three days to portage across the rapids to deeper water. On the day they were to leave, the Nofaronisians accompanied them down to the shore with flowers and singing, and the girls and Tellius were hefted aboard the *Cal Meridian* with Yahto Veli, Wal Wyn, and Rubidius to keep them company. The rest of the crew and the men from the village hoisted the *Cal Meridian* onto sturdy ropes they'd passed beneath it and set it down on cut logs they'd rolled into place along the rapids.

Darcy gripped the railing as the vessel bumped and rolled over the logs, groaning and creaking. She feared that at any moment the repair job to the hull might burst, but the work held and, with a splash, the ship was lowered into the deeper water on the far side of the rapids. The current once again tugged at the vessel, and the sailors, Boreas, and Bayard clambered aboard. They cut the ropes and, like a flash, they slipped down the river.

"All hands to the oars!" Boreas gripped the wheel. "Be ready to row, for we'll not catch a breeze in this archipelago!"

The lilies flew past like white beacons, and the rushing waters spewed them forth into the sea. Once they cleared the lily pads, the current died and the ship drifted for several hundred feet before slowing to a near standstill.

"Row!" Boreas called, and the sailors dropped their oars, their splashes spraying Darcy and her friends where they stood at the railing. "To the fog bank," Boreas called out. "Beyond the fog is open sea, and there we'll catch our bearings and, Pateros willing, a wind, as well."

A wind . . . Darcy thought and perked up. "Maybe I can help!"

"Darcy." Rubidius leaned on his cane. "You cannot produce a wind strong enough to propel this ship."

"I know I can't, but . . . a zephyra could! Do you think she could hear the bone whistle if I blew it?"

Rubidius opened and closed his mouth, thinking. "I suppose it is as good a thing to try as any," he said, "better, probably. I admit that I am most curious to see this object at work."

Darcy pulled the whistle from beneath the collar of her shirt. She wore it always around her neck now. She put it to her lips, closed her eyes, and blew. The high note of the whistle, barely audible, echoed over the waves, sounding just a little different this time, as though it tempered itself to the situation.

Darcy blew until she was breathless and then lowered the whistle. All of the sailors, including Boreas and Bayard, were staring into space with dreamy expressions on their faces.

"I guess now we wait," Darcy said, tucking the whistle away, but almost immediately a breeze tickled her cheek. She turned into it, breathing it in, and toward the fog bank she saw the clouds shift. A figure emerged, racing toward them. The zephyra looked joyful.

"She knew we were calling her!" Darcy waved at the zephyra as the wind spirit swooshed over the ship and circled back to hover within Darcy's view.

"All hands on deck!" Boreas shouted, shooting Darcy and the zephyra a look of awe not unlike the way the Nofaronisians had looked at her.

"Thank you for coming back," Darcy whispered to the zephyra. "I'm sorry for how I treated you before."

The zephyra inclined her head and smiled, showing sparkly teeth.

"Can you help us escape the archipelago?" Darcy asked. "We're afraid we won't be able to get through the fog."

With a look of amusement, the zephyra zoomed upward toward the sails and disappeared. As she vanished, a gusty wind filled the sails, and the bow of the *Cal Meridian* lifted from the waves as the vessel surged forward with such speed that Darcy lost her footing and tumbled over backward. She landed in a heap at the base of the wheel platform with Sam and Lewis, and they laughed.

"Way to go, Darcy!" Sam cried.

Rubidius offered a hand to her and she stood, grinning. Together they watched the fog bank growing ever nearer. The *Cal Meridian* plunged into its soupy darkness, and the momentum of the ship slowed to a crawl. Darcy squinted up at the sails.

The zephyra reappeared, her cheeks puffed out with exertion. She floated out from the main sail and redoubled her efforts, and the *Cal Meridian* picked up the pace once again. Darcy watched the air particles above and raised her arms to clasp hold of them, willing them to split and multiply. With an almighty heave, she threw them against the resistance of the sails, and the *Cal Meridian* shot forward, expelled from the fog like a ball from a cannon. Darcy dropped her arms and collapsed against Rubidius as her vision went black.

"Moderate yourself, my little magician," Rubidius said when Darcy came to just a few seconds later. "Know your limitations."

Darcy pushed herself up from the deck and put a hand to her head. "I helped get us out, didn't I?"

The corner of Rubidius's mouth hinted at a smile. "You did. But you will not always have the luxury of passing out when you overexert your talent."

"Rubidius," Darcy said. "Can you just be happy that we're free? We have Yahto Veli, we have the bone whistle, we got past the snakes, we're out of the archipelago, and we're on our way home. Let's put things into perspective here."

He narrowed his eyes at her. "You have grown up, Darcy," he said as he helped her to her feet, "but you are not yet grown."

"Was that a compliment or an insult?" Darcy closed her eyes and gripped the railing to control another wave of dizziness. "Never mind. I don't really care right now."

The zephyra rested after the push through the fog, but she soon resumed aiding their progress, lending a swift, steady wind. Boreas judged they could be back at the beacon marking Alitheian waters in three weeks' time, and so they settled back into the routine aboard the ship of eating, sleeping, and helping with whatever monotonous tasks they could to pass the time. The boys resumed their morning forms, but Tellius continued to refuse sword lessons with Darcy.

About two weeks out of Alitheia, Rubidius instructed Dean to use his enchanted bow and arrow to send a message to Ormiskos, alerting them of their success and return. A week later, the message came back.

" 'Come quickly,' " Dean read after unfolding the note. " 'Ormiskos in trouble. Warrior needed.' " Dean looked up, past the others, to Perry.

"I'm needed?" Perry frowned. "But that must mean—"

"Tsellochim," Darcy finished. She bit her lip and looked up at Rubidius.

The old alchemist's face was grim. "I will tell Captain Boreas," he said and turned away.

Darcy stood in the bowsprit that night after everybody else had gone to bed. She squinted ahead into the darkness as though her will could force Ormiskos to appear before them. Yahto followed behind her like a ghost and stood silently watching her as she watched the waters. After a while, she couldn't take the quiet any more and rounded on him.

"Yahto . . . did you really agree to that Oath of Service," she asked, "or did Veli pressure you into it?" She sighed, relieved at having the question off her chest.

"It was my idea," Yahto said. He stepped forward to join her and leaned against the railing. "Despite my many failings, I recognize true friendship and bravery, and I hold those qualities in highest regard. I found those qualities in you when you came to rescue us, and there is no person to whom I would rather pledge my service."

Darcy studied his face. He was telling the truth. Yahto never embellished unless it was to look on the dark side of things. "And you're okay with being bonded to me even if I don't end up being queen?"

"You will be queen," he said simply.

"Even though . . ." Darcy swallowed hard as Yahto's dark eyes pierced her.

"Twice wed, yes, I remember," he said softly. "Two weddings. Twice dead, also." He looked away. "For you to be killed, Veli and I will have been killed first, or we will have failed."

Darcy shook her head, not wanting to think about that. "You're the only one who knows that part of my oracle, you know," she whispered. "Please don't—"

"I will keep your confidence, do not worry," Yahto said. "It is part of the Oath of Service, but even if it were not, it is your secret to reveal to whomever you wish."

Darcy let out a relieved breath. "Thank you. But how can you be so certain I will be queen?"

Yahto snorted. "Do you not see how Prince Tellius watches you?"

"Tellius doesn't watch me; Tellius hates me."

"Nonsense. Human foibles," Yahto said. "Tellius *does* watch you."

"Okay then, *how* does he watch me?"

"Like a boy watching his future wife . . . with jealous eyes."

Darcy opened her mouth to protest as a voice cried down from the crows nest.

"The beacon! The beacon is out!"

Darcy and Yahto looked around and stared with the sailors as the pinnacle of rock that held the beacon slid past them in the darkness, its only light a weak sort of flicker.

"What does that mean?" Darcy whispered in horror.

"It means things are much worse than we feared."

Two days later a red glow became visible on the horizon before the dawn. As the sun rose, they could make out the black smoke filling the sky.

"Ormiskos is burning," Boreas confirmed, pressing his seeing glass to his eye.

"They need me," Perry insisted. "We have to keep going."

"Of course we will keep going," Rubidius said, his tone gruff. "Dean, we must send another message. I must know what has happened."

Dean took up his bow as Rubidius scribbled a message to Eleanor and attached it to an arrow.

They spent a nervous hour waiting, approaching ever nearer to the devastation, before the arrow sailed back and came to a quivering halt before Dean's face. Rubidius snatched it down and unfolded the parchment.

"A contingent of malcontents began rioting in Ormiskos Prime several weeks ago," he told them. "They've had a time of it fighting the ruffians and trying to keep the situation under control. Tselloch saw an opportunity and sent in his tsellodrin and tsellochim. The city has not fallen, but they have been fighting for days and need reinforcements. The castle remains secure, but not for long. She, Cadmus, and Tullin are safe." He looked up. "We cannot land in Ormiskos, but we must get close enough to offer aid."

By mid-afternoon, they could see the city clearly. Flames licked the sky from every corner, and the shouts and clangs of battle carried to them across the waters. The gates of the sea wall hung off their hinges and the watchtowers were deserted. Boreas navigated the *Cal Meridian* to within a quarter mile of the city and put down the anchor.

Perry was already prepared. His sword was strapped at his waist and a steely glint flashed in his eyes.

Eight of the remaining sailors were also geared up for battle, and Boreas ordered the coracles to be let down.

"I want to fight," Tellius insisted to Rubidius and Wal Wyn, tightening his cuirass and shooting an obstinate glare at Rubidius. "I am the heir apparent; you must obey my wishes!"

"Not before you are king." Rubidius strapped a sword about his own waist. "I will not allow you to risk your neck because, like a child, you don't want to be left behind."

"But—"

An explosion sounded on shore and Rubidius looked over his shoulder. "Tellius," he said sharply. "No."

The coracles splashed into the water on either side of the *Cal Meridian* and the sailors began climbing down the rope ladders to go ashore; Tellius bitterly watching them go,

The four coracles progressed toward the shore and docked amidst the chaos. The men disembarked and almost immediately began fighting. Perry and Rubidius disappeared down a side street, and Darcy let out a sigh, shooting a glance over at Sam, who was standing with her knuckles in her mouth.

A splash below them drew their attention and they looked down, startled, to see a dark head bobbing on the waves.

"Tellius!" Darcy leaned forward and gripped the railing.

Tellius ignored her and began to swim for shore. A second splash sounded a moment later and Wyn sped off after the wayward prince, stroking beside him toward the docks.

"He'll make it," Veli said in her ear. "He has water magic. He can swim almost as well as a nark."

"Why isn't Wyn bringing him back?" Darcy cried. "He could be killed!"

"Even a nark would not take on a water magician in the water," Veli replied. "Wyn's job is to keep Tellius safe, whatever road he takes."

Darcy still felt a knot of fear in her belly. Didn't Tellius understand how important his survival was to the realm? "Pateros protect him from his stupidity!" Darcy huffed under her breath.

A heavy black cloud hung over the city that had nothing to do with the smoke from the fires; it was the cover the tsellochim generated for themselves when it was sunny out. "There must be an awful lot of them," she murmured.

"An awful lot of what?" Sam asked her.

"Tsellochim. See the cloud?"

Sam paled. "They won't come out here, will they?"

"No . . . the water, remember? It burns them."

They fell silent and watched the city. Around late afternoon, it seemed as though some of the fires had gone out, the smoke less dense in the sky.

Those that had gone to fight didn't return that night, and Darcy and the rest of them slept fitfully and woke early to clamber back to the deck and observe the shore. A few plumes of smoke still rose from around the city, but the heavy black cloud had been driven back into the woods. They were winning.

As midday approached, Darcy felt as though she were forgetting something important. The feeling soon nagged so persistently in the back of her mind that she mentioned it to Sam.

"Me, too. You don't think . . ." Sam frowned. "No . . . it can't be that day already, can it?"

"What—" Someone tugged on the back of Darcy's shirt and she turned around to look. Nobody was there.

"Hey!" Sam said.

"What?"

"Somebody pushed me!"

"Ouch!" Amelia said. "Me, too!"

Darcy stumbled back from the railing as though someone had pushed her in the chest, and something grabbed at the back of her shirt again.

Dean and Lewis, across the ship, were swatting the air at nothing Darcy could see.

"No!" Darcy called. "I'm not ready to go back yet! There's a battle going on, and . . . we haven't even gotten to say goodbye!"

Veli wheeled around, but she was lifted bodily off her feet and hung suspended in the air, well out of his reach.

"What's happening?" Dean yelled, and Sam and Amelia shrieked as all of them were elevated above the ship by an unseen force.

In a moment all five of them were flying through the air, a sixth figure heading toward them from Ormiskos Prime. They sped faster and faster, the water streaking below them, followed by the tower of Kenidros and the trees of the peninsula, as if they were on an invisible line connected to the gateway. Darcy gasped for breath as the air rushed past her face.

And then they were descending through the tree tops, bobbing this way and that to avoid large branches, and with one last flail she was sucked through the gateway and tossed unceremoniously with her friends in a heap of legs and arms on the forest floor in their own world.

Darcy disentangled herself from the others and ran back to the gateway. "No!" she shouted, throwing herself through the two trees and landing with a hard thud. "I *wasn't ready!*" She stomped her foot and punched one of the tree trunks, her arm recoiling as her knuckles protested painfully.

"What's going on?" Perry was turning in circles. "Where's the—what— what happened? I was in the middle of a battle!"

"I guess our time was up," Lewis said, getting slowly to his feet.

"But we were *winning!*" Perry shouted. "All I needed was a few more hours!"

"Do you think they'll lose without you there?" Darcy asked. "Hadn't you already pushed the tsellochim back?"

Perry was quiet for a moment, breathing hard. "I—I don't know. Man . . . I guess they'll probably be okay. Truthfully, Rubidius took out most of them with his water magic. Tellius, too—"

"You saw Tellius?" Darcy asked. "Is he okay?"

"He was fine the last I saw him." Perry shot her a glowering look.

Sam was crying softly, and Amelia put her arm around her. "I didn't want to leave like that," Sam gasped. "We didn't get to see Eleanor again or anything. And we didn't find out if Voitto Vesa is okay. And now we won't know for another whole year!"

Darcy shook her head, resisting the urge to be sick. "This stinks," she muttered, tears threatening at the back of her eyes. She cleared her throat noisily.

"Well, there's nothing we can do about it," Amelia said, looking relieved to be home. "We did what we set out to do this year—we rescued Yahto Veli. We should feel good about that and worry about next year when the time comes."

"Let's not hang around here," Dean said, brushing himself off. "Amelia's right. The gateway's not going to open up again for us for another year. We should head back."

They began the trek to the main body of camp, and Darcy fell back to walk with Sam. She knew Sam felt the separation from Alitheia as acutely as she did, that Sam had formed as deep a bond of connection with the magical land as she had. They walked in silence until they reached the ferry dock and sat on the wooden benches to wait.

"You know," Sam whispered, "I've been thinking . . . about this whole Perry thing."

Darcy frowned and glanced down the benches to where Perry was sitting, looking miserable with his head in his hands.

"I was thinking on the way back about our year, and everything that happened, and . . . I realized that it got in the way."

"What do you mean?" Darcy asked. The foghorn on the ferry sounded from across the bay, and Darcy and Sam both looked up.

"Did you notice that nothing came out of my pouch this year?"

"Sure, but that doesn't mean anything." Darcy replied.

"I'm not so sure." Sam sighed and twisted her fingers together. "I've felt a lot of resentment toward you for a long time. Even over silly things, like," Sam laughed hollowly, "Brandon Cooper."

"*Brandon Cooper? Are you crazy?*"

"It's just . . . boys never look at me, Darcy, and especially not when I'm with you."

"Sam—"

Sam held up a hand. "Let me finish, okay? This isn't about Brandon Cooper; it's about me and how I've been jealous of you. I'd been afraid for a long time that Perry would like you, and after you spent all that time together last year, I could tell something had changed between you two. Seeing you together on the ship this year was just the culmination of a lot of fears and insecurities and . . . I haven't been a very good friend to you. I became . . . the opposite of loyal, but that's what the companion is supposed to be, isn't it? Loyal." She swallowed hard. "If I'm not loyal, how can I fulfill my purpose in Alitheia? When you almost died on Nofaronisi, I checked my pouch every day, sure Pateros would send me something to save you, but it was like he wanted me to feel what it would be like if I lost you. And I've got to tell you; I'd rather have you as a friend *any* day than Perry as a boyfriend."

Darcy bit her lip, her eyes watering. "Thank you, Sam."

"So, about Perry," Sam continued to keep her voice low, glancing over at him, "I think maybe it's time I give it up."

"You can't just *will* yourself to stop liking him," Darcy said.

"No, but . . . my mom says sometimes feelings follow actions. If I start to act as though I don't like him anymore, eventually I should feel that way, too, right?"

They stood together and boarded the ferry, unable to continue their conversation with Perry now sitting so close, but Darcy wanted to encourage Sam. Perhaps it *was* time for her to move on.

Before the ferry reached the other side, Darcy leaned over close to Sam's ear and whispered, "Have you ever thought about going out with Lewis?"

EPILOGUE
THE REAPPEARANCE

Darcy and Sam walked together through the cedar-strewn forest. Amelia had flat out refused to come with them, considering their destination. It was the last morning of camp; the vans and cars were being packed, all the families gathering stray beach toys—and stray children—and regulars like Sam and Darcy were saying goodbye to favorite haunts for another year. Except Darcy and Sam weren't exactly visiting a favorite haunt; they were heading back to East Mooring.

Sam looked grimly determined to stay at Darcy's side, no matter *how* frightened she got, and Darcy was determined keep her distance from anything malicious so as not to give Sam any real cause for concern. They'd decided they couldn't leave Cedar Cove without one further look at the spot behind East Mooring where they suspected Tselloch was forming a gateway—where they were sure Colin Mackaby had disappeared.

"What are we going to do if it's really happening?" Sam asked for the hundredth time. "What are we going to *do* if Tselloch really is making a gateway into *our* world?"

"I don't know," Darcy repeated her usual answer. "But it changes the game a little, doesn't it?"

They left the campsite and continued toward the dark and deserted cabin.

"I wonder how long it takes to make a gateway?"

"I don't know," Darcy said again. "But according to that history Eleanor taught us, it certainly took Baskania a long time. If Tselloch has just started, we may have time to stop him."

They turned right at the cabin and stepped onto the beach.

Sam snorted. "Sure, if we knew *how.*"

"Yeah, well . . . I'm beginning to think all that stuff with the Oracle was a setup, honestly."

"Wait." Sam stopped her with a hand on her arm and they faced each other on the beach. "What do you mean?"

"Doesn't it seem odd to you that the Oracle violated its own code to get an object it could have gotten simply by demanding it as payment?"

"You mean the bone whistle?" Sam asked.

"Yes! And then it gave Voitto Vesa an oracle *so specific* we almost couldn't help but figure it out."

Sam snorted. "It was hardly *easy*, Darcy."

"No . . . but the Oracle doesn't like to make anything easy for anybody, and maybe it wanted it to *seem* hard so we wouldn't figure out we were playing into its plans the whole time."

Sam squinted at Darcy. "Go on."

"So it sets up a *reason* for us to go back to it, and then it gives us the *means*, and then . . . while I'm down in its maze, it *saves* me from this creature, and it stashes both Yahto Veli and the bone whistle in the only portion of its labyrinth I was familiar with."

"But you said it needed you to take them back so it wouldn't lose its power. That's reason enough to make it easier on you," Sam figured.

"But it wouldn't have been in that position *at all* if it hadn't violated the rules of covenantal magic in the first place. I don't think it wanted Yahto Veli *or* the bone whistle."

Sam chewed her lip. "Then what do you think it wanted?"

"I think it wanted to give me something."

"The bottle it put in Yahto Veli's pocket? But you couldn't open it."

"I know . . . but Veli insists the bottle is of great value, and maybe this doesn't make any sense, but the more I think of it, the more I think it's true. You know what else makes me think that the Oracle orchestrated the whole thing?"

"What?"

"After Yahto Veli and I escaped, it—he—didn't kill me. He could have, and wouldn't you think he would *want* to? I'd repaired the breach to the covenant, so why let me escape? *I* would think he'd want to kill me to make sure I couldn't tell anybody else his secrets."

Sam's eyes went round. "You know . . . you might be right! You've got to find out what's in that bottle."

Darcy sighed, looking at the trail ahead. "Come on, let's get this over with. Our parents are going to start wondering where we are."

"All right," Sam said heavily.

They headed across the beach to the game trail and traversed its narrow length into the dark woods behind East Mooring. Darcy kept her eyes peeled for wisps of darkness, but she saw none, nor did she feel the nagging sense of fear she had before.

"I think we might be in luck," she whispered over her shoulder at Sam. "I think that whatever start he made here is gone."

"Darcy!" Sam whispered. "Look ahead!"

Darcy swung back around and gasped. Lying in the middle of the trail, near the pile of rocks where it ended, was a body.

"Colin!" Darcy sprinted forward.

She reached Colin's body and fell to her knees beside it, turning him onto his back. His hair was long and bedraggled, his blonde roots showing, as his apparition had looked the day they'd embarked on the *Cal Meridian* in Alitheia. His clothes were too small, and he smelled horribly pungent, like a burning skunk.

"Is he . . . dead?" Sam whispered.

Darcy studied his face and neck. His eyelids were closed and his cheeks were flushed. She put her face down close to his mouth and nose and felt a soft whisper of breath on her cheeks. "No . . . he's alive."

"What do we *do?*" Sam moaned, dancing on the spot.

"Colin!" Darcy shouted, shaking him hard by the shoulders. He gave no response, his body limp to the touch. She grabbed his wrist and felt his pulse; it was slow and getting slower.

"Sam, do you have your cell phone on you?"

"Yeah, but . . ." Sam scrambled it out of her pocket. "I don't have any reception out here!"

"Run back to camp then and get help," Darcy said. "Call 9-1-1 as soon as you have a signal, okay? I'll stay here with him!"

Sam made a squeak of protest in her throat, but Darcy shouted, "Hurry, Sam! I think he's dying!"

Sam spun around and dashed back up the trail, holding her phone out in front of her like a baton.

Darcy looked back at Colin's unmoving face. "Come on, Colin," she whispered, her fingers at his wrist. "Don't die on me."

THE GATEWAY

CHRONICLES

BOOK 4

THE ENCHANTED

CHAPTER 1

THE PHONE CALL

"Guess what I found." Sam breezed into Darcy's room without warning.

"Huh?" Darcy jumped and flailed her arms, knocking the plastic lamp off her bedside table. She'd been half-asleep over her laptop, trying to finish a term paper for history class. She blinked at her screen where a long line of dashes took up more than three pages. She must have had her finger on the key when she dozed off. Embarrassed, she tried to discreetly delete them as she turned half her attention on Sam, who had plopped down on the mattress at the foot of her bed. "What'd you say?"

"Look." Sam handed Darcy a stiffly creased packet of stapled pages.

"What is this?" Darcy abandoned deleting the dashes halfway through and took the packet from Sam.

"It's my parents' old contact list from Cedar Cove, like, ten years ago, or something."

"So?" Darcy felt fuzzy in her head as her brain slowly awoke from her nap.

"Look at the name I circled for you!" Sam jabbed her finger at the page.

Darcy looked down and felt her exhaustion slip away. "Mackaby," she said, sitting forward. "Long Island, New York. There's a phone number. Is that where they live? Do you think this number could still be good?" She set her laptop aside, term paper forgotten, and swung her legs over the side of the bed.

"It's worth a try, isn't it?"

Darcy snatched up her cell phone and began dialing the number.

"Wait, Darcy—what are you going to say?" Sam twisted her fingers in her lap.

"I don't know, I just want to see if it's the right number."

"You should think this through. What if you only get one shot?"

Darcy blinked down at the completed number on the screen. All she had to do was hit "send" and she could be on her way to finding out some answers to the mystery of Colin Mackaby. But Sam was right. If the number was correct and she *did* get through to Colin, she might have just one chance to get information from him. She sighed and put her phone away. "I'll think it through and try later tonight."

"Okay, good." Sam sounded relieved she wouldn't be there. "Besides, you have to get changed for fencing club. Lewis will be here to pick us up in ten minutes."

****

Darcy sat and stared at the number she'd keyed into her phone. She'd told Sam she would think about what she'd say to Colin before she called him, but the truth was, she still didn't know. It would either come to her or not, and she was tired of waiting.

She hit "send" and leaned over her knees, feeling tense. The phone rang eight times before Darcy hung up, a sense both of relief and disappointment washing over her. It was strange there was no voice mail, and if the number had been disconnected, she wouldn't have gotten through at all . . .

She hit send again. This time it rang six times before someone picked up.

"Darcy, I was wondering when I would hear from you." The voice was both silky and wary. It was deeper than Darcy remembered, but definitely male . . . and it didn't sound like his dad.

"Colin?" Darcy whispered.

"Although, I'll admit, I didn't expect you to call *this* number—"

Darcy felt dumbfounded. "Colin, is that really you?"

"Well, who were you expecting to get?" He sounded irritated—threatening.

"I'm just—I can't . . . how did you know it was me?"

"Do I need to explain to you the intricate and magical world of caller ID?"

Darcy was too surprised even to rise to his sarcasm.

"I suppose I shouldn't be shocked that you got this number." Colin continued as though they were having a normal conversation. "It belongs to my dad's private penthouse in the city. He sent me to live here, you know. All by myself. He wants to keep me quiet and out of sight. Although, truth be told, he gives this number out to anyone—sales people, telemarketers, clients he's finished with, women he doesn't want my mother to know about . . . Of course, what better way to reach an undesirable like me than with an undesirable number?"

Colin's voice dripped with so much bitterness that Darcy cringed. She needed to gain control of this phone call, and fast.

"Listen—Colin—I wanted to ask you . . ." What *did* she want to ask him? "How are you?"

Colin laughed, and there was real humor behind it. "Oh come on, you didn't search out this number to ask me how I am."

"How do you know?" Darcy sat further forward in agitation. "I really *have* been worried about you. Do you have any idea how scary it was to find you on that path at Cedar Cove like that?"

"You were nosing where you didn't belong." Colin's voice dropped even lower.

"Nosing my—" Darcy closed her eyes and took a deep breath. "Sam and I saved your life."

A soft sound came through the receiver, like a swift exhalation through the nose. "Don't flatter yourself. He wouldn't have let me die."

Wanna bet? Darcy thought. "Colin, you don't know what you're messing with—you don't know what *he* is really like. Whatever he's told you or promised you—"

"Oh, do you think it's a secret?" Colin snickered, as though he were talking down to a small child. "I can share, you know. He's promised me relief from this life. From a mother who doesn't know I exist and a father who hates me. If I help him, he'll give me a new life."

"He's *ten times* worse than your father, Colin."

"Don't talk about my father like you know him! You saw him hit me one time and you think you know something about him? You have no idea the things he's done!"

Darcy held the phone away from her ear until Colin finished shouting. "I'm not saying things aren't bad for you, Colin," she said in the wake of his outburst. "And I'm so sorry but—"

"You're sorry? Sorry like the school social workers who told me there was nothing they could do because my father is a 'very important patron of our school,' or sorry like my grandfather who told me to 'be a man and take my medicine'? Is that how you're *sorry*, Darcy?"

"No! I wish there was something I could do to help you, that's why I'm calling." Darcy felt close to tears.

"Don't kid yourself. You hate me just as much as your little friends do. You didn't call to help me, you called to help yourself. But I won't answer the questions you really want answered. I've made a deal, and I don't need your charity or anybody else's. Tselloch has given me a way to help myself."

"Colin, please." She could feel him slipping away.

"See you at camp, Darcy," Colin said, and the line went dead.

Drop Site the game can be purchased at http://www.bellwethergames.com

The White Thread

CPSIA information can be obtained at www.ICGtesting.com
Printed in the USA
LVOW04s2334230115

424116LV00011B/37/P